# QUEEN OF THE CRIMSON THRONE

---

## QUEEN OF BLOOD AND STARDUST
### BOOK 2

## KAITLYN SWANSON

First Edition February 2025

Ebook ISBN: 979-8-9894941-3-2
Paperback ISBN: 979-8-9894941-1-8

Developmental Edit by Caitlin Lengerich
Copy Edits and Proofreading by K. Morton Editing Services
Cover by Moonpress Design | *www.moonpress.co*
Map by Lindsey Staton (@honeyy.fae)

kaitlynswansonbooks.com

# QUEEN OF THE CRIMSON THRONE

KAITLYN SWANSON

To anyone who's ever been told they were
too quiet
*too emotional*
*too defensive*
*too **anything***

# A NOTE TO READERS

This book contains content that may be sensitive to some readers. Please read through the following content warnings before reading.

This book contains themes of death, grief, loss of a parent, loss of a sibling, alcohol use, mention of suicidal thoughts, blood, gore, violence, torture, explicit sexual content, and vulgar language.

# PRONUNCIATION GUIDE

## Characters and Creatures

**Adreona** (Ay-dree-on-uh)
**Alon** (Ay-lon)
**Alvise** (Al-vez-aye)
**Arlo Rossi** (are-lo Ross-e)
**Astria** (As-tree-uh)
**Auden Galtain** (Ah-din Gal-t-ay-n)
~~**Bram Adair** (Br-am Ah-dare)~~
**Caio** (Kay-oh)
**Caspian** (Cas-p-in)
**Caterina Ambrose** (Cat-er-een-uh Am-br-oh-z)
**Cecelia** (Suh-seel-lee-uh)
**Ceto** (Kay-toe)
**Dahna** (Dah-nah)
**Declan Hale** (Dec-lin H-ale)
**Dhampir** (D-hamp-ire)
~~**Elena Adair** (E-lain-uh Ah-dare)~~
**Endora** (En-door-ah)
~~**Enric** (En-rick)~~
~~**Este Rossi** (Es-tee Ross-e)~~

**Elesebetta** (E-liz-ah-bet-a)

**Gael** (Gale)

**Gulia** (Jule-e-uh)

**Hecate** (Hec-caught-ay)

**Hellhound** (Hel H-ow-nd)

**Jasellia** (Jaz-el-li-uh)

**Kahle** (Kay-l)

**Kara Adair** (Car-ah Ah-dare)

**Krissa** (Kris-uh)

**Larissa** (Lare-is-uh)

**Larkin** (Lar-kin)

**Lennox Adair** (Len-nex Ah-dare)

**Lorenzo Rossi** (Lore-en-zo Ross-e)

**Loris Driscoll** (Lor-es Dr-is-cull)

**Luciana Ambrose** (Loos-see-an-uh Am-br-oh-z)

**Luka Rossi** (Luke-uh Ross-e)

**Mara Rossi** (Mare-uh Rosse-e)

**Malina Galtain** (Mal-ee-nah Gal-t-ay-n)

**Nico Elsher** (Nee-ko El-sh-er)

**Nol Adair** (N-ole Ah-dare)

**Odin** (Oh-din)

**Olexa** (Oh-lex-uh)

**Oriza** (Or-ee-zah)

**Quade (Ashford) Rossi** (Qu-ay-d A-sh-f-or-d Ross-e)

**Remy** (Rem-ee)

**Silas Galtain** (Sil-as Gal-t-ay-n)

**Tarick** (Tar-ick)

**Thiago** (Thee-og-o)

**Warren** (War-en)

**Wampus Cat**: (Wom-pus Cat)

**Zienna** (Zee-en-uh)

**Zola** (Zole-uh)

## Places
*Continent of Lethenia*

*7 Courts and their Capitol Cities*

**Lethenia** (Leh-then-ee-uh)
    **Star Court**: Alethens (Ah-leh-thee-ens)
    **Blood Court:** Cel Nox (Sell-nox)
    **Twilight Court**: Verbial (Verb-al)
    **Lunar Court**: Janara (Jan-are-uh)
    **Mystic Court**: Arcadia (Arc-ay-de-uh)
    **Aqua Court**: Salacia (Sa-lay-see-uh)
    **Court of Embers**: Thyrinian (Thigh-rin-e-in)
    **Abode Mountians**: (Ah-bo-dee)

# 1

## LENNOX

The scent of burnt flesh clung to my nostrils as I watched the last of the bodies disintegrate to nothing but ash on the cobblestones. It was reckless really, for me to remain here while the bodies burned.

Anyone could turn the corner into the dark alley and find me, find the High Queen of Lethenia, burning bodies with the embers from her fingertips.

But what could they do?

I was High Queen Lennox Adair. I ruled all.

If I wanted to kill without consequence I would.

If I wanted to bask in the feeling of vengeance I would.

I glanced over my shoulder at the sound of voices nearing. There might not be consequences for my actions, but that didn't mean I wanted to explain myself.

A tingle rushed through my body as I called to my magic and drew water to my fingertips, sending it careening toward the smoldering ashes. The ashes disintegrated in the water as they streamed through the cracks in the stones, mixing with the blood that stained the street as it flowed.

I pressed my back against the side of the building, hiding behind a stack of crates as the string of voices passed. It wasn't until their voices faded, and I could no longer hear their heavy footsteps, that I pushed myself off the wall. I didn't spare the alley a second glance as I pulled the hood of my cloak over my dark hair, casting my face in shadows as I went searching for my next victim.

It was late, the sun had given way to the moon hours ago, shortly afterward was when I left the palace and took to the dark streets of Alethens, as I did most nights.

I could hardly bear to visit the city in the daylight—the sight of the ruined buildings—I couldn't stand to see the aftermath of the attack on my city. The memories of that day—they were too much. I shoved them down and locked them away with the rest of the memories I refused to confront.

On the rare days I offered my assistance in the city, I busied myself with work. I helped clear the rubble from the streets until my palms bled. I relished the pain. It was one of the few times I felt anything but rage and guilt these days. Rage about what the rebel vampire group, the Vanir, had done to my city, my people. Guilt over not anticipating the attack. I let down my guard and my people suffered because of it.

Slowly, ever so slowly, we were building our city back up. The streets had been cleared, and buildings destroyed by the Vanir were being rebuilt.

According to Kara, children were playing in the streets again. Store owners and vendors had opened back up their shops. Our city was moving on, so why couldn't I?

I shook my head. Those were the exact kinds of thoughts I sought to avoid. If I let myself dwell on them, I found myself in a spiral with no one to help me get out.

No one paid me any attention while I wandered the dark streets. With my cloak casting my face in shadows and my glamor hiding the color of my eyes and hair, no one should. No one ever did. Why would anyone expect the High Queen to be out at this time of night in Alethens?

The enchanted sign above the bar glowed in the dim light,

*Atine Tavern*, it read as I ducked inside. The establishment was crowded tonight. The tables were occupied by patrons engaging in rounds of cards as they did most evenings. I scanned the room for an open table, coming up empty. Even the back booth I favored was occupied, it was nestled in the far corner of the tavern, offering a perfect view of the room while allowing me to hide in the shadows.

I planted myself on an empty stool at the bar, lowering my hood as the barkeep approached. The bottom half of his face was covered in a dark beard that extended far longer than any beard should. His hair was the same dark onyx as his beard and was pulled back from his round face. Creases appeared at the corners of each of his eyes as he smiled.

"What will it be tonight, sweetheart?" I tensed. A feeling acute to a dagger nicking my heart brushed through me. I swallowed past the lump in my throat.

"Whatever ale you have on tap." He nodded before turning and fetching my drink. *Sweetheart.* No one had called me sweetheart since—*No.* I shook my head. I couldn't think of him. Not now. Not when I had much more important things to worry about.

The barkeep returned with my drink, placing the foaming mug of ale on the worn wood bar. I slid a coin across the counter as I brought the cup to my lips, drinking half the glass in one go. I cringed. It tasted foul, and I felt like I needed something much stronger right now. But I couldn't dilute my senses too much—not yet anyway.

*After.*

After I completed my task I could indulge as much as I wanted.

I sipped on the rest of my ale slowly as I remained at the bar, my eyes tracking every person who wandered in and out of the establishment, keeping my gaze on the fair-colored male in the corner booth near the front of the room. He had his arm slung around a pretty dark-haired female. The male hadn't been a part of this groups nightly game until a week ago, but he had been here playing every night since. He slammed his cards on the table, a grin spread across his face, causing a dimple to appear in his left cheek. The others at the table groaned and grumbled as the male pulled his earnings towards him.

The female beside him giggled as he placed a kiss to her cheek, before slipping a coin into her hand. The male unwrapped himself from the female and stood, throwing several more coins on the table. He was leaving on a high note, *smart male*. The female remained at the table, immediately fixing her gaze on one of the other players.

*Good.* It would complicate things if she was attached.

I downed the remaining dregs of my ale and tossed another coin on the bar. I pulled my hood over my head and headed out the back door.

☾

"Going somewhere?" I drawled from where I leaned against the wall of the alley between the tavern and the neighboring building. The male paused on the sidewalk, glancing around until his gaze landed on me.

The male's brow wrinkled. "Do I know you?" I pushed off the wall, stepping into the light, and removing the hood so he could see my face.

"No, but you could," I purred. His green eyes glimmered as they roamed over my face to the exposed skin of my chest where my breasts were on full display as they strained against my corset.

I turned and walked down the alley, not needing to look back to know he was following me.

They always did.

Only once I reached the end of the alley did I turn around, finding the male prowling towards me. "Who knew my luck at cards would continue into the night?" He drawled. One of his hands grabbed my hip and he braced the other on the wall beside my head, causing the thin material of his shirt to slip up the pale skin of his arm.

"What a pretty little thing you are." I resisted a shudder as he ran his nose over my cheek, breathing me in as my eyes darted to the dark ink painting the inside of his forearm. I smiled coyly as I looked at him, taking my bottom lip between my teeth as I let my eyes roam over his body.

I ran my hand up his thigh and under his shirt.

"Are you going to fuck me in this alley?" The hand on my hip gripped me tighter as he ground against me.

"Fuck." He moaned. "That's exactly what I'm going to do." He ducked his head, his lips lingering over my exposed collarbone.

A smile ghosted my lips as I wrapped my hands around the male's cock, giving it a long stroke with one hand through his pants as I reached for my dagger with the other.

## 2

## LENNOX

The male didn't notice my dagger had pierced into his side until it was too late. He didn't even have time to scream before I removed it and shoved it through his heart. Blood splattered my clothes, I could feel it against my bare chest as I removed my dagger, stepping back to allow the male to slump to the ground with a thud.

His eyes searched mine in confusion as he lay on the ground, looking for some sign of remorse as blood leached from his wounds, forming a puddle beneath him.

"Does that always work?" A soft feminine voice called from behind me. A voice tinged with judgment, which I had grown all too accustomed to over the past weeks.

"Does what always work?" I didn't look over my shoulder as I knelt next to the male's body, cleaning the blood from my dagger on his shirt.

"Seducing them so they're too distracted to know you're going to kill them?" I rolled my eyes. Grasping the male's arm in my hand, I drew a small ball of flame in the other as I assessed the tattoo on his arm.

The three interlocking circles with an intersecting triangle glared back at me under the soft light. "It makes it easier, that's for sure." The male continued to gasp for breath as I rifled through his pockets for anything of value. "People are a lot less suspicious of me when I'm giving them the impression I'll give them pleasure. It's a surefire way to get anyone stupid enough to work for the Vanir to follow me down a darkened alley."

Finding nothing in the male's pockets, I stood and faced my sister. Kara stood with her arms crossed glaring at me. Her dark cloak concealed her subtle body, revealing only her narrow nose and full lips under the shadows of her hood. Her emerald eyes sparkled in the dim light of the moon.

"You're killing for sport now?" Kara's gaze flitted toward the dying male on the ground. "You didn't even try to get any information out of him before you killed him."

"There was nothing useful he could have given me."

"And how do you know that?"

"I have my ways." She didn't need to know I had killed his friends earlier. That I had taken my time to get the information I needed out of them before I killed them. They had nothing to share I didn't already know. The only piece of information worthwhile was about their friend who traveled with them to Alethens on the Vanir's dime only to abandon them once they arrived. This male might not be working with the Vanir, but he had been associated with them at one point. I couldn't leave any loose ends.

"One of these days this is going to come back and bite you in the ass," Kara countered.

I shrugged. "How so?"

"Someone is going to catch you one of these times, Len," she whispered angrily. I laughed, the sound cold and bitter as it ricocheted through the alley.

"And what if they do? Are they going to report me to the queen? Do you forget who you're talking to?"

Kara let out a harsh breath. "Goddess, I knew it was a fool's errand to try to tell you to be less reckless, but Lennox, I'm worried for you." She approached me, taking my hands in hers. "You need to be more careful."

I pulled my hands out of her hold and crossed my arms instead. "I need to take down the Vanir and stop them from killing any more innocent people."

"And killing them on the streets every night is going to do that?" She took another step towards me. "Tell me, Lennox, in all the nights you've spent out here, stalking and killing Vanir, have you found any information of use?" Her words stung like a blow, my jaw clenching as I rolled over her words in my mind.

"We both know the real reason why you distract yourself with this task every night, Lennox; you come out here and distract yourself with vengeance to keep yourself from addressing what's really bothering you."

I whipped my gaze to her. "You can't avoid it any longer Lennox, you leave for the Blood Court in the morning."

*You don't think I know that.* I wanted to scream. But I didn't. I kept it locked up inside, as I did with all my feelings these days. After that first night, spent with my tears staining my pillows, I hadn't allowed myself to feel sadness for what I had lost that day.

Not for the innocent people lost because of me.

Not for—*no.* I had one more day until I had to confront that. Not yet.

I let all sadness go and traded it for vengeance instead.

Vengeance for my people.

I don't have it in me to get vengeance for my heart. For myself.

I turned my attention back to my sister, taking in her blazing red hair for the first time as she removed her hood.

"Care to explain to me what you're doing here so late?" I raised a brow. "Looking like that?"

"Don't ask questions you don't want to know the answers to." I knew Kara wasn't sitting around by herself at night while I was gone, but I never imagined I'd find her out here, deep in the pit of the city, long past reasonable hours to be out, glamored, to hide her appearance.

I knew my sister; she wasn't out here like me, killing to feel something, but what was she up to? I wanted to ask, the shattered remains of my heart tugged towards her—begging to let her in.

But if I asked questions of her, that allowed her to ask questions of me.

So I bit my tongue.

"I should get going," I turned from my sister's assessing gaze. With the snap of my fingers, the Vanir male's body burst into flames.

"I've got a lot to do before dawn."

# 3

# LENNOX

I pulled my cloak tighter around me as Odin approached the black gates of the palace. Guards dressed in all black held them open on either side as our convoy passed through. A red circle was embroidered on each of their lapels, with lines zagging across the circle in thick red thread, forming two *V's* that resembled fangs, the seal of the Blood Court.

*The Blood Court*—after two weeks of grueling travel, we had finally made it to Cel Nox, the capital city, this afternoon.

There were no Vanir to track, no duties to attend to, no corners to hide in while we traveled. For two weeks, I had maintained my mask of High Queen as I traveled with a group of six Star Court guards.

All I had while traveling was time to think.

Time to think about what I would face while I was here. What I could no longer avoid.

*Who* I could no longer avoid.

It had been six weeks since I held a blade to his throat and demanded him to leave.

For six weeks I had agonized over every decision I had made that led me here. To arrive in the Blood Court to announce my engagement to the Prince.

To the male who had stolen my heart only to destroy it in the end.

He sent letters, of course, he sent letters. They arrived each week like clockwork. I read the first lines of the initial letter before throwing it into the hearth. I blinked back the tears in my eyes as I watched the parchment burn. The rest of the letters that arrived went straight into the flames. I couldn't read his words of remorse. If I was going to survive this arranged marriage, I had to shut myself off from those emotions.

The stones of the Blood Palace were painted black, and even the windows appeared black and clouded, giving the entire palace an eerie feeling. One tower stood taller than the rest at the center of the dwelling. I wondered who got the honor of occupying the tallest peak.

King Arlo most likely. The tallest peak to keep a watchful eye on his city.

*To watch me arrive.*

There was a chill in the late fall air, but that's not why a tremor wracked my body as I passed through the obsidian doors into the palace. I was in the home of vampires.

The *Court* of vampires.

The *City* of vampires.

The home of the vampire who had a hand in shattering my heart. The vampire who—I shook my head, banishing the thought.

*A little while longer.* I had to hold myself together a little while longer.

"Your Majesty!" The males voice boomed across the grand foyer, my guards drew in closer, as the male made his way toward me with a broad smile on his face. "Welcome to Cel Nox. What a pleasure it is to be hosting you." He bowed deeply.

I smiled tightly. "Thank you for having me. And you are?" The male's onyx hair fell past his shoulders, making his pale face appear even more elongated. His downturned eyes matched the shade of his hair.

"My apologies, Your Majesty. I'm Warren, I'm the head of the palace; King Arlo has sent me to welcome you."

"It's nice to meet you, Warren."

My eyes scanned over the faces of the vampires lining the grand hall. The foyer was larger than the one in my own home, it extended far wider with large archways made of a deep black stone on either side that matched the dark color of the walls. The room looked out into a courtyard of sorts, through several rectangular windows trimmed in black.

I hoped in a sea of unfamiliar faces, there might be at least one familiar face, but there wasn't.

Why would he be here anyway? I had been so terrible to him the last time I saw him. I had *ordered* him to leave. Why would he be here to greet me? I was technically his betrothed, I figured he'd be here to welcome me for appearance's sake at least.

"Please follow me," Warren directed as he walked. "I'm sure you're itching to freshen up after your travel, I can show you to your rooms after I take you to meet King Arlo."

My feet stilled, refusing to move. "Is everything alright, Your Majesty?" A line formed between Warren's brows. *The King*, the king wanted to meet me now?

"I would like to freshen up before seeing King Arlo."

"I'm afraid that's not possible, Your Majesty. King Arlo has requested you be brought to him immediately upon your arrival." A knot formed in my stomach. I was already apprehensive about meeting the infamous Blood King, but I didn't expect this—him insisting on seeing me immediately after I arrived. I needed time to prepare.

I needed a moment alone.

I steeled my shoulders. We might be in the Blood Court, but I hadn't forgotten who I was even if they had.

"You can tell the king I am thankful for the warm reception, but I am the High Queen, if I would like to have a hot bath before seeing him, I will have a hot bath before seeing him. If he has a problem with my wishes you should remind him where he falls in the order of things."

Warren scratched behind his ear. "Of course, Your Majesty. Let me show you to your room. I will let King Arlo know you will see him when you are ready."

"Thank you. Please tell him I appreciate his patience."

Warren smiled tightly. "Of course, Your Majesty."

He turned and I continued following him through the throng of vampires, keeping my back straight and shoulders back as I ignored the stares of the vampires, my boots clacking on the deep mahogany floors.

Once we were out of the view I let myself relax slightly, letting out the breath I had been holding as we ascended the staircase carved into the side of the building.

Warren led me to my room, stopping outside the door to rattle off instructions I tuned out, my eyes fixed on the black doorknob.

So close. I was so close.

Finally, he left me.

The minute the door to my bedchamber closed I let out a sigh of relief.

*Alone.*

I was finally alone.

☾

Some while later a knock sounded on my door. I hoped it wasn't my ladies maid, Krissa, again. Twice I had sent her away since I had arrived. Stars bless the girl for trying, but I didn't want her assistance right now. I didn't need her to draw my bathwater or brush my hair. I had grown up accustomed to the company of ladies maids growing up, but I hadn't had one of my own in years, I preferred it that way.

I trudged across my room to the closed door, swinging it

open with force, prepared to give Krissa a piece of my mind this time for failing to stay away until I called upon her.

But when I opened the door it wasn't the female standing there. It was a dark-haired winged male.

"Declan," I stammered. "What are you doing here?"

The harpy's golden eyes narrowed. "I live here, or did you forget?"

"I mean here, at my door."

His voice softened slightly. "I'm here to escort you to see King Alro."

I moved to shut the door, but he was quicker, blocking it with one of his massive arms.

"Fuck," I murmured as I continued my attempt to push the door shut, throwing my entire body against the door.

"I figured you wouldn't be agreeable. That's precisely why I volunteered to come get you. "

I gave up, the harpy was practically a brick wall. I left Declan in the doorway, turning my back to him, and crossed the room towards the sitting room, taking a seat in one of the over-sized chairs.

"It's not that I don't want to go see the king, it's—I'm not ready yet."

"Well, let me prepare you." He tucked in his wings and sat on the couch across from me. "King Arlo has been waiting for the moment he finally gets to meet you. All he wants to do is meet you, to have a conversation. You have nothing to be worried about."

"I'm not worried."

Declan cocked his head and raised a single dark brow. "Even if you were, I'd be right outside the door the entire time," he leaned forward, resting his elbows on his knees. "That's why I wasn't there to greet you when you arrived. I was waiting with Arlo for your arrival."

I said nothing, opting instead to toy with a loose string on one of the decorative pillows.

"Luka and Nico were meant to greet you in the grand hall." My hand stilled on the thread. "You arrived sooner than we anticipated, Luka was out when you arrived, but he was going to be here. He wanted to be here. He should be back soon."

Why was he telling me this? Why did he care? This wasn't the Declan I was used to, I was certain this might have been the most Declan had ever spoken to me directly. Before everything had transpired that day in Alethens, we had become friends— kind of. We were friendly at least. I assumed when things dissolved between Luka and I, it meant I lost Declan and Nico as well. I didn't expect this—this felt like he was looking out for me.

"Fine." I stood, running my hands over my crimson dress. "Take me to see the King."

## 4

## LENNOX

"How is Kara?" Declan guided me through the palace to the king's study.

"She's—fine." I hesitated.

"She's fine?" Declan glanced at me out of the corner of his eye. "And how would you know that? From what I hear you two haven't been speaking much."

"How would you know?" Was it possible Declan had spies in the Star Court? Keeping an eye on me and Kara?

"She told me."

My head snapped toward him. "She told you? Kara told you we haven't been speaking?"

Declan nodded, unfazed as he continued to lead me through the dark marbled hallway.

"She started sending me letters shortly after we left the Star Court."

"And you've been sending her letters back?" He dipped his chin in confirmation. "What do you talk about?"

"That is between me and your sister."

"You told me she said we weren't speaking much!" I argued.

"I only told you because she asked me to look out for you

while you're here." Declan stopped, turning to face me. "She's worried about you, Lennox."

I scoffed, crossing my arms over my chest. "Well, you can write back and tell her I'm fine, and she needs to worry about herself." My chest tightened. Had I cut my sister off so much she was seeking guidance about me elsewhere? She was sending letters to Declan instead of talking to her sister who lived under the same roof...

"Lennox—" I cut him off, raising a hand to stop him.

"No, I don't want to talk about this anymore. If you want to talk with my sister fine, but leave me out of it."

Declan let out a deep sigh. "Fine, we're here anyways." I turned toward the black metal doors looming in front of us. I set my shoulders as he reached for the door handle. It was time to meet the Blood King.

☾

"King Arlo, I present to you, High Queen, Lennox Adair." The king stood from behind his dark obsidian desk as Declan introduced me, but my gaze went to the male standing next to him.

I bit back a snarl at the sight of Lorenzo next to the king.

The Blood Court was full of all kinds of surprises today.

"Lennox Adair, it is a pleasure to finally meet our esteemed High Queen." He gestured to his son at his side. "You've met Lorenzo."

I smiled tightly at Luka's uncle. "Of course, good to see you again, Lorenzo," I lied.

Please have a seat." Arlo gestured to one of the large chairs in front of his desk. "Thank you for escorting her, Captain Hale, you are excused." He looked at his son, "As are you, Lorenzo." The male tensed.

"You said I was allowed to be present while you met the Queen," Lorenzo protested.

Arlo's jaw clenched, "You were. Now, I would like a moment alone with the High Queen."

"But—"

"Captian Hale, escort Lorenzo out." Declan grabbed Lorenzo's arm and led him toward the door.

"I can let myself out," Lorenzo grumbled as he tugged out of Declan's hold. The harpy bowed and looked at me once more. I gave him a slight nod before he turned toward the door.

The door clicked shut behind him as I turned my attention back to the Blood King.

"I apologize for my son's behavior." He let out a long breath through his nose. "I'm assuming your travels went well?"

"Yes, we didn't encounter any roadblocks, which made for quick travel."

I could tell King Arlo was edging close to his first century of life, his chin length hair was still the dark rich color of Luka's, but wrinkles were forming around his eyes—the first sign of aging for most Fae. "Good, good, we wouldn't want anything to happen to our revered queen."

His words were light, but there was a vicious undercurrent to them. Along with the gleam in his dark eyes, even I had the nerve to be cautious sitting across from him. "Would you like a drink to relax after your journey?" He motioned toward the drink car in the corner.

"Sure."

He poured several knuckles worth of amber liquid into two black crystal glasses. "I'm sure you're wondering why I asked you to meet with me without my grandson present."

I remained quiet, taking the drink as he handed it to me across the desk.

"I'm sure you're tired after your travel so I will make this quick and get right to the point." I dipped my chin as I brought my glass to my lips.

"I wanted you alone so I could ask you how you truly felt about this arranged marriage." I jolted back slightly, taken aback by his bluntness, but it reminded me of Luka, the way he spoke his mind without caring if they might make someone uncomfortable. "I'm well aware of Luka's feelings, but I wanted to know how you feel, Your Majesty."

"And how does Luka feel about our arrangement?" I took a sip of my drink, focusing on the burn as it slid down instead of what Luka might have said about me.

Arlo assessed me for a moment, his dark eyes narrowing. "You tell me your thoughts first, then I'll tell you what my grandson said. I don't want his words to sway what you might say."

He leaned back, his chair groaning. He was a smart male, I'd give him that. I appreciated him being upfront, but I didn't have any reason to trust his intentions. Any information I gave him could be used against me.

"I don't know how much Luka has told you, but I am not thrilled at the arrangement. As everyone knows, my parents were mated, I hoped I would find my mate someday. I'm not daft, I know an arranged marriage would be best for my political standing, but it's not what I imagined for my future. It's taking some time to get used to the idea."

Arlo sipped his drink. "And you were not your family's heir, none of this was a future you saw for yourself. I'm sure it has all come as a shock."

"It has."

"I am truly sorry for your loss." His gaze darted to his desk, avoiding mine. "I met your father—and your brother too, they were both great males. All of Lethenia suffered because of their deaths."

I swallowed the lump in my throat.

"Luka on the other hand, has known he would be king from the age he could understand what his title meant. He's been training for this his entire life. He's always known there was a probability he would partake in an arranged marriage if it arose. Never once did he argue against it or speak any displeasure." Arlo took another sip of his drink. "So imagine my surprise, when he came home, from spending time with you, away from his home, and instead of being happy, he came back in the worst mood I've ever seen him in."

Arlo shook his head, his dark hair swaying. "The boy hardly speaks to me, and when he does, his mood is piss poor. All he ever tries to do is talk me out of you two marrying." He set his empty glass on the desk with a thud, resting his elbows on the desk and leaning in close.

"So tell me, Lennox Adair, why is it he never had a problem with an arranged marriage except when it came to marrying you?"

My throat tightened. I truly had wrecked him. Broken him as thoroughly as he broke me. "I—I can't speak for Luka's actions."

Arlo let out a puff of air. "I don't care what happened between the two of you previously, all I care about is the future. A future that is dependent on my grandson marrying you."

I bit the inside of my cheek. Clearly, Lorenzo hadn't divulged everything to his father upon his arrival back in the Blood Court, and neither had Luka. The king appeared oblivious to mine and Luka's relationship. Unless Arlo was as good a liar as me.

"So what I need you to do, Ms. Adair, is to convince my grandson this union is the best thing for him. Maybe hearing it from you will make him see clearly."

I doubted Luka wanted to hear anything I had to say. I doubted he'd even want to see me.

"What makes you assume I can convince him?" Emotions clogged my throat as I steeled my shoulders.

Arlo poured himself another drink, remaining silent as he filled his glass.

"You're a pretty, young thing." He leaned back in his chair. "I don't imagine it will take much convincing."

"Why are you so adamant Luka marries me? He was in line

for a title here. Do you not suppose he will make an adequate king?"

Arlo's nostrils flared. "Quite the opposite, Your Majesty, Luka will make a marvelous king. I would not have put him up for the title of High King if I didn't believe so. Like I said, the boy has been preparing to be king his whole life."

The words, *unlike you,* were left unsaid.

Arlo's voice deepened as he continued, "He was trained by me and his father, who would have made an outstanding king had he not died unexpectedly." Arlo's voice wavered slightly.

"When Luka's parents died, it changed him. There was a while where I thought I wouldn't get him back. He was so lost in his grief—" He shook his head as he stared at his hands. "I was not a present father to my own children, so trying to be a father to my grieving grandson was something I had no clue how to do, but I tried my best, because despite what you may believe, I love my grandson very much, and I want only the best for him. I believe the future my grandson deserves is not here."

He leveled his gaze with my own. "I am only telling you this because you are the High Queen, and I believe you will use this information with discretion. Do I have your discretion, Lennox Adair?"

Anxiety coiled in my gut. *No.* I wanted to tell him. I couldn't handle anything more right now. But I needed to know what he knew.

"Yes."

"Dark things are brewing in our court, things I don't want to leave as a burden on my grandson."

"What kind of dark things?" I pressed.

"That is a conversation of another time, but I will let you know this Lennox Adair—Luka may believe the Blood Court is his legacy, but it's not. He needs to get out of here before it is too late. So when I saw the opportunity to get him out I took it. Despite how angry it might have made him."

I opened my mouth to press him for more details, but he stopped me.

"Please, not now. Not today. I know you are my High Queen, and you have every right to this knowledge, but not today. I promise you another time."

"Fine," I conceded. "But I have one last question. If Luka will not take your crown, who will? Certainly not Lorenzo?"

The king laughed. "So Luka has told you about Lorenzo?"

"He did, and I had the displeasure of spending time with him." Even if it was cut short.

"No, Lorenzo will not get the crown. Although he might think otherwise. I am ready to give up my crown, but I will hold onto it as long as I need until I find another heir."

I had no idea how Arlo was going to find another heir, but I was satisfied with knowing Lorenzo wouldn't be king. And I knew Luka would be too. Not that I had any right to care what Luka might think.

I stood, placing my empty glass on the desk. "It was nice to meet you, King Arlo."

"You too, Lennox Adair. I look forward to many more conversations."

I dipped my head before turning towards the door. "As do I."

"What did he have to say?" Declan asked the moment the door to Arlo's office clicked shut behind me.

"That is none of your business." Declan grumbled as he followed behind me. "I don't need a watch dog, Declan. I can find my way back to my room on my own."

"It's my job to escort you—"

"I need time alone," I snapped. The footsteps behind me stalled, but I didn't bother to look back. I knew the face Declan would be wearing without having to look. I'd be the same face my sister wore more times than not when around me.

I'd seen enough disappointment as of late. I didn't need to see Declan's too.

I continued toward my room alone.

# 5

## LUKA

Smoke was thick in the air, it clogged the crowded street, making it appear later than it was as Nico and I wove through the stalls. We had been making our way through the Stygin market for over an hour looking for a specific vendor to no avail.

The Stygin market was a well-known secret among the Blood Court. All kinds of Fae set up shop in the market. Selling both legal and illegal substances. The palace was aware of the existence of the market but left the vendors alone on the promise they did no harm. Up until the past few weeks, I had only visited the Stygin market once, on a dare from Nico when we were teens. We only made it two blocks before a vendor tried to sell us a crystal. The sight of her smiling with her black rotted gums sent us both running back to the palace without looking back. We were never eager to return after that encounter. Never had a reason to.

But here we were, back at the Stygin market in search of a witch. A witch who possessed a wide variety of ancient texts. She wasn't a frequent vendor here, she only made an appearance every few months, which is why I found myself checking the market once a week, in search of this so-called witch Scribe.

I picked up my pace as I neared the end of the street. I

didn't have all day to wander. I looked both ways before I crossed the alley. We still had several more streets to assess, the market was packed today, making it harder than normal to move through the throngs of people.

"We're running out of time." I ran my hands through my hair. "We should split up."

"Fuck if I'm letting you leave me alone out here." Nico grimaced. "We can come back tomorrow."

"I don't want to come back tomorrow, I need to find this witch today," I insisted.

"But what if she's not even here? There's no guarantee."

I turned and faced my friend. "I need to at least try."

Nico pinned me with a pitying look that made me wince as I fisted my hands at my side.

"Well, let's keep going, brother." I followed behind Nico as he continued down the street, even in the haze of the smoke his icy hair shone. I couldn't lose track of him if I tried. "We should still have a couple of hours until your betrothed arrives. That's plenty of time for us to find this little witchy and get your bride-to-be an engagement present." I ground my teeth, he threw the words around so easily.

*Bride-to-be.*

*Betrothed.*

She and I were betrothed and I had failed her.

I was supposed to protect her. Keep her safe.

Guard her heart.

I had failed her by keeping one little secret from her.

I should have known better. I knew how much she valued honesty.

I knew how much her trust was worth. How hard I had worked to earn it.

I lost it all in the blink of an eye. With one single sentence, everything we built crumbled.

And now we were to be married. She was going to be bound to me for eternity.

Unless I could find Astria's spellbook. Which is why I needed to find the witch Scribe. I would not fail Lennox again. I could do this one last thing for her. Free her from me.

Even if my own heart rebelled against the thought.

I could take the coward's way out.

Marry her. Tie her to me forever.

But that's not what she wants.

It's not what I want either.

I want Lennox to choose me for herself because she wants to be with me. Not because someone forced her to.

So I spent these past two months doing nothing but trying to find Astria's spellbook. If I managed to find it myself and give it to my grandfather, I hoped he'd let Lennox out of our arranged marriage.

He had to.

Which is why I had to find the witch Scribe today. It had been Luciana who turned me onto her. She heard about the ancient Scribe from another witch in her coven. According to Luciana the Scribe held the oldest collection of books in the entire Mystic Court. If anyone was going to have Astria's spellbook it was bound to be her.

It took some inquiring on both of our ends to figure out she traveled from court to court; it just so happened she was due to arrive in the Blood Court this month.

The impending arrival of the witch Scribe couldn't have some at a better time.

Nico nudged me, pulling me from my thoughts as he directed me towards a stall where a small, dark-skinned woman sat. Painted on the banner on the front of her booth was a moon, a sun, and three stars, the signs of each of the witch covens.

A witch, *finally*.

"Let's go." I steered Nico towards the witch.

"Hello, my lady," Nico drawled. "We were hoping you'd be able to help us find one of your sisters."

The witch assessed Nico, her brows pinching and nose wrinkling. "Why should I help you, wolf?"

Nico's brows rose. "How do you know I'm a wolf?"

"Please, I can smell it all over you. You pups stink."

"Hey—"

"Now is not the time Nico." I placed my arm in front of him to draw him back.

"What my friend is trying to say is we've been looking for the witch Scribe."

"What need do you have from a witch Scribe?"

So she wasn't the Scribe. "I'm looking for a book."

The crease between her brows deepened. "What kind of ancient witch volume could a vampire be in need of?"

"That"—I picked up one of the crystals on the table—"is none of your concern."

Time felt like it stretched on forever as she considered my words. I shifted from one foot to another as I tossed the cool crystal in my hands. I needed to get back to the palace before Lennox arrived.

"There is a price for the information you want," the witch said finally.

"Name it, whatever it is, I'll pay it."

"Luka— you can't be serious. This is a witch we're talking about," Nico argued.

The witch threw Nico a glance before breaking out into a sinister smile. "Your friend is right, you are reckless for saying you will jump into a bargain with a witch without knowing what it consists of. What if it's your soul I ask in return?"

"I don't care what the price is. I will pay it."

Nico mumbled a string of incoherent curses. The female's face softened. "You must love someone very much to go to such lengths for them." She was right. But I couldn't admit it out loud. The last time I had tried I found myself on the wrong side of a dagger.

I rubbed at my neck, the phantom sting of the metal sinking into my skin.

"Because you are seeking answers out of love, all I ask is a favor from you. To be redeemed at any time."

"Deal."

I itched at the skin on my forearm as Nico and I crossed the front yard to the palace. The spot where the witch had sliced a dagger across my arm was already healing, but I could still feel the remnants of magic from our deal lingering beneath my skin.

I knew I was reckless to tie myself to a witch, but it was worth it for the information she gave me. The witch Scribe should be arriving in a couple of weeks.

Another witch, the half witch I had tied myself to, was due to arrive in a few hours, giving me enough time to wash the stench of the Stygin market off me before she arrived.

The grand foyer was eerily quiet when we entered. I had expected everyone to be preparing for Lennox's arrival, but no one was to be found.

"Warren!" My voice echoed in the empty space. It took a moment before the vampire's voice rang out in response and he appeared, peeking his head around one of the dark arches, "Yes, Your Highness?"

"Where is everyone? Why are they not preparing for the High Queen's arrival?"

Warren's brow furrowed. "She's already arrived, Your Highness. Her convoy arrived at the gates early this afternoon."

"Fuck." I had missed it, I had missed her arrival. "Where's the high queen now?"

"I believe she finished her meeting with your grandfather and should be heading back to her room."

"Astria's tits," Nico swore. "That's a meeting I would have liked to see."

I swallowed. This is exactly what I had wanted to avoid.

Lennox was strong, she could hold her own with my grand-father, I had no doubt, but I still would have liked to have been by her side—given her a heads up as to what to expect from him. Why did my grandfather ask to meet with her without me?

I'd think about that more later.

I had more important things to worry about.

C☾

I rushed up the stairs towards my bedchamber, taking the steps two at a time, the scent of citrus and lilacs invading my nostrils as I approached the top of the stairs.

She had been here. My stomach knotted. I had thought about this moment for weeks. What I would say to her when I saw her. What I'd do.

But now—all of that went out the window. All I wanted was to lay my eyes on her.

A flash of honey-colored hair snagged at the corner of my periphery as I rounded the corner into the hallway.

She stood facing away from me. Her hand resting on the doorknob. Her gown was made of the color a crimson so deep it reminded me of blood. It hugged every dip and curve of her luscious body. The body I had explored every inch of with my hands and mouth and had been dreaming about for months. As she shifted, her gown revealed a slit up the side and the gleam of metal hid there. My mouth dried.

"Lennox." The words came out a sigh—a plea almost.

*Turn around. Look at me.*

I watched as her shoulders lifted before she turned towards my voice.

Her luscious lips parted in a perfect *o* as those emerald eyes met mine.

Fuck, I had missed those eyes. My body relaxed as her lips tilted upward.

I took a step towards her. I needed to touch her. I needed to feel her—to know she was truly here and happy to see me and this wasn't all a figment of my imagination.

"Lennox." I sighed.

I saw the moment she remembered—when the shock of seeing me wore off.

She clamped her lips together, her gaze turned icy before she turned back around—reaching for the door handle.

"Lennox wait!"

But I was too late. The door slammed shut in my face.

# 6

## LENNOX

I pressed myself against the closed door—balling my hands into fists to try and grasp some semblance of control as my magic pushed and pulled painfully against my skin.

In the weeks we'd been apart I couldn't keep my mind from wandering to what would happen when I saw Luka again.

I had imagined it would be in a large group of people—that I would be able to anticipate the scenario.

I would have my mask of High Queen on. I would be prepared. There would be other people around. I could use as distractions.

Never in all my planning did I account for running into him on accident.

Or the impact the sound of his voice would have on me.

Or that seeing him again would steal the breath from my lungs as his eyes pierced into my soul, lighting up at the sight of me.

When I heard his voice—I forgot for a moment everything that had transpired between us.

That he had broken my trust.

That he had shattered my heart.

That I was supposed to marry him.

At that moment he was simply Luka again.

*My friend.*

My heart clenched. My friend. My lover. *My Luka.*

But he wasn't *my* anything anymore.

He was my betrothed in name only.

"Lennox, please," Luka pleaded from the other side of the door. Every wall I had attempted to build back up over the last weeks threatened to crumble at those two words.

"Lennox, please. I only want to talk to you. Open the door."

I was tired. I hadn't slept well on the trip. I hadn't slept well *in weeks.* That's why my control was threatening to slip so easily. It had nothing to do with the male on the other side of the door.

He was silent, but I could still sense him there. I could smell him. I let myself slide to the floor, clutching my knees to my chest with my back against the door.

"I missed you," he said finally.

*I missed you too.*

I listened as he moved, his back thumping against the door as I assumed he sat as I did with his back against the door.

"I'm sorry I wasn't there to greet you. You weren't due to arrive until later this evening. I didn't want you to arrive here alone. I'm sorry."

"It's okay." My voice was rough in my throat.

"Nothing is okay, Lennox."

He was right.

"How did everything get so fucked up?" he continued. Even through the door, I knew he was running his hands through his hair the way he did when he was anxious.

"We're two fucked up people." I sighed. "We were doomed from the start." I never should have let him in. I knew it would never end well, but yet I had let him in. I was as much to blame as he was.

"Do you ever think about how we almost had it all?" he asked.

I furrowed my brows. What did he mean, *have it all?*

"Those last days before I left everything was so good. You and I were happy. We were together. We were surrounded by the people we loved, spending our nights drinking too much wine and laughing until our sides hurt before we fell into bed together."

I shivered at the memory of the nights we spent together, skin on skin as we discovered one another's bodies. I hadn't let myself remember those nights or the ones spent with Kara, Luka, Nico, and Declan.

Those memories were now clouded with the ash of my burning city. *A city I left unprotected while I relaxed and enjoyed myself. While I let myself get fucked into oblivion.*

"We still had the prophecy and the Vanir to worry about, but we were happy and we had each other. When I had you by my side all of those other things seemed so insignificant. With you and I hand in hand I was confident we could do anything we set our minds to. It was supposed to be you and I, together forever."

*Until the stars turned to dust,* we had promised.

I could hear the smile in his voice. A smile a small part of me itched to see.

"And then everything got fucked up." He sighed. "I know I'm to blame for it, and I'm sorry I lied to you Lennox, and that I broke your trust and—" He swallowed. The words left unsaid hanging thick in the air. *I broke your heart.*

"I think about the choices I made every minute of every day. In my waking hours, and in my sleeping hours, I wonder what would have happened if I had told you about the potential of us being married from the start. Maybe it makes me a terrible person, but I don't regret my decision." That bastard. I'd—

"If I could go back I'd do it again. I'd keep that secret from you if it meant I got to spend the time we had together. If I had told you, you never would have looked at me as someone you could love. As someone you could choose to be with. You never would have looked at me as someone you could see a future with. You would have only seen me as a pawn in this game you wanted to win. So I don't regret what I did. I'd do it a million times over. I'd break your heart and mine over and over if it meant I got to see the way your eyes glow when you're happy. The ways your smile lights up a room. To hear your laugh. To experience what it feels like to be cared for by Lennox Adair, even if it was only for a short time."

My anger vanished as quickly as it came. Snuffed out like a candle in the wind by his words.

"I know that makes me selfish, but I'm done caring. I'm selfish when it comes to you, Lennox. I have been from the start. You do things to me—"

He sighed.

"I'm sorry I broke your trust, but I'd do it again. And I will spend every day making it up to you. That's what I was doing—that's why I wasn't there when you arrived. I was out looking for a witch Scribe with the hopes she could help me find Astria's spellbook."

He was still searching for the spellbook? Even after Hecate's warning? Even though we were set to be married?

"I will keep searching for it day after day until I can find you a way out of marrying me, Lennox. I would love nothing more than to call you my wife, but I know that's not what you want so I'm finding you a way out."

A tear slipped down my cheek, the first one to slip loose since the day I made him leave. I quickly wiped it away with the back of my hand. His voice was determined, but there was a hollowness to it—a sadness. I waited for him to continue, but he didn't. If I wasn't already sitting, I feared my legs would give out from under me. I had known Luka felt strongly for me, but this —I had been so cruel to him by ordering him to leave. But I never expected—*this*. For him to fight so strongly for my freedom to choose who I married. He had the title of High King in the palm of his hands. A title anyone in Lethenia would be eager to take without a second thought.

But not Luka. Would he throw away this opportunity for me?

"Did you read my letters?"

I swallowed. I hadn't felt guilty for throwing them in the fire until now. "No. I—I threw them in the fire without reading them."

"I knew the chances of you reading them was a long shot. But I still had to try, Lennox. You might have stopped thinking about me, but I never stopped thinking about you."

If he only knew—I couldn't think about him. If I had let myself think about him—

"Goodnight Lennox." His voice was thick with emotion. I listened as he stood and took a couple of steps, but he stopped. "Until the stars turn to dust, Lennox Adair."

Only once I could no longer hear his footsteps did I let the rest of the tears fall.

# 7

## LENNOX

I gave myself exactly one minute to wallow before I wiped my tears away and headed toward the bathing chamber.

I splashed my face with cold water, attempting to clear the redness from my face.

Why was it when it came to Luka I had such a hard time controlling my emotions?

I needed—I'm not sure even the Goddess knew what I needed.

I tried my best not to think about Luka over the past weeks. But it was a lot easier said than done. I thought about our last day together over and over again.

The more I let myself stew about it the angrier I became. Not at Luka directly, but at the situation we had been put in.

Even from the beginning, he knew me well enough to decide he shouldn't share his grandfather's proposal with me. We could never reverse time, but I had a hard time believing I would be able to trust anything he did knowing the information from the start.

I grew angry at myself because part of me agreed with Luka's decision. I never would have let myself open myself up to him if he told me his grandfather wanted me to marry him.

Every day I tried to convince myself if I knew that information I wouldn't have let myself fall for him.

I had yet to convince myself of that.

Everything Luka had admitted through the door—

I snapped my head up at the sound of a knock on the door. I took a steadying breath before pushing off the sink and walking to the door.

I hoped it was Krissa with my dinner. I didn't think Luka would try again so soon. I couldn't handle it if it was him on the other side.

When I opened the door I was met with someone who was most certainly not Krissa or Luka.

Instead, I was met by steely blue eyes and hair the color of the moon.

"Nico."

The wolf stood half leaning against the doorway in clothing far more casual than I had ever seen him in, carrying a tray of food in one hand and several bottles of wine in the other. "What are you doing here?"

"Isn't it obvious?" He grinned. "I've brought you dinner."

"But you're not my ladies maid."

He threw me one of his sly Nico smiles that only curved up one side of his mouth. "Are you sure? Perhaps I took up a new profession while we were apart. Being an emissary can get boring. Thought it was time for a change of pace." He winked before pushing himself off the door frame.

I shook my head. "I'm serious Nico, what are you doing here?"

"Like I said, I'm bringing you your dinner?"

I let out an irritated sigh. "But why are *you* bringing me dinner?"

"Because I missed you." I froze, my entire body stiffened at his words.

"Don't look so surprised, L. You make a damn good impression. Now are you going to let me in or make me stand in the hallway all night and eat this food alone?" *L? Where the fuck did that come from?*

I moved aside, allowing him room to move through the doorway before shutting the door behind him.

"C'mon, Lennox. I want to hear all about everything you've been up to these past few weeks."

When I finally turned away from the door I found Nico perched on the couch in the sitting room, filling two glasses with wine before holding one out to me.

He waggled his eyebrows at my hesitation. "I'm not the one who bites, remember?"

I crossed my arms over my chest. "What are you doing here, Nico?"

A crease formed between his brows as he took me in. His expression softened.

"You're my friend and I missed you. I thought this would be a great opportunity to catch up." His shoulders dropped as he looked at the glasses in his hands. "But if you want me to leave I will." He placed the glasses on the table and moved to stand.

"No wait, you can stay—it's—" I let my arms fall to my sides as I searched for the words. "It's been a long time since I've had a friend."

Nico smiled softly. "Well, let me reacquaint you with the practice of friendship, *my queen.*" He gestured to the space next to him on the couch. Hesitantly, I sat, taking the glass of wine from his outstretched hand.

"Typically, when friends haven't seen one another in a while they like to make time to catch up. Usually over wine."

I took a sip. "I can handle that."

"So how have you been? What have you been doing to occupy your time besides dreaming of us?"

A sound adjacent to a laugh caught in my throat. "I've been fine. I've been keeping busy with my duties as High Queen."

"I don't believe you for one second." He stretched a long arm over the back of the couch. "But if you're not ready to divulge whatever secret you're keeping now that's fine." I swallowed. I didn't think I'd ever be ready.

"Why are you here, Nico?"

"I already told you—"

I set my glass on the table and shifted on the couch so I could face him. "But why? You're Luka's best friend. Why are you choosing to come here and talk with me when you're on his side? Did Luka send you here to spy on me?"

He shook his head. "Is that what you think of me? And of Luka? You know he'd never do such a thing."

"But do I? How well do I know either one of you?"

"Lennox, there are no sides in this. Despite what you may believe we're all on the same side here. You and Luka might not be on the best terms, but that doesn't change our relationship." He gestured between the two of us with a finger.

Would they truly not pick sides? Nico and Declan? Maybe it was better if there weren't any sides. I'm not sure I'd have anyone on my side anyway, not with how I'd been treating my sister as of late. I would admit, I missed Nico. I missed his lighthearted spirit, his crass jokes, and the way he was able to make me smile so easily.

Nico placed his hand gently on my leg, his dark eyebrows bunching together as he met my gaze. "What is going on with you, Lennox?"

I took in a shaky breath. "I don't know." My chest constricted, my breaths coming in shallow pants as my magic pushed against my skin.

"You don't have to talk if you don't want to, but I'm here."

I took a deep breath, willing my magic to settle. "Coming here, seeing Luka, it's—it's made me feel confused." Nico took a sip of wine as he waited for me to continue. I hadn't talked to anyone about what transpired between me and Luka that last day. Not even Kara, but Nico—he made it so easy to talk to him.

And I needed to talk to someone. I needed to get these incessant thoughts out of my head.

"I came here convinced seeing him wouldn't change anything between us. That nothing he could say would change things between us…" I came here ready to draw a thick line in the sand. We were to be partners in a business agreement, nothing else. But seeing him and hearing what he had to say—it shouldn't have changed anything. It doesn't, but why does it feel like it does?

"I know it's not my place to speak," Nico's voice brought me back from my thoughts, "but I know how much he cares for you. Maybe your feelings have changed, but his haven't."

I wiped away a tear that threatened to slip out. "I don't want to talk about Luka anymore. Let's talk about something—*fun*." Anything else, I'd rather talk about anything else right now.

A devilish gleam crossed Nico's face at my words. He raised his glass to mine. "To friends."

"To friends." I clinked my glass with his before draining it.

☾

Several hours later, Nico and I found ourselves sprawled across my bed, making shadow puppets on the ceiling using a ball of flame I had created.

What had started as an innocent childhood reminiscing quickly became a dirty game that had us in stitches.

Nico groaned as he rolled on his side to face me. "My head is going to be pounding in the morning, but it will all have been worth it." He poked me in the side. "I got to spend the night with High Queen Lennox Adair."

I giggled as I swatted him on the arm. "You wish."

He propped his head on his hand. "Oh darling, you have no idea. If Luka hadn't already claimed you as his when I first laid eyes on you I would have tried." My smile dimmed at the mention of Luka.

"I'm sorry, L. I didn't mean to ruin the mood by mentioning him."

"No, it's okay." I waved him off, rolling onto my back. "I'm going to have to learn to not flinch every time I hear his name eventually."

Neither of us said anything as we stared at the ceiling.

"How is he?" I spoke into the silence.

"He's—he's okay. He's doing his best despite the circumstances. He keeps himself busy."

"Looking for the spellbook?"

Nico tilted his head slightly in my direction. "He told you about that?" I nodded. "That's all he's done since he got back. He hardly sleeps. Spends all his time researching and traveling around to talk to anyone who might have a lead."

I still didn't know what to make of him trying to get me out of our marriage. I should feel grateful, right? Or relieved. I didn't know how I felt about it yet, but it sure as fuck wasn't that.

"I should go," Nico mumbled as he rolled off the bed. I sat up as he collected his things.

"Nico?"

He turned toward me, "Yeah?"

"Will you tell him—"

Nico held out a hand. "I'm going to stop you right there. Anything you want to tell him you need to tell him yourself. He deserves to hear directly from you. Not from me."

He was right. Asking Nico to tell him was the coward's way out.

"Tell him I need time." I swallowed. "Can you tell him that much, please?"

"That I can do," he said softly.

Some of the pressure from my chest lightened.

I stopped him again as his hand twisted on the doorknob. "Nico."

He raised an eyebrow at me as I stepped into his space

before I wrapped my arms around him. He was stiff for a second before he realized what I was doing.

He wrapped his large arms around me and squeezed. "Thanks for tonight," I spoke into his chest.

"Anytime, L."

# 8

## LUKA

"Come in," I called out, not bothering to look up from the book I was reading at the sound of the knock on the door.

"Do you ever sleep?" Nico chidded.

"You're the one showing up at my room late at night." The smell of lilac and citrus invaded my senses as Nico sat at the chair next to my desk.

I looked up from my book to study him, a burning sensation forming in my chest.

"Were you with Lennox?"

"I was." His lips curved into a smirk. "Jealous?" There was a playful lilt to his tone that made the burning sensation intensify.

I took in his disheveled appearance, his wrinkled clothes, and the smell of alcohol on his breath. Even his silver hair was rumpled. My veins heated.

Nico's expression changed quickly, his eyes going wide and he held up his hands, "It's not what you think, Luka. We were hanging out. As friends." I wanted to believe him—

"Do you think that low of me, Luka? You think I would go after her knowing not only you're engaged, but how you feel about her?"

I scrubbed my hand over my face. "You're right, fuck." I

took a deep breath. "I'm sorry. I know you would never do anything like that." Astria's tits, when it came to Lennox I lost all sense of rational thought.

"You were hanging out as friends?" I pressed.

"Yes, as friends." He sat back in the chair. "Although it took a lot of convincing on my part. You did a number on her, brother."

"What do you mean?"

"She was convinced Declan and I wouldn't want to be friends with her anymore because we would have taken your side."

I knew Delcan and Nico would never abandon her for what happened between us, but she didn't. I'd have to make sure to let Declan know he should try to talk to her too.

"What else did you two do?" Anything, I'd take any scrap of information on her.

"We talked, and drank a lot."

"What did you talk about?"

"My lips are sealed." He pretended to seal his lips and lock them before throwing away the key.

"But she talked to you? Actually talked? Did she seem like she was enjoying herself?" I knew how much I had hurt her. I had hoped she had been able to move on these past weeks, but not knowing if she had, haunted me. I wanted her to be happy.

"She was. We had a fun night. I wouldn't say she's fine, but she's still Lennox. She's still there." I felt like a small weight had been lifted off my shoulders. "It only took some convincing to get her to come out," he added.

"I'm glad she let you in. I couldn't even get her to open the door for me." I pinched the bridge of my nose before resting my elbows on the desk. "When she saw me she slammed the door in my face and refused to talk to me, so like a fucking idiot, I talked to her through the door."

"She said she needs time." He placed a hand on my shoulder. "She told me to tell you that she needs time."

"Time," I murmured. She needs time. Wasn't six weeks enough time? No, she could take all the time she needed. And I would continue to give her space and time if that's what she wanted.

"Will you promise me something?" I asked.

"Anything, what do you need?"

"Promise me you'll keep an eye on her. That you'll be there for her since I can't."

"Luka, you can be there—"

"No." I cut him off. "I can't be there for her." No matter how badly I wanted to, I couldn't. "I hurt her more by being there. But she needs someone. She needs you. Please, Nico."

Before today, I had hoped I'd be able to be there for her, but after her reaction to seeing me—

"Of course. I've got her."

"Thanks." The word came out strained.

"I've got you too, Luka." He patted a hand on my back. "Dec and I both, we've got you too. Don't forget that."

I stared at my palms as Nico stood. "You should get some sleep." He made his way toward the door.

There wasn't time for sleep. Not when I had a time limit as to when I needed to find Astria's spellbook. Soon my grandfather would set a wedding date. Any day now there would be a permanent time constraint on what I needed to accomplish. Sleep would come later.

After I found Lennox a way out of our marriage.

"I'm leaving for Maderia in the morning," I called out to Nico. "I'll be gone a couple weeks. I need you to continue to check the market while I'm gone, in case the Scribe comes while I'm away."

The muscles in Nico's back tensed as he stood in front of the door. He didn't turn as he spoke. "When are you going to stop punishing yourself?"

I shook my head. "What do you mean?"

"You've been waiting weeks for her to arrive and the day after she does you're going to take off?"

"She doesn't want to see me. What do you expect me to do? Sit here and mope around like a lost animal until she's ready to talk to me? Because I won't. She said she needs time, so I'll give her time."

Nico was quiet, I knew he was holding back what he wanted to say.

Finally, he spoke, "I'll look after her. Safe travels."

"Thank you."

Maybe I was punishing myself by leaving so soon after her arrival. I wanted to be here with her. I wanted to be the one looking out for her. But I know she doesn't want me here. If anything, staying here would be a worse punishment. Being here and seeing her and not being able to have her: that might be the worst punishment of all.

# 9

# LENNOX

I had to give it to Luka, I didn't anticipate he'd go to such lengths to avoid me. The morning after my arrival when Krissa delivered my breakfast she had a note from Luka for me. The letter was short and to the point. He had business to attend to out of town, he would be back in a week or two. I was surprised after our conversation the night before. Well, conversation was a stretch, after he talked to me through the door, I thought he'd constantly try to get me to talk to him, to figure things out. I didn't expect he'd leave so abruptly. It made things easy for me at least. All of the planning for our engagement ball was left to me. Not that I liked planning balls, but I was glad at least I didn't have to do it with Luka by my side and pretend everything was fine between us.

And it gave me time to mull over King Arlo's proposition.

He hadn't had time to meet with me again, but he had sent word promising we would soon. He wanted me to spend some time with Luka first and figure out how I might go about things. He seemed as surprised by Luka's last-minute trip as I was.

I spent my mornings training, before taking various meetings in the afternoons. Some days it was ball prep, other days I met with various members of the Blood Court. Although my trip here was for mine and Luka's engagement party, I was using it as a political trip as well. If I was going to spend time in the Blood Court I was going to make connections. If I was going to be tied to this court I wanted to know everything. I had expected to get pushback but was met with little. Most were eager to accept my invitations. During my evenings I surveyed the libraries, scouring over books detailing the history of the Blood Court. Some days Nico pulled me from the library and forced me to have dinner with him. Occasionally, Declan joined us, but it felt weird when it was the three of us. The lack of a specific person was felt more when it was the three of us. It wasn't as present when it was only me and Nico.

I hoped the arrival of Kara today would help ease that strain. Although with how things had been between Kara and I before I left, I doubted her arrival would ease any tensions. It would be a lot harder to avoid her here.

Last night when Nico had brought up Kara's impending arrival he assumed I would be excited. Declan and I shared a strained look that confused Nico even further. Instead of explaining I promptly left.

I'm sure Declan filled him in after.

Now, we all stood awkwardly in the grand hall, surrounded by a group of vampires as we waited for my sister's arrival.

Kara walked through the double doors, flanked by two guards on each side. She was dressed in her leathers, the fabric stretching around her full hips and thighs. Her golden hair was braided in a coronet with several pieces having ripped loose from riding.

"Your Highness!" Warren boomed, in the same way he had during my arrival, "Welcome to the Blood Court!"

"Thank you." My sister smiled sweetly, her eyes roamed around the room until they locked on mine. Her eyes drifted to the males on either side of me, her brows pinching before she fixed her expression. "I'm happy to be here."

"Little Adair!" Nico boomed as he stepped toward my sister. *When had he come up with these nicknames for everyone?*

A full smile bloomed over her face as she moved to embrace Nico, wrapping her arms around him as he lifted her into the air. She squealed before he placed her back on the ground.

"Kara." Declan's voice had a joyful lit to it, causing my brows to lift slightly.

"Declan." Kara smiled as she looked over the harpy before pulling him in for a hug. Declan stiffened as my sister wrapped her arms around him, his wings twitching before he gently put his arms around her.

"It's good to see you," he said.

"It's good to see you too." She bumped him gently on the shoulder, and he smiled as she turned towards me.

"Lennox."

"Kara." Both of our voices were strained as we appraised one another.

We reached for each other at the same time, moving awkwardly into a hug, our bodies stiff as we embraced. I'd never shared such an awkward hug with my sister.

Nico coughed as we pulled apart, sharing a look with Declan.

I glared at him in response.

He smirked at me before turning to Kara. "Shall we escort you to your rooms, little Adair?" He bowed dramatically as he held out his arm to Kara.

"Lead the way, little Nico." She looped her arm through his.

Nico gasped. "*Little?*" He put a hand on his chest dramatically. "I assure you there is nothing little about me, Kara Adair."

☾

Declan and I followed behind Nico and Kara as we ascended the stairs to her room, a couple of hallways from my own.

We all followed inside, taking a spot in the sitting room that led out onto the balcony.

Kara looked around the room, the layout similar to my own only mirrored facing the opposite side of the palace.

"So what have I missed since I last saw you all? And since my sister's arrival?"

"Not much," Declan mumbled.

"You got that right," Nico huffed. "Luka's been looking for Astria's spellbook non-stop, which kept the three of us busy until Lennox arrived last week, and then the bastard decided to go out on his own."

Kara narrowed her eyes. "What do you mean? Luka's not here?"

Declan shook his head. "He left the day after Lennox arrived."

"He left?" she asked again. I shifted in my seat as she turned her attention to me. "Did you even see him at all before he left?"

I swallowed. "Yeah. We saw each other briefly."

"How brief is briefly?" There was a vicious lilt to her tone that made me sit up straighter in my chair.

"That's none of your business,"

"Maybe it's not, but I want to know." She looked at Nico and Declan. "I'll find out one way or another."

I glared at Nico. "Don't you fucking dare."

His eyes widened as he looked between me and my sister. "What the fuck happened between the two of you?"

Kara gave me a pointed look. "You'd have to ask her." Her expression softened slightly. "We might not be speaking currently, but I am a good sister. I don't spill my sister's secrets."

Nico opened his mouth but shut it, the room turning quiet as Kara and I stared at each other.

It was Kara who broke the silence. "So who's going to tell me how brief was brief?"

Nico sighed. "They saw each other in the hallway. Lennox shut the door on him and he talked to her through the door."

Kara's gaze swung to me, she opened her mouth but closed it, remaining quiet for several moments before finally deciding to speak. "So when is *Your Highness* returning?"

# 10

## LUKA

Two days after I arrived in Maderia, a small city in the south of the Blood Court, I realized my search here was a bust. The library in the small village had been destroyed leaving nothing behind. Leaving me to sit and twiddle my thumbs for five days before I gave up due to boredom and decided to head back to Cel Nox. I figured seeing Lennox and not speaking to her would be better than sitting alone in a cottage thinking about her with nothing to distract me from my thoughts.

Usually, when I saw the palace coming into view returning home from travel I got excited to be back home. Not today.

Every step closer to the palace dread settled lower and lower in my stomach.

After leaving Zola in the stables, I took the back stairwell up to my room, not wanting to alert anyone to my arrival yet.

Which is why the last person I expected to see waiting outside my door was Kara.

I had seen Kara Adair in many forms. I had thought I had seen her angry, but looking at her now I knew with certainty I had never seen her *this* angry.

Her eyes were blazing with ire, the way Lennox's did when she was angry, turning the emerald pools to an endless pit of green so dark they were almost black. Her nostrils flared and her lips were posed in a snarl as she stood, hands on her hips outside my door.

She'd never looked more like Lennox.

The look reminded me of how Lennox looked at me those first weeks. A constant state of loathing and apprehension.

"Kara," I said tentatively as I approached. "Would you like to come in?"

"Since I'd prefer not to be attacked during our conversation by one of your guards, I believe that would be wise." My shoulders tensed at the threat. *Astria's tits*, what had gotten her so worked up?

Kara was not the fighting type. She was the mediator of every argument we had while traveling. She was always trying to ease tensions, never igniting them. Seeing this side of her, set me on edge. Kara might not reach first for a sword in a fight as Lennox did, but I had trained with Kara. I knew she could draw blood if she set her mind to it. She *was* related to Lennox after all.

"It's good to see you too, Kara."

She brushed past me, her steps heavy on the wood floor as she entered my quarters. "Cut the shit, Luka."

"For fucks sake Kara, do you care to explain to me why you're here with an apparent vendetta against me? Only *moments* after I arrived back to *my* home? In which you are a guest, in case you forgot."

Kara's sneer deepened. "I've been waiting for two days, since my own arrival, for you to return so I could give you a piece of my mind. Explain to me Luka, why has my sister seen you one time since she arrived? You talked to her through a fucking door, only to leave without warning for a week. Care to explain yourself, *prince*?"

I clenched my fists at my sides, "Watch your tone, Kara. I don't see what I did wrong. Am I supposed to clear every movement I make with your sister? Because that would prove difficult considering she refuses to speak to me."

She leveled me with another glare. Goddess, she was reminding me so much of Lennox right now. "Are you sure about that? Have you even tried to speak to her?"

"Her feelings were made pretty clear when she forced me to talk to her through a fucking door like a whimpering idiot." I shouldn't have admitted to Kara how much it stung to have Lennox reject me yet again, but Kara was a part of this, whether she liked it or not. "Your sister told me she needed time. So that's what I'm doing, giving her time."

"Males are such idiots!" Kara mumbled, throwing her arms in the air dramatically. "She may need time, but what she doesn't need is space!"

"What are you talking about, Kara?"

Her face softened. "You're giving up on her." Her voice was low and thick with emotion.

"I'm not giving up on her."

"That's what it looks like to me." She sat on the arm of one of the chairs, her anger was quickly dissipating, giving way to defeat instead as her shoulders dropped. "I had been counting down the days until Lennox returned to you because I knew you were the only person who could coax her back to life."

"Kara—what do you mean? I'm the reason she detonated in the first place."

There was a pleading tone to Kara's voice now, "You don't know what she's been like these past weeks. She's been so angry. Keeping things from me. She hardly talks to me." Kara's entire body deflated as she let out a shuddering breath. Kara and Lennox hadn't been talking? For how long? Why? Kara and Lennox hardly fought, and if they did it didn't last long.

"I've tried pushing her, but it doesn't work, not from me. I can't take her anger anymore. I hate making her mad, and she's been mad at me for weeks now. She needs you to push her. You're the only one who can." Kara looked at me, her eyes wide and glassy. Was I the reason there was conflict between Lennox and Kara?

"Everything fell apart because Lennox felt guilty for spending time with you instead of preparing for an attack she never could have anticipated. And you broke her trust. But that's only a small part of the problem. Her guilt is the main problem, and her fear of trying again." Kara ran her fingers up and down the arm of the chair.

"Maybe you don't think you're meant for my sister, but only you can restore her hope for the future again."

I shook my head as I took the seat across from Kara. "You don't understand. I broke her."

"Luka, those months you spent with us in Alethens, I got my sister back. You breathed life back into her. When you left she retreated back into herself, but not the sad version she was before she met you. I feel like she's turned off all emotions except anger now. It hurts me to see her like this. Almost more than it did before because I got a glimpse of who she could be again. You didn't break my sister, she was already broken. But, you're the only person who can put her back together. What happened that day in Alethens was a bump in the journey. A roadblock in yours and Lennox's life."

Kara didn't know what she was talking about. She didn't know everything that had transpired between me and Lennox.

"All these weeks I've been counting on you resolving the issues between you and Lennox once she got here," she continued. "So imagine my surprise when I arrive here, expecting my sister to have started healing again, only to learn you've been avoiding her."

"Kara, she commanded me to leave that day. She threatened me with treason if I didn't leave her. If she didn't despise me when we met, she certainly despises me now."

"She was hurting. You know she didn't mean it." I rubbed my hand over my throat, over the phantom touch of Lennox's steel blade against my skin.

"It sure felt like she meant it. There's a lot you don't know, Kara," I said softly.

"Luka," she begged. "You can't give up on her. You can give her time, but don't give her space. She's had too much space already. I need you to be there for her. Don't give up on her. *Please.*" Her pleading tone was so similar to Lennox's, it tugged at the loose threads in my chest.

Her words echoed through the empty part of my heart, the part that had belonged to Lennox and had been ripped out that day in the training center. Her words lit one of the remaining embers, causing the others to stir.

"I could never give up on her, Kara. You know that. No matter how hard I might try. I—I feel strongly for your sister. I probably always will, even if she never feels the same way." Those embers continued to stir to life inside me.

"I've been trying to find a way out of this arranged marriage. For her."

"Include her in it. Let her be a part of everything you do. She needs you, Luka."

Maybe part of me had been trying to protect myself from getting hurt again. Maybe that's why I had kept myself from her. Not only did I want to protect Lennox from getting hurt again, but I was unconsciously trying to protect myself. I knew if I spent time with her again it would do nothing but fuel my feelings for her.

It would give her another opportunity to leave me again.

But Hecate said Lennox and I were tied together. There would be no ridding one another from our perspective lives.

I had hoped that meant there was a future for us where we were more than friends, but maybe that was all we were meant to be. Friends.

I would break my heart over and over again if it meant I got to stand by Lennox's side, even if it was only as her friend.

I'd watch her fall in love with someone else if that's what made her happy.

I'd watch her marry someone else if it meant she got to pick them for herself.

I'd help heal her heart even if it meant breaking mine.

☾

I wiped my palms on my trousers as I tried to steady my raging pulse. I was standing outside Lennox's door, trying to work up the nerve to knock.

I spent all night mulling over Kara's words with a decanter of alcohol and Nico and Declan as my voice of reason. It was because of their convincing I was standing here now. I wanted to spend time with Lennox, I wanted to mend what had broken between us, and I wanted us to become friends again, but I wasn't confident she did.

Declan had insisted I had become too soft when it came to Lennox. *Where is the male that delighted in lighting her fire?* I was still here, but I was afraid to push her in fear of breaking her more. But Kara was right. I had pushed her before when she was broken, I could do it again.

For Lennox, I would do it.

Knocking on her door was the first step.

She had been here a week and I hadn't been able to lay eyes on her. And whose fault was that? I had run like a fucking coward.

Before I could lose my nerve I knocked.

The door opened in a flash of golden hair.

Lennox's hair hung in loose waves, appearing longer than it had before, brighter too against the dark blue of her gown. Her gown—goddess above, it clung to her hips and breasts, leaving little to the imagination.

"Luka—you're back." The only hint of surprise she showed was the slight raise of her brows.

I swallowed. "I am."

She crossed her arms over her chest, further pushing up her

breasts. I forced my eyes upwards. "I realized before I left I didn't tell you where to find the training facility. I'm sure you found your own means of training, but if you're interested there's a private training room with everything you could ever need located on the uppermost level of the palace."

Her eyes roamed over my body before she nodded. "Okay. I might have to wander up there."

"Okay." I knew I should have turned and left, I had no reason to linger, but I couldn't make myself pull myself away from her, not when I finally had the opportunity to look at her again. To talk to her.

"I was going to go for a walk." I ran my fingers through my hair, her eyes tracked the movement. "Do you want to join me?"

"I—I can't." My chest deflated. "But—um, maybe another time."

"Another time," I murmured.

She gave me a sad smile before closing the door.

# 11

## LENNOX

My thighs burned as I trudged up yet another set of winding stairs. I'd be too exhausted from the stairs to work out when I finally made it to the private training room Luka had promised me.

Eventually, I made it to a landing with a door. Thank the Goddess, I don't know how many more stairs I could handle. I pushed open the large wooden door, revealing an open loft space. The room took up what had to be the entire east wing of the palace. Windows surrounded the room on every side, basking the room in sunlight.

The space wasn't fancy by any means. The training facility at home was all sleek lines and steel, but this one—it felt well-used, the floors and walls were all made of well-worn light wood materials. A square training mat sat in the center of the room. A wall of weapons occupied one wall, a row of targets on the opposite side. It was nothing special, it was similar to the general training facility I had been using since I arrived, but this one was private. And that's all that mattered.

No more prying eyes as I trained. Just the way I liked it.

I made my way over to the collection of weapons; I had my

daggers strapped to my side and I grabbed my sword, Minerva, before I left. But my fingers itched towards the intricate daggers thrown about in the collection of weapons.

"You made it." I jumped at the sound of the familiar voice behind me.

"What are you doing here?" I turned to find Luka stalking toward me. There was something different about him today. Yesterday when he showed up in my room he seemed—diluted. He lacked all his normal confidence and charm when he appeared at my door, I had almost thought it was a dream. When I said no to his proposal of a walk I expected a rebuttal, some kind of antic to rile me, but he said nothing. Instead, he turned with his head hanging without another word, leaving me wondering if I had broken him after all. Today he appeared back to normal. The glimmer in his eyes had returned as did his swagger in his walk.

"I'm here to train, why else? I'm the one who invited you after all?"

I bristled. "And you happened to show up to train at the exact same time as me?"

"It's not a coincidence, Lennox. I asked your ladies maid to let me know when you headed here."

"You can't be serious? You're having me followed?" My hand closed tighter around the dagger in my palm. The decorative edge biting into my skin. I'd have a word with Krissa later about sharing my whereabouts with the prince, or anyone for that matter.

"Not followed, I wanted to know when I should arrive." He brushed his hair out of his face as he moved past me to the supply of weapons. "I had other duties to attend to today so I couldn't sit around and wait for your arrival up here all day."

"Why?" I bit out. He didn't respond at first, instead taking his time to select a dagger of his choosing. My fingers twitched around the dagger at my side as his cool fresh scent invaded my senses.

"I wanted to spend time with you," he said without looking up.

I threw my hands in the air, waving the dagger around carelessly. "What is it with everyone's obsession with spending time with me?"

He finally turned and looked at me, resting his back against the shelf of weapons. "My question is, why wouldn't anyone jump at any opportunity to spend even a moment with you."

"I told you I needed time."

"No, you told Nico to tell me you needed time. I am giving you time Lennox, what I am done giving you though, is space."

He took another step towards me. There was only an inch between our chests now as I looked up to meet his gaze. Those blue eyes were full of fire.

"There has been too much space between us, Lennox: courts, cities, doors; I'm done with that. I intend to erase every last inch of space between us." He smirked, the sight causing my stomach to dip. "In time of course."

I should have pushed him away, I should have done something, *anything* to get him away from me. To get space between us. But I didn't have it in me. Maybe I didn't want space between us either, but I needed it. It would be too easy to fall back into a relationship with Luka. Space, I needed so much fucking space.

My heart beating rapidly in my chest said otherwise.

It was Luka who finally took a step back.

"Now c'mon, Sweetheart. Prove it to me, that you haven't lost your touch since we've been apart."

*Sweetheart.* My heart tumbled at that stupid fucking nickname. That stupid fucking nickname I had somehow managed to miss.

☾

Luka and I didn't talk much as we fell back into our training rituals.

After an hour I was ready to call it quits. My thighs still burned from the climb and I needed space from Luka. But the door to the attic burst open revealing a shirtless Nico followed by Delclan and—*my sister.*

"Kara." I sheathed my sword at my side. "What are you doing here?" She pointed to the males beside her.

"These two dingbats refused to leave me alone unless I agreed to come up here."

I looked between Nico and Delcan. The latter's expression remained stoic, Nico on the other hand was smiling like a cat. I was convinced he loved nothing more than riling up my sister.

Nico continued towards Luka and me, slinging his arms over our shoulders. "Look at us, the gang's back together again. Well almost, we're still missing my favorite witch."

I raised a brow. "When was the last time you talked to Luciana?"

He removed his arm from my shoulder. "Now that is none of your business."

I made a mental note to reach out to my cousin later and figure out just how much she and Nico had been keeping in touch.

"Now, who wants to go up against me first?" Nico picked a sword off the rack, examining the blade.

The sight of the four of them standing in front of me, the ease they all carried like they were ready to slip back into old routines without a second thought—I couldn't do this right now. Maybe they could slip right back into things, but I couldn't. Training with Luka this morning was already more than I was ready for. They were trying to resume things to the way they were before.

But that wasn't possible.

The past had been shattered. Luka and I had made sure of that.

"I've got a meeting to get ready for." I didn't look at them as I spoke. I didn't want to see their disappointed faces. Especially not Kara's. All I'd done these past weeks was disappoint her.

At least I was consistent.

No one said anything as I turned and left the room.

## 12

---

## LUKA

Once again I found myself waiting anxiously outside Lennox's door. I prayed to the Goddess she wouldn't reject me again. The sting from two days ago was still fresh, even if she did let me train alongside her since.

But today, I had something better to offer than a walk.

"Hi," she said when she finally answered the door.

"Hi." I braced my arm on the door frame. "Are you busy right now?"

She looked behind her, toying with the end of her braid. "I—"

"I wanted to invite you with me to find the witch Scribe, I don't know if anyone mentioned her to you, but I'm hoping she will have a lead on finding Astria's spellbook. Luciana helped me discover her." I wasn't going to give her an opportunity to make an excuse. "According to my source, she should be arriving this week or the next. I figured you might want to come with me to talk to her."

She let out a breath and her shoulders relaxed. "Sure. Let me grab my cloak." I tried my best to tamp down on my surprise, I didn't expect she'd agree, let alone so easily. I didn't even have to convince her. I had a whole speech planned. I guess I'd save it for the next time I'd inevitably need to convince her of something.

She returned a minute later, fastening her cloak over her leathers, she had yet to change since our training session this morning.

"So where are we supposed to find this so-called witch scribe?" Lennox asked as we made our way down the hallway.

"There is a market that runs several days a week at the far edge of the city. It's a forbidden market of sorts." I questioned how to best describe the Stygian market.

"The market sells many unorthodox and illegal items," I continued.

"Such as?"

"Drugs. And other things."

She looked at me out of the corner of her eye and raised an eyebrow. "Other things?"

"You'll see."

"Hmmm."

"Although the market is technically illegal, my grandfather is well aware of it. As long as no one is killed and they're not trading flesh it can continue."

"I suppose for some it's how they make their income?"

"Yes, when it first started a century ago, the king and queen tried to shut it down, but no matter what they did it reappeared in a different place and by a different name. Finally, the crown gave in, allowing the market to exist under loose guidelines. Those who want illegal items are going to find a way to get them, we might as well provide a channel they can get it without putting their lives and the lives of others in danger and allowing whoever is selling it to make a living."

"Is there much crime?"

"We rarely hear of any if there is. The patrons tend to stick to the rules, they know if they don't it will result in the market being shut down. There are deaths on occasion. Typically whoever decided to break the rules paid the price."

"You're starting to make a lot more sense to me."

I gave her a quizzical look. "What do you mean?"

"Hearing about this market and meeting your grandfather, learning more about your home—you make more sense to me." She tucked a stray piece of hair behind her ear. "You operate by a code of conduct. It's not black and white but more in the gray. You don't believe in killing for sport, but if it's deserved you will delight in taking blood. That appears to be a Blood Court quality."

I pondered her words. I had never thought of it that way, but she had a point.

"I never asked, how did meeting my grandfather go?"

"I was pleasantly surprised. He was actually—nice?" I laughed.

"And that surprised you, him being nice?"

A slight blush rushed to her cheeks. "Yes, well, you never talked too much about your grandfather, only Lorenzo. And your grandfather had a part in our—*arrangement*. I assumed the worst. But from our conversation, I could tell he cares deeply for you."

My steps faltered. My grandfather had never been good at expressing his feelings, that's where my mother got it from. He spoke in actions rather than words. Hearing from Lennox, who knew so intimately what it was like to be loved by a family member, she thought my grandfather cared deeply for me—I wasn't sure how to place how it made me feel.

"My grandfather—he did the best he could with me. I was not easy to be around during the years my parents died."

She dipped her chin. "You told me as much, and so did your grandfather." I looked over at her as we continued through the streets of Cel Nox.

"My grandfather must have liked you to offer you this much information upon first meeting him."

"You know better than anyone I make a good first impression," she remarked. I couldn't stop a laugh from rumbling out of me.

"You're lucky I didn't run right back out the door after those first days I spent in Alethens."

"A weaker male would have." There was a slight tilt to her lips.

"Was that a compliment, Lennox Adair?"

"Interpret it how you want to." I let myself smile at the small pieces of Lennox slipping in. It gave me a small semblance of hope. This entire conversation did. She wasn't shutting me out entirely.

We walked in silence the rest of the way to the Stygian market. Lennox's pace slowed when we reached the first block as she took in the packed city street.

I leaned in close to her as we approached. "Stay close to me." Her eyes widened as she surveyed the street.

A male pulling a street cart bustled past, my hand reached instinctively towards Lennox, my hand resting on her hip and pulling her closer—out of the path of the male. A gasp slipped past her lips as my fingers tightened around her hip.

It took everything in me to let go, but I did.

Lennox followed behind me as I navigated us through the busy streets, weaving in and out of the booths. Every so often I looked back to check on her.

My fingers twitched to intertwine with hers, but I resisted.

Slowly, I needed to take this slowly to not scare her off and shut her down.

Finally, we arrived at the street where I had found the witch before. Sitting in the same spot was a different witch, her table stacked high with books.

I couldn't believe it.

We had found the witch Scribe.

# 13

## LENNOX

Witches have a strange third sense when it comes to meeting other new witches. Each witch gives off a feeling. Typically you are able to sense what coven a witch belongs to, what kind of elements they possess, or what kind of person they are. Like an alarm system of sorts to warn you about danger. Sometimes you get a slight feeling, your magic goes on high alert or there is a slight prickle at the back of your neck. Sometimes you get no feeling at all.

My magic writhed inside me as I took in the witch across the street. All four elements of my magic fought against each other to be released as I assessed her. The sensations coursing through my body put me and my magic on edge.

I had heard stories about evil witches. About the witches who misused magic.

I had a feeling the witch sitting in front of me wasn't entirely good.

"Wait." I held out a hand to stop Luka as he started towards the female. He turned, his eyes going wide as his hand looked at my fingers grasping the firm muscles of his arm.

I immediately let go of him.

"What?"

I tilted my head toward the witch. "I have a bad feeling about her."

Luka looked over his shoulder. "What kind of bad feeling?"

"I don't know how to explain it." I wrung my hands in front of me. "My magic is going haywire. All of my elements are begging to be released. I have a feeling—it's a witch thing."

Luka sighed. "I understand your hesitancy, but Lennox, I've been searching and waiting to find this witch for weeks. This is the closest I've come to finding the spellbook. I have to at least try."

I wanted out of this arrangement, but I didn't want Luka risking himself for me.

"What if I told you I didn't want you to?"

Luka's expression softened. "Lennox—"

"Please, Luka, don't do this," I pleaded. "I can't explain it, but I don't think any good will come from talking with her. *Please.*" My magic pushed and pulsed violently against my skin, begging me to retreat. "You don't feel anything? Your magic isn't reacting at all?" I knew it was unlikely he'd be able to sense anything, but if she was a threat he might feel something. His magic might be on alert if anything.

"No."

I swallowed. "Luka, please, let's go." I took his wrist in my hand and tugged him away from the witch.

He scrubbed his hand over his face. "Fine."

I let go of his hand and as we made our way back down the street, I struggled to keep up with him as he wove through the stalls. He only looked back to check I was still following him a handful of times.

Not even once we exited the market, did he say another word to me.

# 14

# LUKA

I paced around my room, my boots wearing a path in the rug.

I felt guilty about how I had treated Lennox after she begged me to leave the market without talking to the witch Scribe.

I understood her hesitancy, I didn't doubt she had a bad feeling about the witch, but that didn't mean I still didn't want to talk to her.

After weeks of searching, this was the closest I had gotten and I turned around at the command of two little words.

*Luka, please.*

It wasn't often Lennox asked for things nicely, and I was in the habit of giving her what she wanted.

Which is why it was so Stars damned frustrating she wouldn't let me talk to her. I was doing this all for her, didn't she get that? This was all for her freedom.

I'd be damned if I let anyone stand in the way of that.

Even Lennox.

*Fuck it.*

I strapped my sword to my back and took off out the door.

If I had been thinking clearly I would have asked Nico or Delcan to accompany me back to the market, but I didn't want to waste any more time than I already had.

The sun was already setting, casting the market in a dim light. Hiding everything in shadows.

I could have come back tomorrow, in the daylight, but what if the witch Scribe was already gone? I couldn't risk it.

When I finally arrived back at the witches' block I expected to find her packing up, as most of the other stall owners were, but there she sat, surrounded by piles of books, arms crossed over her thin frame, her eyes firmly fixed on me.

"I knew you'd be back, vampire. I could see it in your eyes before." I approached her table without hesitating. "Your companion was smart to warn you away earlier. Witches don't mix well with vampires, no matter what the half-breed witch might try to convince you otherwise."

"Don't talk about your high queen like that," I all but growled.

A feline smile spread on her porcelain face, alighting her upturned eyes. "So the rumors are true, she does have you wrapped around her gilded finger." I ignored her comment, instead directing my attention toward what I needed from her.

"Do you have the Goddess's spellbook in your possession?"

If she was surprised by my inquisition she didn't show it, she only blinked at me. "What does a vampire want with a book like that?" *Isn't that the golden question?*

"It's not for me, I need to find it for someone else."

She tapped a long black nail on the book in front of her. "The answer will cost you."

"I'll pay whatever price you ask." My previous witch scar burned under her stare.

"My answers don't come at such an easy price."

"I don't care, I need that book."

"Stupid boy." I bristled under the name, the witch couldn't be more than a few years older than I.

"My price is linking my life to yours."

"*What?*"

She leaned forward, resting her elbows on the table, her dark eyes gleaming. "I will complete a spell that will bind our lives together. How else do you propose I appear this young? I have lived many lives, boy. Each one runs into the next as the last one comes to pass. I never know when the current life I live within will expire, I like to keep souls ready." My stomach soured. How many lives had this female lived? How many Fae had tied their lives to hers? Was I stupid to consider tying my life to hers as well?

It must have taken a special kind of magic to link lives together. An unnatural kind of magic. That must be why Lennox had been so uneasy. Whatever kind of magic this witch Scribe practiced wasn't natural.

"So, boy, what will it be?" She tapped her nails impatiently. Every instinct in me warned against saying yes. Even my magic, which had been oddly quiet this entire time, was now rioting inside me. I should say no. I could find another way.

The image of Lennox's face in the dining room back in Alethens flashed to the forefront of my mind. The way she had tried to hide her hurt when she realized she was going to have to marry me…

I knew how much she valued the choice of who she married. I wouldn't be the one to take it from her. I would do anything to give her back this choice. Even if it meant tying my life to this witch.

I looked up, meeting the witch's onyx eyes, her piercing gaze sending a shiver down my spine.

"Fine, I'll do it."

The smile that spread across her face chilled my veins.

"I'll enjoy living your days, vampire." She held out a perfectly smooth hand, not a wrinkle in sight. "Give me your palm." I pulled my arm back as she reached for it.

"On one condition." The witch frowned disapprovingly. "If

I'm doing something so dramatic as tying my life to yours, I want more than only your help finding the spellbook."

The witch considered my counter. "You get three questions."

"Deal."

"Now hand me your palm." Hesitantly, I gave her my hand, she turned it over, examining the lines crossing it, running the tip of her nail over the lines.

"Hmmm——" she mused. "It's unclear how many years I'll get from you."

"You can see how long I'll live by examining my palm?"

"Sometimes, but not always. Your markings are clear, but you have the tellings of both living a long life and a short-lived one." A shiver wracked my body. "Your future is unclear, yet to be decided it seems. Interesting." She tapped her nail against my palm.

The words Hecate spoke to Lennox and me those months ago floated into my mind. Maybe this was related to the path of light and dark she had talked about. Perhaps my lifespan was linked to each of those paths. I—I couldn't consider that now. I had far greater worries than how long I would live. All that mattered was getting Lennox out of this marriage.

The witch Scribe drew a small dagger from the pouch at her side, not at all surprised by the sight of the blade. I was all too familiar with witch magic now and the need to bind it with blood. She drew a precise slice over the lines crossing the center of my hand. I winced against the sting.

Red blood pooled in my palm as her hand cradled mine.

She discarded the dagger on the table and searched for her pouch again, this time retrieving a small vial. The sun had all but disappeared now, making it impossible to see the contents. She uncapped the bottle with her teeth, spitting the cap on the table before shaking the contents onto my bleeding palm. The substance came out in flakes, causing a sting as it mixed with my blood.

"Close your fist," she instructed, finally letting go of my hand, only to repeat the process on her own palm. When she was finished, she grasped my hand again, motioning me to open it. As I did she pressed our bleeding hands together and mumbled under her breath.

The air around us seemed to still, the chatter of the market silenced as if we were the only two people remaining.

My skin that touched hers burned as she continued to speak the spell in a language I was unable to comprehend. The burning intensified, seeming to seep its way into my blood and into my veins, spreading the heat and burn throughout my body. I winced under the pressure, so intense it threatened to take my legs out from underneath me.

The witch's voice became more urgent as I gritted my teeth against the pain. What the fuck was this magic?

In an instant, the pain stopped. The sounds around us returned and the witch opened her eyes, removing her hand from mine.

A wicked grin spread across her ageless face. "It is done."

I swallowed and looked at my palm, the line she had sliced across now bore a black mark that glittered red as I moved it against the moonlight. "It will disappear in a couple of days." I'd have to hide it from Lennox until then. She'd gladly slice my neck for coming back here.

When I looked back at the witch, she had all but dismissed me, returning to packing her books.

"What about my questions?"

"Ask away, boy."

"Where can I find the goddess Astria's original spellbook?"

The witch didn't bother to look from her books as she answered, "No such thing exists."

"What do you mean it doesn't exist? There are people across Lethenia searching for it!"

"Astria never had a spellbook, she was never truly a witch,

she was a fallen star, so she never needed spells. Her magic has no restrictions as spells do."

"But that doesn't make any sense, what is it that everyone is looking for?"

"I cannot tell you what your seeker is truly looking for, but I can tell you there is an original spellbook, but it does not belong to Astria, it belongs to Hecate, the original witch."

*Well, wouldn't it have been convenient if the original witch had mentioned that?*

"Although, I don't believe Hecate's spellbook is what your sender is searching for. I suspect they have discovered Astria kept journals."

"Journals?"

"Yes, journals. Stories say that's where Hecate got the idea for the spellbook, from Astria's detailed retellings of her experiences in her journals."

"Where can I find these journals?"

"That I do not know." She flipped through the book in front of her.

"What? All this and you don't even know where the journals are?" I pressed.

She turned her gaze on me, "Remember who you speak to, boy, I could turn you to ashes with the flick of my fingers."

"So could I," I said through clenched teeth.

We stared at one another, neither of us daring to look away first.

She rolled her eyes and sighed. "But now that you know they exist, I imagine you could do a spell to find them." Good thing I knew of a couple of witches who could help me with that.

The Scribe looked up suddenly, her irises burning red. *Goddess above—* "You should go, boy, something dangerous lurks in the darkness. Something not natural is coming."

I was about to question what she was talking about when my magic lit up inside me, churning viciously. Maybe it was still a reaction to her, or maybe it was something else. Either way, I wasn't going to wait around to find out.

"Thank you," I told the witch before turning back down the street at a quick pace.

I continued making my way back out of the market, only a few vendors remained, the rest having closed up shop long ago.

How long had I been with the witch Scribe?

As I continued to make my way through the winding streets, the hairs on the back of my neck raised.

I had the distinct feeling I was being followed.

I knew it was risky to travel alone to this part of Cel Nox at this time of night. I only hoped I wouldn't pay for my stupidity. I took a random turn down an alley, hoping to brush them off my scent if they were in fact, following me.

I wasn't familiar enough with this part of the city to use my enhanced speed, the streets were too close together. I'd have to stop every few feet to ensure I didn't run into anything. Once I got back to the main part of the city I'd have a clear shot back to the palace.

But as I returned to the main road, the feeling continued. *Fuck.*

I decided to risk it. I used my speed, stopping a few feet ahead, before moving again.

Still, the presence followed.

A rancid smell filled my nostrils as I continued and a rustling sound filled my ears as I approached the entrance to an alley. I should have continued forward, I was almost at the stretch where I would be home free to the palace, but I looked down the alley.

A form cast in shadows was bent over a body lying in ribbons on the ground. Blood pooled around them, dripping down the cobblestones and the stench—that was where the smell was coming from. I covered my nose with the back of my hand.

I needed to get out of here. There was no saving whoever that was.

I backed down the alley, unable to look away from the scene before me. I stumbled, catching myself on the side of the building as my foot hit a crate. Causing the person to look over their shoulder at me.

No.

Not a person.

A creature or something. I didn't know what this thing was. *Something not natural.* The witch Scribe had said. This was certainly not natural.

Its body resembled a Fae, but it was all wrong. They were all skin and bones and long, gangly limbs. Even under the dark light, I could tell they were not alive, or not fully alive anymore. Their skin was the ashen color of a corpse. Had they somehow been brought back to life?

A growl left the creature's lips as it surveyed me. Giving me only a moment's notice before it bounded towards me.

I ran.

Even as I ran away from the creature, its smell followed me. It reeked of death and decay.

I used my enhanced speed, appearing at the end of an alley instead of the street. *Fuck.*

I cursed as I came to a dead end. In an instant, the creature was on me. Its long nails dug into my back as it leaped for me, pushing me to the ground. A groan fell from my lips as I landed on the bricks.

I rolled to my back and kicked my legs out, hitting the creature in the chest, pushing it back an inch, giving me the space I needed to reach for my sword at my back.

Blood spilled from the creature's lips from its last victim, landing in droplets on my face. He hissed as its claws ripped into my side, exposing the irregularly long fangs protruding from its mouth. I gritted my teeth against the pain in my side as I kicked again, this time pushing the creature back far enough so I could roll out from under it.

I rose to a crouch as the creature turned its attention back on me, its eyes were hollowed and rimmed in red. Its pupils wholly black. Whatever in the goddess name this thing was, it needed to die right fucking now.

The creature charged towards me again, flashing those impossibly long fangs and claws.

With one swift arc of my sword, the creature's head fell from its neck. Black rotted blood spurting me in the process.

I didn't care to stay and see if the thing was dead.

The wound in my side wasn't healing. I could feel my blood staining my clothes.

I needed to get back to the palace before I was unable to move.

I resheathed my sword and pressed my hand to my side, gritting my teeth against the pain.

I used the last bit of strength I had to propel myself back to the palace, to get myself back home.

I received many looks as I deposited myself at the gates, but I didn't stop there. I moved through the halls until I landed in front of a large wooden door. I pounded my fist against the door several times before I slipped down the wall, tumbling in a heap against the door frame.

I banged my head against the wall over and over again. I hoped and prayed it would open before I passed out. Dark spots danced in my vision. Maybe I shouldn't have come here. But it was too late for that. I doubted I could move again.

After what felt like hours, the door finally opened. I slumped against the doorway, somehow managing to tilt my head upwards to spy the female standing before me.

My eyes roamed up the tanned legs blocking my vision, my fingers, despite my current state, itching to run up them to what I knew lay between them, underneath the flimsy nightdress she wore.

When I finally met her gaze, I couldn't tell what she was thinking. Her emotions were too muddled. Or I was too delirious.

"Good evening, Sweetheart."

## 15

LENNOX

I stared at Luka slumped against my door frame, unable to comprehend what was in front of me. Red and black blood stained his clothes and sprayed across his face and neck like dark freckles.

His face was ashen, the color fading more and more every second I stared at him. Why was he here? What trouble had he gotten himself into since I left him a few hours ago?

And why did he smell like rotted flesh?

"I got myself in a bit of trouble. I need your help," he slurred. Was he drunk?

"What are you doing here, Luka?"

Even in this state, his eyes roamed over my body hungrily, taking in all the areas of exposed skin. I tried my best not to shiver under his gaze as I clamped my thighs together.

"I need your help." He moved his hand from his side, his palm coming away stained red. "I got a little scratch here that won't heal."

Everything came crashing back to reality at that moment. He wasn't drunk. He was hurt.

And by the looks of it not healing.

"For fucks sake, Luka. Who did that to you?" I knelt beside

him, my hands reaching for the wound. "You should have said something right away."

"Sorry," he murmured. "I got distracted." My cheeks reddened. Goddess he was a never-ending flirt. It would be the death of him. My fingers skimmed over the ripped flesh. The wound wasn't big—only a few deep scratches. Where they came from, would be a question for later. But why weren't they healing on their own?

"Here, let me help you inside." I wrapped my arm around his waist, his arm circled my neck and I helped him stand. He wobbled against me as I led him into the room. I looked between the bed and the couch. He was covered in blood and reeked of something foul—but bedsheets could be washed.

I helped lay him down carefully on the bed.

"You want me to heal you? Is that why you came to me?"

Luka's eyes fluttered. "No, I don't need you to heal me. I need you to get Nico or Declan."

"Why?"

"I need— I need blood." My stomach tightened. That's why he wasn't healing.

"Here," I held out my wrist to him as I sat on the bed. "Feed from me."

He shook his head, turning his head away from me. "No. I won't feed from you. Not like this."

"Luka." I let out a long breath from my nose. "You're injured and need blood, feed from me for fucks sake."

"No." Even in his distressed state, his words were firm. Leaving no room for argument. I sighed. I didn't have time to argue with him.

"I'll be right back." I stood, brushing my hair from my face with the back of my blood-stained hand. "Try not to die while I'm gone."

☾

I sat in the chair in the corner, watching Luka as he slept on my bed.

He was clean now, as was my bed. After Nico arrived and got Luka to feed from him, much to Luka's protests, Nico and Declan cleaned him up. Now he was asleep on my bed as he recuperated.

"How long had he gone since feeding?" I asked the two males who resided next to me.

Nico shrugged. "I'd say three maybe four weeks."

"He's been trying to stretch it as long as he can," Declan added.

"Why?" The two shared a look, a silent conversation occurring between the pair. "For fucks sake, one of you spit it out already."

It was Declan who finally spoke. "You can't figure it out?" I glared at him, my eyes narrowing into slits.

"He only wants to feed from you," he finished.

My throat dried. "What do you mean?" I choked out.

"I don't know, it's some weird vampire shit. But once a vampire takes a liking to a certain person's blood they have a hard time feeding from anyone else." Nico leaned back in his chair. "He used to not mind the taste of our blood, but now he says he hates it. That it tastes foul." Nico waved his hand around dismissively.

"But why wouldn't he feed from me when I offered?"

Declan shrugged his shoulders, his wings twitching with the action. "Your guess is as good as mine."

"I think he's afraid he'd take too much, and in his delirious state he wouldn't be able to stop himself," Nico mused.

I opened my mouth to respond but stopped at the sound of sheets rustling. Luka's eyes fluttered open like he knew we were talking about him.

"Good morning, sleepyhead," Nico cooed. "Glad you could join us." Luka sat up, rubbing the sleep from his eyes.

His eyes scanned the room, his brows furrowing as he tried to figure out where he was until his gaze landed on me.

Nico and Declan stood abruptly, making their way towards the door.

"We will leave you to it." The wolf looked between the two of us. "You have a lot to talk about."

"But you will be filling us in later," Declan added, giving Luka a stern look as he passed.

The door clicked shut behind the pair as Luka and I continued to stare at one another.

"So——" he finally said. "I owe you an explanation."

"You mean an explanation as to why you showed up at my door, delirious, covered in blood, not healing, and barely conscious, refusing to feed from me even though that's what you needed? Why ever would I need an explanation for that?"

I stood and started pacing. Now that I knew he was okay, my anger was rising to the surface. Why did he think he could show up like this? This wasn't who we were anymore.

We were partners in an agreement. Not friends.

"I went back to the witch Scribe." I froze, whipping my head towards him.

"You did what?" I seethed.

"I went back to the witch——"

"Even when I asked you not to?" The words came out harsher than I intended. "For fucks sake, Luka, I knew you could be reckless but——this——" I shook my head. "This is a whole new level."

"Can you blame me, though? I did it for you. I needed answers and I got them."

"At what cost? What was the cost of those answers? Was it the witch who gave you those injuries?"

He rubbed his hand over the back of his neck. "No it wasn't the witch, I'll get to that——just let me explain."

"Fine." I huffed as I continued to pace.

"Can you stop that?"

"Pacing is the only thing keeping me from strangling you right now."

"Lennox, please." Stars above, there they were again. Those words.

"Fine." I sat myself on one of the chairs in the small sitting area across from the bed.

Luka stood, the toned muscles of his chest moving and flexing as he made his way to the sitting room, sitting in the chair across from me. My fingers itched to run along the defined ridges of his chest. I shook my head, instead focusing on the lines of his tattoo that peaked over his shoulder.

"Can you put a shirt on?"

Luka smirked, the action warming my insides to a dangerous temperature. "Why? Is my lack of a shirt distracting, Sweetheart?"

"Get on with your story, won't you."

He sighed. "Even though you told me not to, I returned to the witch Scribe. I knew she had the information I needed, and I was right. She said the Goddess doesn't have a spellbook, but a journal instead. The spellbook belonged to Hecate. The librarian couldn't tell me where the journals are located, but she said now that we know what we're looking for, we can use a spell to locate the journals."

"And what was the cost of this information?" I wasn't surprised what the king was looking for wasn't a spellbook after all, Hecate had told us as much. Although this information was helpful, it couldn't have been worth whatever Luka had traded for it.

He turned his hand over, revealing a thick black line across his palm. "She linked my life with hers so she can continue to have eternal youth."

My stomach knotted. "You did what?" No wonder my senses had warned me of the witch. Magic like that was dangerous. Surely she didn't devote herself to a coven, none of them would allow such magic.

If Caterina learned of her—I shuttered, turning my attention back to Luka.

"You're so unbelievably stupid. Magic like that comes at a cost, you better hope it only impacts her and not you."

Luka shrugged. "It was worth it."

"Stupid, insufferable, idiot," I muttered. "But how did you get injured?" I pressed.

"I ran into a creature of some sort." He shivered, his face paling slightly. "It looked like it was dead, maybe a vampire at some point, but its fangs were unnaturally long, everything about it was wrong."

"You sure have a knack for getting yourself injured," I mumbled.

"Only when I know I have you looking out for me, Sweetheart." He smiled sheepishly as he threw me a wink.

"How come you wouldn't feed from me?" His face fell. "And why have you been going so long between feedings?"

He remained silent for a long time. "Luka," I prodded.

"The only blood I've been craving is yours."

So Nico was on to something. "What does that mean?"

He combed his hands through his dark hair. "I don't know how to explain it. Every time I've fed from someone since I fed from you, their blood tastes rancid. I have to choke it down." He took a deep breath. "I've never had this happen before. I've tried feeding from multiple different people, and they all taste the same." My stomach soured at the idea of him feeding from someone who wasn't Nico or Declan.

"Has this ever happened to anyone else before?"

"Not that I know of. The only instances I could find were from mates." My heart froze. *Mates.* "Once they were mated they were repulsed by feeding from anyone else."

A couple of instances recorded of this happening between mates didn't mean Luka and I were mates.

"How come you wouldn't let me feed you last night?"

Luka finally looked up to meet my gaze.

"You know why, Lennox." I swallowed, memories of the last time he fed from me flashing to the forefront of my mind. His hand around my neck, our slick bodies pressed together as he drank from me while pumping inside me.

"Can we not talk about this anymore?" His voice was strained. "Let's talk about how we're going to locate the journals.

I swallowed. "About that, I have an idea."

# 16

# LUKA

Later that afternoon when we all returned to Lennox's bedchamber, I found myself looking at a mirror lying on the table in the sitting room, staring at my reflection in the clouded glass as everyone surrounded the table.

"You will be able to contact Luciana only by using your necklace and the mirror?" Nico asked skeptically.

Lennox moved her hair to the side, unclasping the purple amethyst necklace hanging around her neck. "She used a forbidden form of magic to spell the stone." Her gaze flicked to me, presumably the same kind of magic the witch Scribe had used with me. "It's called Ichor magic. It's different than regular witch magic. Typical witch magic uses spells to pull magic from the earth–Ichor magic on the other hand, pulls magic from everything—typically the witch who wields the spell."

"What does that mean?" Nico pushed in closer to get a better look at the mirror.

"When we use our magic it doesn't take anything from us physically, because we have claimed our magic, yes we can run out, but the magic belongs to us. Ichor magic only belongs to itself. It pulls energy from the witch wielding the spell in addition to any other magic being collected from the earth."

"Why is it forbidden?" Declan asked quietly.

"Your body can only take so much—especially if it's pulling in additional magic that isn't your own. Eventually—"

"You could die." Kara finished for her.

Lennox glared at her sister. "Yes, that is one outcome, but before that happens typically the witch goes mad. They are consumed by the magic. But it's all speculation anyhow—the magic is forbidden for a reason."

A shiver wracked my body as I thought of the witch Scribe. She had to be close to the Ichor magic taking over her if she was claiming others souls—or it had already taken over.

"Anyways, enough of this morbid shit." She took the pale amethyst stone in her hand, pulling her dagger from her side and pricking her finger with the tip. My throat dried and my nostrils flared. I closed my hands into fists to prevent myself from bringing that finger to my mouth and licking it clean.

I watched with rapt attention as she smeared the red liquid onto the stone before closing her hand around it.

We were all silent as she murmured a spell under her breath before opening her eyes and placing the necklace on the mirror in the center of the table.

The mirror rippled, its glass becoming dark as Luciana's form manifested in the glass.

"I was wondering if you'd ever put that stone to use," the witch princess remarked with a sly smile. "What do you need, Lennox?"

Lennox tucked a lock of honey hair behind her ear. "Why do you assume I need something? Perhaps I'm reaching out to chat."

Luciana laughed, the sound low and twinged with danger. "Because I know you, Lennox, you wouldn't use Ichor Magic unless it was necessary."

"Fine," Lennox admitted. "You're right we need your help."

"What can I do?"

"We discovered the book we're looking for isn't Astria's spellbook, but instead her journals. We need your help casting a spell to locate it." Lennox and I had filled everyone in on my findings from the witch Scribe before we called Luciana.

"We don't have anything directly linking us to Astria for the spell, but I thought we could try using Hecate's spellbook and see if it works since they might have come in contact with one another at one point in time."

"Give me a minute." The mirror darkened—Luciana's form disappeared into the glass without saying goodbye.

"Where did she go?" Kara leaned over the mirror.

Lennox shrugged. "I don't know. She severed the connection. But she said she'd be back."

"I guess we wait," I concluded.

"Do you think this will work?" Declan asked. Lennox and Kara shared a look.

"It's worth a shot. There's no guarantee any spell would work without a direct link to Astria or her journal, but it's worth a try."

A breeze filtered through the room, ruffling the curtains to the balcony.

Like she was carried on the breeze, Luciana appeared before us.

Kara jumped, placing a hand on her heart as Declan drew his sword.

"Relax, Dec," Nico said. "It's Lucy."

*Lucy?* I mouthed to Declan. He furrowed his brows before resheathing his sword.

"Surprise." A slow smile spread across Luciana's face.

I looked to Lennox, expecting to find her smiling at the appearance of her cousin, only to find her face etched with concern and anger.

"Don't tell me—"

"Shhh—Lennox." Luciana raised a finger to her lips. "Remember, don't ask questions you don't want the answer to. I'd say this trick is rather convenient, don't you? It would have taken weeks for me to get here, but with this"—She waved her arms dramatically.—"I'm at your door in the snap of your fingers."

I looked between the cousins, trying to figure out what was going on between the pair.

"Wait," I took a step closer to Luciana. When she was in the mirror her reflection had appeared smudged. But here standing before me she looked fully corporal. She wasn't simply a reflection of Luciana she was— "You're here. In the flesh. Not a reflection."

Nico's brows raised as he took a step towards Luciana and poked her on the arm. Luciana swatted him away.

"It is you," Nico marveled.

"A fun little trick isn't it, a spell of my own creation."

"A dangerous trick," Lennox crossed her arms over her chest. "Luce, we talked about this."

Luce rolled her eyes. "We did, and I told you not to worry about it, Lennox. I'm here. It's already done, let's move on."

"I for one am glad you're here," Nico added. Luciana gave him a sly grin.

"I'm sure you are, pup."

"Thank you for coming," Lennox added.

"You needed me, so I came." Lennox smiled slightly before pulling her cousin in for a hug.

"I worry because I care," she said into the witch's hair.

"I know," Luciana murmured. "Now," Luciana let go of her cousin, "I believe we have a spell to do."

# 17

# LENNOX

With the snap of her fingers bags appeared next to Luce, as if they had been waiting in hiding until she was ready to reveal them. "I brought supplies, I figured witch relics are not easily obtained in the Blood Court.".

"You assume correctly," Luka confirmed.

Luce wasted no time, pulling items from her bags, placing candles and vials of witch relics on the table along with a map of Lethenia.

I took the map from her, spreading it out on the table and using the bottles to secure the edges.

"What can I do?" Kara asked.

Luce pulled Hecate's spellbook from her bag and handed it to her. "Find the page with the location spell."

Magic flooded my fingertips at the sight of the book. Magic oozed from the book, sending a tingle down my spine. Kara shuttered as she took the book from Luce's hands.

"What is that?" Declan's gaze was fixed wholly on the book.

"Hecate's spellbook," Luciana answered.

"Why does it feel like that?" Nico shuttered.

Luciana looked up from her bags. "The book is powerful. It hosts the origins of the witches. It's a magical book."

"The pages are blank," Nico mused. Kara looked at him quizzically as she flipped through the pages.

"You can't see the words?"

Nico shook his head. "Neither can I," Luka added.

"Like I said, it's a magical book, only those who it allows can read the book."

"Well, aren't you special?" Nico joked.

"You won't get the book to show you anything talking like that, wolf boy."

"So how does this work?" Declan approached the table, tucking his wings in tight to make room for us all.

"I'll use the book as a beacon to help find the journals, once the ingredients are mixed together I will put them on the map. When the spell is complete the map should reveal to us where the journal is."

"And we're supposed to trust this spell?"

Luciana gave Declan a seething gaze. "Half of witch magic is about faith. Try to have a little, bird boy."

Declan's black wings rustled behind him as he crossed his arms. "It sounds risky," Declan continued.

"Sometimes you gotta take risks, Dec." Nico slung an arm over Declan's shoulder only for the harpy to shrug out of his hold.

"I found the page," Kara interjected.

"Perfect. Set the book on the table," Luce directed. "While I gather the ingredients, can you light the candles, Lennox?"

I spread the candles out along the perimeter of the table before lighting them with the flick of my fingers.

"Ready, Luce?"

"Ready."

Luce dumped the contents of the bowl onto the map. "Will you light them, Lennox?"

I sparked a flame onto the piles of herbs.

"We have a better chance of it working if we all try together." Luce reached out her hands to me and Kara.

Kara, Luce, and I all grabbed hands. Our eyes closing simultaneously as our hands linked. Luce began chanting the spell, after saying it once, Kara and I joined in, the three of us saying the words in unison.

A light wind blew around us, causing the smoke from the herbs to drift to my nose. Luce's hand squeezed mine at the same time a burst of magic jolted through me, like a tiny lightning strike, slowly traveling from my hand through my body as I continued to chant.

We continued until the wind and the magic buzzing in my body stopped.

I opened my eyes, immediately finding Luka staring at me in awe.

I tore my gaze from his and looked at the map. The herbs still smoldered, but they had shifted to form a small circle on the map.

"It worked," Luka whispered in awe.

We all leaned in closer to see the location the spell had revealed.

Chills ran down my arm when I realized where it was circling. "That's the location of Hecate's cottage." I meet Luka's gaze. "The one Luka and I visited."

"Well, it looks like we're all in for a little adventure." Luce grinned. "I've never tried transporting more than one person before."

I whipped my head in her direction. "You want to transport us all?"

"Why not? Time is of the essence here is it not? You two are not in a position to up and leave for several weeks, and based on your last experience with Hecate I doubt she'd talk to any of us."

"So the three of us." Luka looked between Luce and me. "We'll go back to Hecate's cottage."

"No way am I getting left behind this time," Nico protested. "I'm coming too."

Luce shrugged. "Fine with me."

"If he gets to come I get to come, too," Kara added.

"So I get to stay behind while you go off on a ridiculous chase," Declan grumbled.

"Don't pout, bird boy, you can come too if you want." Luce looked at him over her shoulder.

"You can bring all of us?" I questioned.

"I can't see why not. It's good practice."

I sighed. I didn't like how comfortable Luce had become with practicing Ichor Magic.

"It's settled then, we'll all go," Luka said. "Tomorrow night? That way we won't raise suspicion that we're gone?"

We all nodded in agreement.

"Tomorrow we go back to the Mystic Court."

# 18

# LUKA

When we originally discussed Luciana transporting us all to the Mystic Court, it sounded like a great idea. But now, standing back in Lennox's room as she explained to us how this would work—*should* work—I was having second thoughts. I wasn't too keen on the idea of traveling between time and space like a speck of dust as my body morphed to accommodate the magic.

"I don't think we should do this," Declan brought my thoughts to life.

"No one is making you come with, birdy, I've been practicing this magic for a long time—and I'm good at it. Really fucking good at it. Ichor Magic might be forbidden, but it's not an easy magic to harness. I've been doing it with ease for years." Luce looked between us all before landing back at Declan. "So either get on board or leave." She raised a singular dark brow at the harpy.

Declan's wings rustled behind, he crossed his arms but remained silent.

"C'mon, Declan, it will be fine." Kara nudged him slightly with her elbow. All he offered was a grunt in return.

"Whoever is going to come with, join hands," Luciana directed.

I grabbed Lennox's hand and reached for Nico's with the other. Declan begrudgingly stepped into our circle, grasping Kara's outstretched hand.

Luce completed the circle before closing her eyes and chanting the spell.

Slowly the world shifted around us. The room blurred out of existence until there was nothing but darkness. Darkness so dark I couldn't see *anything*. My mind felt disconnected from the rest of my body as I tried to ground myself in this space in between.

I squeezed the hand in mine, wondering if I could still feel Lennox. If she could feel me.

Her squeeze in response grounded me, I wasn't floating about. Lennox was still here. We were both still here.

Wherever *here* was.

Slowly, the world reformed around us. The light filtered back in as the world became corporal again, revealing a familiar grove where Hecate's cottage sat, the same as it was before.

I looked over at Lennox, who stared at the depleted cottage.

"I never thought we'd be back here," she muttered.

"Me either." I was still holding her hand in mine, I gave it a reassuring squeeze before letting it go.

"So this is Hecate's cottage?" Kara confirmed.

"I expected more from the original witch." Luce elbowed Declan and the harpy hissed in response.

"Watch your words, this is the first witch you're talking about," she scolded.

"She has a point Dec, I've met her, and she's not someone you want to anger."

"I still can't believe you got to meet her. The vampire prince has met the original witch and yet, I, heir to the witch throne, haven't." Luciana crossed her arms over her chest as we all continued to stare at the cottage.

"Well that's about to change isn't it." The excitement in Kara's tone was evident.

"Well, what are we waiting for?" Lennox said. "Let's go inside."

We all followed behind Lennox as she approached the house. The outside looked the same, but something was off. Something felt different than before.

I stood beside Lennox as she knocked on the door. "Hecate?" She asked hesitantly. We all waited, my heart thudding rapidly in my chest.

Not a sound came from within the cabin.

Lennox knocked again, calling out for the original witch once more.

"Should we go in?" Nico asked.

Lennox shrugged. "I guess. But I don't think she's here."

"Hecate?" She pushed the door open. We filed into the cottage behind Lennox, quickly filling the space, the abundance of us making the cabin appear tiny.

"She's not here." Frustration quickly built inside me. "We came all the way here and she's not even fucking here." I slid one of the worn wooden chairs out from under the table and collapsed into it.

"Maybe the journals are here somewhere, that's why we were led here," Kara offered.

"I doubt it." The defeat was clear in Lennox's voice.

"Hecate hasn't been living here, I doubt she'd leave the journals here for anyone to find if people across Lethenia are searching for them," I added.

We were fucked.

*Again.*

"Hecate doesn't have the journals anyways." Lennox ran her hand over the shelf lined with relics, her fingers dusting over the glass jars.

When she came to the end of the row she turned and headed back out the open door without another word.

I followed Lennox to the porch and sat next to her on the

sagging front step. "You knew she didn't have them? And she wouldn't be here?"

"I had a hunch." She looked out into the woods before us, to the same woods we had crossed through together this summer, only a few months ago. "She knows we're here. She'll come."

"Are you planning on staying here until she does?"

She took a dried leaf in her hand and crushed it, letting the pieces drift from her palm on the light breeze. "I guess I didn't think that far ahead. I thought she'd be here soon after we arrived, like she'd know I was here or something. But maybe I'm wrong."

"She'll come," I assured her.

"The boy has faith—now that is unexpected." We both jumped at the sound of the familiar voice behind us, looking over our shoulders to find Hecate and two of her Wampus Cats approaching from the forest.

I shuttered as I took in the two beasts—hoping and praying they wouldn't come any closer.

"Don't worry boy, they'll behave this time." I had a hard time believing she had that much control over those creatures.

"I knew you two would be back—But I didn't anticipate it would be so soon." Her red eyes roamed between the two of us before looking behind her into the cabin. "And you brought friends."

"We did, I hope that's okay,"

"Depends."

"On what?" I asked.

The witch ignored my question and ushered us into the cabin instead. "Let's meet them, shall we?"

Luciana's gasp rang throughout the room as we reentered the cabin.

"You're Hecate," she stammered.

Hecate smiled. "The witch heir—I was wondering if I'd ever get to meet you." Her gaze scanned the room. "And the Star Princess." Her gaze continued around the small room.

"Quite the interesting group you two have gathered here."

"It's an honor to meet you." Luciana was unable to hide the awe from her voice.

"And you, Luciana." Hecate nodded her head toward the witch. "My magic suits you. My book is well used in your hands." A half smile curved on Hecate's lips.

"You know I have your book?"

"Of course, I don't let my spellbook land in anyone's hands." Luciana's mouth formed a perfect *o*.

"But be careful, Ichor Magic has a price," Hecate warned.

Luciana sobered. "I know."

Hecate only dipped her chin in acknowledgment. "Well, should we get on with it? Why are you all here?"

"We're still looking for the journals." Lennox wasted no time.

"I should have known you wouldn't give up on those damned books." She shook her head. "I don't have them."

"I know," Lennox continued. "But you have the information we need."

"Is that all I'm good for? Information?"

"That is why you were sent back is it not?" Lennox braced her hands on her hips as she faced off against the original witch.

"Cunning girl." Hecate smiled wickedly. "What is it you want to know?"

"Where can we find the journals?" I pressed.

"I cannot tell you where the journals are."

"What—"

"*Patience*. But I can direct you to who can." She looked between Lennox, Luce, and Kara. "Your family has been looking for these journals for a long time."

"What?"

"It is my belief your father and brother died protecting their location."

"You can't be serious." Kara's mouth fell open.

Hecate turned her attention toward Kara. "I can't confirm

if that is why they were killed. Just as I can't see if the Vanir are connected to the journals, but your brother and father knew about the journals."

"Okay, but what good does that do us? They're dead. We can't exactly ask them where the journals are." Lennox pressed.

"Right, but they were not working alone." Her red eyes fixed on Luciana. "Your mother was working with them."

"My mother? That can't be right."

"Why don't you go ask her yourself?" Hecate raised a dark brow.

"I can't. She'd never reveal that to me."

"But she might to me." Lennox looked over at her cousin, the two sharing a look before Hecate spoke again.

"Looks like you're in for a family reunion," Hecate crooned.

"Alright, let's go. Luce, bring us to your mother."

"Wait, now?" Luciana stammered. "You want to go see my mother now?"

Lennox shrugged. "I can't see a reason to wait."

"We're standing here with the original witch, my mother can wait."

"If you are no longer in need of me, I'll see myself out." With the wave of her finger Hecate was gone. Lennox didn't bat an eye, continuing to meet Luciana's gaze as Nico's mouth fell open.

"Did you guys not see that?" Nico looked between us, eyes wide.

Lennox waved a hand. "She does that. Now there's nothing standing in our way, let's go see Caterina."

"People will be looking for us soon, Lennox. We can't disappear without explanation," I countered.

She drew her bottom lip between her teeth as she crossed her arms over her chest.

"Besides, you two have a ball to attend tomorrow," Nico added.

"A ball?" Lennox narrowed her eyes in my direction. "What ball?"

Fuck, I had forgotten about the star's damned ball. "Krissa didn't tell you? We were invited to a ball by one of the dukes who takes up residence in Cel Nox. We need to make an appearance for at least a little while or it will seem suspicious. You know as well as I do, Lennox, we have to make our engagement believable, even if we are trying to find a way out of it."

She sighed. "Fine. But the night after we're going to see my aunt." I dipped my chin in agreement.

"What if I see if I can get any information out of her tomorrow?" Luciana suggested. "She might not be willing to give anything up to me, but if I mention you, she might give me something. If she doesn't, you come the next day and we can approach her together."

"Okay, I like that." Lennox's face softened as she looked at Luciana, her brows drawing together. "You're sure it's okay to travel this much?"

Luciana waved her hand dismissively. "It will be fine. I'm not worried."

"I'll come with you." We all looked at the wolf.

"What do you mean you'll go with her?" Declan and I asked in unison.

"We can say I arrived as a messenger from Lennox."

"I wouldn't have to tell my mother I've been using Ichor Magic if Nico came with me." Luce and Nico shared a look. "You're not as dumb as you look, pup."

He winked at her. "I'm more than just a pretty face, Lucy."

# 19

## LUCIANA

It had been months since I'd seen my mother. My task of keeping my eye on the witch covens throughout the Mystic Court kept me away from the capital city of Arcadia, where my mother reigned from.

But this was the longest I had been away from my mother since I left her womb.

I missed her, but I didn't mind the space. It allowed me the opportunity to explore things she wouldn't approve of, like Ichor Magic.

My mother would figure it out one of these days, she was smart after all, but I wanted to avoid the lecture for as long as I could.

And my mother loved giving lectures, especially to her one and only heir.

It wouldn't help that my visit would be unexpected.

Or that I would be arriving with a wolf emissary from the Blood Court.

She was not fond of when I veered from her plans. My welcome home would be short-lived once she realized these things.

"We'll tell her we ran into one another on our way to Arcadia," Nico said as we rode alongside one another through the forest, pulling me back to reality.

I had transported us to a village outside Arcadia where we purchased horses to further convince my mother of our ruse while Nico yapped on obsessively about how excited he was to be back in the Mystic Court.

It had seemed like a good idea at the time, having Nico come with me, but now I was having second thoughts. We had gotten on well enough during the weeks we spent together this summer while Luka and Lennox had gone to find Hecate, but he was unpredictable.

You never knew what was going to come out of his mouth. He was a charmer, which would be helpful if my mother was easily charmed.

She was a charmer herself. A mask for what hid beneath.

"Lucy?" Nico's voice finally cut through my thoughts.

"Hmm?"

"Did you hear anything I said?"

"You talk too much, I've taken to tuning you out," I lied.

"You're a spectacular travel partner, you know that?"

"We've been riding for less than an hour, is your attention span that short?"

"Sorry if I like to participate in conversation to pass the time." He tucked his moonspun hair behind his ear.

"Sorry if I like to travel in silence."

"Well, that's no fun. I gave you silence the first half, now you need to talk to me."

I ignored him, keeping my focus ahead.

"Are you nervous about seeing your mother?"

I fisted the reins in my hands tighter. "That's a complicated question."

"How so?" He pressed

My chest constricted. "My mother and I—" I considered how to put my mother and I's relationship into words. "My mother and I have a complicated relationship. We're close, but we're also not. She has high expectations of me."

Nico blew out a breath. "I worry she's going to be suspicious of me arriving here unprompted. It will raise a lot of questions," I continued.

I wasn't due back in Arcadia for another month, that was where I was to return after Lennox and Luka's engagement party in a few weeks, to meet up with my mother before we would travel to Alethens for their wedding shortly after.

"Sounds like my relationship with my parents." There was a seriousness to Nico's tone, a sadness almost, that I had never heard before.

"Do you see them often?"

His body stilled, his back going ramrod straight in the saddle. "I haven't seen anyone in my family since I left almost two years ago to be Luka's emissary."

"Was that intentional?" Nico was one of the friendliest people I have ever met, he cared for Declan and Luka like family, *stars* he even treated Lennox, Kara, and me like family. Him having a strained relationship with his family wasn't something I had ever considered.

"That's a complicated question," he said finally.

"You don't have to talk about it if you don't want to."

"No, it's okay. It's just—it's hard to talk about them sometimes because we are…were close? Are close? I don't know what we are anymore." He sighed deeply. "I don't know if we're close anymore. We had a falling out of sorts and that's why I decided to leave. Luka had been asking me to become his emissary for a long time so I took the opportunity to get out. I needed space from my family so I left."

"You haven't talked to them since?"

"They sent me all kinds of letters at first, my parents and siblings." He shook his head. "I've seen some of my siblings over the years, but I haven't seen my parents since I left two years ago."

What had happened to make Nico avoid his family to this extent? I saw how much he cared for others—for him to abandon his family—

"You were right, silence is better," he finished.

We didn't talk again until we entered the capital city.

C

Walking into the city of Arcadia felt like getting a hug from a relative you weren't fond of, but were obligated to anyway.

It was my home, and at my core, I did love it. But it also held resentment.

Once I became queen I would be chained to this city.

It was my mother's idea to send me out to the villages this past year. My one last opportunity to travel and get out of the city before I bore the weight of the crown.

Her way of easing her own guilt over me being her only heir.

"Your Highness, what a surprise! We were not expecting you." Larkin, one of the palace guards, greeted us at the gates.

I forced a smile onto my face. "I know, it was a surprise on my end too." I dismounted my horse and handed the reins to Larkin. "And I come with a guest." I motioned to Nico. "This is Nico Elsher, emissary to the Blood Court. I ran into him on our way here and offered to be his guide into the city."

"The Blood Court?" The male's face paled.

"Don't worry, bud." Nico said, slapping the male on the shoulder. "I'm not a vampire." He smiled wildly, revealing his lack of fangs. "I'm a wolf."

I rolled my eyes. "He's harmless, Larkin. Is my mother in?"

The male tore his terrified eyes from Nico. "She is, I believe she's in her office."

"Perfect. Have a meal ready for us in a bit. We are hungry after our travels. And make sure my room is ready, along with a room for Nico."

"Yes, Your Highness."

"C'mon, pup." I gestured for Nico to follow me. "Time for you to meet my mother."

☾

I knocked once before entering my mother's office.

Caterina wasn't one for surprises and she might have been Queen of the Mystic Court, but she was still my mother.

"Who do you think you are to enter my office without—" My mother froze mid-word when she looked up to find me in her doorway and not whoever else she thought it might be, her dark eyes, a mirror to my own, going wide.

"Luciana." Her accent only came out in occasional words. One of them was when she said my name, with a slight accent on the *n*. Her slight lilt soothed an ache in my soul I didn't know was there. "What in the Goddess are you doing here?" She didn't hesitate—immediately rising from her chair and moving around her desk to embrace me.

"Mama," I said into her dark curls as they surrounded me.

"What are you doing here, *Lulita*?"

"I came to see you." She shifted, moving to see around me.

"And you brought a guest?"

I removed myself from her embrace. "This is Nico Elsher." I gestured to Nico who took a step forward. "He's the emissary to the Blood Court." My mother's dark brows rose an inch.

"Emissary to the Blood Court? Well, aren't you a long way from home?" She looked between the two of us. "And what are you doing here with my daughter."

"It's a pleasure to meet you, Your Majesty." Nico bowed slightly before taking my mother's hand in his own.

"You remember Lennox is engaged to the Blood Prince." My mother's eyes widened at my informal mention of Lennox.

She squared her shoulders before speaking. "Yes, I am aware of our High Queen's engagement."

"He knows everything Mama, Lennox and Kara told him."

"Did she now?" I quickly explained Luka's injuries in the forest and Lennox's need to use her powers to heal him, revealing her witch heritage.

"I see. But that still doesn't explain why you're here together."

"We ran into one another outside of Arcadia, Lucy was nice enough to ride with me the rest of the way. After I berated her to the point of annoyance."

My mother cracked a half smile as she turned her attention to Nico. "You'd be good for her."

"*Mama.*"

"What?" Her mouth lifted in a half smile. "You can be so serious. You need someone to loosen you up." She winked at Nico, whose mouth fell open before breaking into a smile.

"We are not discussing this now," I interrupted before the conversation could go any farther. I shouldn't be surprised by my mother's brashness; she took any opportunity she could to try and set me up. She had taken over the crown alone, but she did not wish for me to bear that burden alone.

"Nico comes with a message from Lennox." I needed something, anything to change the subject from where it was currently heading.

My mother snapped back to attention. "Well, why don't you two have a seat? I'll have some refreshments sent in."

Nico and I took seats in the twin chairs in front of her desk while my mother called for a staff member.

"So, what news do you come with from my niece?" In true fashion, my mother cut the pleasantries and went straight to the point.

Nico leaned back in his chair, crossing one leg over the other. "I don't know if Luciana mentioned it to you, but when we all visited the Mystic Court this past summer we were in search of a book."

My mother narrowed her eyes in my direction, I did my best to keep my back straight under her gaze.

"No, Luciana didn't mention that. This is the first she and I have seen one another since the beginning of the year."

"The information Lennox shared with me was not something I wanted documented in a letter."

My mother dipped her chin. "Continue, Lord Elsher." We'd discuss my lack of communication with her later in private I'm sure.

"While they were in the Mystic Court this summer they had no luck finding the book, but we've now gained additional information. It is not a book we are looking for, it's Astria's journals."

My mother's brows rose an inch, but she said nothing.

"So we were directed to you."

"To me?" My mother placed a hand on her chest. "By who?"

"By Hecate," I interjected.

"Who spoke to Hecate?"

I opened my mouth to say all of us but stopped myself.

My mother's gaze narrowed on me. "Nico, would you mind checking on the tea for me? I'd like a moment alone with my daughter."

"Anything you want to say to me you can say in front of him."

"Are you sure about that?" I said nothing, meeting my mother's challenging gaze.

"Fine. Let's have it out then. Who spoke to Hecate? All of you? You didn't run into him outside of town did you, Luciana? Did you think I wouldn't be able to smell the reek of Ichor Magic on you?"

"Mama—"

Her tone sharpened. "I warned you, Luciana. I warned you there are consequences for using such magic. And to transport not only you, but others? How stupid and reckless are you?"

"I should go," Nico mumbled as he stood.

"No, Luciana wanted you here, so here you shall stay." He fell back into his chair cautiously, his gaze falling to the floor.

"I've been practicing Ichor Magic for years without a hitch, Mama. Lennox needed me so I went. We can discuss your disapproval of my decisions later, now we have more important topics to discuss."

My mother tapped her long fingernails on the desk.

"Hecate told us Nol and Brahm were looking for these journals and since they are dead we should ask you about them instead. What do you have to say about that mother?"

"Where is Lennox now? Why didn't you bring her back with you?"

"She had a prior commitment," I said through gritted teeth. I was having a hard time remembering why I volunteered to have this conversation with my mother without Lennox.

"When can you get her here?"

"What do you mean?"

"If we're going to have this conversation I want her here."

"Okay," I said hesitantly. She knew something. She had information.

"Her and Luka had to attend an event tonight, but they can be here tomorrow," Nico said.

My mother looked at me, "And you can ensure they get here?"

"Are you telling me to use Ichor Magic?"

"No—I'm simply asking if you can ensure they get here by whatever means necessary."

"Yes. I can."

"Fine." She looked between the two of us. "I assume the two of you are staying here tonight?"

I looked at Nico. "Yes, we will remain here tonight and retrieve the rest in the morning."

"Fine. Well, I have work to do. I will see you both at dinner." She turned back to the work on her desk—dismissing us.

Nico and I stood without another word, both of us remaining silent until we reached our rooms.

"You mother—she's intense."

I slumped against the door with a thud. "That's one way to put it."

I had forgotten how much energy it took to verbally spar with my mother.

"I need a nap. I'll find you before dinner."

# 20

# LENNOX

I had to go to a ball.

I had to go to a ball with Luka.

I had to go to a ball with Luka and act like we were happily in love and engaged and not like my heart shredded further every time I was around him.

And the last time we were at a ball together—those memories alone were enough to send me into a spiral.

But this wasn't something I could avoid. This was the first of many balls and events I'd have to attend with him by my side. I needed to get used to putting on a face while I was next to him and pretending I wasn't dying inside.

The knock on my door told me there was no more ignoring him.

I opened the door, finding him standing in the hallway, waiting for me. He was dressed in head-to-toe black, his shirt was unbuttoned on the top and his sleeves were rolled up, exposing his corded forearms. Why did he have to be so stars-damned attractive?

He looked almost nervous. Anxious even? Emotions I wasn't used to seeing on him.

The moment his eyes took me in, any nervous energy dissipated. He took his time looking me up and down, not even trying to hide his open perusal of my body.

"You look—*wow.*" He scrubbed his hand over his chin, over the thin layer of stubble coating his jaw.

"I mean, you did pick it out for me." The dress had arrived this afternoon, with a note from Luka, insisting I let him help me make sure I was properly dressed for my first Blood Court ball. I was ready to toss out the dress, not willing to let him help me, but then I looked at it. It was a stunning black and gold dress with a low back and plunging neckline. I couldn't resist a dress like that.

"Yeah—but seeing it on you is a whole different experience." His eyes darkened. I knew exactly what thoughts were filtering through his mind. We had a similar conversation before, one that ended with us fucking against a wall. "I think—"

"Don't." I stopped him before he could get the words out. "You can't make comments like that anymore."

"C'mon, Sweetheart. We're engaged. If my fiancè looks good enough to fuck, I should be able to tell her such."

"Keep your filthy thoughts in your head."

"Or what? You'll stab me?" He placed his hand dramatically on his chest as he followed me into the room.

"It's been a long time since you stabbed me. You know how your violence turns me on. You and those daggers." He was practically panting now.

"Thoughts. Keep them in your head," I scolded.

"Fine. I'll keep my thoughts about fucking you in that dress in my head."

"You're infuriating."

"And that's why you—"

We both froze. The unsaid words hanging in the air.

"We should go." The words were thick in my throat.

He scrubbed his hand over his neck. "Yeah." He looked at the floor. "After you.

Luka held out his hand to me and guided me from the carriage. He linked my arm through his as the cold winter chill nipped at my skin. Forgoing a cloak was a decision I was now regretting.

He leaned in close, his lips brushing the shell of my ear. "Remember, we're supposed to be happily engaged. So you're going to have to pretend to like me tonight."

I swallowed, still on edge by how close his mouth was to mine. "Good thing I'm a master at putting on a mask."

Something I couldn't place flashed across his features before he pulled back and guided me inside the manor.

We walked through the gilded doors into a darkened entry where we were immediately passed glasses of a dark liquid in a tall glass by a masked servant.

My eyes scanned the darkened room, searching for any sign of the ball Luka had promised, but there was nothing, the room was empty besides a few masked staff. The curtains were drawn, keeping out any light from the moon. Only a few bulbs were lit, casting the room in a dim orange light.

"You won't find anything in here." I remained silent, taking a sip from my glass as he continued to lead me through the room until we came to a lighted path. We followed the path down the hallway until we were led to what I assumed was the ballroom.

The curtains were shut in here as well, but candles and lanterns were scattered throughout the room along with small strings of lights. The lighted path we followed into the room continued into the ballroom spreading out like lighted roots in the dim room to guide us through.

There was no room for dancing, booths, couches, and daybeds were scattered around the space instead. Fabric dividers were placed strategically throughout the room to create the illusion of privacy, but everything was still out in the open.

Partygoers were scattered around the room, the sounds of

their pleasure mixing with the dark seductive music playing from musicians hiding somewhere in the dark room.

I swallowed thickly as my gaze flicked to the pair of males on the couch beside us. Our arrival did nothing to slow or stop their exploration of one another.

"Is this what you were expecting?" Luka said as he leaned in close to not disrupt the males.

"No." My voice was rough in my throat. No. This was not what I was expecting at all.

"I'll explain in a moment." Luka pulled me along. "Let's find a spot first."

I stopped in my tracks. "A spot—I'm not finding a spot with you Luka."

"Shhh—" he warned. "We're happily engaged, remember? Just follow me."

I did so hesitantly. We passed a small dance floor, where a female danced seductively for a small group of males and females who reclined against a mass of pillows and blankets.

Luka continued to weave us through the room until we came to an unoccupied day bed in the far corner of the room.

"Sit," Luka instructed me. I didn't argue, I sat against the pillows, and placed my empty glass on the table beside the bed.

"Explain." Luka settled in close to me, his leg brushing against my exposed thigh. I ignored the spark that nipped at my skin from the contact.

"Blood Court parties are meant to be an opportunity to let loose. Experience your darkest inhibitions free without judgments. Couples will come here together only to spend the whole night with another and leave together at the end of the night."

"So this party is essentially a high-class sex club?"

Luka chuckled. "Call it what you want." He swiped a bottle of wine off a passing tray.

"I'm not judging. I'm trying to wrap my head around the concept." He held his hand out to me and I passed him my empty glass.

"So—" I asked hesitantly as I took my refilled glass from him. "Do you typically partake in these parties?"

He pushed the hair back from his face. "Yes and no."

A knot formed in my stomach at his non-answer.

"I never came here seeking out pleasure—but if pleasure sought out me I didn't typically say no."

I cursed the goddess-forsaken knot in my stomach for tightening at the thought of him here with another even before I had met him. If I hadn't come here with him tonight, would he have turned someone away if they approached him? Even if he was technically engaged to me? He said there was no judgment for couples who sought out others at these parties—did that include royally engaged couples?

"I know what you're thinking—and no." With a single finger on my cheek, he turned me so I looked at him. "I may be trying to find you a way out of this marriage, Lennox, but you are mine and I am yours. You don't need to worry about me straying—no matter the circumstance." My heart squeezed. My stupid fucking heart. I knew by the look in his eyes he meant it. Luka always meant what he said. He opened his mouth—I thought he might say more, but instead, he let go of my face, shifting back to his seat. The place where his finger was, left a brand on my skin.

We sat in silence for a while—each of us watching the events taking place before us.

"Why did I have to be here if we are going to sit in the corner and watch everyone else?"

Luka's brows rose. "Are you saying you want to do more than sit in a corner?"

I choked on the wine. "No—I mean. You said we were expected here. We're not talking to anyone and I doubt anyone is paying us any attention so why are we here?" Luka chuckled.

"The duke knows we are here, he will call for us later. He's probably giving us some time to enjoy the party first."

"What do you mean enjoy?"

A smile crept up his face. "I think you know."

"We're not doing that." Although the idea of letting Luka touch me didn't repel me at all. It sent a small spark through my body instead.

"You said you didn't think anyone was paying us any attention, there's a way we can change that."

"No."

He laughed again. "You make it too easy to rile you up."

My cheeks heated as I silently cursed myself. I hated how easily he could get under my skin.

"You know I'd never make you do anything you didn't want to do." I eased slightly. I did know that.

"But I will warn you, if anyone pays us a visit you might have to sit a little closer to me. You're making it hard to believe we're happy together."

I grumbled in acceptance as I took another sip of my drink.

"Why are we here anyway?" Attending a ball together was one thing—but this party—I had a hard time wrapping my mind around why we were expected to be here. Especially if no one was paying us any attention as they were wrapped up in their own *experience*.

"You'll see soon enough."

"Luka," I said, my tone sharp.

"Can you trust me, please?" He sighed and ran his fingers through his hair. "The duke is in charge of the city watch. My grandfather claims there haven't been any Vanir attacks on the city since I've been back, but I don't exactly believe him. I wanted to see if I could get an answer straight from the source."

"What makes you think he'll give you the information you want?"

He smirked. "When someone has their hand wrapped around your cock, information slips from your lips real easily."

"Luka," I hissed. "I am not touching him."

"I didn't mean you," his eyes darkened, "You will not be touching him. There are plenty others here that will be at his disposal, but we need to be there when it happens, while he's distracted."

Before I could press about it further Luka stiffened and shushed me.

"What?"

"It's the duke." He spoke through his teeth. "The moment he spots us he'll surely make his way over here. Now's the time, Sweetheart, pretend like you like me."

I stiffened as he snaked an arm around my waist and pulled me closer to him. "Anytime now." He murmured as his lips pressed into the side of my neck. An involuntary shiver wracked my body at the feel of his lips moving across my neck, placing soft kisses wherever they traveled. I shifted so one of my legs draped across his lap, intertwining with his. I closed my eyes and exposed my neck further to him. Moaning slightly as his fangs scraped over my heated skin.

"Keep making sounds like that, Sweetheart, and I'll think you aren't pretending."

"Don't ruin it." I panted as I gripped my hand in his shirt pulling him closer, causing the hand on my back to tighten.

*Too easy*, it was *too easy* to fall back into his arms.

"Well, isn't it the happy couple?" A male voice interrupted the exploration of his lips. Luka bent forward, resting his forehead in the crook of my neck—breathing me in before he sat up and turned toward our visitor. The duke's golden hair was cut similar to Luka's, the longer pieces were mused, as if someone else had been pulling at the strands. His white shirt was unbuttoned, exposing his muscular chest.

"Caspian." Luka gave me a hard time about the face I put on as queen, but he did the same as he addressed the duke and his companions. "I was wondering when you'd find us."

"I've been previously occupied." The male's blue eyes glimmered as he looked at the male and female beside him before breaking out into a grin. "As I see you have been too."

"Yes, I don't think you've been introduced." Luka stood

before giving me his hand and pulling me to stand next to him, wrapping his arm around my waist as he tucked me into his side.

"This is High Queen, Lennox Adair."

The duke's smile faltered for a second.

"My Queen." He bowed. "What an honor it is to meet you and have you in my home. I'm sorry I didn't know of your arrival sooner I would have—"

"There is no need." I interrupted the male. "We are all here to have fun are we not? My arrival should have no hinderance to that."

The male opened his mouth, but Luka interrupted him. "Lennox and I are engaged. We are here so she can see what she is marrying into."

"And are you enjoying yourself, Your Majesty?"

"Very much so."

"I would love for you and Luka to come and join me in my suite."

Luka's grip on my waist tightened, but he smiled. "We would love to."

# 21

# LUKA

It was a shame I liked this particular duke because right now I'd like nothing more than to tell him to fuck off, so I could go back to making Lennox make those little sounds I loved so much as she arched into my touch for the first time in months.

My hand remained on her back as Caspian led us through the ballroom into his private suite. It would be a lot harder to fake our relationship in his private room. There would be fewer eyes on us, but Caspian would be watching closely—it was the opportunity I needed. I just hoped Lennox was ready for what would come next.

We followed Caspian out of the ballroom and down a narrow hallway lit by torches, stopping when we came to a door.

Lennox's eyes were wide as she took in the room. The entire suite was bathed in red light and was smaller than you would anticipate. A bar took up the left side of the room, manned by a single masked barkeep. It was typical for any staff at such parties to remain masked to keep the illusion of anonymity for everyone. There were several tables and booths in the center of the room, occupied by other invited guests.

I ushered Lennox along, following Caspian and his companions to an empty table in the center of the room. The duke and his companions slid into the bench seat, Caspian in the middle with each of his companions on either side of him, leaving Lennox and I to sit in the chairs across from them. Lennox aimed for the chair next to mine, but I pulled her into my lap instead, causing a small squeak to leave her mouth.

"Play along," I whispered into her hair. She dipped her chin, understanding flashing in her eyes as she quickly relaxed into me, her legs falling between mine as she faced the duke.

I banded my arm around Lennox's waist as the barkeep approached with a tray full of drinks.

"Your usual, My Lord."

"Thank you." Caspian dipped his chin to the barkeep as he placed glasses in front of each of us. "This liquor is the finest in Cel Nox, my family made its fortune from this liquor. If you'd like something else, Your Majesty, Gael can fetch it for you, but I ask you do try this first."

Lennox took the glass of amber liquid in her hands. "He's not exaggerating, this is what I keep in my rooms at the palace," I confirmed.

She brought the glass to her lips, my gaze fixed on her neck as she swallowed, wanting nothing more than to pierce the skin with my fangs.

"So? What do you think?" Caspian's voice brought me back to the present.

Lennox smiled softly. "I think if I drink too much of this, I'd find myself drunk quickly."

Laughter rang out around the table. "You'd be right about that," Caspian remarked. The female at Caspians side ran her hand up and down his arm, catching Caspian's attention.

"Where are my manners?" He looked back at Lennox and me. "I forgot to introduce you to my—"

"Lovers?" The female finished for him.

"Hmmm," Caspian said, "is that what you're calling yourself tonight, love?"

The female smiled coyly as her hand traveled down the

duke's body. Whether this female was his companion for tonight or more, I didn't know, but they appeared to be fond of one another.

Caspian shifted and cleared his throat. "This is Jasellia," gestured to the female, "and this is Thiago."

I nodded toward the two, keeping my focus on Caspian as their hands roamed over the dukes body. Caspain's eyes fell closed. Lennox stiffened as he let out a low groan as Jasellia's hand roamed beneath the table.

"So, Caspian, the city has been quiet lately, how have you been spending your time with nothing to do?"

He let out a deep chuckle. "Who told you that?"

"Lorenzo, of course."

Thaigo disappeared beneath the table. "No offense to you, but your uncle knows shit about what goes on in this city outside the palace walls. The city has been running amok with degenerates, this is the first night I've taken to myself in weeks." So my grandfather had been lying to me, was it the Vanir who were running amongst the city?

"Which is why I'd prefer not to discuss this now."

"If you'd like, we can leave you alone to enjoy your night off." I already knew Caspian's answer, but for Lennox's sake, I asked anyway as Jasellia shifted closer, trailing his mouth down the other side of Caspian's neck. I wanted more information, but he wasn't as loose-lipped yet as I needed him to be.

"No need," Caspian slipped his hand up Jasellia's dress as he looked at Lennox and me out of the corner of his eye. "You know I like to watch." Lennox stiffened in my lap as Caspian winked before turning back to his companions or *lovers*, or whatever they were.

"He likes to watch?" Lennox hissed through her teeth, her body going tense under my touch.

"He likes to watch," I confirmed.

She swallowed. "I see."

"Relax. I'm only going to make it look like I'm touching you.

Tell me if you want me to stop or if I'm making you uncomfortable. If we stay a little long I might be able to get more out of him."

Her chest heaved as she watched the duke and his *friends*.

"Does watching them arouse you, Sweetheart?"

She took another deep breath, causing her breasts to strain against the thin fabric of her gown. "Maybe."

"Mmm." I moved her hair to one side, giving me free rein of her exquisite neck I wanted to sink my fangs into. I ran my nose up and down the collar of her neck instead.

"Should we give them something to look at?"

She remained silent, her gaze fixed on the trio as my hand around her waist tightened, my thumb brushing light strokes on her stomach while my other hand ran down her gown until it found the exposed skin of her thigh through the slit in the fabric.

"I want to make it so you aren't thinking about them. I want to make it so you can't think of anything but *my* touch."

Her breath hitched as my hand closed around her exposed thigh, my fingertips dancing on the metal sheathed there.

"Prove it," she breathed.

I shifted her on my lap, hitching one of her legs over mine. My hand on her thigh skated higher, my fingers brushing light strokes on the inside of her thigh under the cover of her dress.

I placed a kiss on her neck as my hand continued to brush light strokes on her skin, my mouth moving up her neck towards her ear. Her back arched slightly as I took her ear between my teeth and tugged.

"You like it when my fangs are on you, don't you."

She said nothing, only eliciting a slight sigh as my fingers on her thigh drifted even higher.

"I can stop if you want me to."

"Don't stop." Her hand gripped my thigh with brutal force.

I nipped at her ear again, my fingers moving even higher, her legs widening farther. I groaned as she leaned back into me, her head falling back as the tip of my finger brushed the fabric of her undergarment.

She inched forward pressing her center against my hand as I continued to grow hard beneath her. My cock pressing into her ass.

"Fuck, Lennox." I cursed as I brushed my knuckles over the soaked lace covering her.

I dragged a single finger down the lace. She jerked forward, a moan slipping from her lips.

*Too far,* we were taking this too far. I moved my hand back, gripping her thigh again as I tried to gain some semblance of control. If she kept making those sounds, nothing would be able to stop me from ripping her undergarment to the side and shoving inside her. My fingers or my cock, I didn't care. I'd fuck her in this room, on the fucking stage in front of everyone if she let me.

And Astrias tits did I want that.

My cock strained painfully against the fabric of my pants.

"Lennox."

She opened her eyes, her chest heaving as she looked at the duke and his companions. One of Jasellia's breasts was exposed and Caspian took it in his mouth. Thiago was still on his knees under the table.

"Now, ask him now," she breathed.

Her words were like ice water. Dousing all arousal.

"Right." The words felt rotten in my mouth. I had gotten too carried away. I was the one who told her this was all an act anyway, a ploy to get information. I shouldn't be surprised by her words. I knew she never would have let this go any further.

"What of the Vanir?" My hand remained between Lennox's thighs as I spoke, my finger stroking ever so slightly as her head fell back on my shoulder. "Have they made a reappearance?"

Caspain didn't open his eyes. "I swear the bastards never sleep. They're everywhere, all the time." Caspain groaned as his hand fisted in Thiago's hair. "Those slippery suckers—they're too smart, too fast. Always one step ahead of us, anticipating our next moves. We're perpetually too late—never able to catch them."

"Have there been any reports of attacks by a beast?" Caspian pulled Jasellia's lips to his, kissing her deeply with his hand slipping between her thighs.

"Caspian?" He ignored me, too distracted by pleasure now. *Fuck.*

"At least we got some information." Lennox's eyes were locked on the scene playing out in front of us.

"We're going to find somewhere private to finish what we started." I told the duke as I lifted Lennox from my lap.

"Let's get the fuck out of here," I ground out.

Something like hurt flashed across her features, halting me for a second, but she nodded, following me out of the duke's manor—neither of us saying another word.

# 22

# LENNOX

"Luka." He continued ahead of me as we entered the palace. "Luka," I called again.

"Goodnight, Lennox," he muttered, not bothering to face me. What had gotten into him? Things had felt okay at the ball. It had reminded me of before, when we were friends. It gave me a semblance of hope we might be able to make this work. That we could pretend to be a happily engaged couple. Pretending with him was easier than I anticipated, I thought things had gone well.

But now he was shutting down, shutting me out.

And I didn't know why.

I continued after him. My anger rose with every step he took away from me. I had given into his touch at the party—had let myself enjoy his hands on my body and now he wouldn't speak to me. Wouldn't even look at me.

*Bastard.*

"Luka! You don't get to walk away from me like this!"

Finally he turned, his eyes blazing, causing me to stop in my tracks. He had never looked at me like that before. I'd seen him use the expression on others, but never me.

"Why not?" His tone was sharp, it made my spine and

shoulders straighten. "You get to walk away from me over and over again. I think I'm due for a chance."

His words struck like tiny pricks in my chest.

Each one stole the breath from my lungs, but not in a good way.

My anger quickly dissipated.

How many times had I walked away from him, but each time he followed?

"Will you at least talk to me?" I said softly. "What's going on? Why are you acting like this?" This behavior was strange coming from him and it was throwing me off balance. He was the one who helped me stay upright, and now he was the one turning me upside down with nothing to grasp.

"Talk to me." I grasped for his arm.

"Talk to you?" His eyes flashed with anger and something else as he moved his arm out of my reach. "All I fucking do is talk, Lennox. I'm lucky if you even listen to what I say, let alone say something back." He ran his fingers through his hair. "I'm so tired of talking with no response. I know you need time—but right now I can't do this. Right now I need time. I need time and space away from *you*."

My chest tightened painfully. He needed to be away from *me*.

*This.* This is what I had anticipated from Luka when I arrived.

This anger. This resentment toward me.

But he had been fine, or fine adjacent when I arrived. Why was he getting angry now? What did I do to change his feelings?

Before I got a chance to ask him, he was gone and I was left staring at his closed door as it shook against the frame. The echo of the slam ringing through my mind.

☾

I paced across my room as I replayed my conversation with

Luka in my mind and over the events of the night again and again.

I still couldn't figure out what I had done to trigger him tonight, but I couldn't blame him for acting the way he did. I had treated him so terribly since I arrived.

Given him only the tiniest scraps of myself.

But tonight—tonight I had given him more of myself than I had in months. I allowed myself to slip back into us for a short time. I told myself it was all an act, but it wasn't really.

So his rejection—or reaction afterward—stung more than I cared to admit. I had finally taken a step forward and now he was taking a step back.

But why? What did I do?

I knew I wouldn't sleep without talking to him again, without sorting this all out. I had hurt him enough as it was—I didn't know what I had done tonight but I needed to rectify it.

It took him a while before he answered the door—he took two steps back, his eyes going wide before narrowing as he took me in.

"What are you doing here?" His eyes roamed over my body, making me remember I was wearing a nightgown that left little to the imagination.

I crossed my arms over my chest, trying and failing to hide my chest from his wandering gaze. He took a sip of the liquid from the glass resting lazily in his hand. It was most likely the same one we had drunk with Caspian a few short hours ago. "Come in, won't you." His voice was slightly slurred, his movements sluggish as he moved, allowing me space to enter into the room.

He didn't look back at me as he headed toward the seating area in the center of the room, allowing me to take in the space.

The room was tidy overall, the bed was unmade, but everything else appeared to have been returned to its place, with the exception of the books. Books were stacked haphazardly in piles everywhere. On the bedside table, on the coffee table, the floor.

There were so many books in the room it resembled more of a library than a bedroom.

"Care for a drink?" Luka filled his own glass from a bar cart stacked with bottles in the sitting area.

"Sure." I sat hesitantly on the couch across from him as he handed me a glass.

We sat silently sipping on our drinks, it was in fact Caspian's families'. My eyes wandered over Luka's body as he sat lounging lazily on the couch, his fingers tracing the rim of his glass. He hadn't changed out of his clothes from the ball, but he had unbuttoned his shirt, leaving his toned stomach on display. I couldn't keep my eyes from roaming to his exposed skin. I remembered how those muscles felt under my fingertips, every hard ridge and plane—

"Why are you here, Lennox?" Luka's voice stirred me from my wandering thoughts. His voice sounded defeated as he continued to stare at his glass.

"I couldn't sleep knowing you were mad at me," I admitted.

He sighed, sitting up straighter. "I'm not mad at you, Lennox."

"I wouldn't blame you if you were. I've treated you terribly," I said softly, not bothering to look up.

"You have," he scoffed.

Silence stretched between us again.

"What did I do to upset you tonight?" My voice came out more strained than I intended. "I thought we were getting along and—I don't know, you stopped talking to me and wouldn't even look at me." As I said the words it set in how much of an impact they had on me. He was one of the few people who truly saw me—every part of me and he didn't run. But tonight he had.

I didn't know how to handle him not looking at me.

I had thought that's what I wanted but now...I wasn't so sure.

The absence of his gaze left me off kilter.

"You didn't do anything, Lennox." He set his empty glass on the table and sat forward, putting his face in his hands. "It's stupid. I should have known better. I got too caught up in everything. I forgot for a moment tonight was all an act and when you reminded me—fuck I'm so pathetic." My heart lurched. "You didn't do anything. When you reminded me it was all an act—it impacted me more than I thought it would."

"Luka, I—"

"Please don't say anything. I told you I didn't want to talk about it and I meant it. Now can you leave me alone for a night so I can lick my wounds? Alone. *Please.*" The strain in his voice was enough to set my feet moving towards the door—even though it broke me to leave him like this. He said I didn't do anything to make him like this, but that's a lie. I did this. I did all of this.

I had gotten caught up in the night too. When he touched me everything else faded into the distance. Everything between us tonight was real—but my feet continued to walk me towards the door. The pleading tone of his voice and the look in his eyes scalded me, pushing me forward.

I hesitated when I reached the door—daring to look back at him. He hadn't moved. His face still in his hands.

"It wasn't all an act," I whispered, before slipping through the door. Not daring to look back and see his reaction.

I thought he had broken me all those weeks ago—but I had never considered I might have broken him too.

## 23

# LENNOX

Hot tears fell down my face as I tore from Luka's room and down the hallway. I couldn't go back to my room. Not knowing he was next door wallowing in the misery I had caused him.

Not after the parting words I left him with.

I didn't realize where I was going—my feet carrying me up the stairs to the training room on their own accord. Nico had mentioned there was access to the roof from up there.

I tore through the room, looking for the door that would give me access to the roof.

*Air.* I needed air.

I finally found it—tearing open the door. My eyes stung as I ran up the stairs.

The moment the cool night air caressed my skin I felt like I could finally breathe again. I gulped in the air. My lungs were greedy for it. I ran for the ledge—my hands grasping the cool stone as I took deep breaths to calm my raging heart and shaking hands.

I don't know how long it took but finally, my breathing steadied.

"Are you okay?"

I jumped at the deep voice behind me, my hand going instinctively to my chest. How out of control had I been to not notice there was someone else up here?

I turned as Declan approached me. His dark hair was unbound, his wings spread wide behind him.

*Was I okay?*

*Yes.*

*No.*

"I don't know." I turned back towards the sky as he took up a place next to me at the railing. "I don't think I've been okay for a long time."

He was quiet beside me. How pathetic was I? I was now telling my problems to Declan who rarely involved himself in others' personal matters.

"Has Luka ever told you my story?" Declan spoke into the darkness, surprising me with his question.

"Not entirely. He told me it was your story to tell." I thought back to mine and Luka's conversation back in the Mystic Court, what he had told me about Declan.

He sighed deeply. "My mother died giving birth to me. Babes aren't supposed to be born with wings. They didn't expect it. I was considered a freak of nature."

I had never heard of half shifted harpies before meeting Declan, but I didn't realize Declan was the only one.

"My father abandoned me at birth. Lost in grief over my mother and essentially disowning me—his son was born an abomination with wings. The only of his kind. What a disgrace. And on top of that, *I* killed her. That was something my father never let me forget."

I kept my gaze on the dark sky as Declan continued, his hands gripping the railing so hard his knuckles had begun to turn white.

"I was raised for the first seven years of my life by the staff in the palace. The only reason my father didn't kill me was because people knew of my birth. I was supposed to be the highly anticipated heir of the Captain of the Guard, but I had failed him from day one. I saw my father on occasion. He made sure he reminded me I was an abomination and he had disowned me. It wasn't until others inquired about my abilities —if I could fly with my wings…" He let out a puff of air as his wings twitched behind him.

"I was so happy when he finally took an interest in me. I should have known better. He only trained me so he could use me. What a useful killing machine I could be. What a good spy I could be. My training was ruthless. Any wrongdoing was punished. Nothing I ever did was good enough for my father. He looked for any excuse to punish me. I couldn't tell you how many times I had laid on the training room floor unable to move—only to be found by a staff member hours later. The palace staff, they are the only reason I survived. That I didn't end it myself."

Tears pricked at the corners of my eyes.

"And then I met Luka. Or Luka found me, however you want to put it. He was the first person to show me there was more out there than the sad existence I was living. That I could leave. That I could live out from under my father's terror. That hope is what kept me going those last years until I left at sixteen."

I placed my hand over his. "Declan, I'm so sorry."

"I'm not telling you this to get your sympathy." He didn't move his hand out from under mine. "I don't like telling my story for that reason, but I often wonder if being born with my wings is a blessing or a curse."

I furrowed my brows as I tried to follow where he was going with this.

"I go back and forth depending on the day. My wings cursed me when it came to my father. But they were a blessing to bring me, Luka, and Nico together. And flying—" He shook his head, his dark hair swishing with the movement. "There's nothing like flying."

"Why are you telling me all this, Delcan?"

"You need to determine the same. Are your circumstances a blessing or a curse? Are you and Luka finding one another—is this arranged marriage a blessing or a curse?"

*Blessing or curse.* He made it sound so simple. A clear-cut choice.

But it was so much more than that. Wasn't it?

When it all came down to it, it was me and Luka at the core of everything. Was he, was our relationship, a blessing or a curse?

My first instinct was to say it was all a curse. Everything we had experienced was all a goddess-forsaken curse.

But to call Luka a curse—the word got lodged in my throat.

He had infected me, yes. He had infected my life like a virus, spreading throughout my existence and clinging to my every crack and crevice until there was no separating me from him. He was woven into me—unable to untangle where I ended and he began. Even while he was away, I still felt a pull towards him. I ached for him.

Luka was—he was the light in my darkness.

But a blessing, that wasn't the right word either.

Luka was Luka.

I just needed to figure out what that meant.

"You've given me a lot to think about, bird boy." I knocked my shoulder against his. "Nico's going to be jealous when he finds out you and I were bonding."

A sound adjacent to a laugh sounded from his throat. "Is that what you call having a conversation? Bonding?"

"When it comes to you, yes. This is the most words I've ever heard you say in one conversation."

"And it won't likely happen again, so you should consider yourself lucky."

"Oh, trust me, I do, Declan." I gave him a soft smile. "Thank you. Thank you for sharing this with me."

"Being able to help you and Luka by sharing my story—it's part of my way of figuring out if my wings are a blessing or a curse."

"Not that my opinion matters, but I think your wings are a blessing."

# 24

# LENNOX

The smells of Arcadia wrapped around me as the city came into focus around us. Luce had come this morning to Cel Nox to transport us to Arcadia with her, depositing us in the outskirts of the city.

It had been years since I had been to the capital city of the Mystic Court, the summer *Before* was the last time. I loved my time spent in Arcadia, the days spent exploring the palace walls and the city within, learning more about my witch heritage. This place held so many memories.

But I had never been here without my mother.

This was her home.

This is where she grew up.

Everything reminded me of her. The thick forest surrounding the palace was where we spent our days learning and practicing witch magic. We would spend our entire day in the woods, packing a picnic lunch so we wouldn't have to return to the palace. We spent countless days browsing the shops in the city proper, leaving when our arms were full of packages of items we could only find in the Mystic Court. The temple, the palace, *everything* reminded me of her. It would be even worse inside the palace. Memories of time spent with her and Nol within the walls were sure to assault me, along with the various pictures and paintings of her throughout the dwelling.

*I could do this, couldn't I?*

Kara fell into step next to me, taking my hand in hers and giving it a gentle squeeze. Things might still be tense between us, but even so, we'd lean on each other here.

When I looked over at my sister there were tears in her eyes.

"I—" She took a moment to collect her thoughts. "I can feel her everywhere."

I closed my eyes and gave my senses over to my surroundings. I felt nothing at first, but after a moment—I gasped. I felt her—the slight tingle at the base of my neck felt like delicate fingertips in a gentle caress. The smell of my mother surrounded me.

My mother—she was here. I opened my eyes, blinking back tears of my own now.

*I am always with you, my Sitara.*

"Kara." I gasped. "Did you—"

"Yes," she breathed. "I—she's here."

"Lennox, Kara are you okay?" Luce's voice was tentative.

I focused my eyes, blinking back tears. "Yeah." I choked back a sob. "Yeah, I'm okay." I shuttered as the sensation of my mother's magic filled me. I looked over at my sister.

Kara smiled. "It's good to be back in Arcadia."

☾

"My mother is expecting us." Luce led us through the palace gates.

Luka had yet to say a word to me since Luce arrived this morning to take us to Arcadia. How much time did he need?

"My mother and Nico are having *lunch*." There was a sarcastic lilt to Luce's tone as she spoke.

"You left Nico alone with Caterina?" I huffed a laugh. "Brave choice."

"*I* had little choice in the matter. It appears she has taken an interest in the wolf, and you know Nico." She lifted a shoulder. I did know Nico and I knew my aunt—either we'd find the two of them bloody and bruised or chatting up as best friends.

Turns out it was the latter. When we arrived at Caterina's office, the Witch Queen and Nico were lounging like old friends, laughing as they sipped from half-empty glasses.

"Mama." Luciana interrupted. "We're here."

"My dears." Caterina set her glass on the table before she stood, holding her arms wide. "Come here, it has been way too long."

I didn't resist as she enveloped me and Kara in her embrace. I breathed in her warm cinnamon scent as I wrapped my arms around her. When she finally let go she stood back, keeping one of our hands in each of hers, her eyes turning glassy as she looked between the two of us.

"You remind me so much of her. I see her—I can feel her in you."

I could see our mother in Caterina too. Although they were only half-sisters, only sharing their mother, they still held similarities. Caterina's skin was several shades darker than my mother's, but they had the same dark hair they shared with their mother. The biggest difference between my mother and Caterina was their eyes. Kara and I might have gotten our light hair from our father, but our green eyes came from our mother.

"Whew." Caterina released our hands and took a deep breath, wiping the slight wetness from the corner of her eyes. "We will have time for a proper reunion later—this is not the proper way to welcome guests into my court."

She turned towards Luka and Declan. "I hope you both excuse my state—it has been a long time since I have seen my nieces and I was not expecting to react this way." She shook her head, her coiled curls bounced as she did.

"I am Caterina Abrose, Queen of the Mystic Court." Declan and Luka bowed slightly as Caterina continued, "Now which one of you is the lucky broad engaged to my dear niece Lennox?"

A sheepish smile pulled itself across Luka's face. "That would be me." He held out a hand to Caterina. "Luka Rossi. It is a pleasure to meet you." Luka brought Caterina's hand to his mouth, kissing the back of it before releasing it.

"You've got yourself a charmer I see," she said smiling.

"You don't know the half of it," I mumbled, causing Caterina to raise a brow.

"Don't think I won't make you dive into that more later." I knew with certainty Caterina would hold true to that promise.

She turned her attention to Declan. "And who are you? What an exquisite creature with wings like I've never seen. If I wasn't involved, I might pay you more attention."

"Mama," Luce scolded.

Caterina smiled and shrugged a shoulder. "What? I'm only kidding, *Lulita*. Lighten up."

Declan didn't say anything, his same stony expression remained as Kara giggled beside him.

"Declan Hale, Captain of the Blood Court Royal Guard," Luka introduced the harpy.

"Hale?" Caterina questioned. "As in the same Captain Hale of the Twilight Court Royal Guard?"

Declan stiffened, his face pinching. "That would be my father."

Caterina sighed deeply, and her smile softened. "I thought so, you look so much like your mother."

"You knew my mother?" Declan stumbled.

"I did." She looked at us all, then back at him. "Later, dear, the two of us should talk, but not now."

Declan swallowed, his wings rustling behind him..

"So now that we're all acquainted, why don't you all have a seat?" Caterina clapped her hands, the sound clearing the tension radiating in the room. "Pour yourself a drink and we can talk. I don't see the point in delaying this any longer." She took her seat behind her desk.

"Luciana has filled me in on what has led you here. And indeed, I was working with Braham and Nol to find Astria's journals." I knew this was likely—but still, the confirmation rocked me. And by the looks of everyone else in the room, the confirmation shook them too.

"Your brother and father initiated the search. They only came to me in the last few months before their—deaths." Caterina closed her eyes and took a breath before continuing.

"Your father had always been obsessed with history. One of the summers you spent here he found an ancient text detailing a time when vampires tried to reverse the effects of vampirism. In their failure, they created monsters—uncontrollable monsters that were half vampire half beast, Dhampirs they were called.

"After years of failed trials, they concluded what they needed to make the transformation successful was Astria's original spell. It was unclear how they came to that conclusion, but regardless they ran with it. They scoured the continent for Astria's spellbook. And that is where their history ended. We assumed they never found the spell, considering vampires still exist. Your father took an interest in this—leading him to discover Astria had kept journals during that time. This sparked the idea that if he could find the journals and if they did contain the key to reversing—or curing—vampirism he could use it as a bargaining chip with the Blood Court."

"What do you mean a bargaining chip? What did he want from the Blood Court?" Luka asked.

"It was my impression all he wanted was for the tensions to be eased between the Star and Blood Court. To ease the tensions between the Blood Court and all of Lethenia. Maybe he had alternative motives, but that's what he told me. And I know Braham—I believed his intentions were true."

"Did he ever find the journals?" I pressed.

Caterina shook her head. "Not that I know of."

"Wait," Luce interjected. "How did you get involved in all this?"

"I caught him snooping in the archives for the journals." She smiled softly. "Braham was a terrible liar. It took little convincing for him to tell me what he was looking for. He had gotten so far as to convince himself the journals were somewhere in the Blood Court—he believed they were in the possession of the family of the original vampires."

"You mean the family of Astria's former lover?" Luce interjected.

Caterina nodded. "That's when he enlisted Nol to help him."

"Nol wasn't helping him the entire time?" It was Kara who asked the question this time.

"Not at first, your father wanted to involve as few people in his quest as possible. But you know Nol, his love for knowledge knew no bounds. Your father would have been stupid not to ask for his help. And Braham needed a way to get into the Blood Court without raising suspicions."

The air in my lungs froze. "That's why he proposed the arranged marriage."

Caterina's face was solemn. "We didn't know if Nol would have to marry her—it depended on how long it took to locate the book. But Nol was willing." I thought it was strange Nol agreed to an arranged marriage without fight. I had figured he felt it was his duty as heir—but it was so much more than that.

He and my father—and Goddess knows who else were playing a game. Unaware of the consequences it would have when they failed to complete it.

I stood from my chair as I tried to wrap my head around the information she had given us, pacing around the room as I spoke, "So you're telling me I got wrapped up in this entire disaster—this entire mess of an arranged marriage even though it was all a sham in the first place? Nol never intended on marrying into the Blood Court, but because he was murdered I lost the one choice I had left because of a scheme my dead father and brother were cooking up."

I couldn't get air into my lungs.

"Lennox." Caterina's voice was soft. It reminded me too much of my mother.

Too much, this was all too much.

"I need—" I gasped. "I can't—" I bolted from the room, ignoring the voices calling out after me. The walls were a blur around me as I tried to make sense of my surroundings.

I knew this palace, but right now I couldn't figure out where I was. I needed—I needed space. I needed to be alone.

I ran through the great hall, ignoring the looks of the staff as I ran. I burst through the doors, gulping in the chilled air as it seized my lungs.

I tried and failed to calm my breathing as I made my way through the garden. It wasn't much of a garden anymore, only a few late fall plants remained, the rest had all withered away for the winter.

Finally, I made it to the deserted patch at the far west side of the garden—the part that had hosted an array of witch herbs and plants growing up. By the looks of it, it still held those same contents, the plants spelled to continue growing even during the winter months.

When I spotted the old wooden bench, my legs threatened to give out from underneath me. I choked back a sob as I collapsed onto the bench.

My mother's bench.

The sight of her name carved into the wood next to her sisters and my grandmothers, sealed with magic to preserve them, calmed my breathing slightly. My name, along with Kara, Nol, and Luce's were etched into the wood at the bottom. Our script large and sloppy. We hadn't wanted to wait until we were older to carve our names in.

I sat on the bench, not bothering to use my magic to warm me as the air chilled my bones.

I stared at the patch of witch plants. I recited each one in my head, row by row, only looking up when I heard footsteps on the stones.

I expected my aunt or Kara to be the one to follow me, but I shouldn't have been surprised to find Luka appearing from the path.

Relief flickered across his features at his discovery of me, but he remained silent as he sat beside me on the bench.

I continued my mental noting of the plants as we sat side by side. I could feel his gaze boring into me but I ignored him.

His hand moved to the space between us, brushing with my own only for him to immediately pull it back.

He scooted closer, eliminating the gap between us, and put his arm around my shoulders. A complaint was posed on my tongue, but it was momentarily halted by the warm tingling sensation cruising through my body—heating my veins.

Luka's fire scorched its way through me, warming the pointed tips of my ears to my toes frozen in my boots.

"Thank you." Only then did I dare to turn my head towards him. He gave me a slight smile before turning his attention back towards the plants I had been surveying.

"Will you tell me about them?" He dipped his head towards the plants. "They're not any I recognize, I assume they're witch plants."

"They are." I proceeded to tell him the names and uses of all of the plants I could remember and he indulged me. He asked questions and gave comments as he continued to warm my body.

When I had finally described all of the plants to him I fell silent.

"Does it make me a terrible person that I'm mad at a dead person?"

"No," he answered immediately. "I think we spend more time feeling mad at the people we lost than we realize."

"I—" I took a deep breath. "I hate that my current situation is an outcome of a scheme I wasn't even a part of. When it was a simple clear-cut deal between the two courts it made sense. My brother was set to partake in an arranged marriage, and one of us had to take his place. I understood it. I didn't like it, but I understood it. That's politics. But this? This mess? This I don't understand." I threw my hands up defeated. "And why didn't they tell me? Why did it all have to be a secret? I'm—I'm so mad at them. Nol especially. This isn't like him to scheme like this."

"Maybe he truly believed the journal held that much power."

"Maybe." I sighed. "I hate that we both got brought into this mess with no say in it."

"I could have had a say in this." His voice was soft. "I could have passed off the prospect of marrying you to Lorenzo. If you think about it, I'm playing the same role your brother was."

I mulled over his words. Was he? Luka had come in knowing he might have to marry me if he couldn't find the book—but his and Nol's circumstances were different.

"No, you're not in the same position. Nol would have married Larissa if it came down to him not finding the book in time. You—you are fighting tooth and nail to ensure we don't have to get married."

Silence stretched between us again before I broke it.

"I don't know if I ever told you, but I forgive you for keeping that secret from me. I did a long time ago," I said softly. "And I don't blame you for any of this—and my outburst in there had nothing to do with you but everything to do with our circumstances."

Luka sighed deeply. "Sometimes I feel like we're pawns in a game much bigger than ourselves—that we have no control over our lives. That every choice is dictated by some higher power."

"It does feel that way doesn't it?"

"If only we could find a way out from under them," he said softly.

"If only."

His hand brushed over mine and I let him intertwine our fingers. I had missed the feeling of his rough palms against my own.

"I'm still broken." The words came out more choked than I intended.

"I know." All the words he left unsaid—all the words he had spoken to me before reverberated in my mind.

*I will take all of you. Even the parts you think are too damaged.*

*I know you think you're broken beyond repair, but I don't think that.*

I told myself I wouldn't let fear get in the way of my happiness—but this, this wasn't fear. This was something else altogether.

I had let Luka in once and it almost ended me. I couldn't risk that again.

I could not do that again.

I would either enter into a platonic marriage with Luka or remain alone for the rest of my life if that's what it took to protect my people.

To protect myself.

No matter what I felt for Luka, I had to keep it to myself.

But friends, maybe we could be friends again.

I had missed him. I had missed his quiet comfort. The way he pushed me. I missed his soft smiles and the feeling of his hand in mine.

If I couldn't have him as my lover, I could have him as my friend. Right?

☾

Luka and I remained in the garden a while longer. Our hands intertwined as we stared out at the frozen garden until even with Luka's fire warming me the chill seeped in.

Reluctantly, we headed back inside. I knew I needed to

continue the conversation we had started with Caterina, but I didn't know if I was ready for that.

"Lennox." Caterina stood, concern clear on her face when we reentered the study. The males were gone, only Kara and Luce remained.

"Are you okay?"

"No." There was no use in lying.

"I'm sorry. I didn't mean to upset you." I let her pull me in for a hug.

"It's not your fault my father and Nol left me in this mess."

She pulled back from our hug, taking my hands in hers. "Still, you've had enough upset in your life, I hate to add to it."

I gave her a weak smile. "Can I share with you the rest?" She looked towards Luce and Kara. "We've been waiting for you."

"Might as well get it over with." I sat in the chair, noticing Luka still stood awkwardly in the doorway.

"You can stay," Caterina said. "If it's okay with Lennox."

"Stay, please."

Luka gave her a tight smile. "Thank you. I can fill in Declan and Nico later if that's okay."

Caterina dipped her chin. "Okay, where did we leave off?"

"My father and brother were scheming to find Astria's journals, tying my brother to an arranged marriage so he could get access to the Blood Court."

"Right." Caterina breathed.

Luka huffed a breath and I looked at him out of the corner of my eye—he only shook his head.

"Nol had only visited the Blood Court a couple of times—never enough that he could get any leads on who the original family was. He was trying to find ancient texts that might give any information to them, but there were none in the libraries he had access to."

"Luka, do you have any idea who the original family was?" I turned toward him.

He shook his head. "We learned the history of them, the legend, but it never included names. None that I had learned anyway." He leaned forward, wringing his hands through his hair. "That's strange, isn't it? I never realized but it's strange it never included their names. There are family archives, located in an isolated wing in the palace in Cel Nox. I wonder if there would be any information in there."

"Can you get us in there?" Luce asked.

"I can get in there, I don't know if the magic has anything against non-family visitors, but it's worth a shot. If anything I can find books and bring them out for all of us to read."

"Is there anything else we need to know?" Kara asked.

"I don't think so. That's as far as they had gotten." I chewed on the information she had given us. It was more than we had gained in our months of searching. Although I hated what it revealed, I was glad we at least had more to go off of than empty words.

Caterina sighed. "There is one more thing. Luce told me about the prophecy Hecate revealed to you. I for one wasn't surprised a prophecy would strike someone in our bloodline. It was only a matter of time."

"What do you mean it was only a matter of time?" Luce questioned, echoing my thoughts.

"This can't leave this room." She looked directly at Luka. "You understand that."

"Yes," We all echoed.

"Our family are descendants of Hecate."

# 25

# LUCIANA

Holy fucking stars above.

I was descended from Hecate.

I was related to the original witch.

"Witches tits," I swore, earning a scathing look from my mother.

Kara remained impassive, staring at the space ahead of her. Luka was slack-jawed in his chair.

"We're related to Hecate. Why did we never know this?" Lennox pressed.

"No one knows. The only living people who knew until this moment were me, Endora, and my mother. And now you lot."

"But why?" Kara pressed.

"Our mother never knew?"

My mother shook her head. "No, I only found out a few years ago while looking through a book of our family tree. I assume it remained hidden because people are afraid of power." She turned to Lennox. "Why do you think your parents hid your fourth element? Your power should have been your first sign your ancestors were those of great power."

Her gaze turned back toward me. "Why do you think Ichor

Magic calls so strongly to you? Who do you think created Ichor Magic in the first place?"

My heart beat faster in my chest. "Hecate created Ichor Magic?"

My mother nodded, her curls bouncing. "She did. It was after Astria returned to the sky. Hecate wanted more power than what Astria had bestowed to her so she found other means." Her eyes burned. "Why do you think Hecate's spellbook calls so strongly towards you, *Lulita?*"

*My magic suits you.* Hecate had told me. I hadn't thought on it but—

"Hecate's magic is strong, but it's not only Hecate's power that runs through you, but the Goddess' magic is in your blood." My breath stalled in my lungs at her words. At the consequences of knowing this information.

"Holy shit," Luka murmured as he looked to Lennox, "Your theory that you could harvest more elements because of your witch magic was true. But it's because your magic is stronger."

I locked eyes with my cousin. "Do you believe that's true?" she asked.

I looked between the two. "It might be."

"Let's not get off track here," my mother interrupted. "You can discuss this all later. The reason I'm telling you this now is because if you can't find the answers you need in the library, there is one more thing you could try."

"What is it?" Kara prodded.

"You could try and summon Astria."

"You can't be serious," I said. "We can't summon the Goddess. That's impossible."

"Not when you have the Goddess' magic running through you." She smirked.

"How could that even be done? No one has ever done that before. Have they? Would she even answer?" Lennox wondered out loud.

"I don't know if she would answer, but it is possible. The

only person I know who has done it was Hecate herself. I believe the guidebook to find it should be in Hecate's spellbook."

"I've never seen such a spell though." I sat back in my chair. "I've read through the book countless times and I've never seen anything about a spell or anything to summon the Goddess."

My mother took a deep breath. "That's because you don't have the completed book."

I whipped my head towards my mother. "What do you mean I don't have the whole book?"

"What you've been using is only half of the book. The other half has been hidden away."

"Why?" Lennox pressed as she leaned forward in her chair.

"You know as much as I do witches are fickle creatures. They like their secrets. Astria and Hecate were no different."

I shook my head. "Fucking witches."

My mother gave me a disapproving look. "Careful how you speak about your people," she scolded.

I waved my hand dismissively. "Yeah yeah." I loved my people, but sometimes they were infuriating.

"Where is the other half of the book?" Kara asked, directing the conversation back.

"In the Goddesses catacomb." My stomach dropped.

"For fucks sake. You're seriously sending us to the Goddess catacomb?"

"I'm not sending you, dear. I'm telling you where the other half of the book is if you need it." She surveyed us all. "What you do with the information is up to you."

Goddess, my mother could be infuriating when she wanted to.

I looked over at Lennox and Luka. "Can you manage to be away from Cel Nox for another day without raising suspicion?"

"I told my grandfather I was showing Lennox a city outside Cel Nox for a couple of days. I can tell him we got delayed if it comes to it."

I stood and turned toward the door. "Well, are you guys ready for an adventure tomorrow?"

# 26

# LUCIANA

We all sat around the large round table in what my mother considered the family dining room. It was the room where we ate as a family or when we had a small number of guests. The room had a much warmer feel than the large formal dining room with its extended rectangular table.

Several bottles of wine were passed around the table as everyone filled their glasses.

My mother's consort, Endora, sat beside her, having arrived back from her day out of the palace. The pair sat with their hands intertwined on the table.

I had seen my mother with her fair share of lovers. She was never the kind of mother to hide her exploits from me. If anything I thought she shared too much: Too much about everyone except my father. I didn't even know if he knew I existed.

He had to though—he had to know the Queen of the Mystic Court had a daughter. Unless he didn't know my mother was the heir when they were together. These were the thoughts I spiraled over time and time again.

But Endora, Endora had been different from the start.

She was the first and only consort my mother had ever taken.

They had been together for almost five years now, but she officially became the queen's consort shy of a year ago.

My mother loved her passionate love affairs, moving from one to the next after she grew tired of them. I think that is what kept her from making Endora her queen alongside her. My mother still worried she might tire of Endora, or the other way around. Not that I thought it would happen, but it wasn't my battle to wage.

My mother ensured she had an easy escape route if needed.

Her sister's murder only furthered that need.

If my mother and Endora were still together ten years from now, my mother might consider making Endora Queen, instead of simply her consort. Or maybe I'd be Queen and none of it would matter.

"It's so nice to finally meet you, Endora," Kara said from across the table.

"Yes," Lennox added, turning her attention to Endora. "We've heard so much about you. We're excited to meet the female who has captured our aunt's attention as it's not an easy feat."

"And I should say the same to you, shall I not?" Endora moved her long ebony hair over a thin shoulder. "It appears you have quite the reputation that precedes you." She glanced toward the vampire prince at Lennox's side.

"Unfortunately, you're correct," Lennox grumbled, but there was a teasing lilt to her voice. Laughter rumbled throughout the room at her comment. I enjoyed seeing these little peeks of my cousin creeping back out from the darkness.

"From the sounds of it, I might get along better with the Blood Prince than you, *Your Majesty*."

"Considering Lennox doesn't get along well with anyone, I think you're correct." Luka laid his arm across the back of Lennox's chair.

My mother chuckled and clapped her hands. "Oh, Lennox, you truly have found one that keeps you on your toes haven't you, how wonderful."

Lennox glared at Luka, who only smiled at her. "If anyone is keeping one on their toes it's Lennox." He elbowed her gently. "Isn't that right, Sweetheart? I never know what I'm going to get with you."

"I'll tell you that you're going to get, a swift kick to the shin if you keep talking about me like this," Lennox responded. I hid my smile behind my glass. I loved watching her and Luka go back and forth, it brought back the sparkle in her eyes.

"I'm sorry if I started something," Endora said sincerely, a pale blush rising to her porcelain skin.

Nico laughed. "Don't worry about anything, this is basically foreplay for these two." I about spat out my drink. Did Nico have a death wish?

"Ouch!" Nico wailed as he reached under the table and gripped his leg.

Lennox smiled sweetly. "Sorry, my foot slipped."

"You're lucky it was her foot." Luka sat back in his chair. "Could have been her dagger."

☾

"So where exactly are we heading tomorrow?" Declan asked as we continued to pass the remaining bottles of wine around the table. My mother and Endora had left us on our own well over an hour ago. We remained, taking advantage of my mother's exquisite wine collection.

"It's called the catacombs—they are like a maze of sorts leading to the place where Astria last remained before returning to the sky."

"A maze with a terrifying backstory," Kara added.

Nico rubbed his hands together. "Care to enlighten us with said terrifying backstory?"

"It's only a tale of reckless childhood nonsense," Lennox said plainly.

"You can't go into the story without telling them the lore first," I added. "That's half of the allure."

"You're right. Tell them the story, master story keeper." *Master story keeper*, that was a title I hadn't heard in ages. Not since—not since the last summer Nol was here. He was the one who gave me the ridiculous nickname in the first place. I've loved stories for as long as I can remember—particularly anything to do with witch lore. I felt like that's all I read growing up. There were days when my cousins visited where we'd all sit out in the grove of trees past the garden and read all kinds of books on witch lore, sharing the stories we loved as we read. Kara and Lennox usually got bored after a few hours and left to find something else to do, leaving Nol and I to read for hours on end.

Whenever we'd visit one another, the first thing I'd do was fill him in on all the witch lore I had learned while we were apart. He listened with intent, and one year he bestowed upon me the title of master story keeper.

"They say the catacombs are where Astria and Hecate performed the spell or ritual—or whatever the fuck it was—that allowed Astria to return to the sky and it left a lot of magic residing in the land there," Lennox continued.

"What was the ritual or whatever it was?" Nico asked.

"Wouldn't we all like to know?" Kara sat back in her chair and crossed her arms over her chest.

"What she means is none of that is documented anywhere. There is only lore," I explained. "Anyways, whatever was performed there fucked up the land—making it tumultuous. Lore claims the magic created monsters—abominations of magic."

"And we're going there?" Declan's brows pinched as he leaned forward in his chair.

"Yup," Lennox said dead-faced.

"But you've all been there before?" Luka looked between the three of us.

"If you can even call it that," Lennox added. "We made it to the top of the catacombs, heard one sound, and ran for the hills."

"You're kidding?" Luka laughed.

Lennox shoved him in the shoulder. "You're telling me you wouldn't run from an apparent monster when you were fourteen? We barely knew how to hold a weapon or harness our magic. Stories of the catacombs are what our parents told us to keep us from sneaking out at night. I wasn't taking my chances." Lennox crossed her arms over her chest defiantly.

"It was Kara who ran first, we had no choice but to follow after her," I added.

"Hey!" Kara protested. "I had never even held a sword back then, I would have been easy prey!"

"We're losing track of the point here," Declan said, attempting to steer us back on track.

"Anyways, we will need to enter the labyrinth tomorrow and find the center, Astria's catacomb, where the spellbook should be residing." My head pounded at the idea of entering that space.

"We should all head to bed. It will be an early morning with a long day ahead of us tomorrow." Declan concluded.

We all mumbled in agreement before we wished one another goodnight.

When I returned to my room, sleep was the last thing on my mind. I had several hours to research everything I needed to know about the catacombs.

I quickly changed into something more comfortable before heading to the library—my favorite place in the palace. The library took up an entire wing of the palace. Every previous ruler was tasked with making sure the library remained stocked with all the newest text, and the Scribes were tasked with finding any ancient text to add to the collections. Some of them roamed the continent their entire lives, hoping to find titles to add to the library.

If I wasn't heir I would have loved to be a traveling Scribe. They never stayed in one place for too long, they got to explore all of Lethenia, in search of books. What a dream.

But that's exactly what it was. A dream.

I used my key to unlock the towering double metal doors and entered the main room of the library. At this hour the floor was deserted, no one manned the massive circular desk in the center.

I bypassed the desk and ascended one of the twin metal staircases that curved around the desk, heading for the third floor.

When I arrived, I quickly scoured the shelves, having memorized where all of the books resided, hauling every book on the catacombs to my reading nook.

When my mother finally got annoyed half of the library would reside in my bedroom, she had a space created for me in the library where I could read comfortably.

My little corner resided towards the back wall on the second floor of the library, pressed up against four large paned windows, allowing for plenty of natural light during the day and the perfect view of the moon and stars at night.

The space had a large plush rug, a long couch, two oversized chairs, a desk, a coffee table, and of course, a bar cart.

Books were already stacked on carts surrounding the area so I placed my findings on the coffee table and got to reading.

I didn't know how much time had passed when I heard the door to the library open, even two floors up the metal creaking of the doors was distinctive. I had no idea who would be in the library at this hour—it was rare anyone ever entered the library in the first place besides the Scribes. Maybe one of them had come back to get some more work done. I leaned forward on the couch, trying to catch a glimpse of whoever had arrived.

My stomach did an involuntary flip at the glimpse of hair the color of moonlight making its way up the staircase.

"Is this your room?" Nico asked, his surprise evident as he took in my state.

"No, this is my reading nook."

"Okay." He sat beside me on the couch. "Reading up on the catacombs, I assume?" He picked up a book from one of the piles and surveyed the cover.

"How'd you guess that?"

"I didn't take you for someone who did anything without being properly prepared."

"More like properly researched."

"What I didn't take you for is a library girl."

"Why's that?" I tucked my braids over my shoulders.

He shrugged. "I don't know. I guess all the people I've met that like to spend time researching in libraries don't also know how to fight a male with a sword within an inch of his life."

"People can surprise you."

"You surprise me." His words sent a tingle down my spine.

"What are you doing here anyways?" I asked, trying to ignore the impact his words were having on me.

"I figured you might need some company."

Nico was a distraction I didn't need when we were short on time. But if he could manage to stay on task it might allow me to get a couple hours of sleep in between the two of us reading.

Against my better judgment I handed him a book from the pile on the table and stretched across the desk for a pen and paper, passing them to the wolf. "Here, write down anything you find about the catacombs or the labyrinth or anything about the spell that got Astria back into the sky."

"I'm not really the reading type." He flipped through the book.

I glared at him. "Then what are you doing here?"

"I wanted to help you, I didn't say I wouldn't read them, I was only trying to make conversation, Lucy."

I huffed a breath. "We don't have time for conversations Nico, I only have a limited time to do all the research I can before we leave in the morning." I narrowed my eyes at him, trying to ignore the wounded look on his face. "So are you going to help me or not?"

"Got it, I'll shut up and read."

"Thank you."

Dawn was still several hours off when we left for the catacombs. Nico and I had stayed in the library until—*late*. Only allowing for a couple of hours of sleep at his insistence.

If it were up to me I would have stayed up all night.

We were silent as we departed on our horses. The catacombs were about a two-hour ride from Arcadia. We had decided we'd travel by horse so I could save all the magic I could for whatever we might encounter. If all went according to plan we should arrive with the sun.

I could feel it as we got closer. The air became thicker, it was rimmed with magic. I could feel it pressing up against my skin, it made me uncomfortable, magic like this, when I had no control over it. There was no controlling the magic of the catacombs.

Up ahead, Lennox and Luka had stopped at the top of the hill, when I joined them I did too.

The catacombs resided in a landform similar to a bowl. It was curved on all sides. The terrain was hilly and hosted mouths to a handful of caves. Discovering which cave led to the labyrinth was part of the trick. A dark, shimmering mist covered the land—making it appear even more eerie.

We left our horses at the top of the bowl and carefully made our descent down the hill.

The air got thicker the farther we descended into the bowl. The sounds of leaves blowing in the wind and animals scurrying about halted—they were exchanged for the low groans and guttural roars of the creatures of the catacombs. As we made it to the bottom of the bowl, the mist swirled around us on a phantom wind, seemingly stirring the catacombs to life.

It was aware of our presence. I could feel it. The mist pressed thicker against us as we pushed forward—blinding us from seeing anything more than a couple feet ahead of us.

"Everyone still here?" Declan called out.

A murmur of yeses were called out in response.

"Stay close," I said. "It will be easy to get separated. The land will try its best to do so."

"I hate magical land masses," Nico mumbled.

"What other magical land mass have you been to?" I asked.

"None. This is my first, but I don't like it."

"How do we know which cave will lead us into the labyrinth?" Lennox asked.

"According to my research, it will only reveal itself if it wants to. The catacombs will try everything in its power to trick and deceive you, Astria designed it as such. It's up to us to show it we deserve entrance to the labyrinth, that we are worthy of entering Astria's sacred place."

"And how do we go about doing that?" Luka pressed.

We continued to press through the mist. I kept my senses open, feeling for any kind of pull—only to have my senses pulled in five different directions.

"I never found any explicit directions," I continued. "But I have an idea. First, we need to make it to what we can assume is the center of the catacombs."

I looked over towards Declan, his face was half covered in the mist, but his golden eyes glowed through the fog.

"Would you be able to fly over and direct us to where the center is?"

"I can, but I doubt we'll be able to see one another."

"If you talk to us we should be able to hear you, and as for you seeing our location…"

I looked towards Lennox. "Think you could put up a tower

of flame so he can direct us where we need to go?" She placed her hands on her hips and smirked.

"Of course I can."

"Alright, Declan?" I looked toward the harpy again.

With a dip of his chin, he flapped his mighty wings and took off to the air. The movement of his wings momentarily cleared the fog, giving us a larger view of the rocky landscape around us.

"I think it's that cave," Kara gestured to the rocky arch in front of us.

"It's not."

"How do you know?" Lennox pressed.

"That would be too easy. That's the whole game of the catacombs. It's trying to trick you into thinking what it wants you to believe. I'm sure there's a nasty monster in there waiting for easy prey."

Kara shivered, her cheeks and the tips of her pointed ears turning a shade of light pink.

"Hey." I placed a hand on her shoulder. "Don't be ashamed of thinking that was it. I did a ton of research last night to find out these things, why would you know?"

"Let's keep going." She shrugged out of my hold and nodded toward Lennox. "Luka and Lennox got the tower up."

I turned to find the pair staring up at the column of flames balancing on Lennox's palm.

"Well, that'll do it," I murmured.

We walked forward, straining our ears for directions from Declan. Maybe we wouldn't be able to hear him through the mist after all.

"Keep straight." His deep voice came from faintly above.

Kara let out a sigh. "Worried about bird boy?" I elbowed her.

"You weren't?" The tone in her voice was cutting—a rarity coming from Kara.

"To the east." Was his next direction.

We all shifted slightly, Lennox and her flames guiding us from the front with Luka by her side. Lennox might be determined to keep Luka at bay, but he was determined to stay by her side. Lennox stumbled slightly, her foot hitting a small rock. She righted herself, but not before Luka's hand reached out, grasping her arm.

She gave him a tight-lipped smile before continuing. Luka released her arm, his hand flexed by the small of her back before moving back to his side.

"A little more to the east."

We shifted again. "Now continue forward."

We continued through the mist.

"Stop." The mist swirled around us as the sound of Declan's wings drew closer before he dropped to a crouch beside us, the mist parting around him.

"Well, that wasn't dramatic at all," Nico said.

"From what I could tell this looked like the center of the bowl. The entire area is shrouded in mist."

"Nico, you still have my pack?"

"You know it." He set the pack beside me and I opened it, pulling out my relics.

"You're going to do a spell?" Lennox asked.

I looked up from where I knelt. "I need your and Kara's help too."

Kara knelt next to Lennox. "Tell us what you need us to do."

"My hope is if we all combine our power, it will amplify our ability to sense which cave is the entrance. And if we use my half of the spellbook as a beacon, it should help our magic search for the other half."

"Seems easy enough," Lennox said.

"Is it dangerous?" Luka peered over Lennox's shoulder.

"I'm not using Ichor Magic, *Your Highness*. You can back off, I'm not putting your bride at risk."

I didn't look up from the bowl I was mixing the ingredients

in. I had no desire to see the scathing looks they were both throwing my way. If they wanted to live in ignorance, fine, but I wasn't going to play into their game.

"I need some of both of your blood in the bowl." I directed the sisters. Lennox didn't hesitate, pricking her finger with the tip of her dagger before handing it off to Kara. Lennox let the blood pooling at the tip of her finger drop into the bowl as Kara repeated the action before handing the blade to me.

"Lennox, can you ignite the bowl?" With the flick of her fingers, the bowl erupted into flames. I placed the blazing bowl on top of my half of the book. The mixture hissed, sending up a plume of smoke that moved to mix with the mist above us.

"Ready?" Lennox, Kara, and I joined hands.

I closed my eyes, inhaling the scent of the smoldering offerings before I started my chant.

As I chanted, Lennox and Kara repeated after me, our words churning in an echo in the catacombs.

There was a slight tingle in my palm, like a tiny jolt of static. It moved through my palm and up my arm. I felt it in my chest before it returned to my other arm, zipping through my palm. Lennox jolted slightly as it entered her palm.

We were connected. I could feel it as Kara and Lennox's power intertwined with my own, caressing itself around the threads of my magic.

"Now that we're connected we need to search for the other half of the book." I removed my hand from Kara's and placed it on the book.

"C'mon, where are you Hecate?" I muttered.

I closed my eyes tighter, envisioning the path towards the cave that would lead us to the Astria's chamber.

*"Where are you?"* I gritted.

My vision steered in every direction. Zipping from one cave opening to the next.

"C'mon." I felt for Hecate again. She was in me. I could feel her. It was her blood in my veins, fueling my magic.

My vision took a sharp turn, guiding me towards a cave to my left and stopping. There was a dead patch of flowers outside the cave, like all the others, but this one had one living flower that stuck out among the dead ones. A single red bud in the decay.

"There." I gasped. Gripping the book and Lennox's hand tighter. "That's the cave."

"I see it," Lennox murmured.

"But how do we find it?" Kara asked.

As if the magic heard her, the illusion slowly backed away from the cave, tracing the path backward until it reached us.

When I opened my eyes there was a path through the mist.

"I think you guys passed the test." Nico's icy eyes sparkled as I met his gaze.

I let out a shuddering breath. "I think so."

# 27

# LENNOX

"Okay, me, Lennox, and Kara are going to go in and find the book, while you guys stay out here," Luce directed as she rose to standing.

"Fuck that." I met Luka's gaze. "Do you think I'm going to let you go in there while I stay out here and hope and pray to the Goddess you don't get attacked by some magical monster?"

He looked over at Luce. "There is no way I'm staying out here."

"I agree with him, Lucy," Nico added.

Luce rolled her eyes. "I figured you guys might throw a fit. Now I have a plan b, but I don't think you're going to like it either."

"Let's hear it," Declan said.

"I know a spell that can connect us temporarily. For a short period of time, we'll be able to communicate mind to mind."

My brows rose. I had never heard of this sort of spell, which meant— "but it uses Ichor Magic, doesn't it."

"Well of course," Luce answered. "What? It's one little spell and it will solve our problem." She looked at Luka. "I figured he wouldn't let you out of his sight."

"Fine." I sighed, she was right. "Tell us what we need to do."

"Are you sure about this?" Luka eyed me questioningly.

"Luce uses this magic all the time, I'm sure it will be fine."

"But do you want to do it? I like the idea of being able to communicate with you while you're in there, but don't do this for me. I won't let you put yourself at risk for my ease of mind."

Ichor Magic had so many unknowns, but it was true. Luce used it all the time and it was created by Hecate... One spell should be fine. I had no intention of making the use of Ichor Magic a frequent occurrence, but I wasn't crazy about the idea of him being out here with those creatures without a way to communicate.

"I want to do it. Being able to communicate with you while we're in there will be helpful."

"Okay." He turned back to Luce. "Tell us what we need to do."

"We will each partner up, Declan and Kara, me and Nico, and you two, *obviously*," she muttered under her breath. I rolled my eyes, sass ran from the Ambrose side of the family after all.

We all listened intently as Luce rattled off the instructions. They were oddly simple for a forbidden form of magic.

"Sounds easy enough," Nico muttered after Luce was finished. He drew his dagger from his hip and shifted toward Luce.

Luka took my hand in his, turning it over so my palm was facing up. "You ready?" I winced as he drew his dagger across my palm, the blade cool against my skin. He repeated the motion with his own hand before we pressed our palms together, our blood mingling before releasing them.

I took out the stardust from my pocket Luce gave me, removing the cork from the vial with my teeth before spitting it onto the ground. I sprinkled the luminescent substance over our palms to mix with our blood.

"Okay, now we press them back together." I looked beside us, finding Luce, Nico, Declan, and Kara repeating the same actions.

Luka took my hand in his again, interlocking our fingers.

"Ready when you are, Sweetheart." I swallowed, focusing on the feeling of the sticky blood marring our palms instead of the feeling of his hand in mine.

I closed my eyes, reciting the spell as Luce had instructed. My chest tightened to an almost painful pressure, my head spun as the pressure traveled to my head.

I squeezed my eyes tighter, trying to ease the pain and pressure as it continued to mount. Luce said the sensation of Ichor Magic was intense, but this—this was more than intense—it was *painful*.

I gritted my teeth as the magic made its way through me.

"Breathe," Luka reminded me, his thumb brushing over the back of my hand.

"I can't—" I gritted. My legs shook from the intensity of the unusual form of magic working its way through my body.

"Yes. You can." I jumped at the feel of Luka's cool hand at my neck. His thumb brushed a line behind my ear, making me shiver despite the intense heat of the magic invading my body.

He pressed his forehead against my own. Our intertwined hands now pressed against our chests. I could feel the erratic beats of both of our hearts between us.

"Breathe Lennox, *breathe*." His breath was warm against my skin. "Breathe."

I tried, my breaths were still coming in short pants, but I focused on his voice, on where his skin touched mine until my breaths were in sync with his as I continued to mutter the spell once again.

*You're okay.*

"Thanks to you."

"Wait, you heard that?" Luka took a step back, his brows pinching as he looked me over.

I opened my eyes. "You didn't say that out loud?"

*No.* His mouth didn't move, but his voice rang clear in my mind.

"Holy shit."

*Can you hear me?* I asked in my mind.

*Yes.*

*Well, this is freaky. As if you weren't already in my head enough.*

Luka smirked. *Careful, Sweetheart.*

"You guys ready?" Luce interrupted, pulling us from our silent conversation.

"As ready as we can be," Kara responded.

*Be safe, Lennox.*

*I will.* I told him in response before disappearing into the mouth of the cave.

I brought a ball of flames to my palm, illuminating our path into the labyrinth. "If you each want, you can use my flames to create your own."

Kara and Luce paused, each of them closing their eyes and opening their palms as embers from my fire drifted toward each of them.

"I forget how cool this is." Kara mussed as she shifted her palm, the flames moving with it.

I flipped my braid over my shoulder. "Flames are the most badass element."

Kara and Luce both scoffed but said nothing more. They knew better than to argue with me about my flames.

We continued down a single path, until we came to a crossing where one path diverged into three.

"Which one do you think it is?" Luce put up a hand to silence Kara and closed her eyes. I could feel Luce's magic surrounding me and curving around the wall of the cave.

She opened her eyes. "That way." She pointed to the path farthest to the right.

Neither of us questioned her, following Luce as we moved along the path to the right. At every intersection we came to, we followed Luce's direction as she felt for the book.

*Is everything going okay?* I jumped slightly at the sound of Luka's voice in my head.

*Yeah. We're still making our way through the labyrinth. Luce has a good feel for where we need to go.*

*Good.* He responded.

*Is there anything interesting on your end?*

He chuckled. I couldn't believe I could hear his laugh through this spell. *No. Nico tried to get us to play a game. Declan and I quickly shut him down. We decided we didn't want to draw any unnecessary attention to us if we could help it.*

*I'm sure he took it well, too.*

*He's currently sitting on a rock pouting.*

I laughed. *If only I could send images through this bond.*

*If only.*

I could picture it though—Nico sitting on a rock pouting with his chin rested on his fist like a child, his silver hair falling across his dark face.

Luce came to a halt again as we came to a crossroads, I mentally shut off my connection to Luka and focused my attention back on my cousin. This crossing had three different entrances. Luce stood assessing all three for far longer than the previous times.

"Do you know which path we need to go on?" Kara pressed.

Luce shook her head. "I can't feel anything." Her shoulders slumped.

I moved, intertwining my hand with hers, closing my eyes, seeing if I could sense anything—or help her sense anything. Not that I had any clue what I was looking for.

I pushed out my magic, feeling for any connection to Hecate, Astria, the book, or *anything*.

I felt—*nothing*.

Luce let out a frustrated sigh. "I don't understand why I can't feel anything. It's like the sensation suddenly stopped."

"Maybe it means we're getting close," Kara offered as she came in line with us.

"But still, I don't understand. I've been able to feel everything up until now."

"Let's try again," Kara said calmly. "Let's all try."

We all grasped hands and tried again—still, I felt nothing.

"Do we just pick one?" I asked.

"I guess." Luce sighed.

Luce closed her eyes again, I assumed to feel for anything to direct us in any direction.

She opened one eye. "Let's go left?"

"Okay," Kara and I said in unison. Any feeling was better than nothing.

We ventured down the path to the left—it appeared the same as all the rest. Although this path felt like it continued on forever—far longer than the other paths.

"Did we chose the wrong path?" Kara asked finally.

"I don't know. I—"

The cave shook around us. I braced myself on the wall to keep myself standing as the ceiling shook. Small rocks and dust fell from above. I moved to a crouch, covering my head with my arms as I looked at Luce and Kara, finding them doing the same.

Visions of the room shaking around me in the palace flashed before me. Of the ground shaking beneath me in the grand hall as my city was destroyed. My throat felt like it was closing—I couldn't get enough oxygen to my lungs as pressure clamped on my chest.

This wasn't happening. *Not again.*

*Lennox.* Luka's voice was laced with panic as it ripped into my mind. *Lennox, what's happening?*

*There's a land tremor in the tunnels.*

*Are you okay?*

*Yes, no. I'm—I—I can't stop thinking about the last time the ground beneath me shook.*

He was silent for several moments. Did something happen at the mouth of the cave as well.

*Are you all okay?* His voice finally came through again.

*Yes. It stopped now.* It had. The rumbling had stopped. A few small stones still fell from the ceiling and dust clouded my vision, but the shaking had ceased.

*Good.* Luka's voice came through my mind again. *Put one hand on your chest and one on your stomach, and take five deep breaths. Focus on the feeling of your stomach moving as you breathe. If your heart isn't back to breathing regularly after the five breaths take five more.*

*Okay.*

*Do you want me to count for you?*

*No, I can do it.* I counted as I breathed, I took five breaths and five more while Luka waited.

*How are you feeling?* He asked after several minutes.

*Better.* My heart was almost back to normal. *I can breathe freely again.*

*Good.* He paused. *Remember, you are in control of your body.*

*Thank you.* I took another deep breath. *Are you still okay out there?*

*Yeah, we got a little bit of the tremor, but not much. But I hope it doesn't wake anything.*

I hadn't thought of that. I looked around for Kara and Luce, the dust was still thick around us, I coughed as I stood, my eyes burned against the dust. I summoned a ball of flames to my palm, the previous one was extinguished in the tremor, I assumed Luce and Kara's had been too.

"Kara? Luce?" Dust invaded my lungs as I spoke.

"Yeah. I'm here." Kara's voice rang through the tunnel.

"Me too," Luce responded. The pressure on my chest loosened as they came into view.

"What the fuck was that?" Luce asked.

"I don't know I—"

The ground shook again, but it was different this time. Smaller. It came from the part of the cave we had come from, not above. The sound shifted, it was no longer a rumbling. It sounded like—footsteps.

There were footsteps shuffling on the hard floor.

*Luka?*

*Yeah.*

*Are you guys still at the mouth of the cave?*

*Yeah, why?*

*We have company.*

"Kara, Luce. We're not alone." They turned and looked down the path where the sound was coming from.

The whine of my sword reverberated in the empty cavern as I drew it to my side, my magic wrapping around the blade.

"Do we wait or do we run?" Luce removed her staff from where it rested across her back.

A chorus of roars sounded, rumbling throughout the cave—they were getting closer.

"Run," I answered without hesitation.

We ran, taking off in the opposite direction of the creatures, trying to get as much distance between us and them as possible. We kept running, the flame in my palm lighting the way a few feet at a time through the dusty tunnel.

"Fuck." I screeched to a halt as the path before us ended, leaving us panting in front of a cement wall.

Luce slammed her fist against the wall. "Fuck! Fuck! Fuck!" She screamed.

*What's going on?* Luka's concerned voice pierced through my mind once again.

*We were running from the creatures that appeared, but now we've come to a dead end.* I looked toward the dark path we had come from. *They will catch up to us any moment.*

*What kind of creatures?*

*Something that growls.*

*Astria's tits. Let me know if you want us to come and help. I don't doubt you all can handle them, but—*

*Luka?* Silence rang through my mind.

*Luka?* I asked again. *Luka!*

*It looks like we will have our hands full out here as well. The quake did wake some monsters after all.*

Before I could reply, the monsters rounded the corner. *Six* monsters—there were six of them. Their bodies were massive and they each had three heads, each bearing a resemblance to a different creature. What in the Goddess name kind of magic created these mutations?

I ran towards the first creature. My sword cut through one of its heads, the one resembling a boar with its massive curved horns protruding from its rectangular snout. The creature's blood sprayed. I couldn't tell what color it was in the dim light, but it didn't look red and the smell was foul. Certainly not normal blood.

I tried for a second head, but the creature snapped its jaws, its long snake-like fangs scraping my arm, clear through the fabric of my leathers. I hissed and took a step back. I clenched my jaw against the force of the blow as my sword thrust through the monster's body, the cut on my arm burning.

The two remaining heads let out a shriek before its body collapsed onto the floor in a heap. I didn't spare them a second glance before I bounded towards two more monsters that entered the dead end, shooting out with my flames in one hand and my sword in the other.

The creature hissed as it erupted in a ball of flames. My sword found home in the other creatures leg, it limped slightly as it came towards me again, its three heads growling at me as slobber—or poison—dripped from their maws.

I grabbed the daggers from my side and flung them, one after another toward the beast, but it didn't slow them.

It ran toward me, its growl shaking the tunnel as I speared my sword through one of the skulls as another one dipped low for my leg.

I screamed as its teeth pierced through my leathers into my thigh. *Holy stars.* I clenched my teeth as the creature tightened its hold, its teeth puncturing through flesh and bone. I removed my sword from the creature with all the strength I could muster.

*Lennox. Are you okay?* Luka's concerned voice pierced through my mind. How strong was this fucking bond?

*Fine.* I bit out. *Only a little scratch.* I panted.

I moved through the pain, slicing my sword up through the creature's chest. It removed its grip from my leg and I screamed, stumbling back, my sword ripping from my grasp as the creature reared back and growled as it assessed me.

*Fuck.*

I could feel the blood gushing from the wound on my leg. My blood soaked through my leathers and dripped down my body. The ground beneath my feet was slippery from it. I took a deep breath and blocked out the pain.

*Later.*

The creature regained its posture and came barreling towards me again with my sword still embedded in its chest and one head hanging lifeless at its side.

I kicked out with my non-injured leg, forcing it back a step as I stumbled, my injury screamed under the pressure, but I clenched my teeth and tried again to block it out. Wounds would heal, but I had to make it out of here alive.

I closed my hand around the dagger strapped to my other side but turned at the flash of movement at my back.

I wasn't fast enough. The creature I had left in flames had recovered. Its charred body was still quick as it scraped its claws down my back.

I screamed, my dagger clamoring to the floor.

*Lennox? Lennox, are you okay?*

I stumbled for my dagger, my back screaming as I stood. The creature with my sword still embedded in its chest swiped for me with its barbed tail, hitting me in the chest and slamming me against the wall of the cave as its barbs pierced through my leathers. I tried to take a step, but the creature lashed out with its tail again. This time my head slammed against the stone wall of the tunnel.

*Lennox.*

Stars danced in my vision. I tried to blink them away, trying to stay standing as the world became blurry around me. I could still hear Kara and Luce fighting around me.

The tail came again. My entire body slammed against the wall. I screamed as the raw flesh of my back scraped against the wall as I slid to the floor.

I tried to stand—the hilt of my dagger bit into my palm as I gripped it tighter.

I need to stand.

I needed—*Lennox.*

That voice. I needed to get to that voice.

*Lennox!*

*LENNOX!*

The voice rang in my mind as my eyelids slid closed and I let the darkness seep in.

---

# 28

# LUKA

*LENNOX.*

*Nothing.* There was nothing on the other side of the connection. It had gone dark. I couldn't feel, hear, or even sense Lennox like I had been able to since she spoke that spell over us.

Something was wrong

Something was *very* wrong.

I swiped at another mutated creature in front of me. Wiping the rotted green blood from my face with the back of my arm.

I needed to get to Lennox.

Something had happened to her. She needed my help.

"What's wrong?" Declan killed another monster, his sword arcing through the air gracefully. The creatures kept coming and coming in a constant stream.

"It's Lennox. She's not responding," I told him as I swiped toward another creature.

"I'm sure she's busy fighting her own monsters." Nico shifted back from his silver wolf form.

I shook my head. "No. I can't feel anything from her. Something is wrong. I need to go find her." I *know* something is wrong.

"There's no way you'll find them," Declan pressed. "They've been in there for hours, Luce and Kara have her."

"How do you know that?" I killed another monster that came toward me.

"I can ask Luce," Nico offered.

"Please," I pleaded.

I cut down another creature, keeping an eye on Nico out of the corner of my eye. The knot in my stomach twisted when his face paled.

"What?" I pressed. Blood sprayed as Nico's ax met its mark.

"Tell me Nico or I'll—" The wolf shuttered as he closed his eyes and took a deep breath before opening them again.

"Lennox got hit hard. She took several hard blows and passed out. Luce and Kara are still fighting off the monsters; they can't get to her yet."

Panic seized my body. I removed my sword from my latest kill. My mind already made up.

"I'm going after her," I declared.

"You are not," Declan bit out.

"The only thing that will keep me from going to her is if I pass out myself."

"Luka," Delcan growled. I knew he was considering it.

I took off running into the cave before he could act. "Luka!" I ignored Nico as I charged forward, drawing a flame to my palm.

Lennox needed me, nothing would stop me from getting to her.

I tore through the tunnels. When I came to the first divide in the paths I didn't think twice before continuing—my body seemed to know where I was heading. It knew what to do. At least I hoped it did, otherwise I was fucked.

Delcan was already going to kill me for going alone. If I didn't even make it to Lennox and I got myself lost here I'd never forgive myself. I'd gladly rot here in this cave.

The cave kept going on and on. I was starting to think I'd gotten lost.

I stopped when I came to another crossing. I panted, placing my hand against the wall.

I needed to find her. Who knew what was happening? She could be dead, torn to shreds by those monsters.

I shuddered.

I couldn't think that way. I would find her.

I closed my eyes, straining for any remaining shred of the bond that would link me to her.

*There.*

It was a tiny pull, maybe I was making it up, but it was there. It was something. A tug urging me toward the left.

I pushed off the wall and jogged down the path.

Maybe I was delusional, but I was going to follow any inkling if it might lead me toward Lennox.

The sound of fighting traveled down the path.

It was them.

I picked up my pace, coming face to face with Kara and Luciana as they fought off the last of the creatures. There was an orb of flames in the corner, illuminating the space in a dim glow.

Five or six creatures were already slain, lying in heaps on the ground, pools of blood surrounding them. They were different from the ones outside. The creatures at the mouth of the cave were mutations of creatures, but they only had one head. These creatures—they were utterly disturbing.

Blood pooled on the ground, splashing up over my boots as I ran through it.

Kara's eyes met mine over the three-headed monster, green blood was splattered over her face and *panic*, there was panic in her eyes.

"She's behind us."

I continued through the wreckage, scanning for Lennox.

*There*, she was lying against the wall, eyes still closed.

"Lennox."

I leapt over the bodies of the monsters, making my way toward her.

Her dagger lay in her open palm like she held onto it until the last moment.

I knelt beside her, my fingers instantly going to her neck.

Her pulse fluttered under my fingers. *Alive.* Her pulse was weak, but she was still alive.

*For now.*

"Lennox, wake up." I shook her lightly, but still nothing. Not even a flutter of her eyes or a stir on her features.

I scanned her body for injuries. There were slashes through the fabric of her leathers on one arm, revealing four gashes that were starting to stitch themselves back together. *Good. She's healing. That's good.* My eyes roamed lower, snagging on the dark patch on her leg. Several puncture wounds oozed blood. *Astria's tits.*

My stomach pitched. A wound of that caliber would need more than her natural healing abilities.

I brushed the hair out of her face. Blood was splattered across her features, but she still looked so beautiful even with the several small cuts painted on her skin. Good thing the creatures were already dead.

I scooped her up in my arms, grabbing her discarded dagger and sheathing it at my side. She was limp in my arms as I made my way to Kara and Luciana who were removing their weapons from the dead monsters in front of them.

"Is she okay?" Kara's voice was thick with concern.

"Her smaller wounds appear to be healing, but the larger wound on her leg isn't, and she's still not waking up."

"Put her down," Luciana directed. "I can heal her."

I shook my head. "I'm not letting her go." Luciana and Kara shared a look before Luciana turned her attention back to me.

"Fine, but will you sit at least?"

I looked around until I found a spot against the wall of the cave that wasn't covered in blood. Carefully I lowered myself to the ground, still holding Lennox's limp body against my chest.

Luciana and Kara knelt in front of me. Luciana placed her hands on Lennox's wound.

"It might take a while." She met my stare.

My body felt numb. "Promise me you can heal her."

"I don't like to make promises," Luce swallowed, "But I am a damn good witch, Luka."

Luce's hands glowed as she pushed her magic into Lennox's body. I had to remind myself to breathe as I waited for any indication what Luciana was doing was working.

I didn't know how much time had passed. We were all silent as we waited. Silent tears streaked down Kara's face as she stared at her sister. She didn't attempt to wipe them away as they made tracks through the green blood crusting her face.

Slowly the color came back to Lennox's features, easing the pressure in my chest slightly.

I held my breath as I waited for her to open her eyes.

*Please, Lennox.* I pushed the words through the faint bond between us—if there even was one anymore. The spell could be gone for all I knew.

*Lennox, wake up. Please.*

I stroked her hair, letting my hand move to her cheek, my finger dragging over her blood-speckled skin as I held her tighter against me.

"C'mon, Sweetheart."

Her eyelids fluttered, causing a spark of hope to flicker in my chest.

They fluttered again, this time they opened and I was met with those emerald eyes.

Her brows pinched. "Luka?"

I forced a relaxed smile onto my face. "Hey, I'm here." My voice stuck in my throat.

"You're here? What happened?"

"You let those creatures get the best of you, but Luciana

healed you." I looked up at Luciana, giving her a smile. "You're all good now."

She shifted in my arms, wincing slightly. "I must have got hit hard. My body fucking hurts."

"I healed your injuries, but you might be stiff for a couple of hours," Luciana told her.

"Thank you," She rasped.

Lennox shifted again, moving to sit up.

I banded an arm around her waist and took one of her hands in mine as I helped her stand.

Lennox looked around. "How did you get here?"

"Yeah," Kara and Luce echoed. "It took us a long time to find our way here, you made it here only minutes after I told Nico Lennox was hurt."

"You told Nico I was hurt?"

"Luka made him ask about you."

"Our connection quieted. I couldn't hear you or sense you at all. I knew something was wrong, I had Nico confirm it. Once I knew you were hurt, I somehow made my way here." I scrubbed my hand over the back of my neck. "I can't explain it, but I knew where to go and before I knew it I was here."

"Interesting." Luciana mused as she flipped her braids over her shoulders. "Well, I guess you're stuck with us now, vampire. Ready for another adventure?"

Luciana gestured behind her, my mouth falling open at the hole in the wall that hadn't been there before. A smile curved up the witch heir's face. "Because we passed the next test."

# 29

# LUCIANA

I stared at the opening in the stones where there once was a wall. A wall Luka had sat against holding a limp Lennox in his arms as I healed her.

But no, my eyes were not deceiving me, there was magic in these tunnels that revealed the opening.

"Whoa," Kara breathed. "Looks like your research was correct.

The research hadn't been detailed about the trials we'd have to face to get to the center of the labyrinth, to Astria's chamber, but I hadn't been anticipating a fight against the beasts to be part of it. Kara looked relieved at the opening, but I was certain this was not the end of our trials. All of the texts I found recorded there were several trials we would have to face. We found the cave and fought off the beasts, but there would likely be one more task for us to complete before we would be able to leave with the spellbook.

"We still need to be careful," I told the group. "There will likely be more traps for us to avoid."

"Luka and I should go first," Lennox offered. I was ready to argue against her and by the looks of it, Luka was too. Lennox had been knocked unconscious by beasts after all, but she summoned a ball of fire to her palm before I could say a word. "You'll need us to light the way."

"Fine." I sighed, looking at Luka. "But you stay by her side." I shifted my attention to Lennox. "You just underwent major healing, there's no way to know if your body is back to normal yet."

She opened her mouth to argue but closed it. "Fine," she conceded.

Her and the vampire prince turned toward the opening, Luka's hand resting on the small of her back as he led her through, and Kara and I followed behind.

We entered the dark chamber, the only light coming from Lennox and Luka's flames.

"There are torches." Kara's voice pierced through the darkness as she approached the outer wall, brushing her fingers over the wooden handles. "Lennox, can you light them?"

Lennox shifted her fingers, but Luka stopped her with a hand on hers. She glared at him, but he gave her a soft smile. "Let me, we don't know if you need to save your energy."

Lennox sighed deeply, crossing her arms over her chest. "Fine."

I rolled my eyes at the two of them, shifting my attention back to the room as Luka's magic lit the torches lining the chamber.

The space looked eerily like a tomb. The chamber wasn't circular like I had first thought, but more of an octagon, with the room coming into points at various junctions. Where we were standing was the highest point of the room. Steep stairs made of a deep red stone led into a bowl, where a dais sat at the center, where Astria and Hecate had conducted the ritual to return Astria to the sky, I assumed.

Drawings and words in an ancient language were painted and etched into the walls. I ran my fingers over the indentations.

"What language is this?" Lennox asked.

"It's the ancient words of the witches," I breathed. "Witches used it initially after their creation to keep their stories to themselves. It died out after a hundred years or so." I read about the ancient language many times. It was the witch's attempt to keep their stories and spells a secret.

"Can you read it?" Kara looked over my shoulder.

I shook my head. "Not all of it. I recognize some of the markings, but I never tried to learn the language in its entirety." Part of the reason why it died out was because the language had no true key. Every story had its interpretations and new words had to be created. There became too many inconsistencies across covens for the language to be worth upkeeping.

I ran my fingers over the marks, scanning for one I did know, "This one stands for the Goddess." The symbol in the middle resembled a woman's form, with a small waist and full hips and three stars dancing above her head with a crescent moon on each of her sides. I ran my fingers over another symbol of the seven-pointed star appearing as it was exploding. "This one is for Hecate." I didn't recognize any of the other symbols. If only I had thought to bring a text with me. But none of my research had said anything about having to read or decode messages in the ancient language. Or anything about the ancient language at all.

"I wonder if it's the story of Hecate and the goddess?" Kara offered.

I moved from the walls, turning my attention back to the group.

"Shall we?" Luka gestured toward the stairs.

"I suppose," Lennox, Kara, and I responded in unison.

One by one we filed down the steep red stairs toward the bottom. Making our way towards the large stone structure in the center. It was on a raised dais, the same markings from the top of the chamber were etched into the outside of the square structure, but these etchings had colors added to them. Even in their old age, the vibrant purples and blues remained as they told a story we were unable to comprehend. Stars above did I wish I could decode it. I tried to etch the markings into my mind so I could try to decipher them later.

"Do you think the book is in here?" Luka assessed the stone structure.

"Maybe." I moved my fingers over the markings on the stones. I could feel a pulse of magic emulating from them. A small tug, like I had in the tunnels that guided us here. But this tug, this pull, was stronger. The sensation in the tunnels had come from my gut, this one tugged at my heart, like there was a delicate string wrapped around my heart urging me forward.

I brushed my fingers over the marking of Hecate carved into the stones.

"Luce?" Lennox questioned hesitantly. "What is it?"

"It's Hecate's magic. It's here." The pull in my chest tightened in response, as if to say, *yes it is her magic.* "The book is in here."

"How do we get it out?" Kara asked. They all turned their attention to me as I pulled a dagger from my side. "According to my research, we need to deactivate the spell encapsulating the book using blood from Hecate's bloodline. She sealed the spellbook with her blood, like a form of Ichor magic before it even existed, to ensure the other half of the book wouldn't get into the wrong hands. The spell ensures only descendants of her bloodline can access it."

"Witches are rather paranoid aren't they," Luka commented.

I pricked my finger with the tip of my dagger. "You have no idea." I let the blood from my finger drip onto the top of the stone structure. It hissed as it hit the stone, the red liquid pooling in the carvings, but nothing happened.

We all waited with bated breath, but still, nothing happened.

"Were there any other directions?" Kara asked hopefully.

I shook my head. "No, I never found any specific details as to how to deactivate the spell." I balled my hands into fists. "Fuck!" I slammed a fist on the makeshift altar.

"Maybe I should try my blood?" Lennox offered.

"Do you think that would work?" Kara's eyes were wide. If only I could have a smidgen of her optimism.

"It's worth a try." Lennox pricked her finger with the dagger, letting the blood drop onto the stone next to mine. Still, nothing happened.

"Well Kara might as well try." I huffed, crossing my arms over my chest. I racked my brain, reminding myself of every-thing I read last night as Kara dripped her blood onto the stones. I had no intention of leaving the cave without the other half of the book.

The stone hissed as Kara's blood dropped. The three drops of blood moved across the surface, smoke rising as the blood pulled together in a perfect drop. The dot moved precisely through the etchings in the stones like water moving through a stream before it disappeared into the stones.

The chamber around us shook. I placed a hand on the wall to steady myself, but the shaking stopped as quickly as it started. I looked up to find Luka with his arm around Lennox's waist, holding her up as she thanked him softly.

He gave her a soft smile before letting her go.

Small fissures worked their way through the stone covering the top of the pillar. Each one branched off into another until the entire top was covered in cracks and the top dissolved in a puff of dust.

I coughed as the dust invaded my throat and blinked back the tears that burned in my eyes. When the dust finally cleared, we all leaned over the structure. A large leather-bound book, identical to the one in my pack, sat in the center of the now open altar.

"Witches tits." I breathed. "It's the other half of the book. I can't believe we found it."

I reached inside the hole and picked up the book. It was heavy in my hands, but it felt almost identical to the one I already possessed. Except this half reeked of power, power so thick it made my head dizzy.

"Stars above." Kara marveled as I held up the book for us all to admire. I pulled the other half of the book from my bag, I wanted to see them side by side. See if something happened when we combined them.

But then the howling began.

Luciana shoved the book in her bag as we all took off running back up the stairs. My chest and legs burned as I bounded up the final three stairs to the top of the cavern.

"Wait!" Kara's voice reverberated through the cavern as we climbed the final stairs. "Which way do we go?" I turned to find my sister looking around the room. There was no longer one entrance to the room but one in each wall of the cavern.

"We should go back the way we came," Luce continued toward the tunnel we had come from.

"But what if one of the other ways is a quicker way out?" Kara asked.

"Or a trap," Luce countered.

"We proved our worth to get into here, why wouldn't the magic continue to reward us with an easy way out?" Kara persisted.

"There is never an easy way out." Luce declared, planting her hands firmly on her hips.

They both looked at me expectantly. "I—" We all turned as the growls rumbled through the room.

"I think we should go in the opposite direction of the

growls," Luka finished for me. "If we end up farther into the labyrinth so be it, I'd rather be lost than dead."

"He has a point," I agreed. The growls grew louder. "Let's get out of here." I grabbed Luka's hand and tugged him along, toward one of the new entrances as Kara and Luce followed at our heels.

"If this doesn't get us out of here I'm blaming you, vampire," Luce said.

"Hey, it was Kara's idea," he interjected.

"Yeah well, I'm still blaming you, it's more fun that way."

I chuckled. "I'm inclined to agree with Luce."

Luka looked at me as we ran, a smirk pulling at his lips. "Well, I can say the same about you, Sweetheart. You're fun to provoke."

Kara and Luce laughed in agreement. I wrenched my hand from his. "Traitors, all of you," I seethed.

Our conversation ceased as we continued our pursuit away from whatever beasts lurked behind us.

"Look," Kara said. "I see light."

"Thank the Goddess," Luce remarked as she kept up pace beside me.

As we drew closer to the light I could make out a figure pacing at the mouth of the cave, Nico turned as we approached.

I could *feel* the sigh he let out at our arrival, the tension visibly leaving his body.

"You made it back."

"Worried about us, pup?" Luce threw him a wink as we exited the cave.

"I'm glad to see this one is still in one piece." He jabbed a thumb towards Luka. "I was trying to figure out how I'd explain what happened to his grandfather without getting myself killed."

"Have a little faith won't you, Nico," Luka chided.

"Faith?" Nico said dramatically, placing a hand on his chest. "I have faith that if I returned to Cel Nox without you and your fiancée your grandfather would make a meal out of me before sending my corpse back to my family." My stomach twisted at the image he conjured in my mind. Was King Arlo truly that cruel? Or did he care that deeply for his grandson he'd do such a thing in retribution for Nico letting him out of his sight?"

"He would do no such thing." Luka slung his arm over Nico's shoulders. "If anything, it would be Declan's wrath you'd have to fear."

Nico shook his head, his silver hair swinging with the motion. "About that one." He jutted a thumb toward Declan. "He's been practicing his lecture for you since we slayed the last beast. You're in for an earful."

"I'm sure it's nothing I haven't heard before," Luka responded.

Delcan glared at him. "I take it you're not even sorry about your actions?"

"Nope," Luka said definitively. "Lennox needed me, so I went to her. I'd do it again."

"Stupid fucking fool," Declan swore.

"Don't take it the wrong way, L, we're glad you're okay. We're glad you're all okay, we're just mad at this idiot for making such reckless decisions and leaving us to deal with the aftermath," Nico informed me.

I forced a smile onto my face, this entire conversation was making me uncomfortable, tightening the growing knots in my stomach. "No, of course, I understand." I understood their frustrations and concerns yes, but Luka's concern over me? That I still couldn't work out. Why he would keep putting himself in danger over me—

"You guys can continue your little scolding later." Luce looked around anxiously. "I, for one, would like to get the fuck out of here before another monster appears."

Without another word, we made our way out of the catacombs.

The next morning we all gathered in Luka's office; Luce had transported us all back to Cel Nox after we arrived back in Arcadia. Luka didn't want to press our luck being away any longer.

We had decided to put off opening the book until this morning, at Luce's request that we bathe and sleep first. I was ready to argue with her, my impatience over wanting to know what was in the book threatening to take over, but I remembered I was caked in blood of a variety of colors, my body ached from my injuries, and my stomach gnawed with hunger. And once the adrenaline fully wore off I knew I'd have a hard time keeping my eyes open.

So we all said our goodnights and planned to meet in Luka's office first thing in the morning.

I had been unaware he had even possessed an office until last night, but Luka argued that was what made it the perfect place for us to meet and look over the book.

"Alright, open it already." Nico rubbed his hands back and forth as we all stared at the two halves of Hecate's spellbook on the coffee table in front of us.

"I can't believe you waited for us all," I told Luce.

A flash of guilt flicked across her features. "Well, I did try to open it last night before I fell asleep. I couldn't resist myself." She winced slightly. "But it wouldn't open with only my blood, I'm assuming it needs all three of ours again."

Without saying a word the three of us pricked our fingers, letting our blood drip onto the faded leather cover.

Our blood sizzled before turning into a puff of red mist and disappearing. As the smoke dissipated, it revealed the cover was no longer blank, but Hecate's name and the ancient symbol bearing her likeness marred the cover in dark glimmering ink.

Luce's fingers danced over the worn leather, but she hesitated before opening the book.

"What are you waiting for?" Kara asked.

"I— I don't know." She opened the cover.

We all crowded around the table, peering at the aged parchment. The same symbols and markings that had been in the labyrinth were scrawled on the page.

Luce quickly flipped to the next page, revealing more of the same thing. She continued flipping through the pages as an irritated scream tore from her throat.

"It's all in this Goddess-forsaken witch language!"

"I'm guessing you don't know how to read it?' Nico asked.

"No." She huffed. "I don't."

"Luce, it's okay." Kara placed a hand gently on Luciana's shoulder. "If anyone can translate it, it's you."

"It will take time." She looked between me and Luka. "Time we don't have."

Luka stiffened beside me.

"It's okay." I sat up straight on the couch. "We will figure out things on our end, you do what you need to do."

Luka swallowed. "Yeah, don't worry about us." His words lacked conviction. "While you try and decode a clue as to how Lennox and I can get out of this arranged marriage, we have an engagement ball to attend."

I knew he was trying to lighten the atmosphere of the room, but his words nagged at something in me.

"Right," I bit out. Luka and I had a tumultuous track record with balls. And considering we had yet to truly discuss the fallout after the last ball, I wasn't ready to be his swooning fiancée in a matter of days.

How could I pretend to be happily engaged when I was at war with my feelings for Luka? And after yesterday—he had run into that cave after me knowing there was a higher chance he'd get lost in the labyrinth than find and help me.

But yet he still took the chance.

I wondered if there would be a day when he would stop taking a chance on me.

# 31

## LUKA

---

Tonight was the ball formally announcing my and Lennox's engagement to the Blood Court.

The news was not a secret, many already knew of our pending marriage, but after tonight, it would be official in the eyes of the people of my court.

Lennox Adair was to be my bride.

As if I wasn't already painfully aware of the marriage I had trapped her in.

Lennox was warming up to me, surprisingly enough. She was willing to talk to me again. But we continued to get ourselves into situations where I made my feelings toward her abundantly clear, which left me feeling like a fool afterward.

I was trying to be her friend. A supportive person in her life, because that's what I know she needs right now. But at the catacombs, during Caspian's party, and in the garden in Arcadia— my actions had been more than that of a concerned friend.

After the events of the past week, I expected Lennox to run in the opposite direction. I expected my actions to cause her to pull away, but it felt like they were having the opposite effect. I could tell Lennox was inching toward friendship territory with me again. I should be ecstatic. That was what I had been hoping for while we had been apart, that despite everything we might be able to be friends again. This should feel like a step in the right direction.

But everything changed when I laid eyes on her again. And it got worse with every moment we spent together since we reunited.

Friends were the last fucking thing I wanted to be when it came to Lennox Adair.

I would get there. If that was all she was willing to give me I would gladly take it—it's more than I had hoped when I left her in Alethens.

But I didn't want to be her fucking friend.

I wanted to fuck the word friend out of her mouth.

I wanted to be her everything.

Her friend, her confidant, her partner, her lover. I wanted it all.

But I doubted she'd ever give me that.

I don't think she'd ever give that to anyone—not after how she blamed our relationship for distracting her leading up to the attack on Alethens.

She said she had forgiven me, but I knew she didn't forgive herself for letting her guard down.

It would take time, but I would wrap my head around being friends with Lennox. I *had* to.

But not tonight.

Tonight we were to be a happily engaged couple in front of my court and I was going to milk it for every second it was worth.

☾

I shouldn't have been surprised by Lennox's appearance as she opened the door—*Goddess above she was breathtaking.*

She stole the breath from my lungs in her gown, the color the deep red associated with the Blood Court. The top was fitted like a corset, the thin fabric covering her breasts strained against the fabric, but the rest of the bodice was sheer. The bottom half of the gown fitted to her body, different from the flowing skirts she typically chose. But as always, there was a slit up the side that traveled so high I wondered what it might expose if she moved just right. On her exposed thigh sat a dagger, both the pommel and blade a glimmering black.

"You look stunning." I murmured.

"You don't look too bad yourself." My own attire matched her gown, the red accents of my black suit making us appear as the engaged couple we were. Her eyes roamed up and down my body, as I stood in the doorway. *Fuck,* I loved having her gaze on me. It sent fire straight to my veins and blood rushing to my cock.

"Are you ready, *my queen?*" I offered her my arm. If we were left alone much longer with her looking like that I wasn't sure what I might do.

"As ready as I can be." She laced her arm through mine and followed as I led her through the palace towards the ballroom.

"Now, this ball, is it an actual ball? Or is it a ball like the one at the duke's manor?" A smirk formed on her lips.

"I hate to disappoint you, but this is a more typical ball. Any acts of lust will occur out of the sight of others."

A slight blush rushed to her cheeks. I hoped it was the thought of what had occurred between us at the last ball that caused it. "What a shame," she admitted.

I stumbled slightly, as the memory of her on my lap made its way to the forefront of my mind. Of how smooth her skin felt under my fingertips. Of how sweet those little breathy sounds were that slipped from her lips.

I cleared my throat. Now was not the time for such thoughts.

"Here we are," I announced as we approached the doors leading to the ballroom. "Are you ready for your official welcome to the Blood Court? You're about to be the envy of many." I said, trying to direct the conversation in a direction that wouldn't make my cock strain against my pants any more than it already was.

"You think that highly of yourself?" Lennox asked.

"No, it's—be careful. The engagement will be a surprise to many."

She pressed a finger to my chest. "They will be upset their prized stallion has been taken off the market?"

"You could say that," I mused. I had never been one to keep to myself—especially after my parents died. I hated being alone. I sought company wherever I could find it and oftentimes it was found in the warm body of another.

"The people of my court like to fight over my attention. I assume the same will still occur tonight, particularly to see your reaction."

"My reaction?" Her brows furrowed and I stifled a laugh.

"They will expect you to be jealous of their vying for my attention. Or maybe not even jealous, they'll want to see what kind of reaction they can get out of you."

Her eyes stayed focused on the door, but her grip on my arm tightened. "What kind of reaction should be expected of me?"

"It's up to you." I took a deep breath. "It's not a secret our marriage is due to a political alliance. The court will be trying to see if you and I are—" I didn't get time to finish before the doors opened and we were blinded by the bright lights of the ballroom. Our voices muffled by the sound of chattering voices.

Lennox's hand on my bicep squeezed harder as I led her into the room.

"Your Royal Majesty, King Arlo Rossi would like to formally announce his grandson, Prince Luka Rossi's engagement to our Royal Majesty, High Queen Lennox Adair!"

We stepped into the ballroom as a round of cheers broke out at the announcement.

"They are to be married in the first moon cycle of the new year in Alethens."

Lennox stiffened at announcement, her steps faltered as her

hand squeezed my arm even harder, her nails biting into my skin through my jacket.

I placed my hand on top of hers, giving it a reassuring squeeze before leaning in to whisper in her ear, "We knew this was coming, don't let them see you falter."

She dipped her chin and straightened her shoulders. "It's only me and you, Lennox." I brushed my lips over her temple, causing her eyes to flutter closed. "Just me and you."

She took a deep breath and opened her eyes. I expected her to look around the room, but instead, her gaze fixed on me.

Every pair of eyes in the room was fixed on our interaction, but all I could see was her.

"You ready?" I asked.

"Sure."

I tore my gaze from hers and led her through the throng of people. The crowd was hushed, they murmured to one another as we passed.

When we made it to the throne, I helped Lennox to her seat. Every time I saw Lennox on a throne I got the overwhelming sense she belonged there. Even on the dark obsidian throne of the Blood Court, she looked like she belonged.

A servant came and passed us each a glass of sparkling wine. "You were right about this party being different than the duke's. Much milder." She sipped from her glass.

"If you want to sit on my lap, all you have to do is ask, Sweetheart."

Her cheeks flushed. "That would surely make all your former suitors jealous."

"Why don't we try and see."

A smirk pulled at the corner of her lips. "Nice try. It will take a lot more than that to get me on your lap again."

"Are you sure about that, Sweetheart? It was pretty easy the other night."

She shot daggers at me with her eyes, her empty hand fisted on the throne, her nails digging into the stone. I had no doubt if we were alone she would have kicked me for making such a comment.

"That was different." She gritted her teeth.

I leaned over closer. "Was it though?"

"I'm done with this conversation." She turned her attention back to the crowd.

"Suit yourself." My chest felt lighter than it did before. These conversations with Lennox were natural. These conversations I could participate in and not worry about the consequences of my words.

We sat up on our thrones surveying the ball as it continued around us. People came up and congratulated us on our marriage in which we thanked them with tight smiles plastered on our faces.

After a while, we were called to the dance floor.

"Our first dance as an engaged couple." I held out my hand for Lennox. She placed her hand in mine and let me guide her from the throne to the dance floor. I placed my hands on her hips, a slight gasp leaving her lips as I pulled her towards me.

She looped her arms around my neck and I shivered at the feeling of her fingertips grazing the skin at the base of my neck.

"Do you remember the last time we danced at a ball?"

"I do." She swallowed. "That was quite a night."

"That was the night I realized I had feelings for you," I admitted.

Her gaze jumped to mine, her brows furrowing slightly in an adorable way.

"You took my breath away when you walked down those stairs. And when I had to watch you dance with the other male —" I had never been so jealous. "I vowed that day I'd never see another male's hands on you."

"Luka—"

"You don't have to say anything. I just wanted you to know."

She opened her mouth but was interrupted as a petite, dark-haired female approached.

"Prince Luka." She beamed. Lennox and I stepped apart, allowing Dahna room to skate her hands down my arm. "It's been ages since I've seen you. Where have you been hiding?" Lennox stiffened as she raked her eyes over Dahna.

"I haven't been hiding anywhere. I've been previously occupied, that's all." I snaked my arm around Lennox's waist, pulling her to my side.

"I'm sure you heard about my engagement. Dahna, this is my soon-to-be wife, High Queen Lennox Adair."

Dahna looked at Lennox for the first time, who had a tight-lipped smile plastered on her face.

"Yes." Disdain leached into Dahna's voice. "We were all surprised to hear about your engagement."

She moved her gaze back to me, dismissing Lennox entirely, causing rage to simmer inside me. Dahna and I had shared many nights, but that was it. *Nights.* And here she was trying to dismiss Lennox. To dismiss our *High Queen*... My magic pressed against my fingertips.

"That is not the proper way to greet your queen now is it?" I said, my tone sharp.

Dahna stumbled back, her brows pinching together as she looked at me. "I—" She looked back and forth between Lennox and me several times as she struggled for words. "I'm sorry. It's a pleasure to meet you, Lennox," she finally stammered.

"It's Your Majesty to you."

"I'm sorry, Your Majesty," Dahna stumbled.

"And I believe a proper courtesy is to bow to your queen," I added.

"Bow?" Dahna paled. "You can't seriously expect me to bow, Luka." She reached for my arm, but Lennox stepped in front of me, blocking her.

"Your Prince asked you to bow to your Queen. Now *bow.*" There was no room for debate in Lennox's tone.

I stepped around Lennox, placing myself at her side again

as Dahna looked nervously between us. "Unless you'd like to be thrown in the dungeon, I suggest you bow."

Dahna bowed deeply. As she rose, Lennox interrupted her. "I didn't tell you to rise."

A vicious smirk graced her face as Dahna fell back into her bow and I pulled Lennox tighter to my side.

"I love seeing your vicious side," I whispered into her ear causing a smirk to form on her lips.

"You may rise," she told Dahna finally. "Now, let me make one thing clear, *Dahna*." Lennox's voice was sweet, but laced with venom.

"Luka is my fiancé. *Mine*. If I hear you ever lay a finger on him I will personally make sure those fingers are removed from your body." Dahna paled as I failed to hide my growing smile. "Second, if you ever disrespect me or your prince again, I will ensure you never live another day." She turned her attention to me. "And I keep my promises, don't I, Luka."

"You do, Sweetheart." I placed a kiss on the skin beneath her ear. "Every violent one."

All color was now leached from Dahna, her confident facade nowhere to be seen as she clasped her shaking hands in front of her.

Lennox turned, lacing her arms around my neck and winding her hands through the hair at the base of my neck. "You may leave now." Her eyes didn't move from mine as she dismissed Dahna.

"Looks like you are a good actress after all." I pulled her against me, hovering my lips over hers as her body bowed to my touch. "Jealousy suits you."

"Turns out it's a lot easier than I thought," she admitted as her lips dusted over mine for a moment before she pulled back.

"How recently have you been with any of your—" She pulled her bottom lip between her teeth as she searched for the right word. "*Lovers*."

"I wouldn't go so far as to call them lovers." She raised a

single brow. When was the last time I had been in bed with another? "I suppose it was sometime the week before I left for Alethens."

Lennox's steps faltered, my hand on her back catching her to prevent her fall. "You mean to tell me you haven't been with anyone since you met me?" Her eyes searched mine for the lie.

"Only you, Sweetheart." It hadn't been intentional. There had been nights in Alethens, out with Declan where I had been posed with the opportunity, but turned it down. At the time it had been due to my fascination with Lennox and my determination to keep my eye on the goal.

At some point it shifted, my abstinence became solely about Lennox. I didn't want anyone else. Even since I had returned to Cel Nox. After we had broken one another's hearts it would have been so easy to bury my heartache in another, but I couldn't get myself to even try.

My heart belonged to her even if she didn't want it.

"Why?" She stammered. "Why haven't you been with anyone since you've been back in Cel Nox? Surely the opportunity has presented itself."

"It has, but I would never do that to you. We're engaged."

"But not really. You're trying to ensure we don't remain engaged, so why haven't you sought out others?" I could hear her emotions rising as she spoke—I could feel them too. Her magic quickly rising to the surface.

"Engaged or not engaged, my soul belongs to you, Lennox. If we get married you can be free to have whatever lovers you want if that's what you desire." My stomach recoiled at the idea of her with another while married to me, but if seeking her pleasure elsewhere, if that's what she wanted, I'd give it to her.

"My heart will always belong to you. Maybe someday I'll be able to move on, but for now, I am set on you. No one will ever compare to you, Lennox Adair." I swept a loose hair from her face, letting my finger move down the side of her neck as I fixed my gaze on her full bottom lip.

I should have stopped talking. I had already made myself a fool for Lennox too many times only to be rejected by her each time. But I needed her to know how I felt. If there was even a sliver of a chance she'd ever see me as more than a friend again I needed her to know how I felt.

"You can't say that," she stammered, the panic clear in her voice. "I'm no one special. You can't put your life on hold waiting for me."

"I already have, Lennox, I did the day you walked down those stairs and hurled insults at me like it was your first nature."

She opened her mouth only to shut it again.

"I've told you countless times and I'll tell you again. I will wait for you, Lennox. However long it takes. I'll even be your fucking friend if that's what you need me to do right now. But there is no one else. There will never be anyone else as long as you are still in this realm."

I wanted to tell her I loved her. I wanted to tell her I loved her until she believed it. I knew nothing would make her believe it until she wanted to, but I had already scared her too much. Pushed her too far. It was clear by the look on her face.

"Luka—I." Her hands dropped from where they had rested around my neck.

"I need some air." She turned to the door.

"Let me escort you."

"No, I need—" I grabbed her hand in mine and turned her toward me as the crowd looked on and murmured around us. I took another step toward her in an attempt to keep our conversation between the two of us.

"I know you need a moment away from me. I'll give you that, at least let me escort you." She nodded in agreement and let me lead her towards the door to the patio.

The patio was mostly empty, as was expected at this time of year, but a few people were littered around the open space. I led Lennox past the patio, intending on leading her to a secluded space in the garden where she could be alone with her thoughts.

When we rounded the first hedge we came face to face with a hulking silver-haired wolf.

Nico smiled brightly as he took in the two of us hand in hand. "Well isn't it the couple of the night. Out for a little alone time?" He waggled his eyebrows.

I looked at Lennox out of the corner of my eye, who was visibly pale under the light of the moon as she stared straight ahead.

"Nico, can you escort Lennox to a private garden spot?" The wolf eyed the two of us curiously. "Lennox needed some air." Understanding flashed across his features.

"Of course." He held his arm out to Lennox and she took it without hesitation. I watched as Nico led her deeper into the garden. The knot in my stomach tightening with every step Lennox took away from me.

# 32

# LENNOX

I gripped Nico's arm with an iron grasp. Fearing if I let go I might sink to the ground as Luka's words swam in my mind.

I felt like I had drank too much wine—my mind was foggy, nothing was making sense, although I'd only had one glass.

"What did Luka say to freak you out now?" Nico continued to lead me through the garden. "You don't have to tell me if you don't want to but—"

"I— he—I don't know." Tears prickled at the edges of my vision.

Nico led me to a bench and I sat, immediately putting my face in my hands as I tried to process what happened.

"I think he loves me," I said finally.

"No shit."

I whipped my head up to look at him, but his expression remained neutral. "What? Are you telling me you're only figuring this out now? I could tell he was falling in love with you the first day I arrived in Alethens. He has it bad for you, Lennox."

I wasn't just figuring it out. He had tried to tell me he loved me that last day in Alethens, but I hadn't wanted to believe it. I had hoped it was something he tried to say in the heat of the moment.

"We can't be together." The words felt rough in my throat.

"Why not?"

"It—it's too complicated."

"I think the two of you getting married would solve a myriad of our problems."

I put my head back in my hands. "Since when are you so reasonable?"

He sighed. "What did he say that made you want to run for the hills this time?"

"He said he'd wait for me. That I am it for him. That I can take other lovers if I want to, but he never will." The idea was baffling. He would sit by and watch me fall in love with someone else if that's what I truly wanted. Who did something like that? Not that I had been able to bed anyone else since he left. And I tried. I had sat in taverns flirting but when it came time to leave I never could.

I had never dwelled too much on it, but was it because of Luka? I had considered maybe I wasn't ready to move on, but...

"Lennox?" My sister's voice pulled me from my thoughts. I looked over to find her emerging from deeper into the garden with Declan by her side.

I narrowed my eyes at Declan as he removed his hand from my sister's back.

"Are you okay?" Kara asked.

Yes. No. I don't know.

"Luka said something that made her spiral." I gave Nico a seething look as he stood. "She's done talking to me. Kara, why don't you take over?"

I shook my head, how pathetic was I? Nico and Kara taking shifts to help me sort through my feelings. To figure out my impossible situation.

"I don't know if she wants to talk to me—"

I fixed my gaze back on the ground in front of me. "Of course she does," Nico said. "I'll leave you two to it." I didn't dare look at my sister.

I listened to the sounds of feet walking farther and farther away and one pair moving closer until Kara sat next to me. Approaching me like a scared animal who might bolt if you made a sudden movement.

"What's going on, Len?" My sister placed her hand lightly on my shoulder. "You haven't talked to me since—" she trailed off. Since those first days after I made Luka leave. Even then I had only given her the briefest details. Unable to speak without pain ripping through my chest. Before I shut it all out. Refused to talk to her.

To talk to anyone.

"If you'd rather talk to Nico I can get him back." She moved to stand, but I pulled her back with a hand on her arm.

"I didn't mean to talk to Nico and shut you out." The only reason I had shut her out in the first place was because I knew she was the only person who could talk sense back into me. I didn't want that those first weeks. But the longer I shut her out the harder it was to let her back in. Especially after she became upset with me.

"Nico came to me the night I first got here and he knew Luka's side of the story and it made it easier to talk. He already knew things. With you—Kara you know me too well." She saw right through my arguments. Poked holes in my defenses because she knew me, knew my weaknesses. She and Luka are the people who know me best. Goddess, I hoped those two never teamed up against me. I would be defenseless.

"I understand. I'm not mad, only hurt you feel like you can't talk to me."

"It's not that I can't talk to you. I—I don't think I'm ready to hear what you're going to say."

Kara let out a light laugh.

"I've made some choices when it comes to Luka that I'm not proud of. I made them selfishly—to protect myself." My chest felt heavy as I remembered the day in the training center. I never wanted to feel like that again.

"After the explosion and Lorenzo telling me Luka and I were going to be married, I was so upset Luka had kept his involvement from me, but I understood why he didn't tell me. I reacted stronger than I should have, but the way I felt when I learned he had kept it from me—it hurt. It hurt so fucking bad so I wanted to make him hurt so he would leave me. But it didn't work." I let out a deep sigh as my sister placed her hand on my back and began rubbing soothing circles like our mother used to.

"He tried to tell me he loved me and I was so afraid of those feelings I commanded him to leave while I held my dagger to his throat." I wrapped my arms around myself.

"Len."

A sob caught in my throat at the memory. "I hurt him so badly that day and he continues to care for me. To want the best for me."

"Kara," I all but sobbed, "I don't deserve the way he treats me. He sees a side of me I don't think exists outside his eyes."

Her hand on my back stilled. "Lennox, that's not true. You're so hard on yourself. Luka isn't the only person who sees you that way. I know I do. I know Luce does. I'm sure Nico and Declan do. We all love the messed up person you are because that's what makes you you." She put her arm around me and pulled me to her side, I let my head rest in the crook of her neck.

"How do I make him stop loving me?" The words speared my chest in half as they came from my lips in a whisper.

"Oh, Len." The tears were coming hot and fast now. I couldn't stop them from falling.

"You can't. I watched him fall in love with you. Once he started there wasn't any stopping him. You tried to push him away but you weren't able to, I doubt you can reverse it now."

She squeezed me tighter. "I just—I wish you would let yourself be happy. That you would stop resisting all of this."

"Kara— "

"I know, I know why you do. I—I love you so much, I hate seeing you torn up like this because you don't want to get hurt or hurt anyone else."

"It's not only that. I let the ball drop. People died because I was too preoccupied with Luka."

"You could have never predicted that attack, Lennox. Even if Luka had left, there was still nothing you could have done. Declan wasn't preoccupied and he didn't anticipate it either. And you know Declan. He's on top of everything all the time."

"I don't know what to do. Tell me what I should do." I wiped the tears from my face with the back of my hand.

"I can't, Len. This is up to you."

I sighed. "I can't go back in there." Not only was I sure I looked like a mess, but I couldn't face Luka again. Not right now.

She rubbed circles on my back again. "I'll cover for you. You go."

I wiped the remaining tears from my eyes. "Tell Luka—" What should she tell Luka? I'm sorry? The words seemed insignificant after everything he had confessed to me.

"I'll handle it. You go."

"Can you get Declan? He knows all the backways. I don't want to be seen."

"Give me a second."

She returned a minute later, Declan in tow.

"You ready?" I nodded despite the hollow aching in my chest.

We were almost to my room when I stopped Declan with a hand on his arm. "How was Luka? Is he okay?"

Something flashed across his features, and his wings twitched. "He will be. He was agonizing over everything he told you. He's afraid he scared you off."

A rough laugh slipped from my lips. "I don't know if scared is the right word. He shouldn't regret what he said. I needed to hear it, but I need some time to process." I looked at the harpy. "Can you tell him that?"

"Of course."

"Thank you."

# 33

# LENNOX

"Where are you going?"

Luka's voice from behind stopped me, my foot stilling mid-air on the stairs. I cringed, my hopes of escaping the palace walls quickly dissipating.

"Nowhere."

Luka's steps moved closer. "Dressed in your leathers? I have a hard time believing that."

Fuck, I was screwed now. I had been able to avoid Luka for the last day after the ball, having kept to my room, but I was going stir-crazy. I had too much energy built up that I needed to get out. I had planned on wandering around the city looking for any signs of the Vanir. If I happened to shed some blood while I was exploring it would be an unexpected bonus.

"Tell me where you're going, Lennox."

I thought I'd be able to sneak out undetected, but it appears I was wrong. I took a deep breath, still refusing to turn around and face him. "There's no way you're letting me get out of here alone, are you?"

"Nope, not unless you're going to your room, which happens to be in the opposite direction." I finally let myself turn around, keeping my gaze on the ground instead of the vampire before me in an attempt to keep everything he had said to me at the ball out of my mind. I was trying to get out of here to distract myself from those thoughts in the first place. And now here he was.

"I was going out to explore Cel Nox this evening. I haven't had a chance to explore the city much." The lie rolled off my tongue easily. It was a partial truth after all.

"I'm sure you won't mind if I join you, I can be your tour guide."

I gave him a fake smile. "I would love that," I bit out.

He sighed. "Don't lie to me, Lennox. If you're going to get yourself into trouble, I'd like to be there to help you if I can." His tone turned serious.

"You sure you can handle me all by yourself?" I knocked my elbow against his.

He put his hand to his heart dramatically. "You wound me, Lennox. You know perfectly well how well I can handle you alone. Or do you need a reminder?"

"No." I stammered. *Fuck.* One of his infuriating smirks pulled at the corners of his mouth. I needed to get out of here. Away from *him.*

"But I like what you're thinking, Sweetheart, let's see what Nico and Declan are up to. Maybe they want to come along." Well, there goes my plans. There's no way I'd accomplish my goals with those two in tow. "And Luce and Kara are still here for another couple of days, aren't they? Maybe they'd want to join us, too."

"The more the merrier," I said with as much fake enthusiasm as I could muster.

☾

A while later the entire gang was gathered at the front door, cloaks slung over our shoulders as we exited the palace. It hadn't taken long to convince everyone to join us according to Luka. It looked like we were truly going to have a night out.

"Where are we headed?" Nico's arms were slung over mine and Luce's shoulders as we walked.

"I was thinking of going to Yalla. They have decent ale and there's sure to be some kind of entertainment," Luka offered.

"To Yalla, we go!" Nico bellowed, earning a laugh from the group.

My leathers kept the chill away on the long walk to the tavern, but I welcomed the heat of Nico's arm on my shoulder, the wolf was practically a living furnace.

When we finally arrived at Yalla, the tavern was packed. There didn't appear to be an empty table in sight, the tavern was bustling with people talking, dancing, drinking, and indulging in whatever they desired.

Nico and Luce volunteered to grab us all a round of drinks while the rest of us searched for a table, finally settling for a rounded booth in the far corner.

We all squished in around the horseshoe-shaped table. Somehow I ended up between Nico and Luka.

I tried my best to ignore the feeling of Luka's thigh pressed up against mine as we passed the ale around the table.

I wished it was something far stronger.

"So, Lennox, what made you want to come out tonight?" There was a mischievous twinkle in Luce's eye.

"I wanted to explore the city, that's all." I took a sip of my drink.

"C'mon, L," Nico elbowed me in the side, "we all know that's a lie." I was not about to reveal my intention to spend the evening hunting Vanir in a crowded Cel Nox bar crawling with vampires.

"You're right, I wanted some piss-poor ale," I said instead.

Nico barked out a laugh but held up his glass to mine. "Cheers to that."

We all laughed, but it was lined with tension.

"I know what she was up to." Kara sipped innocently from her drink.

I kicked her under the table. "Ow!" My sister threw me a dirty look.

All eyes turned in my direction. "How does she know what you were planning?" Luce demanded.

I threw Kara a pleading look, begging her not to give me away... I knew not including her initially would come back to bite me in the ass.

"Because she was doing the same thing back home up until the night she left. I figured it was only a matter of time before she continued her hunting here."

"Hunting?" There was a steely undercurrent to Luka's voice that made me sit up straight.

"This is not the place to discuss this," I seethed, lowering my voice. "There are too many prying ears."

"Well, that's an easy fix." With the snap of her fingers, I felt Luce's magic washing over me, sealing our voices in her bubble. "Now talk, Lennox."

"Fine." I knew they wouldn't drop it. "I've been hunting Vanir in my spare time."

The table stilled. "You've been doing what?" Declan's voice was lined with icy rage.

"By yourself?" Luka asked quietly.

"Yes, by myself!" I snapped. I looked at him, surprised to find his face etched with concern.

"How'd you find them?" Declan pressed.

I took another sip of my drink. "I blended in. I listened. Earned contacts. When they were least expecting it I killed them when they outlived their usefulness."

"Impressive." Nico leaned forward, resting his elbows on the table.

"Did you ever gain any significant information from them?" Declan asked.

"No," I let my frustration leak into my voice. "None of them knew anything I didn't already know. So all I accomplished was ridding my city of their filth."

"Vicious creature," Luka mumbled.

"So that's what you were planning to do tonight? Hunt down Vanir?" Declan pressed. I could see the cogs turning in his brain as he took it all in.

"Caspian told us they are all over the city and I figured they might have more information than any I came across in Alethens. And when I get stir crazy, I like to shed blood."

Luka shuttered beside me. His hand balled into a fist on his thigh.

"And you were going to go have all the fun without us, Sweetheart?"

"I didn't think you'd want to be included."

"Did you forget watching you draw blood is one of my favorite pastimes?" I let my eyes meet his, the fire in his blue gaze sending a shiver through me.

"I mean I don't share the same fucked up sentiments as Luka, but I also love a good fight," Nico added, but I didn't take my gaze from Luka's. He would truly follow me anywhere, wouldn't he? And he didn't say he'd try to stop me—I finally tore my gaze away from his, turning my attention back to the rest of the group.

"Well how about this, we enjoy our fun night tonight, but another night we can all go out and hunt Vanir together," Nico proposed.

"Sounds like fun to me" Luce sat back in her chair, crossing her arms over her chest.

"Planning murder with three of the monarchs of our continent, can't say that's anything I ever imagined I'd participated in," Declan muttered before finishing off his ale.

Luka raised a brow at me. "You in, Sweetheart?"

I shook my head and rolled my eyes. "I don't have a choice, do I?"

Luka looked at me, placing a hand on my thigh as he did,

his face serious as he spoke. "You always have a choice, Lennox."

"If we're going to be bathed in blood, I guess we might as well be bathed in blood together," I said in return.

The table erupted in cheers as they raised their glasses, signaling a toast. I tried and failed to hide my growing smile as I clinked my glass with theirs.

What a bunch of fucked up idiots we were.

☪

The ale never stopped flowing as we all sat around the table.

As we sat, talked, and laughed, I realized I didn't think I'd ever had a group of friends. I had my siblings and Luce growing up—and they were who I spent the majority of my time with. But they were my family—not friends I made outside of the palace. I didn't have any friends outside the palace walls. Not unless barmen counted.

I had acquaintances. I participated in idle chit-chat with visiting males and females, but once we returned to our perspective homes we didn't talk to one another. We did our duty and returned to our perspective lives. And it wasn't on them. It was on me too. I didn't try to pursue those relationships—or any relationships. Platonic or romantic. Any romantic relationship I pursued ended before they or I could get attached.

Maybe my issues were more deep-rooted than I had thought.

I had never felt left out—I had never craved those relationships since I had my siblings.

But now, after sitting around this table tonight laughing and drinking with my friends—I thought for the first time I might have been missing out on something all this time.

These people—they all knew me to various degrees—and yet they were still here. They knew me and still wanted to be my friend and spend time with me.

They would follow me into darkened allies and kill the enemy without question.

Who did that?

Friends, I guess.

"Let's play a game," Nico suggested as Luka appeared with another round of drinks. This time another tray of shots along with our ale.

"What game?" Kara finished off her glass and reached for another.

"It has to be something simple," Declan amended. "None of you have the wherewithal for anything else right now."

I laughed. He had a point, I didn't think any of us could handle anything too serious right now. Declan on the other hand had hardly touched his second drink.

"Hey." Kara shoved him slightly. "Are you saying I've had too much to drink?"

"No. But if I take your money in this situation it would feel like stealing."

"Let's bet on something else," Luce suggested. "We play a simple game of whoever has the highest card wins and the lowest card loses. If you lose the draw you either have to answer a question from the winner of the round or take a shot."

"I'm in," Nico said immediately, shuffling the cards before placing one in front of each of us, not giving us a chance to argue.

I picked up my card. A six. Not too bad, but not enough to make me feel comfortable about my odds.

"Flip your cards in three, two, one…"

We all flipped our cards and I looked around the table eagerly.

"Dammit," Nico swore while Luce clapped eagerly. "Looks like I get to ask you a question."

Nico leaned back. "Bring it on, Lucy."

Luce debated for a minute before asking her question, "What's hidden in your bedside table?"

Nico's eyes widened, his mouth falling open. "How do you know about that?"

Luce grinned widely. "I walked in on you one morning and you were in an awful big rush to hide whatever's in there from me."

We all looked at Nico expectantly. "You're no longer my favorite." He pointed a finger at Luce. "But I am no quitter. So if you all must know, I sleep with a stuffed wolf every night, that's what I was hiding in my drawer."

Luka choked on his drink as I failed to stifle a laugh. "How is this the first I'm hearing of this?"

"Awe, how cute," Declan added, a small smirk pulling up one side of his mouth.

"Adorable," Kara cooed.

"One question. That was the rule." Nico picked up a shot and drained it. "If you want another you'll have to earn it."

"Fine." Luka picked up the cards, shuffling them before dealing out another round.

We all flipped our cards again, this time Kara was the winner.

Kara looked around the table assessing until they landed on Luka's two placed in front of him. "Luka." Her smile was vicious, one borrowed from my own book. "Have you ever been in love?"

The table quieted. Apparently we weren't playing around.

"Yes." He said without hesitation. His gaze locked with mine. "Once," he admitted.

The breath in my lungs stilled as we continued to stare at one another.

Nico coughed into his arm. "Next round."

Kara dealt the cards again.

"Fuck." I laid down my three and looked around the table. Declan smirked at me, his card displaying a twelve flipped in front of him.

"Lennox, what's something you regret?"

Did I have regrets?

I wasn't one that regretted much. Everything happens for a reason. My eyes itched to look towards Luka.

He might have been my biggest regret. Letting him go. Refusing to let him back in.

I reached for a shot. Not hesitating before I slung back the alcohol. It burned as it went down. Almost as much as the regret of not answering the question.

I guess I had plenty of regrets now.

I ignored everyone's stares as I set the glass back on the table, harder than necessary.

"Next round." I shuffled the cards.

Luce won again.

"Nico, have you ever had more than one partner at the same time?"

He smiled like a wolf. "On several occasions." He leaned forward, taking one of Luce's braids between his fingers. "But if you want to know about my sexual exploits all you had to do was ask, Lucy."

She swatted at his hand and leaned away. "It's only a game, Nico, don't work your pretty little brain too hard."

"You think I'm pretty." He beamed.

"I think it's time to go," Delcan declared.

"Yeah if we stay too much longer we might see one of Nico's sexual exploits," Kara remarked.

"Kara!" Luce screeched.

"What?" My sister shrugged. "I'm only saying if you two are going to fuck, I'd rather it not be on this table in front of us."

"Little Kara Adair." Nico beamed at her before placing a hand on each of her cheeks. "I love you." He planted a kiss on her forehead and let her go.

"Okay, now we really need to get out of here." Luka took me by the elbow and led me toward the door. "When Nico gets like this there's no predicting what's going to happen."

I let out a small laugh. "I have to admit, I kind of want to see what might happen."

"There will be plenty more opportunities for that, Sweetheart. I promise." I looked over my shoulder to see if the rest were following. I laughed at the sight of Declan herding them toward the door like animals.

My head was feeling light, I was buzzing—we all were. Turns out shedding blood wasn't the only thing that could ease my tensions.

I had fun tonight, we all had.

Nico walked in front of me now, his arms slung loosely over Luce and Kara's shoulders while Declan walked beside them.

Luka and I fell behind. Both of us shaking our heads at Nico as he sang an out-of-tune song as he swung between Luce and Kara.

"Has he always been like that?"

"Loud? Obnoxious?" Luka offered.

"I was going to say happy, but those work too."

Luka sighed. "He's been like this to a degree, but don't let him fool you. Nico has a lot going on you don't know about. That even I don't fully know about. He uses his personality to distract others—to distract himself from what's going on inside."

I chewed on the inside of my cheek. "I can understand that," I mumbled.

"I bet you wish you had more of a sunshine disposition to hide your feelings?" Luka nudged me with his elbow.

"Hey." I nudged him right back. "Not everyone is meant to be sunshine and rainbows."

"I know. You know how much I love your vicious, angry side."

"Oh, I know."

His hand brushed against mine, sending my nerves tingling up my arm.

"Luka—"

A crash came from the alley beside us, sending us all careening. Luka's hand pressed against the small of my back as my hand closed around my blade.

"What was that?" Declan's voice was serious as he approached the alley—hand rested on the daggers sheathed at his side.

"The last time I was in an alley it didn't end well." Luka moved his hand from my back and reached for his sword.

"You don't think it's one of those creatures do you?" Kara's brows pulled together.

"There's only one way to find out." Nico took a step into the dark alley.

"You can't be serious?" Luce stopped him with a hand on his arm.

"What? Are you scared, Lucy?"

She scoffed. "Not scared—I have a sense of self-preservation, unlike someone." She swatted him on the back of the head. "We're not heavily armed and you're drunk. If it is one of those creatures Luka saw before, we're not properly prepared."

"She's right," Luka spoke up. "Those creatures were deadly. Kara, do you even have a dagger on you?"

"Of course I do—I am an Adair after all." She pulled two knives from beneath her dress. "But unlike Lennox, I don't love fighting if I can avoid it."

"We should go," I said quietly.

I hated running from a fight, but they had a point. I wouldn't risk others because I didn't want to back down from a fight. If it was a Vanir, I would be confident we could take them, but whatever was in that alley felt wrong. Every instinct made me believe it was the creature Luka had encountered.

Another sound came from the alley, like nails scraping on the stones, drawing our attention back as a shadow emerged.

"We might not have much of a choice, now," Luka muttered, his hand flexing on his sword.

The creature crawled closer, its feet scraping on the ground. Red eyes glowed from the darkness.

"Run," Luka gasped. "It's one of them." He grabbed my arm, attempting to pull me away, but I couldn't tear my eyes from the creature. It was massive, walking on two legs, but looking far from normal. A low growl fell from its mouth, revealing its foot-long canines, dripping with blood.

"Lennox." Luka was pulling me along now. "What are you doing? RUN!"

The creature lept, its massive, razor-sharp claws swiping for the air I had occupied a moment ago. That I would have still occupied if Luka hadn't pulled me out of the way.

We ran down the street as the creature chased us, I looked over my shoulder to find two more creatures emerging from the alley and taking chase.

"Fuck! There's more." Luka looked back. "If we keep running they're going to find someone else in the city to terrorize."

"You're right." I agreed. The rest of our group was already far ahead of us.

Good.

Hopefully, they were safe. Luka and I could handle these creatures alone.

"You ready for a fight, Sweetheart?"

I tore my sword from its sheath, its whine echoing through the street as I stopped and turned toward the approaching monsters.

"Always."

# 34

# LENNOX

The first beast met my sword, its warm blood spraying. The impact of our clash reverberated through my body. I clenched my teeth as I removed my sword, kicking the creature with a boot to the abdomen. It stumbled back on the sidewalk until it collapsed on the ground dead.

Well, at least it was easy to kill.

Luka fought alongside me, slicing his blade across the neck of the monster, spurting black blood over his body.

The monster fell to a heap at our feet as three more monsters leaped toward us.

"What are these things?" I questioned as my blade swiped across a monster's arm. An arm that looked an awful lot like a Fae arm.

"I have no idea!" Luka yelled from beside me.

The monster in front of me continued its pursuit, its red eyes glowed in the dark night, but there was something different about them. About the monster's entire face. I blocked it with my sword, holding it in both my hands as the creature's claws continued to try and swipe at me as I moved us toward the bulb of light on the building.

I studied the monster's face again. Black veins spread over its face, some of them were split into festering gouges. Its red eyes were sunken as were its cheeks, but its nose, the shape of its brows, and the curve of its lips, those were Fae features.

Like it was a fae-turned-monster.

It couldn't be though. Could it?

The monster used my distraction to finally push my sword away, it fell to the ground with a clamor.

I screamed as I blocked its advance with my arms, its claws ripping through my leathers. I ducked, kicking out with my feet to attempt to knock it over, but it only stumbled.

I scrambled back looking for my sword as the creature lunged for me.

An ax arched through the air, slicing straight through the monster, its black blood raining on me before it fell to the ground in two halves.

"You came back." I looked up at Nico. His silver hair was speckled with the black blood of the monster.

Nico smiled. "We weren't going to let you and Luka have all the fun." He gave me his hand and I took it, letting him pull me up.

Between the six of us, we quickly dismantled the remaining three monsters, until all that remained were piles of flesh around us.

"What in the actual fuck were those?" Luce's chest heaved.

"I don't know, but can we discuss them later? When we're inside the confines of the palace?" Kara's face had a greenish tint to it as she looked away from the piles of flesh.

We all nodded in agreement. I brought flames to my fingertips, intent on burning any evidence we had been here, but stopped before I let the sparks reach the bodies.

"We should keep one." They all gave me a curious look. "We have no idea what these are, the only way to find out is to bring one with us."

"She's right," Luka agreed.

"Nico, help me carry one." Nico groaned but followed Luka as he searched for a beast that was mostly whole.

They carried the beast between the two of them, receiving questioning looks from the guards at the gate when we returned.

"Get him to the dungeon." Luka directed two guards once we entered the palace. "But keep this from my grandfather and Lorenzo. Got it?" The guards nodded before departing with the corpse.

"What now?" I asked after they departed.

"Sleep." Luce yawned, as she leaned against the wall. "Sleep first. Talk in the morning."

"She's right," Declan agreed. "Let's all get cleaned up, get some rest, and we can figure out what those monsters are in the morning."

We all mumbled our goodnights before heading in our separate directions, Luka by my side as we headed for our rooms.

My legs wanted to give up as we ascended the stairs.

Goddess, I was more exhausted than I had realized now that the adrenaline had worn off, but I paused when I made it to my door. Luka did too, resting his head against the frame.

Blood coated every inch of exposed skin on my body. It itched where it was dry, but still, I didn't open the door.

I wanted to ask him to come stay with me. I wanted the comfort of him sleeping beside me after tonight.

I turned toward him. Trying to work up the courage to ask him, I knew if I asked him he'd stay.

Just this once.

"Goodnight, Lennox." He sighed before he disappeared into his room, closing the door behind him.

# 35

## LUCIANA

As tired as I was after the events of the night, I couldn't sleep.

I slept for a few hours after we first arrived back at the palace, but after I awoke I couldn't fall back asleep. My wind whirled with too many questions. Too many theories.

There was so much to do and too little time to do it.

That's how I found myself decoding the second half of Hecate's book until the sun rose.

I had still failed to uncover anything helpful, but I was getting faster at decoding the book. I rewrote everything I translated, that's what took half the time.

If only I could uncover a spell that could transcribe the book for me, wouldn't that be helpful? But I wanted to get as much done as possible before I had to leave back to Arcadia this afternoon. As much as I wished I could stay here, I still had duties to attend to, duties my mother would not let me abandon much longer, no matter the circumstances.

So this afternoon I'd say goodbye to my friends and transport back to Arcadia to continue to prepare for a crown I had no interest in.

I'd much rather continue to spend my days lost in ancient witch texts.

I made my way to the palace dungeon, where we had all agreed to meet this morning to figure out what the abomination was that attacked us last night.

Whatever it was, it was rotting. I could smell it already from the top step of the descent into the dungeon.

No one else had arrived yet, so I let myself into the cell. It was unlocked and unguarded, stupid, even if it was dead.

I summoned air to my fingertips and made a barrier around the corpse. It didn't block out the stench entirely, but it helped.

I knelt next to the corpse, surveying the rotting flesh as best as I could.

Lennox was right about what she said, the creature had features that resembled a Fae. I had a hunch someone was messing with a dark form of magic, turning fae into killing machines. But why?

I turned my attention to the door, as everyone else arrived in the cell.

"What the fuck is that smell?" Nico's face scrunched as he entered the cell, everyone else following behind him.

"That is the smell of rotting flesh. Be glad I already put a barrier around him."

"Any idea what it is?" Lennox pushed past the rest of the group.

I shook my head. "No, but you're onto something. I think it was made, but I don't know how. Or why."

They all remained silent as we stared at the corpse.

"I have a theory," Luka said. I stayed crouched by the body but looked at the vampire prince. "Do you remember the story Caterina told us about when people were first trying to reverse vampirism?"

I don't think any of us could forget that story. "She mentioned in their failures, they created monsters, abominations, Dhampirs she called them."

"Witches tits." I met Luka's gaze. "You think these monsters are the product of someone trying to reverse vampirism again."

His throat bobbed. "There's no way to know for sure, but it seems like a pretty big coincidence." My mind whirled as I pieced together the information we had. "I looked into the story Caterina mentioned, about the Dhampirs, last night. When they tried to reverse the vampirism spell or curse or whatever you want to call it—the person's soul left their body. Essentially, they died, but left a functioning body behind. All that was left in the remnants of their body was a monster. A killing machine. That's why they finally stopped—the Dhampir's got out of control. Because there was no longer a soul in the body, it decayed and mutated as it tried to sustain life in a dead body."

"Did you ever see any pictures?" Lennox asked.

I shook my head. "No, but there were descriptions. "The Dhampir's fangs mutated—sometimes they shrunk into nothing, other times they grew to a foot long. Their features mutated, but you could still see their resemblance to their Fae self if you looked hard enough."

Lennox's eyes met mine. "If these are Dhampirs—" She shuddered. "I want to see if it has the Vanir mark anywhere, they have to be the ones behind this." Lennox kneeled next to the body. I joined her, searching the Dhampirs body, but we found nothing.

"It doesn't mean it's not associated with the Vanir," I offered.

Lennox sat back on her heels. "I need something to make sense." The defeat was clear on her face, and I hated seeing it. She had been through so much, suffered so much, and now she was left with all of this.

I could do this for her.

"I have an idea." I stood. "I don't know if it will work, but it's worth trying." They all stared at me expectantly. "I might be able to use Ichor magic to figure out how this was made. Or what it was made from."

"How?" Luka pushed off the wall and came to my side.

"I've never tried it before, only read about it, but there are cases where witches have used magic to dismantle a being, to figure out how it was created. There's no guarantee it will work, but I'm willing to try to prove our theory."

"Not if it will come at an expense to you. I won't let you," Lennox argued.

I rolled my eyes. "It will be fine. I want to do this." A small thrill ran through me at the possibility. I had wanted to try this kind of magic, but never had the reason to.

"I'll use a preservation spell and bring it with me when I leave this afternoon. I'll keep you all updated on any progress I make." If anything, It will give me something to look forward to while back in Arcadia.

"It will take a while, but if it works, it might give us the answers we need."

We all looked at Lennox, who stood with her arms crossed over her chest. I'd do it even if she told me not to, there was no use in fighting it.

"You want to do it, you're not just doing this for me?" Lennox searched my face for any sign of hesitancy.

"No, I want to do this. It will be fun."

"Fine." She conceded. "But if anything feels even slightly wrong or bad or anything, you stop. Promise?"

"Promise." The lie slipped off my tongue easily.

# 36

# LENNOX

I stood outside the closed door, flanked by two of the remaining guards. They had begged me not to come here, but I had to see it for myself. I had to see it to believe it was true.

The metallic scent of blood invaded my nostrils as the door slowly opened.

Blood.

There was so much blood.

It ran in rivulets across the floorboards. I was certain the liquid would stain the room for eternity. I would let it—leave it as a reminder as to what occurred in here.

Something wet landed on my exposed collarbone.

Tears.

I was crying. Again.

The tears mixed with the blood staining my chest, creating a trail through the dried red streaks.

I turned my attention back to the room. There was nothing left to identify.

The scraps of fabric were undetectable as they mixed with the ribbons of flesh heaped on the floor.

Ribbons of flesh.

That's all that remained of my parents and Nol.

*Piles of mutilated flesh.*

*Gone were their smiling faces. Torn to shreds by vicious bloodthirsty monsters. Dark spots appeared in my periphery. I stumbled as I moved closer to their remains. I willed a flame to my fingertips. Only a small spark flickered.*

*They deserved better.*

*They deserved so much better than to be reduced to this.*

*I directed my small flame toward the piles of flesh.*

*It took a few seconds for the spark to catch.* "What are you doing?" *A voice came from behind me, one of the guards that had accompanied me.*

"Releasing their souls." *My entire body felt numb as I watched my family's remains burn.*

*My mother, father, Nol, this is what they would have wanted. They wouldn't want anyone to see them like this. They wouldn't have wanted me to see them like this.*

*Why them? The three of them were all in here together. They were trying to escape.*

*They were trying to get to me and Kara. Why had I been able to escape, but they didn't make it?*

*Why did they leave me behind?*

*Why didn't Olexa get to them faster?*

*Where were Olexa's remains? Where had the vampires found her and reduced her to shreds?*

*Vicious sobs wracked my body as I watched the shreds turn to ashes.*

"I'll love you until the stars turn to dust." *I choked out between sobs.* "Be at peace."

*I focused on the burning center of the flames as my vision grew darker until my legs gave out from beneath me and I gave into the darkness.*

☾

I twisted and turned in my bed as the memories assaulted me.

One after another.

They appeared so vivid. I could smell the burning flesh as if it were occurring in my bedchamber right now and not on that night three years ago.

*Three years.*

Tears stained my cheeks and the pillow beneath me. I couldn't stop them from coming.

It had been three years since I last laid eyes on my parents.

Three years since I had seen my brother's smiling face.

Three years since my life was torn apart.

Three years since I had become the High Queen of Lethenia.

Three years of suffering and I still felt like I was back there that night, experiencing it all again.

I never slept on the anniversary, but I usually had methods of distracting myself.

The first year I had ventured into town and drunk myself into a stupor before falling into someone's bed, only to awake to a startling nightmare.

The second year I crawled into Kara's bed. Holding her tight as we both shed silent tears.

But she had left two days ago, Luce transported her back home before returning home herself.

So tonight I was at a loss. I itched to get out of this room. To take to the streets in search of blood. But I would be stupid to go out this late by myself after our encounter with the Dhampirs the other day.

I reached for the empty glass on my bedside table, moving across the room to fill it again as I wiped the tears from my face with the back of my arm. Even the alcohol was failing to aid my sleep or calm my racing thoughts. My magic pushed and pulsed against my skin as the memories continued to berate me.

The idea I had been debating flickered across my mind again. It was still early in the night—it would be a long night ahead of me if I couldn't manage to relax at all.

I threw back my drink, relishing in the burn as it slid down my throat.

What did I have left to lose?

*Nothing.*

*Everything.*

I could however gain some comfort, maybe even sleep.

I poured myself one more drink before I headed towards the door.

My bare feet were silent in the hall as I padded towards the neighboring door. My hand froze over the knob.

My heart hammered. If I went in, there was no going back.

I twisted the knob and pushed open the door, cringing as the door creaked open. But the figure in the bed didn't rustle.

I closed the door behind me, pushing my back against the door as my eyes remained fixed on the bed. Still, he slept. His chest moved up and down slowly. He looked so peaceful.

A few rouge pieces of hair fell over his face making him look younger.

I should let him be.

I should leave.

I turned back towards the door, pulling it open to make my escape. I shouldn't have come here.

"Lennox?" Luka's voice was thick with sleep as it called to me. My spine stiffened and my hand halted on the door handle.

Slowly, I turned towards him. He scrubbed at his face as he sat up, the sheet shifting to reveal his bare chest.

"Lennox, what are you doing here?" His eyes scanned my face, his brows knitting with concern. "What's wrong?"

I opened my mouth, but nothing came out. If I started I wouldn't stop. I closed my mouth, remaining with my back pressed against the door.

"Lennox." His voice was soft.

I swallowed. "Can I stay with you?" I wiped a tear from the corner of my eye. "Only for a little bit."

He dipped his chin. "Of course, you can stay as long as you need." He pulled back the sheets and shifted, making room for me next to him.

My feet were silent on the wooden floors as I slowly made my way to the bed. I should have felt some sort of regret or embarrassment for coming in here, but I didn't.

I needed him tonight.

"Thank you." I crawled in next to him.

He pulled the blankets over us and I wrapped my arms around his middle, pulling him close and resting my head in the space between his shoulder and head.

He tensed for a second before embracing my hold, wrapping his arms around me in return.

We said nothing as we lay there. His fingers running a constant trail over my bare shoulder. He didn't say anything as he continued to wipe the tears that streaked down my face. I didn't know how much time had passed when I finally spoke, breaking the silence.

"It's the three-year anniversary of their deaths."

His fingers stilled for a second before continuing again. "This night is always hard. I can never sleep. The memories flood my mind. I—I couldn't be alone."

"You don't have to justify anything to me, Lennox. I'm always here if you need me."

I moved in closer to his neck, inhaling his scent as I wrapped my arms tighter around him.

"Do you want to talk about any of it?"

I wasn't sure if talking about it would make it better or worse. But maybe talking was better than silence. Than thinking.

"Tonight I had a nightmare about when I was brought to see their bodies." I swallowed. "They were practically unidentifiable. I don't even think the vampires had drank from them—I don't know how it would have been possible with so much blood staining the study. They had been ripped to shreds."

He said nothing, continuing his soothing strokes on my shoulder.

"I burned their bodies right there. It's a witch thing, but

when someone dies an unexpected death sometimes their souls can be trapped in their bodies from the trauma. We burn them to ensure their souls are released."

"That's beautiful. Although I'm sure it was hard to see them like that, I'm glad you got to do that for them."

"It was my first act as High Queen."

His fingers resting on the small of my back flexed. "I wish you didn't have to do that alone," he added.

That was the first of many things I did alone. I didn't even ask Kara to come with me. I didn't want to expose her to that. "I passed out after I burned the bodies," I admitted. "That was the last time I let myself grieve or show weakness in front of others."

His movement on my shoulder stopped and he pulled me closer instead, resting his chin on my head. "I know I've told you this before, but you are stronger than anyone I've ever met."

"I don't feel like I am."

"I wish you could see yourself for how I see you, Lennox."

"Why do people keep saying that?"

Luka laughed, low and deep. The sound reverberated through my body. "Who else told you that?"

"Kara."

"Kara and I have a lot in common don't we."

"Yeah, you're both a pain in my ass."

He laughed again and poked me in the side, causing me to squirm in his hold.

"It's only because we care about you."

We both fell silent.

"Try and sleep now, Lennox, I'm right here if you need me."

I pulled myself closer to him. He shuffled, moving to place a kiss on my forehead before he smoothed my hair with his hand.

"Goodnight, Lennox."

"Goodnight, Luka."

I slept.

When I finally awoke the sun was high in the sky, basking the room in warm morning light. The night was over. I had made it through.

I rolled over, surprised to find the space next to me was empty, I ran my hand over the dip in the bed, where Luka had laid. The spot was still warm, he hadn't been gone long.

I sat up and rubbed the sleep from my eyes.

I couldn't believe I had slept.

I should have been ashamed for coming to Luka last night. For asking for him to comfort me, but I wasn't.

I needed him last night.

I had to remember that sometimes it was okay to lean on others. To need others.

I could hear sounds coming from the bathing chamber, that must be where Luka was.

Goosebumps covered my body the minute I left the warm comfort of the bed. I had been sweating last night in my room from my nightmares, but now—it was colder than a witch's tit in here. I wrapped my arms around myself, rubbing my hands up and down my arms as I searched for something to keep me warm.

One of Luka's long-sleeved shirts was slung haphazardly over a chair. I didn't care if it was clean or dirty, I pulled it over my head. It instantly offered more warmth than my silk night-dress, even if it only fell mid-thigh. The fabric was thick and warm, that's all that mattered.

However, my feet were still freezing. The fire no longer flicked in the hearth. I sent my flames careening towards the smoldering ashes while I went in search of socks.

How in the goddess had Luka let it get so cold in here? He must have slept the whole night too if it had gone out.

I looked around the room, past the towering piles of books and clothes strewn about, my eyes landing on a chest of drawers adjacent to the bed.

I padded over to the dresser, immediately reaching for the top drawer when my eyes snagged on the small painted portrait resting on top.

The painting was tiny, small enough to easily fit in ones pocket.

I traced the small golden frame with my fingers as I surveyed the people within it.

The female was thin, her dark, curly hair cut just above her shoulders. She smiled tightly, but her blue eyes glimmered. The older male looked identical to Luka, but with longer hair that fell past his shoulders, stopping mid-chest. A youngling sat in front of the pair. The face was younger, rounder, and his hair longer, floppier, but it was him, it was Luka. He smiled brightly in the painting.

It was a portrait of Luka and his parents. My heart caught in my chest. I had never seen a picture of the three of them together. There weren't any of his parents or anyone in the palace. They looked so alike—it made me yearn for my own family. I blinked back the wetness forming at the corners of my vision.

*Fuck.*

Socks, I needed socks. I reminded myself as I blinked back tears.

I set the portrait back on the dresser, my gaze landing on a small glass bowl made of a dark green stone. In the bowl sat a bracelet of sorts, made up of grass and flowers. Magic emulated off the object, it had been spelled to keep the plants from dying I assumed. I picked up the bracelet, tracing my fingers over the intricate weaving of the blades of grass.

It was the bracelet I had made for Luka the afternoon we spent at the lake this past summer.

"I asked Kara to spell it for me when we returned from the Mystic Court." Luka's arms came around me on either side, caging me against the dresser, his fingers brushing over mine as they examined the bracelet. "She used her earth magic to bring the flowers back to life and spelled it so they'd live forever."

"I can't believe you kept it." I turned around in his hold, his arms still on either side of me resting on the dresser as I looked up at him.

"Of course I did." He moved his arms, his fingertips grazing the backs of my arms in the lightest touch, sending shivers scattering over my body. His fingers rested lightly on my elbows as we both looked at the bracelet. A lot had happened since I'd made him that bracelet.

"I didn't mean to pry. I was looking for some socks and I got sidetracked."

"Here, let me." He moved around me, gently pulling open the second drawer and pulling out a pair of socks.

"Thank you." I reached for the socks, but he stopped me, pulling them out of my reach.

"No, let me." Before I could protest he was on his knees in front of me. I was suddenly too aware of how exposed my legs were. Images of him kneeling in front of me in an entirely different scenario burned in the back of my mind.

"Foot." He gently tapped my foot and I raised it for him. He ever so carefully rolled the sock on my foot, taking extra good care to roll it up my leg to where it rested mid-calf.

Every brush of his fingers on my leg sent desire straight to my core.

"Other foot." He directed me as he put my foot back on the ground and tapped the top of my remaining foot. I tried my best to steady my breath as he rolled the sock up my other foot, trying to steer my mind from the filthy thoughts that kept berating me. Of where else on my body I'd like his fingers.

Goddess, I hated that he had this effect on me.

As he finished, he let his hands drag up the back of my legs; I took a deep breath as they danced in a feather-light touch on the back of my knees. Although I was afraid to look, I was certain his gaze was fixed where it shouldn't have been.

"I should go," I all but panted.

He swallowed. "Okay." His voice was strained, but he stood and I met his blazing eyes.

I turned to put the bracelet I was still grasping back on the dresser, but he stopped me with a hand on my wrist.

"You should keep it."

I debated it for a moment. Part of me wanted this small piece of him.

"No. I want you to keep it. I made it for you after all." I placed it in his palm, closing my hand around his. "Thank you again for last night."

"Did you sleep the whole night?"

"I did, thank you. You're like my own personal dream-catcher or comfort blanket or something."

"Or something," he murmured.

"I should get going." I stepped out from around him and headed for the door. "I'll see you at training in a bit?" I called over my shoulder.

"Yeah, I'll see you in a bit."

# 37

# LUCIANA

The scented candles flickering on every open surface of the cabin overpowered the smell of rotting flesh.

For two days, the body of the abomination, the Dhampir we encountered on the streets of Cel Nox, has been sitting waiting for me. Luckily, the suspension spell I placed on it before we left Cel Nox had kept it from rotting any further, but the candles would help me from wanting to vomit from the vile smell while I worked. That and the bundle of herbs I tied around my neck.

I had spent the last two nights in the library, making sure I had all the information I needed to complete the spell.

It was a complex spell, but I was confident I could do it.

I had Hecate's magic running through me after all.

I palmed the dagger in my hand before raising it over the Dhampir's body. Its chest was marked with the same black webbing covering the Dhampir's face, the markings coated the creature's entire body, like its blood itself was rotting it from the inside out.

I placed the tip of the blade below the creature's neck, pushing the tip in until a tiny bead of black blood formed under the blade.

Perfect.

I pushed the blade in deeper, pulling it across the Dhampir's chest with force until I reached the bottom of its stomach, right above its pelvis.

I removed my dagger, taking a step back to survey the incision I'd made through the Dhampir's body.

Black blood had already begun to ooze from the wound. I turned my head to the side as I balled my hand into a fist, shuttering against the sound of cracking bone and ripping flesh as I used my magic to rip open the wound.

When I looked back at the body there was now a gaping hole in the Dhampir's abdomen.

I turned from the body, retrieving the bowl I left sitting beneath a dark cloth. I had mixed the ingredients for the spell together two nights ago with a large offering of my blood and allowed them to meld together under a dark cloth until they were needed. Exactly as the spell had specified.

Slowly, I poured the liquid inside the beast's exposed chest cavity. Once the bowl was empty, I returned it to the counter, exchanging it for a vile of stardust.

I sprinkled stardust in the chest cavity, it hissed and smoked as it met the blood mixture, as the spellbook said it should.

I put the stardust back and searched for my dagger.

I sliced the dagger across my palm. I squeezed my hand into a fist, letting the blood pool for a few seconds first before I moved my hand over the open wound. I opened my palm, letting my blood drip into the body.

I closed my eyes and chanted.

☾

Sweat dripped down my brow, and my body trembled under the strain of the magic, but I persisted.

My blood continued to flow from my wound into the Dhampir's chest as my magic worked its way through its body, following the trail of blood as it wove itself through the abomination.

My magic followed the blood as it moved slowly through the body. Searching for any evidence of the magic that created it. Searching for any trace of magic of any kind.

Even when my body threatened to crumble beneath me, I stood.

I gritted my teeth and chanted.

Louder.

Faster.

*There.* A small silver thread appeared in my mind. I surged for it. I pulled the thread, gently at first, but it didn't move. I tugged at it again, the thread gave way to a dark hole, I tumbled into the darkness.

Screams pierced my ears, echos of screams rang through my mind rattling my brain, causing a pressure to mount in my head.

But I continued to follow where the magic led me.

*Pain.*

I didn't know how, but I knew there was pain in here. It felt like the creature, the Dhampir, was being ripped apart, torn in two.

I felt like I was being ripped in two.

I screamed against the pain as it consumed my body.

I wobbled, catching myself on the table as white dots speckled behind my closed eyelids, but still I chanted as the blood continued to ooze from my palm.

☾

I tried to open my eyes, but they resisted. The weight of them felt too great. The ground beneath me too hard.

Where was I? Not my bed, or in the library.

I tried again to open my eyes, slowly they opened a crack.

The room was dark, making it hard to make sense of anything. My throat felt raw, my tongue stuck to the roof of my mouth. Water. I needed water. I ran my tongue over my cracked lips.

Finally, my eyes opened fully, but it only made the throbbing in my head worsen. Blood was caked to my palm, dried in some spots, but sticky in others as my wound still oozed.

*My wound.*

The spell.

I tried to stand, gripping the table for support as my legs wobbled beneath me. I must have passed out during the spell.

Fuck.

I'd been close, I'd gotten glimpses of the creatures creation, but it wasn't enough. I needed to try again.

I looked at the unhealed wound on my hand.

Later.

I needed food and water first. Then I would try again.

# 38

## LUKA

I laid in bed staring at the ceiling. Every sound had me turning my attention to the door.

I knew it was a one-night thing, but it didn't keep me from hoping she'd walk in my door again.

It had felt so good to have her in my arms again. Although now I'd crave it every night. It had been so long since we'd shared a bed, it was easy to fall asleep alone before. But now— with the scent of her still lingering in my sheets...

I snaked my hand underneath the sheets, giving my cock a long hard stroke.

I jerked up at the sound of a knock at my door.

Goddess above, of course Lennox would interrupt me the moment I decided I needed to take the edge off.

"Luka!" Lennox's voice came from the other side of the door.

"I'm coming." I quickly adjusted myself before making my way to the door, halting when I found not only Lennox at the other side of the door, but Luciana as well. Perhaps I should have put clothes on. Having Luciana see me in nothing but my undershorts wasn't what I had been antic-ipating.

The witch raised a perfectly arched brow as she scanned me. "Is this how you greet everyone who arrives at your door?"

"It's how I greet guests who knock on my door in the middle of the night." Lennox avoided my gaze, looking at the door frame instead. Besides training, I hadn't seen her since I about came in my pants after putting socks on her feet.

"I found something," Luce continued.

"And it couldn't wait until morning?"

"I was under the impression time was of the essence. Or am I misinformed." She rapped her nails against the door frame.

"Fine. I'll get dressed and meet you all in my study. Unless this is so urgent I don't have time to get dressed."

"Put some clothes on, princeling. Lennox might enjoy seeing so much of you but the rest of us have no interest."

Lennox's mouth fell open, but before she could say anything Luciana gripped her wrist and pulled her down the hall. "Enough of this, let's go."

I smiled after them for a moment before returning to my room to get changed.

☪

Several minutes later we were all gathered in my study, all but Luciana looking like they'd rather be back in bed sleeping. She had even managed to transport Kara back from Alethens for this *special* midnight meeting.

"Alright Lucy, what was so important you had to wake us all in the middle of the night? And not in a good way." The witch glared at Nico.

"I found something." She took the halves of the book from her bag. I shuttered at the presence it evoked. Even I could sense its power, it raked down my skin like invisible claws.

"Nothing I've translated so far has been of any use, but I did manage to translate a name." She flipped through the pages until she came to the one she wanted.

She pointed to the symbol on the page. "Galtain."

"Galtain," I repeated.

"Does the name ring any bells?" Lennox asked.

"No." I scrubbed my hand over the back of my neck. "But I might know how to find out."

☾

Sneaking into my grandfather's office was a stupid fucking idea.

A stupid fucking idea that I shouldn't have even brought up in the first place.

But once I brought it up to Lennox, there was no going back.

My grandfather possessed the Populus, the book containing all of the families who ever lived in the Blood Court and where they resided along with their family tree. He prided himself on keeping it update and maintaining the Blood Court's rich history. If we could get access to the Populus we could look for the Galtain family and see if it could help us figure out how they were related to Hecate's book.

However, my grandfather was out of town for the next week. After much debate it was decided we would sneak into his office to search for the Populus instead of waiting until he came back. I floated the idea of sending him a letter asking for permission, but Luce's argument won out. We needed the information sooner rather than later with mine and Lennox's wedding date quickly approaching.

So we were breaking into my grandfather's office, which would be fairly easy, there was only one obstacle standing in our way: Lorenzo.

Which is where Luciana came in.

Luciana was going to occupy Lorenzo for as long as she could by playing the role of a visiting heir over lunch. Lorenzo loved "taking the place" of my grandfather while he was away. He was overjoyed to find out *he* got to host our visitor.

The moment Lorenzo left the dining room, Luciana would let us know through the crystal Lennox wore around her neck.

I stood behind Lennox as she painted a symbol using her blood on the door of my grandfather's office, a spell Luciana had taught her last night to unlock doors.

Her blood hissed on the door before disappearing in a mist as Lennox whispered the spell under her breath.

"Here goes nothing," Lennox muttered. Her hand twisted the knob. It clicked faintly before opening.

"Good job, Sweetheart." I placed a hand on her back as I guided her into the office, closing the door quietly behind us.

"Where do we start?" She looked around the office.

"Why don't you begin with the shelves and I look through the desk?" My grandfather's office was small, the only furniture in the room was his desk and the bar cart, hopefully, that would make it easier to find what we needed.

Lennox dipped her chin and headed toward one of the bookshelves that lined the wall.

My grandfather's desk was a mess. Empty glasses and half-smoked pipes littered the counter along with papers.

I scanned the documents, looking for anything of significance as well as the Populus.

Reports from cities across the Blood Court lined the top along with general reports from his correspondents.

I moved to the drawers next, sifting through drawer after drawer of random shit: pens, scraps of paper, half-smoked pipes, and spools of thread, I was ready to give up when I came to the bottom drawer. Underneath the bottle of alcohol and shards of glass from a broken decanter was a black-bound journal, tied closed with a leather strap.

The Populus.

I let out a sigh of relief. "Lennox, I found it." I removed the leather strap and flicked through the book as Lennox looked over my shoulder. I flipped through the sections until I came to the letter G. Her lavender scent invaded my nostrils as she leaned over further, strands of her hair brushing against my neck.

I returned my focus back to the Populus as I continued to flip through the pages but found nothing. I flipped back to the beginning. Flipping each page carefully, making sure I didn't miss it, but nothing.

There was no family named Galtain in the Blood Court.

"Fuck."

Lennox stood straight again. "Well, at least we can check it off, they're not in the Blood Court."

I leaned back in my grandfather's chair, running my hand through my hair. "Yeah, but now we have six other courts to search." I reached for the Populus again, as I picked it up papers slid out from inside, falling to my feet. I reached for the scraps, my eyes scanning over the words as I shuffled through them. "Holy shit. Lennox."

"What?"

I swallowed, looking up to meet her eyes. "I think my grandfather knew your father and brother were looking for the journals."

"Why do you think that?"

"Because my grandfather has their research."

# 39

# LENNOX

My eyes scanned over the papers in Luka's hands. Papers scrawled with a combination of Nol and my father's handwriting. My father's writing was nearly indecipherable, but I would recognize Nol's perfectly printed small script anywhere.

"How?" I whispered.

"I— I don't know." Luka rubbed his hand over the back of his neck. "Why does my grandfather have these? Where did he get them?"

Luka's questions echoed my own.

"Do you think—" Pressure mounted in my sternum. "Do you think your grandfather had something to do with their deaths?"

The color leached from Luka's face.

"I mean—these had to come from my father's study. The study—that's where they found their bodies that night." Luka didn't move, his back straight as he stared at the papers with a haunted expression in his eyes as I continued, "That's where I burned their bodies." I blinked back the wetness forming in the corners of my eyes. "I haven't been back in the study since, but—"

I closed my eyes to fight back the dizzying sensation blurring my thoughts. "But what if someone had been looking for something in his office—"

"Like clues leading to the cure for vampirism," Luka finished for me.

"And my father found them," I continued. "And—" I closed my eyes, the image of the blood staining my father's study burned into the back of my eyelids. The smell of the burning flesh invaded my senses like I was back in that room again. I grasped the edge of the desk to steady myself as my legs trembled.

Luka's hand on the small of my back brought me back to reality. The gentle arc of this thumb reminded me I wasn't back there.

"Do you think—is your grandfather working with the Vanir?" I whispered. Before meeting Arlo, I might have been more likely to believe it, but after meeting the Vampire King I wasn't so sure. Was he capable of that? I didn't know him well enough to make assumptions, but Luka did.

"I don't know."

Luka slammed the papers on the desk and ran his hands through his hair, pulling at ends as he paced across the small office. "This doesn't make sense—I don't think it's something he would do but how else would he get those documents? Either he got them himself—"

"Or he sent someone to get them for him," I finished for him.

My mind whirled as I tried to comprehend how that was possible. How had Arlo known my father was looking for the journals? Or maybe my father told him and Arlo wanted the information to himself, without the entanglement of a marriage. But that wouldn't make sense, if he didn't want a marriage why was he pushing for one now? My head pulsed behind my eyes.

"What if it wasn't the Vanir that night that killed your family? What if it was vampires sent by my grandfather to get this information and it all went terribly wrong?"

"But how does that explain the other Vanir attacks?" I asked. How many enemies were we facing here?

"What if the Vanir are a separate entity from the people searching for the book—from my grandfather and whoever he's working with?"

"Luka, what if your grandfather is working with the Vanir? He's been hiding their presence in the city since you arrived back—it's not out of the realm of possibility."

He stilled, fisting his hand at his side as his mouth set into a firm line. "Luka—" I reached for him but stopped at the sensation of warmth radiating across the bare skin of my chest. The pendant on my neck heated, sending a jolt of magic through me.

"Luce and Lorenzo are done with lunch." I met Luka's gaze, we'd have to finish this conversation later. "We need to get out of here."

Luka gathered the papers scattered across the desk stacking them together before reaching for the bottom drawer.

"Wait." I halted him with a hand on his wrist, reaching for the stack of papers in his hand.

"What are you doing? We need to get out of here." I pulled the papers out of his reach.

"Lennox." There was a warning edge to his voice this time.

I scanned the desk. "We need these papers. I want to see if I can duplicate them with a spell."

He halted before retreating a step. "What do you need?" He asked.

"I need blank papers."

Luka moved to the drawers on the opposite side of the desk, pulling out a stack of blank parchment from the second drawer and handing them to me.

I laid my father's documents out on the desk, keeping an eye on the door as I placed the blank parchment on top of each sheet. I didn't have everything I needed, but I hoped I could still make the spell work.

I reached for the crystal ashtray on the desk, emptying the ashes into the garbage at my feet. I used my dagger to pierce the tip of my finger, dripping a steady stream of blood into the bowl. I balled up the blank parchment and dipped them into the ashtray, roughly covering the parchment in my blood before laying them back over the original papers.

"If this doesn't work my grandfather will kill me," Luka muttered.

"Well, we better hope this works." When all the documents were covered with the blood-soaked parchment, I brought fire to my fingertips, making a ball of flames and directing to the corner of the first sheet of blood-soaked parchment. The corner caught, and the parchment sizzled as the fire spread across the paper until it dissolved into smoldering ashes. I repeated the process with the remaining documents until all of the pages were covered in smoking ashes.

I leaned over the surface of the desk, with a light blow of my breath the ashes scattered, dissolving into the air, revealing perfect duplicates of the documents.

"Way to go, Sweetheart." Luka squeezed my arm lightly, there was a slight air of wonder in his voice as he assessed what I had done.

"Thanks." I couldn't believe that worked. "That was the first time I did that spell, I'd only ever read about it."

Luka snaked around me, grabbing the documents I stared at. "Appears you're pretty talented." He placed a kiss on my temple, catching me off guard.

He carefully placed the original documents back in the bottom drawer, while I gathered the duplicates before we both headed towards the door.

Luka stood behind me, looking up and down the hallway as I repeated the spell to lock th door behind us, letting out a sigh of relief at the sound of it clicking back into place.

"Let's get out of here." I followed Luka as we rushed down the hall.

We had only made it a few feet when Luka halted abruptly, causing me to run into the back of him.

"Ouch." I brought my hand to my nose, rubbing over the tip that had met Luka's back.

"Fuck," Luka swore. "Someone coming."

I froze, straining for any indication he was right. Sure enough voices and footsteps sounded in the distance.

"What do we do?" Arlo's office was the only room in this hallway. If anyone found us here it would raise suspicions.

The voices became louder, every footstep bringing them closer to exposing us. Before I knew what was happening, Luka wrapped his hand around my wrist, pulling me around the corner into a shadowy alcove. Once we were covered in the shadows he spun me, pulling my back against his chest and banding a strong arm around my waist.

I opened my mouth to protest, but he stopped me with his hand over my mouth. "Quiet, Sweetheart," he whispered against my skin. "We don't want to be discovered do we?" I shook my head. "Good, then play along." He released me, removing his hand from my mouth before spinning me and pressing me against the wall.

"What are you doing?"

"We need to make it believable to anyone who walks by." His nose dusted over my collarbone and up my neck. "Can you make it believable?"

All I could manage was a nod as his hands tightened on my hips drawing me closer. I moved my hands up his body, letting one rest on his shoulder, and winding the other through his hair as my body bowed to his.

He groaned, the sound vibrating against my neck as I tightened the grip on his hair. It took everything in me not to roll my hips against his to get any kind of friction.

He shifted so our faces were touching. My cheek flush against his before he tilted his head to hover his lips over mine. I could feel his breath against my lips. One small movement and they would be on mine.

My body was coiled tight, heat emulated from every place we touched. If the people had passed I had no idea. All there was in this moment was me and Luka and his hands on my body, his lips on my skin. His hand moved up my leg, finding the slit in my dress as he was so skilled at doing. He continued his exploration until his fingers were gripping the hilt of my dagger. He hoisted my leg up, his hand slipping higher, his calloused fingers skimming the globe of my ass. I wrapped my leg around his and shifted my hips, earning a groan from his lips. I bit my lip to stifle my own.

I dragged my hand from his hair, drawing it across his firm jawline, down his neck and across his chest, until I made it to the hem of his shirt and slipped my hand underneath the fabric, scraping my nails against the muscles beneath.

I yelped as he nipped at my ear and tugged.

His lips moved from my ear back to meet my own, brushing my lips in the lightest of kisses, my breath hitched. I resisted the urge to press in closer. To press my lips against his again.

His hand under my dress moved higher, his hand squeezing the flesh beneath his hand, causing me to shift against him in search of any form of friction against my center.

I held back a moan as he licked and sucked at the skin on my neck. *More.* I wanted more.

I wanted his fangs scraping my skin before sinking in.

I wanted his lips on mine.

I wanted him to slip his hand into my undergarments. To slip a finger inside me.

I wanted him moving and pulsing inside me.

*This*, this we could do. Just this once. No talking, just coming together as two bodies.

"Luka—" I pulled him closer, grinding against him again. I could feel how hard he had grown in his pants. I skated my hand between us and stroked him through the fabric. He swallowed as he placed his forehead on my collarbone.

"They're gone." His voice was hoarse.

He pulled away, slowly removing his hands from my body. The space where they rested instantly going cold.

"Thanks for playing along." He didn't meet my eyes as he spoke. "I'm going to go and find everyone and tell them we found something." He ran his hands through his hair. Taming back the locks I had messed up.

He took a step back. "I'll meet you in your room in a bit."

And with that he left, leaving me in the alcove alone.

☪

We all gathered in my room a while later, my mind still reeling over what had transpired between Luka and me in the alcove.

I couldn't stop thinking about the feeling of his hands on my body. The trail of heat they left. It left the pulsing need at my center unfulfilled.

Luka was the last to arrive despite being the one going out and finding everyone. He didn't even look in my direction before sitting on the couch opposite me.

Everyone looked between me and Luka. I ignored them as they shared looks I didn't care to dissect.

It was Declan who finally broke the silence. "What did you find?"

I tore my gaze from Luka, who was looking out the window instead.

"I guess I'll be the one speaking." I let my irritation leak into my voice. Was he going to make a habit of this? Ignoring me every time I let him touch me?

Luka continued to look out the window as I revealed to everyone what we found in the office. Including my theory about Arlo being involved with the Vanir, before placing the duplicated documents on the table.

"You really think Arlo is behind all this?" Nico asked.

"I don't know him well enough, but why else would he have these documents? They're from my father's study."

"What if Braham sent Arlo the documents? Before he died? They were in communication." Luce drummed her nails on the table. "I will ask my mother if she knows anything about it," Luce added, glancing at Luka out of the corner of her eye.

"Thank you."

"Did you two read through all of the documents?" Declan looked up from the papers in front of him, a piece of dark hair falling across his face.

"We didn't exactly have time to examine them closely." I made my way over to the harpy. "Why did you find something else?"

"Is there a reason why your grandfather would be keeping documents detailing missing vampires?"

"Missing vampires?" Luka's brow furrowed. "When?"

Declan continued to shuffle through the papers as we gathered around him. "There's hundreds of them."

"Hundreds? I feel like if there were hundreds of vampires going missing I would know about it." Luka grabbed the papers from Declans hands. "This can't be right."

"I would have thought I would have been privy to the information too, but clearly I'm not," Declan added.

"So Arlo is hiding these disappearances?" I mussed. "But why?"

"These go back years," Luka muttered. "Starting with the disappearance of my cousin."

I whipped my head toward Luka. "Your cousin?"

He nodded solemnly. "My cousin Este and her friend disappeared out of the blue one afternoon. They wandered into the forest and never returned. They were never found." Luka swallowed, his eyes fixed on the document in his hand. I remembered him telling me about her, the evening we spent under the stars during the ball last spring. "The date on the oldest report is from the day she disappeared, seventeen years ago."

"There are no reports documenting disappearance before that one?" Luce asked.

Declan shuffled through the papers again before finally shaking his head.

"Clearly, your grandfather must believe the disappearances are related, but that doesn't explain why he's kept them hidden," Kara wondered out loud.

"Wait." I sat up in my chair. "When I first met with Arlo when I arrived he alluded to dark things happening in the Blood Court, do we think he meant these disappearances?"

Declan shrugged. "Maybe, but there's no way to know for sure."

I hadn't thought too much about our conversation, especially considering Arlo had denied every meeting I requested since to follow up on our conversation. I hadn't thought about it before, since Arlo had been traveling frequently, but maybe he was avoiding me. Avoiding telling me whatever these *dark things* were.

"We're missing something," I mussed, tapping my fingers on the arm of the couch. "The Vanir and these disappearances, Arlo having my father's research, they all have to be connected somehow." I forced myself to look at Luka, my chest squeezing at the dejected look on his face. "And King Arlo might have been that connection."

The room was silent, none of us daring to say anything or even look at one another, lest acknowledge the potential truth of my statement.

"What do we do next?" Kara finally asked.

"We need to go back Alethens," Luka said, turning our attention to him.

"What do you mean we go back to Alethens?" We couldn't leave. Not when we were finally getting somewhere.

"You're due to go back in a few days anyway. Instead of

waiting a couple of weeks for the wedding, I'll come with you now. I'll make up some excuse to my grandfather."

"You don't have to," I argued.

"Yes, I do." He ran his fingers through his hair. "I can't be here with my grandfather right now. I—" He sighed deeply. "I need some time to sort this all out."

"Okay," I said softly. "If that's what you want we'll do it."

"It is," he confirmed.

"I have an idea." Luce looked up from her lap, meeting our expectant gazes. "But I don't think you're going to like it."

"Spit it out," I pressed. *Anything*, I'd do anything if it had the potential to help us.

Luce let out a deep breath. "Once we get everyone back to Alethens, we need to summon the Goddess."

## 40

## LUKA

My room was out of liquor.

I don't know how, but I had a sneaking suspicion it was due to a certain silver haired wolf. Which is how I found myself scouring through the deserted palace kitchen in search of something that would help curve my never ending thoughts.

I didn't want to talk to anyone about it. I turned away Nico and Declan when they arrived at my door earlier tonight. I needed to be alone with my thoughts to sort them all out without anyone else's opinions first.

I didn't have many people in my life that cared about me. So the idea my grandfather could be behind such heinous acts... I had talked myself in circles trying to convince myself he had nothing to do with the murder of Lennox's parents, or the Vanir, or disappearing vampires.

But the evidence was fucking compelling.

It appears like I might know my grandfather even less than I thought.

That was the circle I found myself in hour after hour until I had finally had enough and went in search of a drink, only to find my bar cart in my room empty, sending me on my little search to the kitchen.

Finally, I found a bottle of liquor, stashed in the far top corner of the pantry. The clear liquid had no label and was half empty—surely something the staff kept hidden for times of need.

I took a long swig straight from the bottle, it burned sliding down my throat.

"Fuck." I winced, wiping my mouth with the back of my hand.

Whatever it was, it was fucking strong. I left the kitchen, taking the bottle with me. I'd replace it another day with something far tastier, but I'd suffer through drinking it tonight. Anything to numb my thoughts.

"Luka?" I stilled at the sound of Lennox's voice drifting toward me from behind. I looked over my shoulder, she still wore her dress from earlier. The same one I had roamed my hands under in the alcove.

My cock stirred at the memory of my hands digging into her ass and the little sounds that fell from her lips as I pinned her to the wall.

"What have you been up to?" I willed my thoughts to take a much safer path.

She fell into step next to me. "I was on a walk. I needed to clear my thoughts."

I scoffed. "Your method sounds a lot healthier than mine." I held up the bottle for her to see.

"But yours is much more fun." She took the bottle from my hand, bringing it to her lips.

"I wouldn't do that if I was you."

She rolled her eyes as she brought the bottle to her lips.

"The fuck is this shit?" She coughed, the liquor spitting everywhere.

I couldn't help myself, I laughed.

"It's not funny! You asshole." She slapped her hand against my arm.

"Hey, I warned you."

"Not well enough."

"I can't help it if you're not a very good listener."

"I assumed you were being greedy. Usually everything you drink is good."

"Everything I drink is good. This isn't mine. Somehow my bar cart ended up empty. This is all I could find."

"Well next time you come find me. I've still got the good stuff."

"Noted, Sweetheart," I told her as we made it to our doors, my hand twisting on the knob as I pushed it open with my shoulder.

"Aren't you coming in?"

Lennox stood in her open doorway, brows raised expectantly. "I said I have the good alcohol."

I let myself smile slightly. "You know I can't say no to you."

☾

I had told myself I would have one drink with Lennox, but here I was, still in her room three drinks later, sitting beside her on the couch in front of the fire as we continued to chat idly. After each drink I told myself I was going to leave.

But then she asked if I wanted another one and I could never get myself to say no.

But now I needed to go.

Lennox sat next to me, her head resting on the back of the couch with her eyes closed.

"I should get going," I announced. "It's late and it's been a long day."

Lennox opened her eyes. "I suppose you're right."

I held out a hand and she took it, allowing me to help her stand. I pulled her to me, tucking a strand of hair behind her ear, letting my finger linger on her jaw.

"Do you—" She closed her eyes and took a deep breath. "Do you want to stay here tonight—with me?"

"Do you want me to stay here with you?"

"Yes." Her eyes fell shut as I let my fingers dance down her neck.

I dropped my hand and took a step back before I let my touch linger any longer.

"I'm going to go get ready for bed, but I'll be back." I forced myself to take a step back, keeping my eyes on her until my back hit the door.

Maybe staying was a bad idea—especially after today.

But fuck it. I needed her tonight.

I quickly readied for bed and when I returned to Lennox's room she was dressed in one of her goddess forsaken nightgowns. This one matched the color of her eyes, it made her skin appear tanner, even in the dead of winter. The silk fabric left little to the imagination. The hem of her nightgown rose to reveal even more of the smooth skin of her perfect, toned thighs as she climbed into bed. If the nightgown had been any shorter I would have gotten a fantastic view of her perfect ass I wanted to sink my teeth into.

I fisted my hand on the dresser, the wood groaning under the pressure as my cock stirred to life in my pants. Staying here with her was a bad fucking idea.

How I'd be able to keep my hands to myself when she was dressed like that—I took a deep breath before I made my way to the bed and crawled in beside her. I laid on my back with my hands fisted at my sides.

"Luka." I dared to look at her out of the corner of my eye. She was lying on her side, one of her hands propped under her head like a pillow, her golden hair flowing behind her. Her other hand dragged down my bare chest, her fingers tracing the lines of my muscles.

I should have kept my shirt on.

"You're not going to sleep like that all night are you?"

I opened my mouth and quickly shut it, clamping my jaw shut tight. I wanted to touch her, to pull her to me—or settle in between her thighs and devour her with my mouth until she was screaming my name. My control was thin right now. *Too fucking thin.* I doubted I'd be able to stop myself if I started. I wanted her too badly.

"I can leave if you want me to. If I'm making you uncomfortable," she said softly.

*Fuck.* "No, it's—" I stammered. "If I let myself touch you, I might not be able to stop."

Her breathing hitched and her hand stilled on my chest. She shifted, the warmth of her body closing in on me, her lavender scent invading my senses as she rested her head on my chest, nestling into me.

"When I asked you to stay, I didn't intend on you staying on your side of the bed. If I wanted that I would have let you go back to your room. I want you to hold me, Luka."

She hitched her leg over mine, wrapping our legs together as her hand roamed up and down my chest.

"Lennox," I all but growled.

"I promise I'll behave. Just—hold me. Please."

I groaned. "Those words are my undoing, you know that right?"

She shrugged against my chest. "I guessed as much."

I let out a small laugh. I gave in and wrapped my arms around her, my palms running across the thin fabric of her nightgown covering her back.

She wiggled, her leg tightening around mine, she was practically straddling me now.

"Sleep, Lennox," I grumbled.

"You're no fun, Bloodsucker."

*Bloodsucker.* How long had it been since she'd called me that? Used that teasing nickname?

*Too fucking long.*

"Bloodsucker, huh? You haven't used that term of endearment for a long time." I stroked her hair with my other hand.

"Is that what you think it is? Bloodsucker is a term of endearment?"

"If it's not, what is it, *Sweetheart?*" I placed a kiss on the crown of her head.

"I-I don't know." She stammered. "If you don't like it, I won't use it again."

"Well, that's a first." Her laugh rumbled against my chest. "No, I like it when you call me Bloodsucker. I missed it."

"I missed you calling me Sweetheart," she admitted quietly.

My hand stilled on her back.

"You did?"

She nodded against my chest. "I don't know why. The nickname infuriated me at first, but somewhere along the line that changed."

"I've always loved it when you called me Bloodsucker," I admitted. "Made me feel real special."

I jolted as she poked me in the side.

Her breathing became shallow as we let the silence take over. When I was sure she was asleep, she spoke again.

"Do you remember that night at the tavern, when we played the game and Declan asked me what my biggest regret was and I drank instead of answering?" Of course, I remembered that night. That stupid fucking question. I thought for sure she'd say she regretted me. I tried to prepare myself for the sting her answer would give, even though it never came it hurt just as much.

"I think my biggest regret—my only regret, is ordering you to walk out of the training center that day." I closed my eyes, unable to stop the shutter that wracked my body at her confession.

"After the attack on Alethens, I used to think back on those days leading up to the attack, after we returned from the Mystic Court. I'd replay those days over and over again and think about what I would do differently. I still do sometimes, but I've come to the conclusion there wasn't much I could have done differently. I did everything I could. But I still remember the look on your face when I told you to leave. It haunts my night-mares. Every time I close my eyes I see the pain and hurt on your face." Her voice broke.

"I regret asking you to leave. I regret not going after you." She paused. "I regret not asking you to stay. Every day I wonder how different things might have been if I'd asked you to stay."

"You still can—ask me to stay," I said quietly.

"I can't." Her voice was pained.

"Why not?"

"I'm afraid of what you might say." She was quiet for a moment. "Afraid you might say no." She paused. "Afraid you might say yes." Her hand flexed on my chest. *Time,* she still needed more time.

"When you're ready, ask me again." She clutched me tighter, closing her eyes as she buried her face into my neck.

"Goodnight Lennox." I placed a kiss on her forehead." She was silent for several moments before her voice broke through the silence.

"Goodnight Luka."

# 41

# LUCIANA

Two days later I met Lennox, Luka, Declan, and Nico in a forest outside Cel Nox to transfer them back to Alethens to save travel time.

Time is always of the essence these days.

Which is why I had been running on close to two hours of sleep every night.

After spending all day attending to my duties as crown princess, I alternated spending my nights researching in the library and working on my spell with the Dhampir. Both projects had resulted in nothing of use so far, which made my lack of sleep even more frustrating.

Each night I felt like the moment I got close to reaching for the magic inside the Dhampir I passed out, waking later to a wrung-out body and a crusted wound on my hand.

If I was going to lose sleep, I'd at least like it to be for some reward.

I gave Lennox two days to get her affairs in order before I returned so we could summon the Goddess.

We were going to summon Astria.

Like a bunch of fucking idiots.

No one had ever been successful in summoning Astria. Some said it was a crime to do so and interrupt her. But damn interrupting her. We needed her help.

And if anyone would be able to summon Astria, it would be me, Kara, and Lennox.

Three witches whose Hecate's blood ran through.

And we possessed Hecate's full spellbook.

My mother had prepared me as much as possible. Telling me any information that might be useful to help in our pursuit.

She even sent me with relics and herbs from her personal garden.

I pretended I didn't know she had a secret garden. And hadn't been using the herbs for years.

I hauled the leather strap of my bag farther up my shoulder as we continued into the woods beyond the palace, past the training center, until we came to an area far enough away that we wouldn't attract any unwanted attention.

Once we found a place we all found suitable, we set out on the tasks we had discussed beforehand.

Declan and Kara got to work setting up a perimeter around us, ensuring no one would find us, while Luka and Lennox set up the fire.

"Do you think this will work?" Nico asked as he helped me unload my bag.

"There's only one way to find out." I shrugged. "No one has ever been successful before, but maybe we will be the first."

"I'm not getting my hopes up," Lennox added, her and Luka had returned, each holding a pile of sticks in their arms. We needed a large fire for the spell, making an actual fire would be more efficient than relying on magic to sustain it. And I needed Lennox to focus her attention on the spell, not keeping a fire burning.

"C'mon Len," Kara chidded. "Why do you have to be so pessimistic?"

"It's called being realistic." She dropped her pile of sticks to the ground.

"Whatever you want to call it," Nico mumbled.

Lennox flipped him off before returning her attention back to helping Luka start the fire. He had set up a perimeter of rocks and was now carefully placing the sticks in the shape of a pyramid.

I sat cross-legged in the grass, with Nico across from me, placing my stone bowl between us. He had my bag at his side, ready to pass me what I needed. One by one I asked Nico for the relics and herbs, consulting Hecate's spellbook to make sure I was adding everything in the correct order and in the right amounts.

It didn't say if those details were critical to the spell, but I wasn't taking any chances.

I placed the last ingredient in the bowl, letting out a deep sigh as I looked at the fire now blazing behind Nico.

It was time.

I stood, taking the bowl and the two halves of Hecate's spellbook with me as I approached the roaring flames.

I set the two halves of the book before the fire and the bowl on top of them before looking at Lennox and Kara.

"You ready?" The sisters nodded, reaching for their blades, each of them slicing open their palms and allowing a steady flow of blood to drip into the bowl.

Once our blood was mixed with the relics and herbs, I used my blade to mix them all before lifting the bowl over the flames.

Kara and Lennox stood around the fire, following my instructions and waiting for the next step.

I muttered the spell, completing the first part before dumping the contents of the bowl onto the raging fire.

It hissed as the blood mixture hit the flames. It dulled for a moment before rising higher as I continued the spell under my breath.

"Now," I directed my cousins. They each sliced their palms

again and I did the same before we all joined hands, our blood mingling together as we chanted the words we had memorized.

The fire blazed higher as the magic swirled around us. The air became thick with magic, even with my eyes closed I could see the blaze as it grew higher.

Sweat coated my brow, dripping down my face as we continued to chant.

The magic thrashed around me, sending my knees buckling —but I held strong.

I gritted my teeth and forced my tongue to continue with the spell. It was as if my magic was at war with the words—trying everything in its power to get me to stop chanting.

We had to be getting close. We had to if the magic was trying to stop me.

I managed to open my eyes and caught a glimpse of Kara and Lennox.

They were struggling too. Their bodies shook and their faces were etched with concentration and pain.

We could do this. I knew we could.

Maybe it was a trick of the mind, but I swore I could see the magic swirling around us. Stars danced on a phantom wind even though it was the middle of the day. The sky grew darker and darker—more stars coming into focus.

I repeated the spell again and at once the magic ceased. It wasn't gone, but it lessened, no longer did it press against my skin, but danced around me like a phantom breeze.

The fire died, it was nothing but burning embers now as more and more stars came into vision.

In the space where the flames had once been appeared the thickest concentration of stars. The formation of stars became thicker and thicker with each passing second—they appeared to almost be forming a shape—like a constellation coming to life.

It looked like— "Holy stars," Lennox murmured.

"It's —"

I swallowed—my throat suddenly dry as I realized who stood in front of us.

The star-flecked figure turned, focusing its starry eyes on me.

"I'll give you dears a moment to get over your shock—but I would love to know why I was summoned by three of Hecate's descendants."

# 42

# LENNOX

"Is it really you?" Kara's voice filled with awe. "You're the goddess Astria?"

The figure shifted, her body made of stars moving as she did. "I am." She spread her starry arms wide.

She was beautiful. Even if this wasn't her true form it was still breathtaking. Her body was made up of stars, dark and light contouring the shape of her body. She wore no clothes, only the stars covered her exposed skin. Her hair made of stars falling to her waist, covering her breasts.

"I can't believe it worked," I murmured.

Her lips curved up, "You should have more faith *Queen of Blood and Stardust*. You will never be the answer to the prophecy if you do not have more faith, my dear."

"The prophecy—you can tell us about the prophecy?" I asked eagerly.

She held up a star-flecked hand. "I cannot—that defeats the point of a prophecy. That you must discover for yourself." I rolled my eyes as Astria's gaze shifted behind me.

"And you even brought the king." She smiled. "I do love seeing you rekindle your love for one another."

"Love, we're not—" She held up her hand again.

"We do not have time for your denials tonight. I do not know how long your spell will allow me to be here. You must get on with what you summoned me for."

"We're looking for your journals," Luce cut in.

The goddess's lips turned down. "I feared you would not give up this search easily." She shook her head, her starry hair moving with the motion like a mass of stardust.

"I will tell you where to find them, on one condition." She paused, eyeing us all. "Only if you promise they will not leave your hands."

"That defeats the point," Luka said as he moved to stand at my side.

"We need the journals to get me and Lennox out of this arranged marriage. My uncle and grandfather are searching for them."

The goddess narrowed her eyes at Luka. "They cannot have the journals. If you give the journals to them they will only cause destruction. The destruction I already sense is brewing."

"But I don't understand," I protested. "What is in those journals?"

"What you have heard is correct. The ones who are truly searching for those journals are hoping to find the cure to vampirism. They are hoping it will reveal a way to reverse the spell." Well, at least that answered one question.

"Unbeknownst to them, the journals will only put them farther into their pits of despair."

"What do you mean?" Luce tucked a braid behind her ear.

"There is no cure to vampirism," Astria said matter of factly.

"Why not tell them?" Luka questioned, pressing in closer to the Goddess.

"Because living with hope keeps them from falling over the edge into destruction." I let out an irritated sigh. Couldn't someone give us a straight answer for once?

Astria stared at Luka. "If anything, when you find those

journals you should destroy them so no one will ever know the truth."

She turned her star-flecked gaze to me. "If you want to save Lethenia you will keep those journals hidden or destroy them entirely."

"How do we find them?" It was Nico who spoke this time.

Astria's face softened as she looked at the ground between us. "You must find the Galtain family. That is what you were searching for, hmm? Answers as to how to find them?" There was a different tone to her voice as she spoke now, almost a sadness. "The Galtain family lives in the Blood Court, in a tiny village to the south of Cel Nox, almost at the border of the Court of Embers. You won't find it on any map though. They have the journals."

"If they live in the Blood Court why were they not on the Populus?"

Astria met Luka's gaze. "The Galtain family has been scrubbed from history."

"Why?" Luce pressed.

"That is not my story to tell."

For fucks sake. I hated all this secrecy.

Astria maneuvered her hand, the stars around her moved, coming together to form an object in her hand.

"This map will lead you to them." She manipulated the stars until the map rolled up, and she bound it with a star-flecked string.

She held out the map to me, I took it hesitantly. The end that met my hand turned to parchment. As Astria lifted her grip on the map the entire thing became solid.

"Use the map to find the Galtain family. Do whatever you must to destroy those journals if you choose to seek them out."

I looked around. Defeat and confusion was written on all of our faces. All this time and energy spent towards finding these journals for it to end like this.

"We should have followed Hecate's directions the first time," I murmured.

"It's my fault," Luka admitted. "I'm the one who's been obsessing over finding them to get you out of marrying me."

Astria tapped her chin. "That is something I could never understand—why are you both so determined not to marry? Have you ever taken a moment to think what a true joy your union would be?"

I spared a look at Luka. There were so many emotions written on his face. Defeat, confusion, *hope*.

"It's hard to see the joy in an arranged marriage," I said finally.

Astria's stars flickered out one by one. Her form was becoming less and less like a person and more like the starry sky.

"Wait, what can you tell us about King Arlo and his involvement with the Vanir? Was he the one who orchestrated my family's deaths?" I took a step toward Astria as her form continued to dissipate. She couldn't leave yet. We still needed answers. "What does any of this have to do with the disappearances Arlo has been cataloging?"

I don't know how it was possible, but Astria's face paled, causing my stomach to drop. She opened her mouth, her throat bobbed before she closed it again, her lips forming a thin line.

"Part of of being able to see all means I cannot share information openly." Her entire shape deflated. "The Stars do not allow me to share what I know about any of what you ask."

I swallowed a scream as I balled my hands into fists. Of course, she couldn't tell us anything. That would make this all too easy, wouldn't it.

I'd have a conversation with the Stars one day and let them have a piece of my mind.

"But I can tell you this." She looked around to all of us. "Be careful who you trust, but do continue to trust your instincts, all of you. They have not led you astray yet."

Her form grew more faint as she looked toward me again.

"Lennox." There was a hint of urgency to her tone now. She took my hands in hers, they somehow felt real despite being made up of stars. "Listen my dear." Her voice lowered to a whisper only I could hear as her stars closed around us, hiding my friends from view.

"Look past the arranged marriage. If you take away everything that has put you on this path, look at who you are standing here with. Everything that has led you to him. You are focusing on the wrong thing my dear." Her stars continued to wink out, her form becoming translucent. "I've already said too much, but Lennox, some things are more simple than they seem. Some problems are easily avoided if you let your heart be free." She placed the waning form of a hand on my chest. "Your heart is still in there. All of it. We're all rooting for you. All we want is for you to be happy."

"All?" *We?* My chest constricted.

She nodded. "All. We all want you to be happy again."

A tear slipped down my cheek as the last of the stars making up her form winked out and daylight crept back in.

# 43

# LUKA

That was it.

After our encounter with Astria, we all headed back to the palace.

We were all quiet as we mulled over what happened, none of us muttering a word on the long walk back.

All of this time and effort spent trying to find the journals—months of searching—all for Astria to tell us to keep them hidden.

Or destroy them.

I didn't know how much power the Goddess could have on us from the sky, but I didn't want to risk disobeying her. Clearly, she was watching us from wherever she resided.

"So what do we do now?" Nico asked.

"Nothing," Luciana discarded her bag on the ground with a thud before falling back into the chair. "Didn't you hear what Astria said? Those journals need to stay hidden."

"She said we should destroy them," Lennox looked up from the spot on the carpet she stared at. "We need to find the Galtain family and destroy those journals."

"Are you sure that's a good idea?" Declan's wings were tucked in tight behind him as he looked out onto the balcony.

"No," Lennox responded. "But it's the only way to ensure they remain hidden."

"She's right," I interjected. "We need to go and get those journals. Either keep them in our possession or destroy them. That's the only way we can ensure they don't get in the wrong hands." That was the truth, a truth I didn't like, but I wasn't ready to give up on this quest, not yet. I wanted to see what was in those journals. They couldn't help mine and Lennox's situation, but I still wanted to see this through. We were all eager to see what lay in those pages.

"When are we leaving?" Nico interjected.

"You think this is a good idea?" Luciana questioned, throwing him a look over her shoulder.

Nico ignored Luciana and looked at me. He had been the one who accompanied me on all my fruitless quests to find information about the journals. "If Luka thinks it's a good idea I'm with him."

If looks could kill, Luciana's look would have sliced clear through Nico.

"I have a few things I need to attend to here over the next few days," Lennox said, steering my attention back. "But I could go in three days time." She looked to Luciana. "Does that work for you?"

She took a deep breath. "I can take you anywhere you need in the evening. My mother has been keeping me busy during the day."

"That's fine," Lennox agreed. "It's settled, in three days we'll pay the Galtain's a visit."

Everyone mumbled agreement before slowly dismissing themselves until it was only Lennox and I left in the room.

"Are you okay?" she asked.

I kept my gaze on the floor. "I will be." She moved, the sound of her filling a glass at the bar cart filling my ears.

The couch dipped as she sat beside me. "Here." She handed me a drink.

"How are you so calm about this?" I brought the drink to my lips.

She sighed deeply. "When Astria spoke to me, she told me something."

She took another sip from her glass, I watched as she licked a drop from her lips.

"What did she say?" My voice was rough in my throat.

"She—she said some things that have gotten me thinking—I can't make sense of it all yet, but she said I needed—that *we* needed to look past the arranged marriage. To instead look at how we got here and who we got here with."

She set her glass down and rested her head between her hands. "She said things are more simple than they seem."

I drained the remaining liquid in my glass before setting it on the table next to hers. "I feel the complete opposite," I mumbled.

Lennox reached behind her, grabbed the bottle, and filled both of our glasses.

"Things have never been simple when it comes to you and me," I muttered.

"Isn't that the truth?" she agreed as she took another sip. "But we both need to accept we're getting married. Hecate told us we would be tied together. This must be what she meant."

I scoffed. "After all this you're going to accept this marriage so easily?" I had no qualms in marrying Lennox. I loved her for fucks sake. I'd marry her tonight if that's what she wanted, but it wasn't. She didn't choose me for herself. She was stuck with me.

"Luka." Her hand rested on my leg. "There are worse people I could marry."

I shifted so her hand fell from my leg. I was being more stubborn about this than I should have been, but I couldn't understand why she was suddenly so okay with this.

"Isn't that a nice sentiment?" I muttered.

"Luka." She reached for me again, but I stood, moving out of her reach.

"Don't." I shook my head, trying and failing to right my thoughts. "I'm sorry, I shouldn't act like this, I need some time to process this." I sighed.

I took up my spot next to her again. "I just hate the idea that I am someone you're stuck with."

I could feel her gaze bearing into the side of my face, but I remained looking forward. "Don't you understand? I don't see it that way, Luka. You are—" She stood, pacing as she wrung her hands.

"I know we've had our ups and downs, and most of that is due to me, but Luka—you mean more to me than about anyone. Yes, I always dreamed I could marry for love, but I also thought if I'd be forced into an arranged marriage it would be with a stranger, someone I didn't know. I worried they'd be a cruel, terrible person I could never get along with. I never imagined I'd be in an arranged marriage with *you*. With my *friend*. With someone I care about so deeply—" There was a waver to her voice, but she continued.

"Someone who cares about me more than I've ever been cared about. Someone who sees me for me, who takes care of me, who pushes me to be a better person. Someone who will go to all ends to ensure I am happy and I get what I deserve, even if I think I don't deserve it. You never gave up on me even when I was so broken and cruel and a shell of a person. I am so lucky to get to marry you."

She took a deep breath. "I know you think you don't deserve me Luka, but I don't deserve you. I've dragged you through hell and you're still here, wishing better for me." She stopped her pacing to look at me. "You are better Luka, and I need you to realize that."

There were times when I thought Lennox and I couldn't be more different, but in times like now, I was reminded how similar we were.

"We're two fucked up people aren't we." I leaned back on the couch and she collapsed beside me.

"More fucked up than anyone else I've ever met." It would take me a while to adjust to the fact we would indeed be getting married. Even if it wasn't what either of us wanted. But we'd figure this out. Somehow, we'd figure this all out.

I wove my fingers through hers and brought her hand to my mouth, kissing the back of her hand, her skin was smooth against my lips. Astria's tits did I want to kiss more than her hand.

"Thank you—for saying all that." I sighed. "I've got issues, clearly."

"If anyone has issues it's me." She squeezed my hand. "But at least we've got each other." I laughed. Stars above, I loved her.

I met her gaze as both of our heads rested against the couch, "Until the stars turn to dust, Lennox Adair."

"Until the stars turn to dust, Luka Rossi."

# 44

# LENNOX

Two days later, Luce transported Luka, Declan, and I to the small town outside the Southernmost border of the Blood Court. After much debate it was decided Nico and Kara would stay back—we figured the smaller number of unannounced strangers arriving to the family's home the better. Only Luka and I would try to talk to the family, while Luce and Declan would stay out and stand guard outside.

We headed through the dense woods the map Astria had given us deposited us at, finally coming to a cottage with smoke rising from the chimney.

"Someone's home," Declan noted. "Luce and I will stay hidden out here. Let us know if you need us." I grasped the purple stone around my neck; we had no idea what we were walking into, the stone's connection to Luce could save us if we needed. I released the stone and turned toward the cottage.

Our boots crunched on the snow as we approached the dwelling. Snow hadn't reached the North yet, but winter was in full swing in the Southern part of the continent. The cottage reminded me vaguely of Hecate's, if her's has been upkept. It was larger, but not by much, and had no front porch, instead, there were two wide wooden stairs leading to the door.

Both of us hesitated at the threshold—there was no going back after we knocked on the door.

"Ready?"

"As ready as I can be." I was trying to muster as much confidence as possible. I knew we were likely not going to like what we found out today. Or what we might have to do. The thoughts had hung heavy over the both of us for the last two days. I rested my hand on the handles of the daggers at my side as Luka knocked on the door.

There was shuffling on the other side before it finally opened.

A young male opened the door. His dark hair curled around his face in loose waves as he stood with his hand on the door frame. "Can I help you?"

"We're looking for the Galtain family," Luka said. "Is this the correct residence?

The male paled slightly. "Yes, this is the Galtain residence." He moved so his body covered the majority of the door frame. "What business do you have?"

"We were hoping to speak to the head of the household," I interjected. Keeping my voice as level as possible to not frighten him any more.

"Son, who is it?" Another male approached the door. This male's dark skin creased around his eyes and he had the same dark curly hair as the younger male, father and son I assumed. The male held a pot in his hand, a towel in the other as he dried the dish.

"This is my father," the younger male confirmed, stepping back to let his father into the door frame.

"Silas Galtain. And you two are?" His dark brows furrowed as he looked between me and Luka.

"We're travelers passing through, we heard you might have a story to tell us." The lie we had practiced slipped easily off my tongue.

"We're not interested. Sorry folks." Silas moved to shut the door, but Luka was quicker, blocking the door with his boot.

"You're going to want to let us in," Luka insisted.

Silas crossed his arms. "And why's that?"

Luka and I shared a look. He rose a brow and I dipped my chin in confirmation. We had anticipated this, not expecting we would be let in without revealing our true identities, but it was worth a shot to see if we could remain anonymous.

I turned my attention back to the males and removed my hood, tucking my hair behind my ears, revealing their delicate points. "You're not going to leave the High Queen out in the cold now are you?"

Both of the male's eyes widened.

"Or your prince?" Luka removed his hood.

"You're—" Silas looked between the two of us.

"Holy stars," the son mumbled.

"It can't be," Silas mused.

"High Queen Lennox Adair and Prince Luka Rossi at your service." Luka bowed dramatically.

"Please come in." Silas stumbled as he moved aside. "Please excuse my behavior. I—I never would have said such a thing if I knew who I was talking to."

I put my hand on Silas' arm gently. "No hard feelings. We cannot blame you for being cautious."

"Have a seat." Silas gestured towards the small kitchen area. A large rectangular table took up the majority of the space. Counters lined both of the walls, piled with dishes and cooking supplies. Heat radiated from the small stove in the corner, a kettle steaming on the top. Eight chairs squished around the table, the center piled high with dishes and other utensils.

"You must have a big family?" Luka noted as he took a seat next to me, his eyes wandering around the home.

Silas smiled. "I do. Auden here is my youngest." He placed a hand on Auden's shoulder. "He's the only one still living at home. My wife is out in town right now. We have four other children, two daughters, and two sons, all married off and living on their own. Lots of grandchildren too." Silas beamed.

"How many grandchildren?" I asked.

"Five." He smiled as he moved towards the mantel, picking up a framed portrait on top. "And one more on the way." He handed me the frame. I couldn't help but smile at the large family captured in the photo. I could pick out Silas' children easily, they all had the same dark hair and tawny skin with bright olive eyes.

"You have a beautiful family," Luka admired as he leaned over my shoulder.

"Thank you." Silas put the photo back on the mantel, taking care that it was put back in the right place. "Can I get you two anything?"

"We're fine, thank you," we replied in unison.

Silence filled the room.

"I'm sure you're wondering why we're here," Luka broke the silence. Silas halted, his back going straight before he sat in a chair across the table from us, next to Auden.

"I am, I'm assuming you're not here simply to visit."

"There is no use in dancing around it—" I shifted in my seat. "We're looking for Astria's journals and we believe you have them here."

Silas's jaw ticked. "And why do you assume I have those journals?"

"Astria herself told us your family has them," Lukas's tone offered no room for debate. "And she gave us a map leading us to you."

"Holy shit," Auden murmured.

Silas elbowed his son. "Manners," he hissed.

Silas turned his attention back to us. "Are you telling me you spoke to the Goddess?"

"We did," I confirmed.

Silas sighed deeply, looking at his son and back at us. "Those journals mean a lot to my family. If I did have them, I have no desire to give them up."

Luka leaned forward, bracing his forearms on the table, "Why are they important to your family?"

"You don't know?" Silas looked between the two of us. "Astria didn't tell you?" We shook our heads.

"Tell us what?" I pressed.

Silas scrubbed his hand over his face. "Why doesn't that surprise me?" Silas took a deep breath. "Astria gave my great-great-grandmother the journals before she returned to the sky."

"Why would she do that?" Luka and I asked in unison.

"She claimed it was her way of saying sorry, her explanation as to why she did what she did." Silas laughed, the sound bitter and hollow, causing a pit to form in my stomach.

"What did she do?" Luka leaned forward further.

"She turned her into a vampire."

"Wait—your great-grandmother was the first vampire?" I gasped.

Silas nodded.

"You're the original vampire family," Luka mused. "But why couldn't I find your family name in the Populus?"

"Our history as the first vampires isn't something we—or anyone in the Blood Court—boasts about. If anything, we're viewed as a disgrace. I'm sure the palace went to great ends to hide our identity, to pretend we no longer exist."

"That's terrible," I muttered.

"There's nothing we can do about it." There was a sadness to his tone.

"But why are the journals so important?" Luka pressed, turning our attention back to our task.

"The journals detail everything that happened between Astria and my grandmother. They wouldn't mean much to anyone else—but to our family—one that is viewed with such disgrace—" Silas gave his son a small smile. "It's a reminder that it was all worth it."

Luka and I shared a look. *That it was all worth it?*

"Astria and my grandmother were in love, but the story is more complicated than the one told across Lethenia. My grandmother, Elesebetta, escaped home to avoid an arranged marriage to a cruel male. Her family was extremely poor, her father promised her to a wealthy male in exchange for a large sum of money without her consent. The night before her wedding she ran. That was when she met Astria.

"They fell in love and planned a life together. But somehow my grandmother's family got a letter to her. Telling her if she did not come back and marry her intended, her younger sister —who was far too young to be married—would take her place."

My stomach twisted and Luka tensed beside me.

"So Elesebetta left Astria in the dead of night without saying goodbye. Only leaving Astria a note telling her she had to leave and go back because she was already married and pregnant with his child. She lied to Astria about the child—she knew Astria wouldn't let her leave otherwise. She hoped lying and saying she was pregnant with the male's baby would prevent Astria from killing the male. Elesebetta hated him—but she didn't feel he deserved to die because of her.

"Astria was furious at Elesebetta for leaving her. For months she plotted her revenge. At this time she had already experimented and created the other types of Fae, so she figured why not create a type of Fae that would not only curse Elesebetta, but her entire family for the rest of time? A curse seemed like a far better punishment to serve than death."

"Astria knew my grandmother, and she used the knowledge to her advantage. She knew Elesbetta had a kind hearted soul— she hated seeing others hurt. So Astria created a curse that would require Elesebetta to hurt others in order to survive. Elesebetta had drained Astria of all joy in her life so she would be cursed to drain the very lifeblood from others." Silas looked at the floor. "When Astria found my grandmother she gave her no time to explain before she turned her into a vampire. Her desire to feed was immediate."

I sucked in a breath.

"It was only in the pleading sobs of Elesebetta's sister as Elesebetta feasted on another that Astria learned the real story of why Elesebetta left. Astria left in a fury of shame over her actions. No one saw or heard from her for months, until one day she returned to find the male Elesebetta had married dead—my grandmother having killed him with her new powers, with her newfound thirst for blood. Elesebetta was so overcome with anger for Astria that when she showed up out of nowhere my grandmother tried to kill her. Astria dropped off the journal and fled. No one ever saw or heard from her again. Until it was told she fled to the sky."

We all knew the history of vampires, the legend of Astria— but not really. We had all been told a version so far from the truth. It wasn't out of revenge—it was hurt that Astria created the vampires. All this time we viewed Astria as a vengeful Goddess cursing the vampires, but it was out of heartbreak— losing the one she loved.

"We bring out the journals every year—" Silas continued, "we share the true history of our family with our younglings— even if the rest of Lethenia views us as the family who brought this plague upon us all—our family will grow up knowing the truth. It was not of our wrongdoing that we were cursed—our ancestor was brave. She gave up her happiness to save her sister."

My chest constricted. The story hit a little too close to home.

"Maybe it's a crime to share the story of the Goddess' mistake, but we've never been punished for it. If anything, I feel like she has blessed us. We always have enough food to go around. Even in years when harvest is poor—there's enough to get us through the winter. When we thought we had gotten to the last of our coins we found one more in the jar. Maybe it's blind hope, but I think Astria is watching over us."

Even if Astria was looking over the Galtain family, it didn't explain why Astria wanted to keep the journal hidden. Why she wanted it destroyed.

"Can we see the journal?" I needed answers. I doubted they laid in the journal, but we were this close, I needed to see it.

Silas nodded solemnly before turning his attention back to Auden. "Go grab it, will you?"

Auden returned a few minutes later, a worn black leather journal in his hands. He returned to his seat, sliding the journal across the table.

I took it in my hands gently.

"This is it?" Luka murmured.

"That's it," Silas confirmed.

My hands shook slightly as I moved aside the leather strap holding the book closed, leaving a strip of leather that was lighter than the rest.

I flipped through the worn pages carefully—although the journal was hundreds of years old the parchment was still fresh. It had likely been spelled to resist aging.

Luka and I sat shoulder to shoulder as we read the book in silence, taking in every page until the writing ceased. I flipped through the empty pages at the end, but there was nothing more. No damning information. No shocking reveal. The journals contained as Silas had promised—the story of Astira and his grandmother. I was about to slam the journal closed in frustration when a sliver of gold writing glinted in the firelight.

I elbowed Luka as I tugged at the paper, causing an entire page to come loose. It was a folded-up square that had been worn with time—unlike the rest of the journal.

I opened up the paper to reveal the scrawled script. Where the journal had been practiced and perfect writing, not a smudge in sight—this paper was a mess. It was the same handwriting, but notes were scrawled in the margins. Lines were crossed out and written over.

*Blood.*

*Spell.*

*Bloodthirsty monsters.*

"Holy stars." I continued to scan the page. "These are the notes she used as she tried to figure out how to create vampires."

Luka leaned in close as we continued reading. The writing was all nonsense—scrawled notes. Details about trials and failures in her experimentations.

I flipped over to the back to find more of the same, except— at the bottom, there was a note that was written more cleanly than the rest.

Dragons blood was circled several times over next to a note that read, *to ensure the spell can never be undone.* My blood ran cold as I read the final note. *If anyone tries to reverse the spell, all creatures created after the original will die.*

# 45

# LENNOX

*All creatures created after the original will die.*

My head spun as I read the words over and over again, ensuring what I was reading was correct. Did this mean what I thought it meant?

I carefully folded the paper back to its original shape. If someone were to successfully undo this spell, all vampires would die? My heart ricocheted in my chest.

If that was true, why did Astria want this hidden? If someone was looking to cure vampirism, shouldn't we use this information to stop them? Or did Astria want all vampires to die? Was she still holding a grudge against the family she cursed?

"I need to step outside for a moment," I murmured. *Air. I needed air.*

I pulled my cloak tight around me, shoving my hands into the deep pockets as I embraced the sting of the cool air in my lungs.

Luka followed me out wordlessly. The minute we were outside I felt his magic surround me as he placed a silencing bubble around us.

"Did you interpret the message how I did?" I asked.

"That if someone cures vampirism all vampires die?" His tone lilted at the end of his word. "Yeah I got that."

I twisted my loose hair in a coil at the back of my head before releasing it again. "None of this makes sense."

"I know." Luka kicked at the snow with the tip of his boot.

If someone cured vampirism, Luka died.

The thought clouded my mind.

If someone cured vampirism, Luka would no longer exist.

Things between Luka and I were complicated. But no matter what we were, I didn't want him to die. If he died—I flashed back to the feelings I felt in the forest all those months ago—when we were simply friends. Barely friends. The panic that surged through me as I saw him slowly dying in front of me. That was *then*. My feelings for him were nowhere near as strong as they are now. The idea of losing Luka—I struggled for breath. My palms were sweaty despite the chill in the air.

Before I could register what was happening, Luka was wrapping his arms around me. He squeezed me tight as if he was trying to squeeze the fear out of me. I looped my arms around him in return.

"It's okay. I'm here," he murmured into my hair. "I'm here.".

"You're here,"

"I'm not going anywhere." The pain in my chest lightened. "It will take a lot more than an ancient spell to take me from you," he said into my hair.

I squeezed my arms tighter around him. "I can't lose you."

"I know."

I shuffled in Luka's arm, causing him to release his hold slightly, but he still held me in his arms.

My chest still heaved—every breath moving against his chest as our gazes locked.

Goosebumps broke out over my body, not from the cold, but from the intensity of his gaze. I shivered, letting my gaze linger on his lips.

He leaned in closer—stopping until there was only an inch between our lips.

Our breath mingled in the space between us, creating puffs of smoke in the cold air.

I wanted so badly to close the gap between us.

"Why do you stop me every time we get closer to crossing that line?" The question had been plaguing my mind since the alcove, since the party at Caspian's manor.

"I'm giving you time? Remember?"

Time, right. He had been so careful to give me time. He pushed me—but never too far when it came to us. If we were going to go down this path it would be because I initiated it. When he knew I was ready.

I leaned forward—a slight sigh escaping my lips as I brushed them against his.

"Oh, pardon me." A cheery voice came from the trees behind us.

I closed my eyes as Luka leaned forward, resting his forehead against mine as he let out a sigh.

"I'm not going anywhere," he whispered before moving to face our visitor.

"I'm so sorry," the female said. "I didn't mean to interrupt you two love birds." I opened my mouth to interject but stopped as Luka's hand on my hip flexed.

"You must be Silas' wife." The female's eyebrows rose at the mention of Silas. "We were inside talking with your husband and son," Luka continued. "We needed a moment to ourselves. I'm Luka Rossi and this is Lennox Adair." Shock colored the woman's face.

"Goodness me. The High Queen and the Prince in my home. Oh, I do hope my husband has welcomed you properly." She smoothed her hands over her skirt. "Are you leaving or may I ask you to stay for dinner?"

Luka and I shared a look. "What do you think, Sweetheart? Are you hungry?"

"Starved," I answered.

We let the Galtain family feed us until we were so full we couldn't move anymore. We proceeded to remain in their company, moving to sit by the fire where we continued to talk and drink for what felt like hours. Silas and his wife, Malina, shared stories about their family and their ancestors—about what it was like when they first became vampires.

Luka placed a hand on my thigh. "We should get going before it gets too late."

"You're right."

I stood, as did the Galtain family.

"Thank you for your hospitality, it was such a joy to meet you all."

"And you too." Silas pulled his wife in close to his side.

"What are you going to do about the journal?" Luka whispered into my ear.

The journal, right. I had forgotten about the journal. About the task Astria had given us.

"We were not honest in our intentions in seeking you out." After their hospitality tonight I couldn't lie to them. I refused to drag things out for longer than I needed to.

"What do you mean?" Malina questioned.

"We were told by Astria when we found the journal we either needed to take them for ourselves or destroy them," I said before I could stop myself.

Sila's eye darted to the journal where it rested on the table.

"I'm not going to destroy it," I added.

His eyes shifted back to me, all the kindness leeching out.

"So you're going to take it?" There was an edge to his voice now.

"No." I kept my voice calm. I felt Luka's gaze boring into the side of my head. "I'm leaving the journal with you."

"Lennox, are you sure that's smart?" Luka warned under his breath.

"No, but it's the right thing to do."

I moved towards the table, picking up the journal, and bringing it to Silas, taking his hands in mine as I placed the journal in his hands. "This journal belongs to your family. It deserves to stay with your family. No matter what Astria might say—the best way to keep these journals safe is to keep them with your family."

"Thank you." Silas' eyes shown with sincerity.

I gave him a tight smile, forcing myself to turn toward the door before I could go back on my decision, not even checking to see if Luka followed behind me.

The warmth left my body with every step I took from the home.

"I can't believe you let them keep the journals," Luka called after me, his boots crunching on the snow.

"You let them keep them?" Luce's voice rang out through the silent forest.

"You don't understand." I quickly filled Luce and Declan in on the events in the cottage.

"So what?" Luce pressed. "Just because they were a nice family doesn't mean they should keep the journals—Astria said to destroy them, or did you forget that tiny detail?"

"I didn't forget it," I snapped. "Those journals were important to them—they will keep them safe."

"You don't know that," Declan argued.

I glared at the two of them, the silence coming from Luka was getting louder and louder by the second.

"For once can you let me do the right thing—the decent thing?" My voice rose an octave. "Those journals mean so much to them—they deserved to keep them. They will keep them safe." I refused to take that one thing from them. That journal had been the bane of my existence for months, but it was their beacon of hope. I wouldn't take it from them for my own selfish gain or the selfish actions of Astria.

"Goddess above, you're stubborn." Luce crossed her arms over her chest.

"Lennox did the right thing." Luka came to stand at my side. "There was no way we could have taken those journals from them."

"It's not like I don't believe you." Luce huffed. "But you're bearing the wrath of the Goddess, not me."

"The wrath of Astria is the last fucking thing I'm worried about."

"You could have at least taken the paper with the notes about the spell and destroyed it," Luce argued.

I felt around in my pocket, my hand closing around the folded up square of paper in my hand. I held the square between me and Luce. "For your information, I did take the important notes. If you'd stop arguing with me for a minute I could have told you that."

Luka's head whipped in my direction. "When did you take that?"

I shrugged. "I slipped it in my pocket when we left to go outside. There was no fucking way I was leaving that information in their hands."

Declan pushed himself off the tree he had been leaning against. "You could have led with that."

# 46

## LUKA

"Do you think I made the right choice?" Lennox asked as we approached her room. She had been quiet since Luciana had deposited us back at the palace in Alethens.

"I do, I believe they will keep the journal safe—they have for centuries, so why wouldn't they now." I ran my hand through my hair, pushing the strands out of my face. "Besides, both of us would have regretted taking the journal from them for the rest of our lives, and you took the important information anyways, that must be why Astria wanted the journals destroyed." Or she wanted to maintain her spin on the story that had been told for centuries, painting her in a more flattering light.

Lennox faced me as we approached her room, sucking her bottom lip between her teeth as she mulled over my words. I wanted nothing more than to take her lip between my own teeth and tug.

"You're right," she conceded, releasing her bottom lip. "I—I didn't expect Luce to react that way. I mean what if Astria is upset?" She shook her head. "You know what—fuck that—I'm upset with her. She was deceptive and misleading, so fuck her and her wants." I huffed out a laugh as she looked up at the ceiling.

"That's right Astria, fuck you." She flipped her middle finger up to the sky.

A laugh rumbled from my chest. "I hope you haven't cursed us with bad luck for the rest of our lives."

"I'm already cursed, don't you think?"

I couldn't stop the twinge of pain that coursed through my body at her words, but I shrugged, trying to ignore it the best I could. "If that's the way you see it."

"Luka I didn't mean—"

"No, it's fine." I stopped her before she could continue. I didn't want to hear what she had to say right now. "I know what you meant." I turned toward my own door.

"Goodnight Lennox." I called over my shoulder.

"Goodnight," she said softly.

I let out an exhale at the sound of my door closing behind me. I needed to stop letting her little comments get under my skin so easily. I knew she didn't mean I was a curse to her—but that didn't stop my mind from thinking I was part of her life she saw as a curse. Our arranged marriage was a curse to her—that I was sure of. I was never good enough for anyone—why would I be good for Lennox?

I inhaled deeply, my head suddenly feeling light. I took a step—only to realize the ground in front of me had begun to shift.

"What in the Goddess—" I reached for something, anything, catching my hand on the dresser and knocking over the contents sitting on top of it. They fell to the ground with a clash. Something was wrong.

The air—it smelled slightly off. Was there something in the air? I stumbled forward, my feet unable to find steady ground.

My vision blurred at the edges. I needed help. *Lennox.* I needed Lennox. I turned back towards the door or where I thought the door was—running into a wall instead.

"Fuck," I grumbled, reaching my hand out toward the wall to help guide me to the door. Only my hands didn't meet a wall.

A chest. My hands were gripping the chest of a large muscular male.

*Fuck.*

I stumbled away from the intruder, fumbling for my sword—its pommel felt heavier than before. Every movement felt languid—it took more effort than normal to raise my sword.

The figure in front of me laughed—low and rough as he easily blocked my sword—sending it careening toward the ground.

I ducked—I think—as his sword came towards me—only for my stomach to be met with his knee. I groaned, kneeling over and gripping my stomach.

"I've waited for this moment for a long time," the male grumbled before his fist met my face. I tried to move, but I wasn't fast enough. The force knocked me to the floor, my head cracking against the wood.

The male was on me before I could move. His body hovering over mine as he punched me again and again. Something cracked—surely my nose. Blood sprayed from my mouth onto the floor as I took blow after blow—unable to fight back as my body failed me. One of my eyes was already swelling—further impairing my vision. Stars danced at the edges of my blurred vision. It wouldn't be long and I'd pass out and the pain would stop.

"After we're done with you, your pretty little bride-to-be will hardly be able to recognize you when she comes to rescue you." He laughed. "If she even comes to rescue you at all."

A trap, this was a trap. Whoever they were, they didn't want me—not really. I was nothing more than bait for the real prize they wanted: Lennox.

Crack, another punch to my jaw.

*Lennox.* I tried to shout out to her, I needed to warn her, but nothing came out.

"Lennox!" I tried again.

*Crack.*
"Lennox—"
*Crack.*
Everything went dark.

47

# LENNOX

*Lennox!*

Luka's voice rang through my head again. The first time I thought it was in my head, a dream but—

"Lennox!"

"What in Astria's tits is he doing," I grumbled as I made my way towards his door.

I knocked on his door sharply—my annoyance rising with every moment passing without him answering.

"Luka!" I rapped on the door again. Still nothing.

"Luka?" I tried the handle—the door was unlocked so I made my way inside. "Luka, you have a lot of explaining to do—"

The words died on my tongue as I took in the room. There were books and broken glasses strewed across the floor like someone had swiped them across the dresser. I scanned the room—where was he? The room was dark—not a lantern was lit.

With the snap of my fingers, my flames bathed the room in a soft glow as it filled the lanterns.

The balcony door had been left open—allowing a cool night breeze to filter in. "Luka?"

I took a step towards the balcony, halting as I stepped in something warm and sticky splattered on the floor.

My chest constricted at the sight of the red liquid under my bare foot. *Blood.* My eyes darted around the room. There was blood everywhere in the entryway.

It lay in a pool and was splattered across the wooden floor.

"Luka!" Panic was rising inside me now, taking control over every rational thought. I ran through the room, my feet tracking bloody footprints as I searched for him, only to come up empty-handed.

I scanned the room again, looking for anything, any clue as to what happened. My gaze snagged on steel gleaming in the light, Luka's sword was lying in the entryway, next to the pool of blood.

Someone was here. Something happened and they took Luka.

That's why he had called for me.

My chest heaved—my breaths coming in short pants.

Panic consumed me. I took off running—Luka's sword in my hand.

I would find him.

"Lennox!"

In my rush, I ran smack dab into Declan. His large hands gripped my arms. "Lennox." His golden eyes scanned over me. "Are you okay?"

"I'm fine. I have to go." I moved to step around him, but his hands held firm on my arms. "What's going on? You're bleeding."

"It's not my blood, I'm fine. I don't have time to explain."

His brows pinched together. "Why do you have Luka's sword?"

"That's what I'm trying to tell you—something happened to Luka."

Declan moved past me, his large strides quickly taking him to Luka's room as I ran to catch up with him.

When I reached the room he was sniffing the air. "I think he was drugged—the air smells unnatural."

"The footprints." He looked at me. "Those are yours?" I nodded.

"Lennox, we'll find him, but you can't run off by yourself. We need a plan."

"We don't have time to make a plan. We need to find him!"

Declan placed his hands gently on my shoulders. "Luka is strong—he can endure whatever they put him through. If he was drugged like I assume, he's passed out and not feeling anything right now. He should be out for a while. If he wasn't drugged he would still be here. He would have fought his way out of it."

He had a point.

"You can't worry about him," Declan continued. "We have to focus on saving him." I wiped away a tear that attempted to escape without permission.

Goddess, why was I crying? Before I knew what was happening, Declan was pulling me into his body and wrapping his arms around me.

I was stunned for a second before I realized he was attempting to hug me. His body was stiff as a board, but I wrapped my arms around him.

"We will find him, I promise."

"Don't make promises you can't keep, Declan"

"I'm not."

☾

A while later we were all gathered in Luka's room. I had stayed back, staring at the blood-spattered floor while Declan had woken the others

"Do we want to split up and search the city?" Nico asked.

Declan rubbed his hand over his chin. "That could take days."

"We could do a tracking spell." Luce looked towards me. "They can be finicky, but with his blood…" Luce looked around nervously. "I think it would work."

"Is a tracking spell the same as scrying?" Nico asked.

Kara shook her head. "Scrying can be used in a more general sense—and you don't have to have a direct connection to who or what you're locating."

"Tracking spells are more specific and reliable. They require a direct link to who you are searching for," Luce continued. "Luka's blood is the ideal conduit for a tracking spell."

"Okay." My voice was rough in my throat. "I'll do it. Tell me what I need to do."

Luce nodded. "I'll go grab what we need. I'll be a second."

"You don't have to do it if you don't want to." Kara placed a hand on my shoulder. "Luce or I can do the spell instead."

I shook my head, my body numb. "I need to do it."

"If that's what you want."

Was it what I wanted? I didn't want to be in this position in the first place—that's what I wanted. I wanted—I *needed* Luka to be okay. That's what I needed.

Luce arrived back a few minutes later, arms full of relics. I watched numbly as she concocted the elements to complete the spell. I turned away as she scraped some of the blood from the pool on the floor and placed it into the bowl.

"You ready?" Luce asked.

I moved to stand beside her. "What do I need to do?"

She instructed me on everything I needed to do to complete the spell.

My hand shook slightly as I took the bloodied stone in my hand, the stone bloody with *Luka's* blood. I squeezed the stone in my hand, trying my best to ignore the feeling of Luka's blood on my palm.

I focused my mind, searching for the connection between Luka and me. I could feel it—it was there. It was nothing more than a thin thread connecting us somehow. The thread stretched and pulled as I followed it through Alethens—towards Luka.

The thread led me toward an abandoned building on the far edge of the city. I followed the thread through the closed door—stunned the spell allowed me. It was like I was there—making my way through the building.

It was mostly empty—whoever had previously owned the building had cleared it out well. But on the far wall of the building, written on the bricks was a symbol only a few would recognize. If you didn't know it, you'd assume it was a random emblem left behind by the previous owners, but to me, it told so much.

The sight of the three interlocking triangles with a larger triangle crossing through them was the sign of the Vanir.

They didn't want Luka, they wanted *me*. This was all a trap —taking Luka to get me to come after them.

Hadn't they learned yet not to fuck with me?

I followed the thread down a steep set of stairs leading to a dark room underneath the building. A knot formed in my stomach as I made my way down the stairs. I wanted to stop, but the thread pulled me forward.

A sob formed in my chest at the sight before me when I rounded the stairs.

Hanging by his wrist from shackles attached to the ceiling was Luka.

His face had been badly beaten, bruises covered his bloodied face. One of his eyes was swollen shut, but it looked to be healing already. Dried blood was caked on his face and chest.

His shirt was in shreds—like they hadn't bothered to take off the entire thing—they let it hang in pieces as they used whatever tool that inflicted the nasty gashes across his chest.

If I had been fully corporal, I would have emptied my stomach at the sight of what had been done to him.

I'd get him out of here. I knew his location—we would get him out.

But still, I couldn't get myself to turn around—to remove myself from this dreamlike state.

I approached Luka, my bare feet sticking to the blood that layered the floor.

Real, this all felt so real.

"Luka." I brushed his matted hair out of his eyes. "We're coming for you." I brushed my thumb across the cut on his cheek.

"I'm coming for you." I placed a kiss on his bloodied cheek. "And I'll kill every last one of the bastards who dared lay a finger on you."

I knew where he was now. We would get him out of there. He would be safe soon. The anger slowly igniting as I plotted my revenge.

A quick death would not be enough for them.

They would find out what happened when you fucked with Lennox Adair.

---

# 48

# LUKA

I blinked my eyes open, wincing at the pain ripping across my face at the action.

I groaned as I tried to shift, balancing on my toes as much as I could to relieve some of the tension on my wrists where the shackles cut into my skin.

I took deep steadying breaths to try and dull the pain coursing through my body.

Everything hurt.

I must have passed out during their last round of torture. I looked at my chest. The wounds were already healing, but the scars were jagged and angry from the rusty blade or whatever it was they ripped across my chest.

I assumed once they realized I was awake they would begin another round. I don't know how long they would torture me. Until I died? It wasn't me they wanted—they wanted Lennox. They would play with me until she arrived—I was the bait in the trap laid for her.

I had dreamed of her—except it hadn't felt like a dream. I tried to shake the haze from my mind.

I swore I could still feel the ghost of her hand on my face and her lips on my cheek.

*I'm coming for you.* She had said. Had she been able to communicate to me through a dream or was it a hallucination? It had felt real.

Either way, she couldn't come for me. I knew she could hold her own, but I was not worth risking her life for. I hoped she remembered that.

Footsteps sounded on the stairs.

*Great*, they were back.

"Perfect. The Prince is awake." The female, Remy, they called her, smiled gleefully.

The hulking male behind her, Tarick—the one who had snuck into my room in the first place—echoed her excitement.

Tarick handed Remy something, I strained to see what it was as she headed toward the corner of the room, her back to me.

Tarick ran his hand over the scars they had created the last time; I winced as he dug his finger into one that wasn't fully healed yet, pressing my lips together to stifle a stream. "These are healing up nicely. Looks like you're ready for more." His smile was wicked, causing my entire body to tense. "Wait until you see what she has planned this time, *Prince*." He laughed, the sound grating against my nerves.

"You ready?" Tarick bellowed.

"Ready," Remy confirmed. I turned my head as far as I could trying to see what she had. My stomach hollowed at the sight of the glowing metal in her hand.

"Tarick, you better hold him so he can't move away. We don't want him to ruin his brand." Remy turned her attention back to me, a vicious gleam in her eyes. "If you can't hold still and mess it up I'll have to do it again."

I gritted my teeth, breathing heavily through my nose.

"This is going to hurt," she crooned.

All there was was pain as she pressed the scalding metal to my chest. I couldn't hold in my screams—they ripped from my throat as I thrashed against my restraints.

Tarick held firm behind me—ensuring I couldn't move, no matter how hard I tried. Sweat dripped down my forehead as I continued to scream. Remy only laughed as she beheld me in front of her.

*LUKA!*

Lennox's voice filtered through the pain—through my screams like a beacon of hope. Maybe it was a hallucination, but like the dream it sounded real. It sounded like Lennox. I tried to respond but all I could manage was another scream of pain.

*Luka.* Her voice was thick with concern—and panic—there was panic in her voice. *Hold on. A little bit longer, I'm coming.*

Lennox was coming. I thought through the pain. She couldn't come.

After what felt like hours, Remy released the brand. My skin still burned, the pain lessening only slightly. With the pain no longer ripping through my body, I again tried to speak to Lennox. *Don't come. It's a trap.*

Was it her or was this all in my head? Either way, I had to warn her if we were somehow able to communicate, perhaps there was still a thread that remained between us after the spell we used to connect us in the catacombs.

Remy laughed again, drawing my thoughts back to the present. "Looks pretty good doesn't it." She stood back so the two could admire their work. "I thought about spraying it with salt water to ensure it doesn't heal, but I decided rebranding him every hour would be much more fun."

I gritted my teeth, biting my tongue so hard I tasted the metallic tang of blood fill my mouth. They wouldn't get a reaction from me. Not now.

*It doesn't matter. I'm coming for you.*

A dream, her voice in my head had to be a dream.

"We'll be back in a little bit," Remy sing-songed as she walked towards the stairs. "Don't get too comfortable."

Only once they were out of sight did I let myself look at the brand on my chest.

The skin was scorched and angry from the fresh burn.

But the image was clear. The symbol of the Vanir was tattooed over my heart.

☾

I fell in and out of sleep as I hung from the ceiling. Trying and failing not to dwell on the pain the brand still inflicted. Trying not to panic over the thought of going through that pain over and over again.

Maybe it would hurt less the next time.

My mind kept drifting back to Lennox's voice in my mind. Was she truly coming for me? I doubted she would heed my warning, if she did hear it. Once Lennox set her mind to something there was little you could do to change it. I doubted my pain-filled pleas would do much.

And most of all, I didn't want her to see me like this. A pathetic mess hung from the ceiling with a brand of the Vanir on his chest.

I wasn't worth saving.

# 49

# LENNOX

I had never been to this part of the city before. It was well past the city center to the south—I wondered if it was even considered part of Alethen's or if it was out of its boundary.

But the building in front of me looked the same as in my vision.

I was still on edge after Luka had called out to me, I don't know how I was able to hear him, maybe it was the effects of the spell still lingering, but it was like I could sense he was in agony. There was a prickling at the back of my mind that urged me to call out to him. Even through the connection, I could hear the pain in his voice. It had caused my own knees to buckle —giving everyone else around me a scare as we made our way through the city.

His screams still echoed in my mind.

Once I recovered, I was more determined than ever to get him out of that hell hole.

Luce figured it was a lingering effect of the spell we used in the catacombs to connect to one another—a lasting effect of the Ichor magic that let us remain connected somehow. I didn't question it—right now I was grateful for it.

We separated when we came to the building—Luce, Declan, and Kara would go around the back and try to find a way in.

Nico and I would walk right in the front door.

We both cringed as the door creaked open, eliminating our element of surprise as the male and female standing in the middle of the room turned towards the sound.

They were both shocked for a minute at our intrusion, but quickly their faces turned to delight.

"The Queen has come to retrieve her Prince," the male crooned.

"Sooner than I anticipated." She tilted her head to the side as she spoke, her light braid falling over her shoulder. "You must love him a lot."

I didn't pay them any attention before I struck. I lashed out with my sword. The female shrieked as my sword slid across her chest. She stumbled forward and I caught her, forcing my sword into her side. When I released her she stumbled to the ground, moaning as she clutched the gash in her side.

I fell to the ground on top of her, my legs falling on either side of her chest, pinning her wrist beneath my knees. Despite her wounds, she squirmed underneath my hold.

"I hope you regret ever laying a finger on him," I all but growled. I slid my dagger through her chest without another thought, my heart pumping in my chest as I watched the life leave her eyes.

I glanced over at Nico, who had the male on the ground at his mercy with his dagger to his throat.

"You have that one under control?"

He threw me a wicked smile. "You go get Luka, I'm going to make sure this one regrets ever going against his Queen."

I dipped my chin and rose to stand, resheathing my weapons as I jogged towards the stairs.

I would have thought the vision would have prepared me for what I found at the bottom of the stairs, but it didn't.

The metallic tang of blood filled my nostrils along with the scent of—*burnt flesh.*

I rushed down the final few stairs—my eyes immediately searching for Luka, hoping and praying to the Goddess I wasn't too late.

Maybe cursing her was a bad idea after all.

For a brief second, relief flooded my system at the sight of Luka still hanging from where I had seen him in the vision. But the relief was short-lived at the sight of the freshly branded skin on his chest.

I placed my hand over my mouth to stifle my sob. They had fucking *branded* him.

They had branded him like an animal with the symbol of their group.

I would delight in watching each and every one of them burn.

I ran to him, his name slipping from my lips. "Luka."

His eyes fluttered open. "Lennox," he breathed. "Is that you?" He lifted his head slightly.

"It is. I'm here." I reached for him. I wanted nothing more than to press myself against him and wrap my arms around his ruined body—but I didn't want to hurt him. "I'm going to get you out of here," I promised.

I let go of him, and looked around the room, my eyes catching on a bucket in the corner. I brought it over and stood on it so I could match his height.

My fingers brushed his blood-matted hair out of his face as I brought our foreheads together. "I'm here. I've got you. I'm sorry it took me so long."

I pricked the tip of my finger with my dagger until it drew blood, sketching a symbol with my blood on each of the shackles on his wrist. "Looks like the spell I learned to open your grandfather's office is coming in handy again," He watched me as I worked, struggling to keep his eyes open.

Once the symbol was sketched on each of the cuffs, I

murmured the spell. There was a hiss before the locks clicked open. I wrapped my arms around his torso as he slumped to the ground—trying to slow his fall as much as I could.

"I've got you."

"Thanks." He panted.

"Can you walk?"

"I think so. I just need a minute to feel my legs again."

"Do you know—was there more than the male and female upstairs?" I flopped his arm around my shoulder.

He shook his head. "I only ever saw them, but I'm sure there are more of them that know I'm here."

"We need to get out of here."

I wrapped my arm around his waist as he continued to lean on me as we made our way up the stairs.

When we made it to the top only Nico was waiting for us. "Where is everyone else?"

"They ran into some company outside—they've got it under control now but I didn't want to leave you two unprotected."

At that moment the three of them came rushing into the building—all of them splattered with blood as their eyes scanned Luka propped against me.

"You ready to get out of here?" Luce asked.

"Fuck yes." The normal cadence of Luka's voice was returning.

Within minutes we were back in the palace.

I wasted no time in giving everyone tasks—needing supplies and a healer to tend to Luka while Declan helped me get him into the bath.

"I'm fine." Luka swatted away Declan as he helped him into the tub. "Stop babying me."

"You were tortured, Luka. Let us help you," Declan argued.

"Fine," Luka huffed. "But I'm not letting you bathe me."

Delcan raised his hands in surrender. "Fine by me."

"Declan, I think I've got it from here."

Luka looked over his shoulder at me. "I can bathe myself, I'm fine."

His face was no longer swollen. The healer had given him a tonic and with mine and Luce's combined healing abilities he was already looking normal, the wounds were healing and the color was coming back into his face. But there were dark circles under his eyes, and blood coated his body.

And that fucking brand, it was starting to heal, but the remnants of a wound that severe would remain.

"Please, let me help you. I want to," I said softly. He eyed me for a long moment before finally dipping his chin.

# 50

# LUKA

Lennox returned a while later, soaps and a washcloth in hand as she knelt beside the tub.

She lathered the cloth in soap before holding it out to me. "May I?"

I didn't take my eyes off her as she tentatively began rubbing the cloth over my skin. She started with my shoulder. Taking her time as she gently scrubbed the blood from my skin. She made her way down one arm before moving to the other.

She didn't look at me as she worked, which allowed me free rein to look at her. Her cheeks were slightly flushed, but there were deep circles under her eyes. I doubted she had slept since before we had left to search for the Galtain family.

I wasn't even sure how much time had passed since I had been taken.

A day at least, judging by where the sun was in the sky.

Or more.

There had been no windows in that chamber.

Once Lennox finished with my arms she moved to my neck and next my face. Ever so gently she brought the cloth over my face. I watched the heavy rise and fall of her chest and she dipped the cloth back in the water before bringing it back to my cheek again.

She dipped the cloth back in the water again, this time she brought it to my chest. I sucked in a breath as she moved the cloth over the brand.

She jerked back and removed the cloth. "I'm sorry," she stammered.

"It's fine."

Her eyes remained fixed on the burned flesh. "Does it still hurt?"

"A little. The skin still feels tender." It hurt my pride more than anything to have the mark on my skin, to know I was marked by them. The skin would heal, but a wound that deep would leave a scar.

"I'm going to find a way to get rid of it," she declared as she dipped the cloth in the water again before getting back to cleaning my chest.

"You don't have to. It's fine."

"No, it's not," she bit out. "It's all my fault." She dropped the cloth in the water and sat back on her heels—staring at her wet hands as they soaked through the fabric of her nightgown.

"What do you mean it's your fault?"

"They took you to get to me."

I grabbed the towel sitting at the edge of the tub, wrapping it around my waist as I stepped out of the tub. I sat against the basin, facing Lennox as she remained staring at her hands in her lap.

"None of this is your fault, Lennox." I took her chin in my hand, tilting it to make her look at me. "They came here with the intention of killing—whether it was you or me or someone else—this is all their fault, not yours." I swiped my thumb over her cheek. "I'm here because of you Lennox. You saved me. None of this is your fault. Do you understand that?"

She closed her eyes but remained silent.

"I need you to answer me, Lennox, do you understand none of this is your fault?"

She breathed deeply before answering, "I understand."

"Good." I swiped my thumb over her bottom lip—the soft sigh that escaped her lips sending blood rushing to my cock.

"Come here." Confusion clouded her features at my demand, but I gave her no time for argument as I pulled her to my lap. "I need to hold you for a moment, is that okay?"

She nodded.

Her bare legs wrapped around my waist as I pulled her to my chest, wrapping my arms around her. Ever so slowly her arms wrapped around me and she rested her head on my chest.

"Thank you for coming for me." I rested my chin on her head. I felt the deep inhale she took in my bones.

"I've tried so hard to keep you at bay—to try and care less about you—so if something happened to you, it wouldn't hurt me, but it never works. Last night—" She shuddered under my hold.

I gripped her tighter, rubbing circles on her back as she searched for words. "When I got to your room and you were gone and there was blood on the floor—I was so terrified I would never see you again. I'm starting to think no matter who you are to me, it will hurt me if something happens to you."

The words were on the tip of my tongue. *I love you.*

I was fairly confident she knew how I felt about her, but if I had died never having told her those three words—I knew I'd regret it.

But I'd also regret telling her that now. She was still figuring out where we stood, what our future looked like. It was still too soon to tell her how I felt. But every day I felt like we were getting closer and closer to bridging the gap between us.

Lennox's breathing slowed as I held her to my chest.

"You should get to bed," I said finally.

"You're the one that was attacked, I'm supposed to be taking care of you." She yawned.

"You already took care of me. Let me take care of you now." She said nothing but remained resting against my chest.

I poked her side. "Bed. Now." As much as I was tempted to let her fall asleep in my lap like this, I also needed my sleep.

"Fine." She crawled out of my lap before silently leaving the bathing chamber.

I quickly dressed, slipping on a loose pair of pants before heading into the bedchamber. My body felt weak, my legs weary. It had been a long fucking week.

I halted in the doorway at the sight of Lennox curled up in my bed.

"I can leave if you don't want me here."

"No, it's—I'm surprised, that's all. Of course, you can stay."

I peeled back the sheet and slipped in beside her, resting my arms under my head as I lay on my side to face her.

Her hand reached out slowly. Her fingers moving up my bare arm to my face. She traced her fingers across my jaw, my cheek, across my brow. "I hate how afraid I am of losing you," she confessed as her fingers moved to my hair, she twisted the damp stands between her fingers.

"You don't need to be afraid of losing me. I'm not going anywhere." I dusted my thumb over her cheek.

"You can't promise me that."

"You're right I can't." Her brow furrowed slightly. "But I will do everything in my power to keep to my promise."

She shifted closer, her one hand still playing with my hair while her leg wrapped around my own, pressing our bodies together.

"Sometimes, I'm so overwhelmed by my feelings for you." I swallowed as she continued. "It's hard to even breathe when you look at me. That terrifies me more than anything, the effect you have on me."

My heart beat so fast in my chest, I feared she might be able to hear it. "Imagine what I feel when you dare to even look at me."

She smiled—a tiny little smile that softened her entire face. "I like it when you look at me. Sometimes I feel like you're the only person who truly sees me for who I am."

She pressed in closer, licking her lips as she traced my own with her fingers.

Her eyes drifted half closed as she leaned forward and brushed her lips over mine.

"Lennox." I pressed my hand into her back, pulling her closer as she arched against me.

Her lips brushed over mine again—testing, teasing.

"Luka." Her lips pressed against mine. The movement so light before she pulled back—her eyes searching mine.

"I can't promise you anything yet," she murmured. "But right now—right now I need to feel you. I need to feel you—to know you're here. That you're okay. That you're alive."

Her fingers tightened in my hair, pulling my mouth towards hers.

"I'm here, Lennox."

I moved forward—pressing our lips together. Lennox didn't hesitate this time. Her hand gripped my neck as she pulled my mouth to hers. Months of built-up tension and emotions were put into that kiss. It wasn't gentle. It was greedy—both of us trying to make up for time lost. She took my bottom lip between her teeth and pulled—eliciting a groan from me.

"You wicked, violent creature," I murmured against her mouth.

She smiled against my lips, her leg wrapping around mine pulling me tighter to her, pressing her hot center against my leg. Her tongue teased the seam of my lips and I opened for her.

Our hands roamed over each others bodies as we continued to kiss for what felt like days, *hours,* as we reacquainted with each other.

Her hands roamed over my chest and back until they finally slipped lower, under the band of my pants, her hand wrapping around my cock. I slipped the thin strap of her nightgown over her shoulder, exposing one of her breasts. I rubbed my thumb over the tightened peak as her grip on my cock tightened as she stroked me up and down. I groaned, dipping my head to take her nipple in my mouth. Her back arched as my tongue and teeth teased the sensitive bud.

My hands gripped the swell of Lennox's ass as she rolled on top of me. Her hands roamed over my chest as her lips moved down my neck. I slipped my hands underneath the silk of her night dress until the fabric bunched at her waist.

"No undergarments tonight, Sweetheart?" Her wet heat slid over the fabric of my pants as she ground herself against me. "Did you have this in mind all along?"

She lifted her head from my chest to meet my gaze, mischief swirling in her eyes.

"You know me, I like to be prepared."

Her lips returned to my chest as she kissed her way lower.

"I better be the only one you were preparing for." I pinched her side and she giggled against my chest.

I winced as her chest scraped against the brand on my chest, the burns still sensitive despite the healing. I hissed, my hand fisting the sheet underneath me.

Lennox stilled, shifting so she sat straddling me, her night-gown out of place, her one breast still exposed as she stared at me, her brows furrowed and lips turned down.

"It still hurts?"

I nodded.

She closed her eyes and took a deep breath. When she opened them she leaned down, pressing her lips to the center of the brand.

"I'll make them pay."

She braced her arms on either side of me, careful to make sure she didn't touch the burn before she pressed a kiss to my jaw and then my lips. I wound my hand through her hair, keeping her lips against mine until she finally pulled away. She pressed her forehead against mine, her hair a curtain around us.

"Sleep," she murmured.

"Sleep," I confirmed. As much as I wanted to continue what we had started, I knew that's what neither one of us truly needed right now.

She sat up and swung her leg off of me. She fixed her night-gown before curling up next to me, resting her head in the crook of my shoulder and pulling the blanket over us.

# 51

# LENNOX

I snuck out of Luka's room before he woke.

I usually relished waking up in his arms. I loved basking in the feeling of being safe, protected, and happy—for as long as possible in his presence.

But not today. Not after last night.

I know I'd have to face my choices later—all of my choices, but that was exactly why I snuck out. I needed to gather my thoughts with a clear head. I needed time out of Luka's arms to do such.

I knew the moment Luka woke up and looked at me with sleep in his eyes, with his hair all rumpled like. I loved, all rational thoughts would scatter and I'd finish what I started last night.

When it came to Luka, I had such a hard time being rational. The way he looked at me—sometimes it made me want to say fuck caution and reasonable thought, and screw my shattered and broken heart because Luka made all those fears seem so much smaller.

But I couldn't do that, because I was marrying him in a little over a week.

I would soon be tied to him for the rest of my life.

If I said screw it and let myself be happy with Luka, what would happen if it all fell to pieces? Not only would I once again find myself shattered—but there would be no escaping him.

But last night—the idea of losing him shook me to my core.

I needed to feel him—to touch him to help quench my worries.

And it did. And then some.

It should have felt like a mistake—letting myself kiss him. But I couldn't find it in myself to call it that. Maybe we could walk this line. We could be friends who were married and also fucked.

That could work, right?

I could contain my feelings towards Luka to strictly friends. Because being with Luka—touching him, kissing him, being with him, it quieted my mind.

And now my mind was anything but quiet.

I had no idea what to do about Luka and I, and on top of that, the Vanir had struck again. And there was the journal. Or the lack of journal. And whatever Arlo had to do with everything. Everything was a fucking disaster and we were running out of time.

But there was one thing I could do.

Trying to summon Astria again might be a stupid idea.

Trying to summon Astria by myself might not even work, but I needed to try.

We had unfinished business and I needed answers.

I pricked my finger, letting the blood fall into the bowl in front of me.

I had come to a cave hidden in the woods—one Kara, Luce and I used to explore as children not far from the lake. I hadn't been here in years, I doubted anyone had, which made it the perfect place to summon the Goddess out of the prying eyes of others.

I hoped it would work by myself.

I dumped the contents of the bowl over the raging fire, setting it on the ground at my feet before closing my eyes and beginning the spell.

The magic pushed and pulled against my skin, I gritted my teeth against the strain. Without Luce and Kara by my side, the magic was more intense than before. It nearly brought me to my knees, but I continued. I opened myself up to the magic, letting it roam through my body as I called for the Goddess.

All at once the magic stopped. I sucked in a breath as my magic returned to its resting place inside me, but the hairs on my arms remained raised. Magic filled the cavern. I could feel it in the air, taste it on my tongue.

When I opened my eyes, the Goddess' starry form was in front of me once again.

"That was less dramatic than last time," I told her.

"I didn't take you for one to care for dramatics."

"You're right." I perched myself on a large rock, crossing one leg over the other.

"So, what do you want from me this time, Queen of Stardust." The Goddess sat herself on a rock across from me.

"You owe me an explanation."

"For what?" She raised a perfectly arched starry brow.

"You lied to us about what's in the journal."

"And you didn't destroy it like I told you to."

I scoffed, "If you're so concerned about it, why didn't you take it back yourself."

She narrowed her dark eyes on me. "You met the Galtain family. You know why."

"But you thought I could go in and do it?"

"You are becoming more and more unpredictable, Lennox Adair." She looked at her nails. "I thought at least one of you would be able to do it."

I doubted anyone who heard the family's story would be able to take the journal from them.

"How long have you been looking over that family?"

"What do you mean?" She snapped.

"You know exactly what I mean. You feel guilty over what you did to the family—you've been trying to make up for your actions for decades, haven't you? Giving them luck and assistance when they needed it.

"Anything they believe is my doing is only coincidental."

I rolled my eyes. "How did you let the story get so twisted anyways? *Why* did you let that happen?"

"The well-known story paints me in a much more flattering light, don't you think?" The smile that grew on her face was cold and cruel.

"You're a monster. You know that? You let that poor family suffer for the consequences of *your* actions."

Astria stood, her form turning darker. "Do you forget who you speak to? I am your Goddess. No matter how you feel about me, you still need to treat me with respect."

"I think we're past that, don't you?" I stood, meeting her eye to eye.

"I could turn you to stardust with the snap of my fingers girl."

"Do it," I gritted. Our eyes locked in a fierce stare.

"I've had enough," she snapped, her form dissipating, the stars winking out.

"Wait!" I reached out, my fingers slipping through her figure.

"If you think I'm going to remain here so you can insult me—"

"I'll stop, let me ask you what I wanted to in the first place." Fuck my temper, getting in the way.

She crossed her arms as her figure reformed. "You have two minutes."

"There are people out there trying to cure vampirism, why

not tell them if they find a cure, it will erase all vampires from existence?"

"You saw those pages. Everything I used to create the spell is on those pages. If that were to get into the wrong hands—it's a free pass to figuring out how to reverse the spell."

"But I destroyed your notes about the spell." I had used my own flames to burn the pages I had stolen to ashes, ensuring no one ever found the information hidden within.

"You might have destroyed the easy route to recreating the spell, but if you read the journal close enough, one could figure out everything I did to create the spell. It would take much longer, but the information is there."

*Fuck.* I should have taken my time, read through the journal more carefully before leaving it behind.

I paced back and forth in the cave. "I still don't understand, why not tell them so they stop searching for a cure? Tell them the consequences?"

"Because what you don't understand is the group who are leading this charge doesn't care about vampires. Why do you think they want to reverse vampirism? It's not because they no longer want to crave blood. They want the race gone altogether. To them, losing all current vampires would be a small price to pay for them to be eradicated from this continent."

My stomach hollowed. "Are you sure they would take that risk?"

The Goddess' shoulders sank. "To them, it's not a risk. I have no doubt they would see it as a reward for their persistence."

"I should have destroyed it." *Fuck*, if the journal got into the wrong hands...

"You should have."

I bit my tongue. "I'll write to them. Tell them why it needs to be destroyed. They might do it."

"I doubt it, that family loves the journal."

"Maybe they can bring it to the wedding and we can do it together."

"Speaking of your wedding, when are you going to give in to the prince? I'm getting tired of waiting."

"My relationship with Luka is none of your concern."

"I beg to differ." The Goddess smirked. "Isn't that the other reason you are here, to ask me about him?"

I opened my mouth, but she stopped me. "Before you ask, I can't say why. But I can say this. You need to stop getting in your own way, Lennox Adair. You try so hard to place blame on everyone and everything around you when you're the biggest obstacle in your way. You're trying so hard to fight what has been set out for you that you've failed to realize what is in front of you, might be what you want. You are too upset about how you got here to realize it."

"I—"

"I'm not done yet." She held up a star-flecked hand. "Don't make the same mistakes I did. When Elesebetta left me I was hurt, similar to the hurt I'm sure you felt when you found out the Prince had been keeping things from you." I stiffened. "But I knew deep down she loved me and there was a chance she would come back to me if she could because we loved each other. But I was so terrified by the small possibility she might not want me that I didn't leave it up to chance. I made it so she could never come back to me. I acted out of hurt and anger and made a choice that prevented my one true love from ever being able to come back to me."

"What does that have to do with me?"

She raised an eyebrow. "It has everything to do with you." She moved, her stars moving with her as she took my hands in her own. "Don't let your own cowardice prevent you from the life you deserve, Lennox Adair. From the life you have earned." She squeezed my hands.

"I see everything. I see the way you and the vampire prince look at one another. And I can tell you with confidence the look is *rare*. You have to trust he will come back to you, even when you are at fault."

I swallowed, looking away to avoid her gaze.

"How long do you expect him to wait? One day he might get tired of waiting and move on. Don't lose your chance."

"But, I—" *I'm scared.* My hands trembled in hers.

"Love is the most terrifying thing I've ever experienced." I almost thought I could see tears in the Goddess' eyes. "Something that has the ability to bring you more joy than you could ever imagine and more pain than you could ever endure should terrify you. But I've never thought of you as someone who balked in the face of fear, Lennox Adair."

I felt her words as they sunk into my bones.

"I'd say I have faith you'll make the right choice *Queen of Blood and Stardust*, but you might fuck it up like the stubborn child you are."

And with that, she was gone. I was left alone in the cave. My mind swimming with all the information I had gleaned.

But one thing was clear. I fucking hated Astria.

# 52

# LENNOX

The entire walk back to the palace I stewed over Astria's words.

So what if she was a so-called "all-seeing Goddess?" What did she know? She didn't know what was going on inside my head.

Either way, she had no business giving me advice when she had made such terrible choices in her own love life. She made a rash decision that cost her a lifetime of happiness and created a species of bloodthirsty vampires. Why shouldn't I take all the time I needed to figure out where I wanted things to go with Luka?

We were getting married. We had the rest of our lives to figure out our relationship. He told me he would wait for me, however long it took.

Astria didn't know shit.

Stars she was infuriating.

If I ever saw her again—

"Lennox."

I looked in the direction of Luka's voice, finding him walking down the hallway towards me. His smile faltered as he approached, his brows furrowing slightly.

"Are you okay?" He placed his hand gently on my arm.

"Yeah, I'm fine—"

"Is this about last night?" His shoulders straightened.

"No, Luka…" I wasn't prepared to run into him again so quickly. I still needed more time to gather my thoughts about what our kiss meant. *Our more than kiss.*

"What is it?" He tucked a lock of hair behind my ear with one hand while the other moved to my waist, drawing me against him. "Lennox, talk to me."

"It's nothing, I—I summoned Astria again." I let the words slip out, there was no use in hiding it from him, it would all come out eventually.

His hand fell from my face. "You did what? By yourself? Why?" He ran a hand through his hair.

"I'm capable of doing things on my own." I crossed my arms over my chest, putting space between us. "And besides, I had something to discuss that was between me and her."

"Okay, sorry. I know you're capable." He met my gaze again. "Do you want to talk about it? You look upset."

"No I'm fine, I just need to process everything."

He swallowed. "I'm here if you want to talk."

"I know." The concern on his face was genuine—it stirred something deep inside me. Something I wasn't yet ready to confront, especially after my conversation with Astria.

I wrapped my hand around his forearm. Him, I needed him, that's what I needed right now.

A distraction.

Heat coiled low in my stomach at the thought of what we left unfinished last night.

I leaned forward, pulling him towards me as I pressed my lips to his. I wrapped my arms around his neck as I waited for him to kiss me back.

After a moment he did. His hands moved to my hips, his fingers digging in slightly as he pulled me against him. I wrapped my fingers in his hair as his tongue found its way into my mouth.

I snaked my hands under his shirt, untucking the fabric from his trousers, allowing my hands to roam over his skin.

"I need you inside me, now," I murmured against his mouth.

He stopped, his feet staying firm in place as I tried to move him toward my room.

"Lennox, wait a second." His hands on my waist held me in place.

I gripped his forearms. "What?" I asked impatiently.

He looked at his feet, causing a lock of now disheveled hair to fall across his face.

"Luka, c'mon." I reached for him again, only for him to pull his hand away and take a step back.

My stomach fell.

"I can't do this right now," he said softly.

"Do what?"

"Be your distraction."

I forced out a laugh, the sound was bitter in my throat. "You're not a distraction."

He took another step back, another step away from me.

"Are you sure? Because that's what this feels like right now."

"Luka."

"No, I—I can't do this right now. Not after last night." He turned away, raking a hand through his hair.

"Luka wait." I placed a hand on his arm.

"I'm serious Lennox." I flinched at the sternness of his voice as he moved out of my reach.

"I'm sorry. I—you can keep feelings separate Lennox, but for me, it's a lot harder. Last night—last night you let yourself feel. Now you've had time to think about it and you shut your feelings off. I know you, Lennox. I can see it in your eyes. I know how your mind works, and how you act. And you might not admit it, but you know me too. And what I need right now is space."

Every word felt like tiny slices against my skin.

That's what happens when you let people see you.

They see past your defenses.

I let go of Luka's arm. He didn't look back as he walked away.

Maybe Astria was right, maybe I had less time to sort things out with Luka than I thought.

# 53

# LUKA

The door slammed behind me, rattling the frames on the wall.

"Who got your panties in a bunch?" Nico called from the couch.

·Great. The last thing I wanted right now was to be around people. I needed time to think. *Alone.*

I collapsed on the couch next to Nico with a sigh.

"You look like you need a drink," Delcan commented from the chair.

"Does that mean your offering?"

Declan raised a brow as he reached for the decanter on the table and filled it with several fingers worth of liquor.

I drowned half the glass in one swallow.

"You going to tell us what's got you all torn up?" Nico asked.

"Lennox and I kissed last night." Declan's brows rose slightly. "And today she summoned Astria."

"She what?" Nico interjected.

"There's more." I swallowed the rest of my drink and reached for the decanter. "Astria must have said something that upset her and she refused to talk about it. She wanted to fuck instead and I turned her down."

"You turned her down?" Declan repeated. "I didn't think that was possible for you."

I laid back on the couch. "I didn't think so either, but—she said she wasn't ready to commit to anything yet, which is fine—I understand. Last night it was fine, but today she wanted to use me as a distraction and I couldn't be that today."

Not after last night. Last night—last night I saw the emotion in her eyes, felt it in her kiss.

All of that was absent when she kissed me in the hallway.

"But I feel like I let her down when she needed me today." She needed me, she needed me as a distraction and I denied her.

"I think keeping sex out of the picture is better for both of you until you get your feelings sorted out." Declan and I both turned our attention to the wolf.

"Since when did you become a relationship expert?" I asked Nico.

"I never said I was, I have common sense. Something you and Lennox both seem to lack." He leaned back on the couch, letting his arms rest on the top of either side.

Declan let out a huff as he sat back and crossed one leg over the other. "He's got you there."

"Who invited you two in here anyways?" I muttered.

"You have the good liquor—that in itself was an invitation." Nico raised his glass in my direction.

"Well if you're going to be in here, shut up. I don't want to talk about this anymore." I rested my head on the back of the couch.

"So what do you want to talk about?"

"Did Lennox fill you in on our conversation with the Galtain family?"

"No, we've all been a little preoccupied with you getting kidnapped, you and Lennox almost fucking, and Lennox apparently summoning Astria on her own. No one tells me anything," Nico pouted.

"You do have a flair for the dramatics don't you, " Declan added.

I shook my head before filling them in on the details of mine and Lennox's visit with the Galtain's."

"So you didn't destroy the journal?" Nico asked. "No wonder Luciana has been so grumpy."

"And since when are you in on the state of Luciana's feelings?" I pressed.

"I'm not in the know of her feelings, but I noticed she's been a little more irritable lately."

I shook my head, I didn't want to dive into my own shit right now, I wasn't going to make him.

"Anyways, back to our conversation, we didn't destroy the journal. Neither of us had the heart to take the journal away from the family."

"Well, it doesn't seem like there was much use for the journal anyways so it should be fine right?"

"Well," I scrubbed my hand over the back of my neck. "There's one more thing I need to tell you."

Both of them leaned forward in their seats. "There was one important detail we gained from the journal. It said if someone manages to reverse the spell on vampires, all living vampires will cease to exist."

"You didn't think to start with that?" Declan protested. I ignored him as he swore under his breath.

"What are you going to do with that information?" he pressed.

I shrugged. "I don't know. It left us with a lot of questions. I'm assuming that's why Lennox summoned Astria again."

Declan stood, his wings rustling behind him. "Let's go find her and ask her."

"Not tonight, please." I looked at them. "Tomorrow. Do you remember why I'm here?"

"Tomorrow then." Declan sat back down. "But no more avoiding this after tonight."

"Fine. Nico, pass the bottle."

☾

Declan was knocking on my door early the next morning, much to the disappointment of my throbbing head.

Nico groaned from where he slept belly down on the couch. Declan was the only one with any self-preservation skills last night.

"How much longer did you two stay up drinking last night?" Declan wrinkled his nose at the sight of the table of empty bottles.

"I don't know." I collapsed into the chair. "I've had a terrible sense of time lately." It was true, especially since my kidnapping the hours had blended together. Nico and I kept drinking until we passed out. Long after Declan left us.

"Well get up and get ready." Declan rolled Nico off the couch.

"Ow!" Nico groaned as he fell to the ground with a thud.

"You could both use a shower." Declan wrinkled his nose. "We're all meeting in an hour. Get your sorry asses ready."

☾

Lennox didn't look up as I entered the room, instead, she continued her conversation with Luciana as her plate of food sat untouched in front of her.

"Good morning."

"Good morning," Kara and Luciana responded.

"Good morning," Lennox said quietly, her gaze finally sliding to me.

"Now that everyone is here, can we discuss why Declan dragged us all here this morning?" Luciana crossed her arms over her chest. "I'd like to hear about your conversation with Astria so I can stop holding this grudge against you Lennox."

"You told her?" Lennox looked at me with narrowed eyes.

"No. I told Declan and Nico." I looked at the two of them. "I'm assuming Declan told her since he was concerned about the information shared about our Galtain visit."

"What information?" Kara and Luciana said in unison.

"You didn't tell them?" I asked Lennox.

"I've been a little preoccupied," she mumbled.

"Obviously," Luciana huffed while Kara eyed her sister curiously.

"In the journal, it said if the curse against vampires is reversed, all living vampires die."

Luciana whipped her head in Lennox's direction. "What in the stars was occupying your mind so much you failed to share that little tidbit of information?"

Lennox's gaze slid to mine before giving her attention back to Luciana. "That's what I was so preoccupied with, that's why I summoned Astria. I needed to get answers from her."

"And did you?" Declan asked.

"Yes and no." She tucked a lock of hair behind her ear. "When I pressed her as to why she wanted us to destroy the journal, why we shouldn't share that information with everyone —she said the people who are looking for the journal wouldn't care about that. According to her, she thinks that will only make their goal come to fruition sooner. It will make their jobs easier in the long run. These people hate vampires so much they'd love to see them extinct."

*Astria's tits.* This was worse than I anticipated.

"Can't Astria prevent that from happening?" Declan asked

Lennox shook her head. "She didn't make it sound like she could."

"So what are we going to do?" Luciana set her glass back on the table.

"I'm hoping I can convince them to destroy the book, if I tell them the circumstances." Lennox chewed her bottom lip.

"Do you think they will do that?" I asked.

"I don't know, but I have to try." We had to try or I might *die*.

"So there's nothing we can do now?" Kara asked.

Lennox shook her head. "I don't think so."

"Luce, have you gotten anywhere with the Dhampir body?" Declan turned his attention to Luciana.

The witch slumped in her chair. "No. Everytime I feel like I'm getting close my magic runs out and I pass out. I can try one more time and then I need to get rid of the body. It can't last much longer."

I kept my eye on Lennox as the conversation continued. Nothing Lennox revealed was new information. We had both already known my dying was a possibility.

She was still hiding something.

☾

"Lennox, wait." I reached for her as I followed her out of the dining room.

"What?" She didn't stop, talking as she continued down the hallway.

"We need to talk."

"Oh, now you want to talk." She stopped and turned toward me, crossing her arms over her chest.

"What else did Astria say to you that you're not telling us." Something flashed across her features.

"Nothing." She shifted from one foot to the other.

"Stop lying."

"I'm not lying."

I took another step toward her, forcing her to tilt her chin up to meet my gaze. "I know you better than you think, you're hiding something."

"Whatever Astria said to me is none of your business."

"It's my business when it makes you act like this to me." She was silent as she looked at her feet. "Whatever she said upset you and I want to help you. Talk to me."

"Despite what you might assume, I don't need your help."

"That's not what you made it seem like last night."

"Fuck you," She spat, her eyes churning violently, the green turning a dark shade, I could sense her magic rising to the surface. "I needed you last night and you left me." She shoved me with a hand to the chest.

"I didn't leave you, Lennox. If you needed me, you wouldn't have tried to get me into bed and would have talked to me instead. You wanted to use me to avoid dealing with whatever is eating you up. If you would have talked, I would have listened. But my feelings are at stake here, I have to have some self-preservation when it comes to you, Lennox."

She looked like I slapped her, but I continued, "I'm not saying any of this to try and hurt you Lennox, I need you to understand that. I want to be able to be there for you when you need me, but I can't risk my own well-being in the process. I'm trying to protect myself, Lennox. Don't you realize the power you have over me? You can shatter my heart with a single word. One fucking word and I'm done for. That's how much control you have over me. You don't realize how hard it was for me to say no to you yesterday but I did. And then I drank myself into a stupor to keep myself from going to you anyway."

Still, she said nothing. Her face blank—I had no idea if my words were even sinking in. If she heard any of them at all.

"Come and find me when you're ready to talk," I told her before leaving her in the hallway.

54

# LENNOX

I stared at the space that Luka left empty.

*Come and find me when you're ready to talk.*

How had I fucked everything up so quickly?

All this time I had been trying to protect myself from Luka hurting me, while he was trying to protect himself from me.

I let his words echo in my mind as I made my way up to my room.

First Astria and now Luka—

"Lennox, what are you doing?" My sister's grip was firm on my arm, her fingers pressing into my skin as she pulled me into her room from the hallway.

"Kara?" My brows furrowed as I looked at my sister. Her eyes were blazing. "What do you mean what am I doing? You're the one pulling me aggressively into your room with no warning."

"What are you doing messing around with Luka like that?"

My mouth fell open. "I'm not messing around with Luka!"

She crossed her arms over her chest. "The conversation I overheard makes me think otherwise."

"You were spying on us?"

"It's not like you were in a secluded location. You were in the middle of the hallway."

I crossed my arms over my chest, making myself a mirror of Kara. "It still doesn't make it okay."

"You know what's not okay?"

I looked at the ground, not wanting to hear her answer, but I knew I'd get it anyway. "Fucking Luka isn't okay. Tell me you're not fucking him, Lennox."

"I'm not fucking him!"

She sighed deeply, giving me a look, *my* look.

"We only kissed," I admitted. She didn't need to know there was more than kissing.

She threw her hands up in the air. "Goddess, Lennox. How could you be so insensitive?"

"Insensitive? How does that make me insensitive?"

She turned from me and paced the room, her hands firmly on her waist. "He would burn the realm to ashes for you if it meant you'd be happy. He'd string himself up if it was what you wanted. And you take advantage of that, Lennox."

"I am not taking advantage of him!" At least I didn't think I was. Was that what I was doing?

"You know he would do anything for you and you take advantage of him. You're playing with his feelings, Lennox."

"I—" My entire body deflated. Everyone was telling me a different version of the same story.

"He loves you, Lennox. You know that, even if you refuse to admit it. He loves you so much he's willing to sacrifice his own happiness for you. He's not someone you fall into bed with Lennox. If you need a good fuck so bad, go find someone in the tavern for all I care. But you can't fuck Luka if you're not going to go all in with him."

"I'm not fucking him!"

"You're not now, but tell me you haven't been thinking about it? Especially if you were kissing him."

"I—" I couldn't lie to my sister.

Kara's face softened. "Len, I know you love being independent. That you don't like to rely on others. I know you think you don't want him, that you don't need him. But Lennox—that's the biggest fucking lie I've ever heard. You want him. You've been a miserable person the past few months without him. You want him Lennox, whether you want to admit it or not. You and Luka are so intertwined—even you can't separate yourself from him."

Was she right? No matter how hard I tried to get Luka out of my life I never could. And I didn't try very hard to remove him from my life did I? What had Astria said? That I needed to accept that what lay in front of me might be what I wanted all along. And Luka was right earlier, I didn't want to think about my feelings from last night. The lengths I would go for him—it was fucking terrifying, so I tried to ignore it. I tried to ignore the hollow ache in my chest that formed when we were apart, the fear that took over my body when he was taken, and the spark he brought back into my life.

"Len, have you ever considered he might be your mate?"

I froze, slowly turning toward my sister. "You're not serious? Luka is not my mate. There's no way. That's insane. He's not my mate."

I would know if Luka was my mate. I would have known the first day I saw him. Or I would have had some inkling since. That's what all the stories about people finding their mates say.

"Is it that far out of the realm of possibility? Think about it, Lennox. You both have had this pull towards one another since the first day you met. You can't resist each other. You tried to stay away from each other, but you can't."

"Maybe we can't stay away from one another, but that doesn't make us mates, Kara. We're fated together for something else—that's what Hecate and Astria implied. Not that we're mates."

"Maybe you are mates, but they could never tell you. Maybe that's the future they keep hinting at."

"No," I grit out. "Stop trying to make the future what you want it to be. You're trying to put thoughts into my mind."

"You need to stop resisting Lennox!"

"I'm not resisting! I'm being rational! Astria's tits Kara, you're infuriating."

"I'm the infuriating one? Lennox, you're the definition of infuriating." She let out a hollow laugh. "You know what Lennox? I'm tired of keeping my thoughts to myself. I think you love him. I think you love him and that terrifies you because that means he can hurt you. Do you know how tiring it is to watch you and Luka resist each other over and over again? Especially since we witnessed for a short period of time what it was like when you were together? You two were magnetic Lennox. I've never seen anything like it. The way you lit up around him— you still do sometimes. I never thought I'd get to see you happy again after Mom, Dad, and Nol died, but I did, and Lennox—"

Tears welled in her eyes. "Seeing you happy again made all the pain and heartache of the past three years worth it. Everything you put yourself through had a purpose—that you would meet Luka." She wiped away a tear that fell from her eye.

"You need to decide Lennox. You either need to leave Luka for good, or be with him."

"I can't leave him, Kara. We're getting married," I said softly.

"So either be clear with him and set expectations that nothing can happen between you two or tell him you love him and be with him."

"It's not that easy, Kara."

"But isn't it?" she said exasperated.

"Goddess, Lennox, you're so stubborn." She stood and headed towards the door.

"I'll give you some time to think. But you need to make a decision, Lennox. You're getting married at the week's end."

"You think I don't know that," I said softly.

"Don't be mad at me, you got yourself into this mess, Len."

My sister was so much like my mother. I know she'd be telling me the same thing. I know she'd be disappointed in my decisions too—the way I had handled things with Luka. But it wasn't that simple. I was tied to Luka for the rest of my life. Everyone else made it seem like this was such an easy decision to make.

But what if I let myself fall back into him? We were getting married. If everything fell apart, there would be no escaping him. I'd have to continue to stand by his side for the rest of our lives. But could I live with the opposite? Could I stand next to Luka, pretending not to care about him, pretending I didn't want to let myself fall into him for the rest of our lives? I didn't know if I could live with that pain.

The way I looked at it, both options could end in pain. Why wasn't there an outcome that wouldn't leave me heartbroken?

☾

Luka all but avoided me for the next several days. We trained but hardly spoke. He left right as we finished, leaving the palace shortly after and not returning until late. I wanted to talk to him —I tried to work up the courage to talk to him, but I lost the nerve every time and before I knew it he was gone. What would I say to him anyway? I still had no idea where I stood—where we stood. Part of me hoped when I finally did talk to him I would know what to say—that I would know what to do. But the opportunity never presented itself.

We are getting married tomorrow.

Tonight there was to be a dinner with all of the monarchs that had arrived for the wedding along with several other important families.

Arlo and Lorenzo would be there, along with Caterina and Endora. The kings from the Aquatic Court, Alon and Ceto, arrived yesterday, as did the prince and princess from the Twilight Court. Nico's sister was due to arrive tomorrow morning as a representative from the Lunar Court. There would be a representative from every court except the Court of Embers, which was a surprise to no one. They hadn't left their court in centuries.

My gown had a fitted corset, with sleeves that fell off my shoulders. The dark green fabric, the color of a deep forest, had an iridescent glow to it—like the fabric itself sparkled.

A crown far more extravagant than I typically preferred rested on my head. My hair was pinned up intricately—the pins Gulia had used already poking into my head. When Kara did my hair she was careful to make sure none of the pins poked me.

But Kara and I had yet to talk to each other since our fight.

It had been a lonely few days left alone with my thoughts.

Luka and I were sitting on opposite ends of the table—what felt like a million miles away. All the people I would have liked to have next to me to keep me company were seated away from me, scattered around the table. I would need to make sure I had a hand in creating the seating chart next time. This one felt like a cosmic joke.

The kings from the Aquatic Court were seated on either side of me. Ceto sat to my left, his dark hair was braided in many small braids, each one banded with gold and silver clasps on the end that complimented his dark skin. His large frame made the chair he occupied look small. His husband, Alon sat on my other side, the complete opposite of his partner with his lighter skin and smaller frame.

I didn't mind conversing with the kings, I would need to make a point to visit the Aquatic Court, but political conversations were the last thing on my mind. While I talked with the kings I couldn't help but let my gaze travel towards Luka. He looked so happy—so content at the opposite end of the table as he conversed with Caterina and Endora. He didn't appear to be bothered by our lack of communication over the last several days, oblivious to the turmoil happening in my mind.

As the servants cleared the last of the plates, Arlo stood, glass in hand. I hadn't had a chance yet to talk with Arlo and Lorenzo, and I didn't know if Luka had either. But his presence in my home set me on edge.

"Thank you all for coming tonight. We are all so excited to celebrate the marriage of my nephew Luka, and our esteemed High Queen Lennox." He looked around the table, giving me a lingering look, causing my back to straighten in my chair. "Our intention with this union is to help unite our continent, especially the relationship with the Blood Court and the rest of Lethenia." Somber murmurs broke out around the table, and Arlo quickly continued, "We have already seen the impact of this union—the Blood Court and the Star Court have never been closer."

I forced a smile onto my face. If only he knew Luka and I hadn't talked in days and we were trying to figure out his involvement with my parents' murders.

Arlo raised his glass. "To Lennox and Luka."

"To Lennox and Luka," everyone echoed.

Arlo's toast marked the end of dinner. I placed my glass on the table before standing and making my way to Kara and Luce.

"Hey." I turned at the sound of Luka's voice. I don't know how he had gotten across the room so quickly.

He took another step closer to me, gently placing his hand on my back. "Is this okay?"

I nodded. "How are you doing?"

"Okay."

"You made it through the dinner, that's one less thing to worry about."

"You're right. If only we could just skip past tomorrow."

"That would be nice wouldn't it."

We both took another sip from our drinks as we looked around the room at the people chatting. We were the couple they were all supposed to be celebrating today, but they all seemed unconcerned about engaging in conversations with the two of us.

Fine by me.

"You've certainly kept yourself busy this week."

A muscle ticked in his jaw. "There were lots of tasks that needed my attention. I think you're familiar with that."

"It's a big palace, which made ignoring me pretty easy." It was a cheap shot, but I needed it. I needed to let it out or I'd keep holding it in. And holding in my emotions never ended well.

"I wasn't trying to ignore you, Lennox."

I shrugged, turning my attention back to the party.

"I told you I needed time. I've been gracious in giving you all the time you need, can't you have the decency of giving me the time I need?" That was the thing about Luka, if I took a shot at him he'd shoot right back if need be.

"You're right, I—I missed you this week," I admitted.

He smiled slightly. "You did?"

I rolled my eyes. "Don't let it get to your head too quickly."

He shook his head, causing a lock of dark hair to fall across his face. My fingers itched to brush it away.

"I missed you too," he admitted softly.

"I'm sorry for how I acted." I let the words slip out before I lost my nerve. But I needed to say them before we were married. Before we were bound together. "You deserve more than my anger," I continued. "And you were right—I was using you as a distraction without realizing it."

"I think you do a lot of things without realizing it."

"Luka, I—"

"There's my favorite couple!" Caterina interrupted. Her arms were spread wide, inviting us both in for a hug. I wrapped my arms around Caterina, watching Luka embrace Endora from over my aunt's shoulder. Caterina let me go and braced her hands on my shoulders. "How are you feeling dear?"

My eyes glanced toward Luka who was engaged in conversation with Endora. "I'm okay." She gave me a small smile.

"I know this isn't what you ever wanted or planned, but I'm proud of you Lennox. You stepped into the role of High Queen so beautifully. I mean look at how you handled this situation. We are lucky to have you as our High Queen."

"Thank you." Her words landed peacefully on my soul, continuing to soothe the ache that had taken place since the crown was placed on my head.

"Luka is a good male, I have confidence he will treat you well, despite the circumstances that brought you here."

"I know." My gaze slid towards Luka again.

"Your parents would be so proud of you." I sucked in a breath. "You know they're watching you." I blinked back the tears in my eyes.

"I love you."

"Oh, my dear." Caterina pinched her lips together and pulled me in for another hug. "I love you too. Until the stars turn to dust my sweet Lennox."

# 55

# LENNOX

I'm getting married tomorrow.

I sat on the chaise lounge on the balcony of my bedroom, staring out at the garden and the starry sky.

Dinner had ended a while ago, Caterina walked me to my room and bid me goodnight. I had wanted to continue my conversation with Luka, but he was engaged in a conversation with Lorenzo and Arlo and I had no desire to interrupt them and get myself roped into a conversation. Now, I was trying to work up the courage to go to his room and finish our conversation. Part of me hoped he'd show up on his balcony, save me a trip, force me into a conversation like he was so good at doing.

Instead, I was sitting alone, the night before my wedding, questioning everything.

I couldn't say I had thought too much about my wedding day, but the events planned for tomorrow were not what I had ever thought my wedding might look like.

Hundreds of people would gather tomorrow for the ceremony to see the High Queen marry the vampire prince. The party afterward would carry on through the night.

I would be forced to talk and mingle with people I had never met before. Spending my wedding celebrations talking and catering to others' feelings and wishes.

I stood and leaned over the balcony, peering into the garden.

All I wanted was a small intimate ceremony where I could celebrate with my friends and family—the people closest to me, as I committed to spending the rest of my life with the person I loved.

Tomorrow would not be that.

And on top of all that, the absence of those I had lost would be felt more than anything.

A soft knock on the door echoed through the room. "Come in," I called out, looking over my shoulder as Luka hesitantly stepped through the door. He looked around for a second before spotting me on the balcony and making his way to me.

"Hey." He stood beside me, placing his hands on the railing next to mine.

"Hi," I murmured softly.

"What are you thinking about?"

"Our wedding."

"Really?" He looked at me out of the corner of his eyes. "What about it?"

"It's—it's not what I had expected my wedding to look like."

"Me either." He was silent for several moments before speaking again. "That's what I came here to talk to you about."

He ran a hand through his hair. "I know this isn't what you wanted in a marriage. I know how important it was for you to get to choose love for yourself. It eats at me every day that I am part of the reason why that choice was ripped away from you."

He turned to face me. "That's why I wanted to give you a choice. You don't have a choice in marrying me tomorrow, but you have the choice in marrying me now."

"Luka—what—what are you talking about?" My mind raced—trying to figure out what he meant. What did he mean *marry him now?*

"I'm giving you a choice, Lennox. You can marry me

tomorrow—in front of all those people, we can do the whole big wedding thing, that will be our wedding. Or—or you can marry me tonight. We can have the ceremony we both want. We get our friends and have a private ceremony. We don't have much control when it comes to this wedding—*our marriage*—but we can have control of this one thing. You can choose to marry me tonight if that's what you want."

"You would do that for me?" I somehow choked the words out through the lump in my throat.

"I would rip the stars from the sky for you if that's what you wanted. Because I love you, Lennox." He brushed his thumb across my temple. "I love you so fucking much and it pains me every day to have taken this choice from you. Let me do this for you. Let me give you back this choice."

Goosebumps scattered over my body. "You love me?"

He shook his head and smiled, letting out a small puff of air. "Yeah, I love you. And I think you already knew that." His hand moved to cup my chin, his other hand resting lightly on my hip, his thumb brushing lightly underneath my ribs.

I had assumed he loved me, but hearing those words from him—it cemented together a broken part of my soul.

"Yes." His brows furrowed. "Yes, I'll marry you tonight Luka."

The smile that broke across his face was so bright—that too mended another part of my soul.

He didn't hesitate as he pressed his lips to mine. His hand wove in my hair as he pulled me closer and I fisted my hands in his shirt.

He loves me. Luka *loves* me.

I suspected what he felt for me, but hearing him say it out loud—hearing that confirmation—my magic swelled inside me, my emotions going haywire over his confession.

Hesitantly, I pulled my lips from his. "If we're going to get married tonight I need to get ready," I panted.

"You look perfect the way you are." He placed another kiss on my jaw.

"If we're going to do this, we're going to do this right." He continued kissing his way down my throat as I spoke.

"I'm going to send for Kara and Luce to help me get ready. Can you, Declan, and Nico get everything else set up?" He halted, his groan vibrating against my skin.

He pulled back and placed another kiss on my lips. "I've got it, Sweetheart. Meet me in the garden in an hour?"

Slowly, he removed himself from me, placing lingering kisses before finally his hands slipped from my body and he walked backward towards the door, smiling the entire way.

"See you in a bit."

I couldn't help smiling to myself as the door closed behind him.

☪

I stood in front of the mirror as Kara and Luce fussed around me. It was astonishing what we put together in such a short time.

Neither of them showed any surprise when I told them what happened between Luka and I on the balcony. Kara had squealed and embraced me before rattling off all the things she needed to gather, but she made sure to tell me, *I told you so*, in a sing-song voice before rushing off to gather supplies.

I had no idea where Kara had found my dress on such short notice, I was thoroughly impressed. The garment was made of a deep blue, the color of the early night sky. The bodice was fitted and the skirt simple. Silver and gold stars adored the shimmering fabric. The back was cut in a deep v. Attached to the sleeves was a train of sorts—made from sheer fabric adorned with stars that matched the bodice.

My hair was down and in loose waves. A simple silver crown

made up of stars and moons rested on my head with clear gems adorning it.

"You look stunning." Kara hugged me from behind, resting her chin on my shoulder.

"I can't believe you're doing this. One wedding is bad enough, choosing to have two…" Luce shook her head but smiled.

"Are you saying you don't dream about your wedding?" Kara asked.

Luce let out a harsh laugh. "I hope and pray to the Goddess I don't have to get married."

"And here I thought Len was the pessimist," Kara chided. "You really don't want to get married?"

"A regular marriage sure, an arranged marriage, no thank you." She threw me a sideways glance. "Sorry."

"I've accepted my fate," I steeled my shoulders and assessed myself in the mirror. I had. Luka was my fate. As was our marriage.

I was starting to think this all might be a blessing. Luka, this arranged marriage. Maybe it was a blessing after all.

"I'm ready."

# 56

# LUKA

I had to admit, we did a pretty good job putting together a wedding on such short notice for three people who knew nothing about weddings.

We had cleared out the center of the garden, moved away the tables and benches to allow room for our small ceremony.

The moon and stars decorated the sky, a mirror of the bulbs of light we had strung throughout the garden.

Declan and I stood waiting in the garden—Nico had gone to find Caterina and Endora. I thought Lennox might want them here.

I shifted back and forth from foot to foot, waiting for Lennox to arrive. Part of me thought she might change her mind, decide tomorrow was what she wanted—and not this choice I was giving her tonight.

The choice to choose me.

To choose us.

I had been mulling over what to do all week, coming up with one last attempt at giving Lennox the life she had dreamed of. The opportunity to choose love for herself. I still didn't know if that's what she was doing in choosing to say yes to tonight, but the look in her eyes—and the way she let me kiss her afterward

—maybe the space apart these past few days had been good for both of us.

The sounds of voices filtered through the garden, but my chest deflated when the people rounding the corner were Caterina, Endora, and Nico, not Lennox.

Caterina approached me, a wide smile brightening her face. She braced her hands on my shoulders, placing a kiss on each of my cheeks. "This was such a sweet thing for you to do for my niece. I like the two of you together." She winked before letting me go and moving to the side where Nico and Declan stood.

Finally, Kara and Luciana appeared from around the hedge, my eyes scanned behind them for Lennox.

My breath stilled at the sight of her.

I had thought she was beautiful the first time I saw her walking down those stairs, but tonight—she was a shining star in the dark sky, and she was coming right toward me.

She smiled softly when her eyes met mine, creating a smile of my own to spread on my lips.

Goddess I loved her.

"Hi." Her voice sounded almost shy.

"Hi." I took her hands in mine, intertwining our fingers. "You look—" I searched for the right words, coming up empty for something that could fully encapsulate how beautiful she looked. "I've never seen anyone so magnificent."

A blush rose to her cheeks. "You look pretty good yourself."

"Are you sure you want to do this?" I didn't even want to ask. I wanted this—for us, I wanted this one moment. But if she changed her mind, I'd give her that out. I'd give her that choice.

She looked at our intertwined hands. "I'm sure."

"Let's do this, Sweetheart."

Our friends made a circle around us as our hands remained intertwined.

"We never discussed this, but is it okay if we incorporate a tradition from the Mystic Court?" Lennox asked.

"Of course." Our ceremony tomorrow would be a combination of the ceremony from each of our courts, but tonight we could make it whatever we wanted. Each court had its own traditions, but the core of the ceremony was the same, the pair vowed to one another and to the Goddess their commitment to one another.

In the Blood Court, it was typical for the couple to exchange blood—something Lennox and I would be partaking in tomorrow.

"Luce is going to light a candle and conduct a spell that will thin the veil around us—allowing the people we have lost into the ceremony."

Her eyes searched mine. "My parents and Nol—your parents. They can be here if they want."

I tucked a strand of hair behind her ear, letting my fingers linger on her face.

The idea of having our families here, even if we couldn't see them— "Thank you."

We stared at one another—neither of us saying anything.

"When you're ready," I hadn't even noticed Luciana completing the spell, but I could sense her magic in the air around us.

"Can I go first?" She asked.

I intertwined our hands again.

"Luka—you're the best person I've ever met. Whenever I find something I don't like about you, you show me a redeeming quality about that trait. You infuriate me. You push me in every aspect of my life. Not to try and get me to be a better person, but to embrace the person I am. You shine a light on the parts of me I think are unlovable and you love them anyway. I tried so hard to keep you out of my life—to keep space between us. To keep myself from falling in love with you, but nothing worked because you refused to leave me. Despite my constant asking and pushing you away—you never left me. Thank you for never giving up on me. I needed that—I needed you."

She looked at her hands. "I need you. I want you, Luka. You

are intertwined into my being as much as my magic is. You have no idea how much it means to me that you have given me this choice. Allowed me to choose to marry you tonight. I'm done fighting against all of this. I'm tired of fighting against us— something that feels so natural. I choose you, Luka. I choose you tonight. I will choose you again tomorrow and every day after that. It's you. It's always been you and I'm sorry it took me so long to realize it."

"You mean that? You're choosing me?"

Her emerald eyes gleamed in the moonlight. "It does. It means I'm yours, Luka. You can have all of me, every mangled, darkened part of me."

She raised up on her tiptoes and planted a soft kiss on my lips. "I choose you, Luka Rossi."

"I choose you too." I kissed her again, twin smiles breaking out on our faces.

"I love you, Lennox Adair, I've been falling in love with you since the first time you scowled at me."

She shook her head and rested her forehead on my shoulder, failing to hide her smile.

"I'm serious." She looked at me again. "My entire life everyone put me on a pedestal—they walked on eggshells and they tried to please me. And then there was you—stabbing me to make yourself feel better after we'd only just meet. You made me work for your love, your affection—I had to earn it, which has made it all the sweeter to know you have deemed me worthy enough to be cared for by you, Lennox Adair. Because as we know you do not give your love away easily. You are my every-thing, Lennox." I pressed my lips to the palm of her hand. "I promise you will not regret choosing me tonight."

I closed my hand around the dagger at my side, her eyes tracking my movement before she reached for her own.

"You ready?"

This was the ceremony we had planned for tomorrow, a combination of Blood Court and Star Court traditions.

I gave her my palm, wincing as she sliced her blade across it, before I repeated the action across hers. I pulled out the vile of stardust Luciana gave me earlier and shook the contents over our bleeding palms. The stardust shimmered as it fell before sticking to our bloodied palms.

I combined our bloodied hands, intertwining our fingers once again.

My palm tingled—the stardust already at work as our blood mingled together—tying us together for eternity.

"I, Luka Rossi, bind my life to yours, Lennox Adair," I repeated the ancient words. "I vow to protect you, to push you, to stand by your side and love you for the rest of eternity," I added. Lennox's eyes glimmered at my additions to the vow.

"I, Lennox Adair, bind my life to yours, Luka Rossi. I vow to stand by your side, to care for you, and to protect you for the rest of eternity."

The tingling in my palm intensified, the sensation moving from my palm and spreading up my arm, sending a shiver down my spine.

I met Lennox's gaze again, her face telling me she was feeling the same sensations I was. I gripped her hand tighter as the magic continued to work through our bodies—working to bind us together.

Finally, the sensation subsided. We removed our hands, both looking at the twin marks marring our palms.

Not every married couple was blessed with a mark. It was all up to the Goddess and the Stars to bless a union with a marriage mark.

Lennox and I appeared to have been blessed. The skin where we had cut one another had healed, but was slightly raised—leaving scared skin behind in the form of a thick line of black ink shimmering in the moonlight. The cut extended up my palm before divulging into two lines that wrapped around my middle finger. At the bottom of the cut, the line extended down my wrist until it slowly faded into my vein.

A light wind whipped around us. Lennox and I both looked as Astria appeared beside us in a hardly corporal form. "Your mark is one of greatest significance. Your blood is now bound together as displayed by the ink over your cuts—so you shall never forget your commitment to one another." She brushed her starry finger over Lennox's palm, tracing the line as it snaked down her wrist. "It fades into your blood—a symbol of your blood now being one."

She squeezed Lennox's hand before releasing it. "I hereby bless your union, from now until eternity may your lives now be bound."

And with that, she was gone.

"That's it?" Lennox looked at me. "We're married now?"

"There's one last thing we're forgetting."

"What?" Her brows pinched together.

"We seal the marriage with a kiss."

She smiled before my lips descended on hers. The kiss was soft at first before turning ravenous. I pulled back—only to be dazzled by the smile lighting up her face.

My *wife's* face.

She wrapped her arms around my neck and pulled me back for another kiss. My arms wrapping around her waist before I lifted her off the ground and spun her.

Cheers and hollers broke out around us and Lennox laughed against my mouth as I swung her around.

*Married.*

Lennox and I were married.

---

# 57

# LENNOX

Luka and I were married.

*Married.*

Holy fucking shit I'm married.

I buried my head in Luka's shoulder as he continued to spin us around as our friends and family cheered.

When he finally put me down the world still spun around me, but I fixed my gaze on Luka. His smile cracked my chest clear apart.

I no longer cared if my heart was in shattered pieces because I had Luka. Whatever state my heart was in it still had the capability to be loved by him and to care about him so deeply. It was terrifying what my fragmented heart could still feel.

"What are you thinking?" Luka stroked a finger down my cheek.

"I'm thinking I'm happy. And I can't believe we're married." A laugh slipped out of my mouth.

"Is that a good thing or a bad thing?"

"I think it's a good thing." He draped his arm around my shoulder, placing a kiss on the crown of my head.

"I think it's a good thing too."

A while later we found ourselves in one of the formal sitting rooms for a makeshift wedding reception.

Kara and Luciana had scoured the kitchen for some food—coming up with some chocolates and cakes for tomorrow they hoped no one would notice were missing. Meanwhile, Nico arrived with his arms full of sparkling wine, but with no glasses, forcing us to pass them around and sip from the bottle.

After toasting us, Caterina and Endora bid us goodnight—allowing us "younglings" to celebrate to our heart's desire.

That had been hours ago.

The deserts had been devoured, only half-eaten cakes and crumbs remained next to too many empty bottles.

"Wait!" Kara wobbled slightly as she stood, a half-empty wine bottle in hand. "Luka and Lennox you need to dance."

I scoffed from where I rested against Luka with his arm around my shoulders. "I don't think so."

"Why not?" Luka played with the ends of my hair. "It is our wedding night. I think a dance is called for."

"There's no music," I protested.

"I'm on it." With the snap of Luce's fingers, soft music filled the room.

Before I could argue further, Luka was standing and offering me his hand. "May I have this dance, *wife?*"

I shook my head, smiling slightly. "I don't have much choice do I?' I put my hand in his, allowing him to pull me to standing.

"You always have a choice with me, remember?" His hand moved to rest on the small of my back. I looped my arms around his neck, meeting his smile with one of my own.

He pulled me closer, there wasn't an inch of space between us as we gently swayed to the music. I wrapped my arms tighter around his neck and placed my head on his chest, closing my eyes as I listened to the beat of his heart.

Tomorrow our dance would be watched by prying eyes. We

would dance the formal dances, I would have to make sure to remember each step as we moved around the crowded dance floor. But this moment—this dance—this was perfect. This quiet moment with our friends was just for us.

I will forever be grateful for Luka giving me tonight. For giving me the opportunity I thought I had lost.

The soft music faded, I moved my head so I could look at Luka. A smile broke out on his face as the music changed—the soft instrumentals switching to an upbeat tune.

Before I knew what was happening he was spinning me around, leading me in a series of swirls and twirls as I smiled and laughed before he dipped me dramatically and kissed me. I met his lips greedily as I clung to him.

When we finally parted I was panting—my heart beating fast in my chest.

"I'm ready to go back to our room now."

"I can walk you back to your room if that's what you want."

I bit my bottom lip. "I said *our* room, are you coming with me?"

Luka's eyes darkened. "Astria's tits you know I'm coming with you." I took his hand in mine and led him towards the door.

"Thank you all for a great night," I called out behind me. "We'll see you all tomorrow."

☾

"So which room is our room?" Luka asked as I dragged him through the palace.

I shrugged. "Doesn't matter to me, as long as we're together."

He pulled me back and spun me until I was facing him. He braced his hands on my hips and pulled me to him. "Look at you being all sentimental."

"Don't get used to it, Bloodsucker."

"What if I told you it turned me on." Desire coiled low in my stomach as he pulled me closer so I could feel how turned on he was.

"I'd say you're a liar." I pressed my hips against his. "Or that there are a multitude of means I'm aware of that turn you on other than me being sentimental."

He groaned as I rolled my hips against his. "Keep that up Sweetheart and I'll take you right here in this hallway."

"You're the one that stopped us in the first place."

"As much as I'd love to fuck you against this wall right now, the plans I have for you tonight are not happening here."

I shrieked as he hauled me up, my world turning upside down as he threw me over his shoulder.

"Luka! Put me down this instant." I railed against his back with my fist, which only earned me a slight smack on my ass.

"You prick!"

"C'mon, Lennox, I know you like it when I spank you." He swatted at me again, the motion sending desire straight to my core.

I bit my lip, not willing to give in at this moment.

"That's what I thought."

I pinched his behind instead which only earned me a dark chuckle that I felt down to my bones.

How many months had it been since we'd been together?

*Too many.*

It wasn't until the door to my bedchamber clicked shut behind us that Luka finally deposited me on the bed.

I glared at him as his eyes roamed up and down my body hungrily.

"You are so incredibly beautiful, do you know that?"

I said nothing, my chest heaving and he continued to look his fill. My skin burned under his gaze. Everywhere it traveled I felt it upon my skin.

Finally, he approached me. His hand tangled in my hair as

he pulled me towards him until our foreheads rested against one another.

"I love you, Lennox," he whispered in the space where our breath mingled.

*I love you too.* The words lingered on the tip of my tongue. This was all happening so fast. I had never been in love before, but these feelings I felt towards Luka, had to be love. What else could they be? But I wasn't ready to take the last leap yet. I needed to make sure what I was feeling was true. I wouldn't hurt him again if I could prevent it.

"I—"

"You don't have to say anything back. I just want you to know."

I fisted the fabric of his shirt. "I've never felt like this with anyone else."

"It's terrifying isn't it."

I nodded against his forehead.

"Take all the time you need, Lennox. I'll still be here when you're ready." He kissed my forehead.

I closed my eyes as his lips moved to my temple, my ear, my neck.

Lower and lower his lips moved until he reached the fabric of my dress.

He bunched the fabric at my waist. "Lift up."

I obliged, lifting my hips so he could remove the garment, leaving me in nothing but red lace undergarments.

His gaze heated. "Please tell me you picked this color for me." He grabbed my thighs and pulled me towards him.

I smirked. "You may have been on my mind when I picked them out." He groaned and pressed his head against my stomach.

"Dangerous devious creature." He nipped at my stomach with his fangs.

"Are you going to feed from me tonight?"

"If that's what you want, I might be able to oblige." My

blood heated. "Perhaps I'll try biting you somewhere else tonight. Maybe here?" He scraped his fangs along my inner thigh, and I whimpered.

He smirked as he rose up, grazing his knuckles over the fabric of my undergarment covering my center. "Or maybe here. This seems like it might be a sensitive area."

His fingers moved again, dancing up my collarbone until his finger caressed up and down the delicate skin of my neck, over my thrumming pulse.

"We both know how much you love it when I bite you here." His tongue lapped at the skin where his fingers had been before his mouth clamped down and he sucked hard.

"But I might like to mark a different part of you tonight."

He moved back down my body. His hands skating across my thighs as he spread my legs apart farther—making room for himself as he kneeled between them.

"What if I start here?" My hips jolted off the bed at the feel of his knuckles dragging across my center through the lace. "You like that, hmm?"

I nodded, not being able to form words as desire overwhelmed my senses.

"Luka, please," I whimpered as he continued to stroke me through my undergarment, his thumb pressing into the soaked fabric.

"Please what?" His finger stilled its movement.

"Please touch me."

"I am touching you." His fingers dusted over my core.

"Bastard," I swore. "More, I need more."

He tisked. "Who knew my wife was so needy." *My wife*, his use of those two words caused my pulse to pick up.

"As much as I'd love to tease you until you were begging for my touch, it is our wedding night." His hands gripped the sides of my panties and he pulled them down my legs.

"Just this once I'll give in." He kissed the inside of my thigh. "But don't forget Lennox, next time I will make you beg."

His lips clamped on my center and he sucked on the bundle of nerves, his chuckle vibrating against my heated skin as I squirmed beneath him.

"Stars, I forgot how sweet you taste." His hands gripped my thighs, spreading me further as he feasted. His tongue lapped at me greedily—stroking up and down my center before returning and sucking on my clit. Every stroke worked me higher and higher into a frenzy.

"Not yet," Luka commanded.

My hips bucked off the mattress as two of his fingers plunged into me. He twisted his fingers inside me and I moaned. In and out his fingers pumped as his mouth continued to suck at my clit.

"Please," I whimpered. Desire coiled tightly at the base of my spine. Higher and higher it crested. Luka removed his fingers and I whimpered at the loss.

I jolted as his fangs scraped over my clit.

Holy fuck—he wasn't going to—

Pain and pleasure erupted as Luka's fangs pierced the bundle of nerves.

I screamed and his hand splayed across my stomach to keep me in place as he took the first pull of my blood.

Another scream tore from my throat—the pain and the pleasure were too much. Stars danced at the back of my vision as the room around me blurred.

Desire burned hotter with every pull of my blood.

He gripped my ass to pull me closer as he drank.

My fingers fisted in his hair; I pulled at the strands as he continued to drink—pressing his mouth closer.

"Luka!" I screamed as my pleasure erupted. My legs locked around his head as his mouth continued to feast. I couldn't even tell if he was still drinking from me any more—the amount of pleasure was too much.

Finally, as the waves of pleasure subsided, Luka removed his mouth from me, wiping the remains of my desire mixed with my blood from his mouth with the back of his hand.

"That was——" I panted.

"I know." He smiled—a smile full of male cockiness.

"Prick." I dragged my eyes over him. "You're still wearing far too much clothing." I quickly discarded his shirt.

I dragged my hands up and down his sculpted torso, my fingers running over every ridge and dip of his muscles.

"My turn." I pushed him to lay on the bed before clamoring for the buttons of his pants.

My mouth watered at the sight of his cock as it sprung free.

I stroked him a few times with my hand—earning a rough groan from him. I gave him no warning before I took his cock in my mouth.

"Fuck," he hissed, his hips bucking off the bed.

I ran my tongue up the underside of his cock as I tried to take him deeper. Choking as his length hit the back of my throat.

"Keep that up Sweetheart and I'm going to come in your pretty little mouth."

I removed my mouth from him with a pop. "Do it," I challenged.

His eyes sparkled. "Do you mean that?" I nodded.

"You want me to fuck that wicked mouth of yours?" Heat pooled deep in my stomach at his words. "I need you to say it, Lennox."

"Yes," I breathed. "I want you to fuck my mouth."

He groaned and layed back on the bed. "Then get to it, Your Majesty."

I closed my mouth over him again, taking him inch by inch into my mouth until he hit the back of my throat.

Luka's hand found my hair, wrapping his fingers in the strands and pressing me forward—forcing his cock further down my throat. I choked, but he held me there.

Tears formed in my eyes before he finally let me go, but it

was only for a second before he started fucking my throat in earnest.

His hips jutted up in time with his hand forcing me forward at a brutal pace as I choked on his cock.

My body burned with desire. I snaked my hand between my thighs, needing to find release of my own.

"Is choking on my cock making you wet?"

I murmured a yes around his cock.

"Good. I want you to come with me. Touch yourself so you'll come while my cum is spurting down your throat."

I strummed at my clit as his cock hit the back of my throat again and again. "Fuck Lennox, your mouth feels so good around my cock. Are you ready to come with me?"

I whimpered around his length as my climax traveled up my spine.

"Good."

I picked up the pace of my fingers as Luka continued to thrust.

He came with a groan, the sound sending me over the edge with him.

My screams were muffled by his cock as I sucked every last drop of his release until I finally removed my mouth.

"Such a good fucking girl." Luka stroked my hair. I shivered under his words and his soft touch.

I crawled up his body until my lips could meet his. "I need you inside me," I spoke against his lips.

"I thought you'd never ask." I straddled him, my knees on either side of his thighs. I took his cock in my hand—already hard despite coming down my throat. I positioned him at my entrance before notching him inside me an inch.

I moaned at the first feeling of him. His grip on my hips tightened—I knew he was trying his best to restrain himself from seating himself inside me in one brutal thrust of his hips.

He was letting me have control of this moment. It was always been a balance of control between the two of us.

I slid myself down another inch—allowing myself a moment to accommodate myself to his size as he stretched me.

"Lennox," Luka warned as I squirmed slightly.

"Patience."

"I'm about out of patience," he growled, his grip on my hips tightening.

I slammed down without warning, his cock seated fully inside me as our hips met.

"Fuck." We moaned in unison.

"You feel so fucking good, Lennox."

I moved on his cock in a slow languid motion. I could see in his eyes my pace was killing him. It was taking all his restraint not to take control of the movements, but he continued to allow me.

His fingers tangled in my hair at the back of my neck. He used his grip to tilt my head back, pushing my breasts towards him.

His tongue flicked out at one of my peaked nipples before his mouth descended on my flesh. He continued his ministrations on my breasts as I continued to ride him slowly. Taking my pleasure from him as I wanted it. I swiveled my hips—as he nipped at my breasts with his fangs.

I slowly increased the pace of my hips as he nipped at my nipple—causing a slight moan to slip from my lips.

"Goddess, I love the sounds you make," he murmured against my skin.

His fang scraped against my other nipple and I moaned again.

"If those are the sounds you make when I only graze your nipples I wonder what would happen if I bit them."

I stopped my movement, tilting my head to meet his gaze. "You wouldn't."

His eyes sparked with the challenge. "You know I would."

I slid myself all the way off his cock until only the tip

remained. I met his gaze as I slammed back down with a violent thrust.

"Do that again." My breath hitched as I slowly moved back up, his cock slipping from me inch by inch as his tongue flicked over my hardened peak.

When only the tip remained he moved his hands back to my hips.

"Ready?"

I held my breath and nodded.

In one brutal move, he slammed me back on his cock at the same time his fangs pierced my breast.

I screamed as he moved me back up only to slam me back down as he took the first pull of my blood.

I threw my head back in ecstasy as he continued the motion over and over again until I felt like I was no longer connected to my body. His thrusts were violent—hitting deep inside me. It was too much—it was all too much. My release crashed over me like a tidal wave.

He licked at my nipple again as he removed his fangs, licking at the skin he had pierced as he continued to thrust his hips up into me, searching for his own release.

As my soul came floating back to my body I leaned forward and kissed him, biting at his lower lip as our sweat-coated bodies stuck to one another as he continued to move inside me.

He came with a groan—our bodies continuing to move in slow languid movements as I tangled my hands in his hair and kissed him.

Eventually, we both came back down, our breathing labored —I could still feel the rapid beat of his heart under mine. Slowly I slipped off of him, my body heavy with exhaustion as I found a place next to his side.

Our limbs were still intertwined—we were a mess, but I didn't care.

My eyelids were heavy with a haze of lust and exhaustion. Luka pulled up the blanket around us and I moved in closer to him. Slowly our breath evened out as we both drifted towards sleep.

This was never how I imagined this would go. I had never let myself think what it might look like if I let Luka in again. If I let myself accept this marriage wasn't any arranged marriage— that it was an arranged marriage to Luka. To my friend. To someone I care so deeply for. I never let myself think about what it might look like to be happy in this marriage with him. I was too preoccupied with trying to protect myself.

What did this mean for us? What would our future look like? Would he move to the Star Court? Would we have children one day? Did I want children? Did Luka want children?

"Stop." Luka's voice pulled me back to reality as he smoothed his hand through my hair.

"I can hear you overthinking. I can feel you tensing."

I sighed. "There's so much we haven't figured out yet."

"I know, but we don't have to decide all that now. We have time."

*Time.* We have time.

We have our whole lives in front of us. The idea was terrifying and thrilling at the same time. I had a whole life with Luka to look forward to that had yet to be decided.

"We will figure it out," I repeated. Some of the tension left my body.

I listened to the rise and fall of his chest as sleep crept in.

"Thank you." I didn't know if he was sleeping yet. I hoped he was still awake. "Thank you for giving me time."

"I would have waited countless decades for this time with you."

I was too afraid to say it, but I would have waited countless decades for him too.

58

## LUKA

I stared up at the ceiling as Lennox lay sleeping beside me. The sun had risen a while ago, we didn't have long until people would come looking for us both to begin preparations for the wedding, but I wanted to savor as much of the morning with her as I could.

The events of last night kept replaying in my mind as I lay there. I was still unsure as to how we got here, but I was so fucking grateful.

Lennox Adair was my wife. *My wife.*

And by her own accord.

She chose me last night.

I brought my hand to my face admiring the mark that now tied me to her. The metallic ink infused with stardust glimmered as I shifted my hand in the sunlight streaming through the windows.

"What are you doing?" Lennox mumbled as she shifted beside me.

"Admiring our mark."

She squinted and brought her own hand in front of us.

"It is pretty miraculous isn't it." I brought my hand next to hers so we could admire the two together.

"Do you regret binding yourself to me yet?" I nudged her slightly.

"Not yet, but give it a few hours."

I tried not to wince. I knew she was joking—I brought the joke on myself for fucks sake, but I wasn't yet confident she wouldn't regret her choice one day.

"Hey." She spoke softly. Her hand cupped my cheek and she turned my chin to face her. "I have never regretted you. Remember that? Even when I was mad at you, I never regretted you. I—I care about you. You're the one that might end up regretting binding yourself to me."

I took her hand from my face and kissed the center of her palm, directly over our mark. "Never."

She smiled, but I saw the caution in her eyes.

I pulled her to me and she rested her head against my chest.

"How about this?" she said finally. "Let's promise one another if we're ever feeling uneasy or unsure or anything about our relationship we will tell one another. That's the only way we're going to make this work. No matter how stupid or insignificant it might be, we tell one another."

"Okay."

"I know you're afraid of the people you love leaving you, but I'm not going to do that to you, Luka. I'm here," she said softly.

I sighed. "I know, but it's hard to remember that sometimes. Especially when everything is going so well." I paused as memories assaulted me. "Everything was going so well before my father died." Before he left me. Before everyone started leaving. Everything was going well before I messed up things with Lennox and she left me.

"We're two fucked up people aren't we?"

"But all of our broken parts fit together somehow." I fiddled with the end of her hair. "How much time do we have before Gulia comes knocking on the door?"

"Not long." Lennox glanced at the door.

I scrubbed my hands over my face. "But you could be in the bathtub when she arrives."

Lennox sat up and looked at me. "You mean *we* could be in the bathtub."

"You're insatiable aren't you."

"We are newlyweds, it comes with the territory after all." She placed a quick peck on my cheek before moving from the bed. She let the sheet fall to the floor as she waltzed towards the bathing chamber. I watched the perfect swells of her ass as she swayed her hips. Her long hair flowed down her bare back in a tangle of waves. Goddess, she was stunning.

She stopped at the entrance to the bathing chamber, placing her hand on the door frame as she looked over her shoulder at me.

"You coming?"

I had made a point to avoid temples since my mother's funeral.

Why it is that they are places where we celebrate new beginnings and also mourn the ones we've lost?

The temple at the center of Alethens was similar to the one in Cel Nox, temples were fairly uniform across all courts. They all had rows of bench seats that led to an altar at the front—used to worship and give thanks to the Goddess and the Stars.

At the center of every temple, there was a scene depicting the Goddess. At the Star Court temple, a portrait of the Goddess creating the first High Fae was etched into the stone. The Fae was kneeling in front of Astria as she held the Fae's face in her hand, her fingers brushing her newly pointed ears. The one in the Blood Court wasn't as flattering towards the Goddess—not that it depicted her in a negative way, but it was a simple portrait of Astria etched into the red stone.

The room quieted around me, a sign the ceremony was about to begin. The rest of the guests filtered in and found their seats. The temple was packed full. Several crowns glimmered in the front rows as their heads turned towards the temple entrance.

Nothing would ever compare to how Lennox looked last night, but nonetheless, she was still breathtaking.

The gown was a stark difference from last night—gone was the dark glimmering gown of moonlight in favor of colors typical of the Star Court. The gown was sleeveless, leaving Lennox's chest exposed with no adornments. The bodice was fitted at the top and was a dark blue that disappeared as the gown flowed, ending in a white as pure as snow. Flecks of gold were scattered throughout the gown, tying in the Star Court's signature color.

Lennox's hair was pulled back and gold gems that resembled water droplets adorned her ears. It was simple and elegant.

I let my gaze drop to her hand, where her marriage mark was hidden. The mark that marked her as mine.

There were murmurs around me, but I couldn't hear them. All of my attention was focused on the female walking towards me.

On Lennox.

On my wife.

# 59

# LENNOX

When Luka looked at me it made everyone else fade away. There were hundreds of people in this temple, but all I saw was him. When I finally made it to the dais he took my hands in his, leading me up the stairs towards the priestess standing at the center, clothed in her golden robes.

Marriages didn't require someone to guide a couple through a ceremony, but in public ceremonies like this, it was common for someone to narrate the ceremony, typically a priestess. I looked at Luka as the priestess addressed the crowd. I couldn't help but notice how different this was from our ceremony last night. All these people dragged here to witness us say a few words to one another—and to make matters worse, we were already married.

Not that anyone would ever know. Luce had placed a glamor over the mark on our hands and would release it at the right moment to make it convincing that we were receiving them during the ceremony.

I turned my attention back towards the priestess as she finally stopped talking. She reached for the goblet behind her and held it between us in her hands.

"By sharing this wine you are both agreeing to bind your lives to one another," she declared.

She handed the goblet to Luka first. He sipped from the glass, smirking at me over the rim. "I bind myself to you, Lennox Adair." He passed the goblet to me.

I sipped from the glass and repeated the words, "I bind myself to you, Luka Rossi."

I handed the glass back to the priestess, and she continued talking, something about the sanctity of marriage.

"And now for the exchanging of blood, as is customary in the Blood Court." The priestess handed a dagger to Luka, her face paling slightly.

The dagger was ornate and I wondered if it had ever been used before, the pommel and blade were gold with raised swirls and whirls adorning it. Even if it was decorative, it was sharp, the steel cut across mine and Luka's palms easily as we repeated the same steps we had last night. When we intertwined our bloodied hands the priestess spoke again.

"All of Lethenia!" she exclaimed as she raised her arms dramatically in the air. "I introduce to you the newly bonded couple in marriage, High Queen Lennox Adair and Prince Luka Rossi!"

Luka took a step towards me, the cheering from the crowd faded into the distance as he kissed me, brushing his lips lightly over my lips before devouring me entirely. His hand at the back of my neck pulled me closer, deepening the kiss as I melded my body to his.

I felt Luce's magic wash over me as Luka's tongue slipped into my mouth. I pulled him closer as my tongue stroked against his.

The priestess made a low sound in the back of her throat. I peeked out of the corner of my eye to find her still standing with her hands in the air as she gave us a disapproving look.

"This is the house of the Goddess, remember," she murmured.

I laughed against Luka's mouth before I removed my lips from his. He took my hand and we turned to face the crowd.

"No turning back now, Sweetheart."

"I'm fine as long as I'm going forward with you."

Several additional tables had been added to the dining room for the meal tonight, all decorated in finery. We'd all eat a grand feast together before moving to the ballroom for the wedding ball. Luka's arm was around my waist and I had a glass of sparkling wine in my hand as we surveyed the room.

"Who's that?" I gestured to the brunette female making her way toward us. I had never seen her before, but something about her felt familiar. Her coiled chestnut hair fell past her shoulders. Her eyes were dark, but her square jaw and the shape of her nose felt familiar.

She smiled when her eyes landed on Luka, sending a pang of jealousy straight to my gut.

Luka smiled big, causing the knot in my stomach to tighten. "That's Zienna."

"Luka!" Zienna exclaimed, throwing her arms around my husband.

"Zee." The two stepped back from one another. "I'd like you to meet my wife, Lennox Adair."

I smiled tightly at the female, still uneasy at her familiarity with Luka. "Lennox, this is Zienna, Nico's sister."

My chest lightened instantly—*Nico's sister.*

"It's nice to meet you."

A wide smile broke out on the female's face. "You too." She embraced me in a hug before I could protest.

"I see where Nico gets his enthusiasm from," I said into her hair. "It must run in the family."

Zienna laughed as she released me. "What else has he told

you about our family?" She asked, her eyes darting back and forth between me and Luka.

"Not much." Zienna stared at Luka expectantly. "He hasn't told me a word about why he left." Zienna's shoulders shrank.

"I tried to get him to talk at first, but he refused. And you know Nico. He will only talk when he's ready." Luka raked a hand through his hair. "But I didn't think it would take him this long to say anything."

Zienna opened her mouth, but Luka stopped her. "I don't want to hear it from you." Understanding flashing across Zienna's features.

"Thank you for looking out for him."

"Of course, you know he always has a place with me." He pulled me into his side. "Even if I am married now."

I nodded in agreement. "As much as I hate to admit it, Nico's become one of my best friends. He will forever have a home with us if he needs it."

"Thank you. Things haven't been the same since he left. He left a large hole in the pack. I was glad for the opportunity to see him."

"Have you spoken to him?" Luka asked.

She shook her head. "I'm not even sure if he knows I'm here." She sighed deeply. "Anyways, congratulations, Luka. I'm glad to see you happy." She placed a gentle hand on my arm and squeezed lightly. "I don't know you Lennox, but I hope I can get to know you. If you're important to my brother and Luka I know you must be a good one."

Luka pulled me closer, placing a kiss on top of my head. "She is."

"You must also be a saint for putting up with the three idiots. Although Declan's not as much of an idiot as he is a mood killer."

I laughed. "I like her," I told Luka, which made her smile widen.

"Right, back at you Queenie," she said with a wink.

"Are you sticking around after the wedding?" It was rare I met females I got on with so easily.

Her lips pulled tight. "That all depends on how my conversation with Nico goes." Her gaze traveled behind us. I looked over my shoulder to find Luce and Nico engaged in a conversation.

"If you'll excuse me."

"It was nice meeting you,"

Zienna made a move toward her brother. "You too."

"If you're still around tomorrow we should have lunch," I called after her.

Zienna paused, looking over her shoulder at me. "I'd like that. It's a date."

"Look at you, making friends."

I poked Luka in the side. "I say that in a good way, Lennox. Zienna is a good one. You will get along well. But I do admit, the idea of you two being friends is slightly terrifying."

# 60

# LUCIANA

I was never certain Lennox would get married. She was so independent. She loved being wild and free· as she flitted from one partner to the next, never getting too attached.

·But in the last twenty-four hours, I'd watched her get married not once, but twice, to the same male.

And she looked happy after all of it.

I was happy for her. Lennox deserved happiness after everything she'd been through.

I hoped it would continue.

"What are you thinking about, Lucy girl?" I rolled my eyes at the ridiculous nickname as Nico held out a glass of sparkling wine. I took the glass, taking a large sip before responding.

"I was thinking about how happy I am for Lennox. And Luka."

"I'm happy for them too, I never thought it would all end up like this."

Neither did I, but for much different reasons than Nico. In reality, this should have been Nol's wedding. The thought was ·like a dagger to the heart.

Fuck, I missed him.

"Fuck." Nico shifted, moving behind me like he was trying

to hide. Only it failed because even if I was tall, I wasn't taller than the wolf and I couldn't hide his massive frame.

"What are you doing?"

"Hiding," he hissed, turning away from me as he pretended to look around the room.

"Nico?" A female voice said tentatively from behind me.

Nico and I turned toward the female in unison, I was immediately taken aback by her striking features.

Her eyes lit up at the sight of Nico, a large smile forming across her face. "Nico." She sighed. "It's so good to see you." She reached out to hug him, but he took two steps back.

"What are you doing here?" I had never heard Nico talk with such venom. Who was this female?

Her smile faltered. "I was invited."

"You didn't have to come."

"Luka is my friend too, or did you forget that when you wrote all of us off?"

There was a dangerous gleam in Nico's eye. "You want to do this here, Zienna?"

Zienna… witches tits, *Zienna*. I looked between the two. "This is your sister?"

"You told her about me?" There was a hopeful lilt to Zienna's voice.

"Yes," Nico ground out. "I told her about you in name only."

Zienna opened her mouth and closed it, saying nothing as Nico glared at her.

"Nico," she said quietly. "Can we talk? Please?"

"Is that why you came? Did they send you here to try and talk to me?" He shook his head, his silver hair swinging with the movement. "Pathetic."

"You know they wouldn't." There was a desperation in her voice now. "I came here to support Luka, and I wanted to talk to you, yes, but no one else knew I was coming. Nico, I want to talk. I'm your sister."

Nico growled, his nostrils flaring as his hands fisted at his sides.

"We both know that's not true now, don't we."

"Nico." Zienna's voice wavered.

"I'm not talking about this at my best friend's wedding." He drained the rest of his glass. "Get the fuck out of here Zienna."

Nico stormed off and I followed after him. I had no idea what was going on with his family, but he needed someone right now, that was clear. I guess that person had to be me.

"Wait." Zienna grabbed my arm before I could get too far.

Tears glistened in her eyes. "Will you please tell him I'm sorry? And that I miss him. We all miss him. And—and if he's ever ready to come home, we will be waiting for him. No matter what, he's still a part of our pack."

"I'll tell him." She smiled softly, blinking back tears. "Now, if you'll excuse me."

I turned from Zienna, trying to see where Nico had taken off to. He hadn't made it too far. His hulking frame was over by the table hosting alcohol; I found him fixing himself a drink.

"Care to tell me what that was all about?"

"Nope." He drained his glass and moved to fix another drink.

"Whatever happened—"

"I said I'm not fucking talking about this right now so I'm not fucking talking about it. Alright?"

I reared back at his tone. "Alright," I said tentatively.

I looked around the room, looking for something to write on, but coming up short.

I reached for a bottle of wine on the table, peeling off the label.

"What are you doing?" Nico asked.

"Do you have something to write with?" His brows furrowed, but he reached into his jacket pocket and produced a pen.

I took it and scribbled what his sister had said to me on the label, when I was finished I folded it into a tiny square.

"Here." I handed the folded label to Nico. "Your sister told me to tell you this and since you don't want to hear it, I wrote it here." He opened his mouth to protest, but I stopped him. "You need to promise me you won't destroy it because I know you might not want to read it now, but someday you will." He sighed and reached for the label, but before he could put it in his pocket I stopped him, closing my hand over his.

"You have a family that cares about you, Nico. They are waiting for you to come back to them. Don't you dare take that for granted."

His expression softened as he searched my face, I looked away before he could look too long and made my way back into the crowd, leaving him behind.

# 61

# LENNOX

"Congratulations my boy!" Arlos's voice boomed from behind us. Luka's shoulders caved inwards as Arlo's hand clamped on his shoulder.

"Thank you, grandfather." Luka let go of me to hug his grandfather.

"Yes, congratulations indeed." Lorenzo appeared from behind Arlo. I tensed at the sight of both of them.

"Thank you," Luka said.

"Yes, thank you both." Luka's arm snaked around me, his hand firm on my hip as he pulled me against him.

"What is this?" Arlo grabbed Luka's hand and inspected it—turning it over and back. "A marriage mark?"

"It is," I answered. "It appears the Goddess blesses our union."

"Blessed indeed," Arlo murmured as he continued to examine Luka's hand.

"And you have one as well?"

"I do, an identical match."

Arlo's eyes glimmered. "May I see it?" He dropped Luka's hand and extended his own towards me.

I shifted, but Luka stopped my hand. "You don't have to show him if you don't want to."

"It's okay." He dropped my hand, allowing me the space to extend it towards his grandfather.

Arlo's finger brushed across the marks. "Remarkable." He reached for Luka's hand again, examining our hands side by side.

Finally, he looked back up at us, his eyes wide and glimmering as he released our hands. "I've never seen anything like it. You two are both truly blessed. Be thankful for the blessing the Goddess has given you."

"We are," we said in unison.

Arlo elbowed Lorenzo, who had been standing strangely quiet. "Looks like we might have a love match on our hands after all."

Lorenzo's frown deepened. "From the kiss at the end of the ceremony, it sure looked that way. Unless she's another one of Luka's conquests."

Luka's hand tightened on my hip. "That is my wife, and your High Queen, you're talking about," Luka growled.

"Lorenzo," Arlo said sharply. Lorenzo's smirk only deepened.

I took that as my window of opportunity. I despised the man. I didn't care if he was Luka's uncle—and I didn't think Luka cared much either. "Just because we are now connected by marriage, do not think I will hesitate to end your life."

Luka's hand relaxed slightly on my hip as Lorenzo opened his mouth, but I continued before he could get in a word. "Not only are you speaking ill towards your High Queen but your High King as well, *my husband*. I know he would not hesitate to see you bleed either. You don't want to cross us, Lorenzo."

"She speaks true," Luka added. "I've been on the wrong side of Lennox's sword, it's a place I never want to be again. She never misses."

"Apologize to your queen, Lorenzo. Or have you gone stupid?" Arlo snapped.

The three of us stared at him, waiting for his next word. Lorenzo squirmed under our cumulative gazes. "I apologize, Your Majesty," he finally managed.

"You owe Luka an apology too," I added.

Lorenzo's gaze was filled with disdain as he looked from me to Luka.

"I'm sorry Luka."

"I believe his title is Your Majesty," I added. Lorenzo grumbled as he looked at his feet.

"I'm sorry, *Your Majesty*," he grit out.

"Now go," I demanded. "We no longer require your presence."

Lorenzo stormed off, stomping like a child as he mumbled under his breath.

"I'm sorry about his behavior, I don't know what has got into him tonight," Arlo apologized.

"He will learn quickly Lennox will not tolerate disrespect." Luka straightened his shoulders.

"As she should not." Alro dipped his head. "I'll leave you two to continue to mingle, congratulations again."

Luka pressed his lips to mine. "Have I told you recently that I love you?"

"Not in the last few minutes."

"I love you." His words sent warmth coursing through my body as he kissed me again.

"I don't know about you, but I've had enough mingling for now."

"I agree." I finished off my glass of sparkling wine.

"Should we get the meal started?" I followed as he led me towards the head of the table.

The crowd grew quiet as we moved towards our spots, everyone shifting around us as they too found their seats. It took only a minute for silence to fall over the dining room. Luka and

I traded our empty glasses for the ones set at our place settings before Luka spoke.

"Lennox and I would like to thank you all for coming to celebrate our marriage today. We are excited about our future together as a married couple and what we can do together to unify our courts and all of Lethenia. As I see it, the future ahead of us is bright."

Luce smirked from the spot beside me. "Such a softie," she murmured. I rolled my eyes and turned my attention back to Luka.

"Thank you all for coming," I added.

"To Lennox and Luka!" Arlo boomed as he raised his glass.

"To Lennox and Luka!" The crowd cheered.

Luka beamed at me as he lifted his glass towards mine.

My lips had only brushed the thin glass when Luce grabbed my arm. "Wait!" She cried. Luka halted, his glass halfway to his mouth, brows furrowed.

"What?"

Her grip on my arm tightened. "I'm not certain, but I think your drink is poisoned."

Luka's voice lowered. "What?"

"Your drinks are poisoned," she repeated.

"I heard that," Luka hissed. "Why do you think that?"

Murmurs broke out around the table as everyone eyed us cautiously.

"I can smell it in the air," she hissed. "I could smell something, but I wasn't sure what it was until it hit me. Lennox, trust me, I know the smell of poison. I've been studying poisons for years—maybe it's not in your drink, but it's in the room somewhere."

I set my glass down. "I trust you."

"Me too," Luka agreed. "Is there any way you can test it?"

"Let me see your drink." I passed her my glass as she pricked her finger, letting a drop of blood fall into mine and Luka's glasses along with her own.

The blood dissipated into Luce's glass, turning the sparkling wine a light blush color. In mine and Luka's glass, the drop of blood maintained its shape and floated perfectly in the center of our glasses.

"Holy Shit," Luka murmured.

"What's going on?" Declan's voice came from behind us. We turned to find Nico and Kara following behind him.

"Someone tried to poison Lennox and Luka," Luce said.

"Not so loud Luce," I scolded.

"What?" She crossed her arms. "Someone tried to commit treason, everyone should know."

"What did you say?" Arlo's voice came from across the table. "What's this about treason?"

"Someone has tried to poison the High Queen and King." Declan's voice was pure steel as he addressed the entire room.

Shock rolled across the room as people looked at one another. "No one leaves this room until they are dismissed," Declan continued as the murmurs grew.

"Whoever did this will pay." Luka's voice rang across the room. "We—"

I ducked, covering my head as the glass windows shattered. Screams broke out around the room as a roar accompanied the shattering glass. I stood up, brushing the pieces of shattered glass from my hair. In front of the broken window, a creature stood from its crouch. The monster looked around the room, its red eyes aglow. Blood dripped from its fangs and claws.

Of all the times for a Dhampir to appear, in the middle of our wedding celebrations was an awful inconvenient time.

Three more Dhampirs bounded through the broken window into the room.

"Astria's tits," Nico swore as he reached for his sword at his side. "Bad day not to bring my ax." Nico took off towards the monster, sword in hand. Declan was already out ahead of him, his sword swinging towards the creatures. Roars echoed in the background in unison with the screams of our wedding guests as the Dhampirs ripped into partygoers.

"Please tell me this is some kind of surprise wedding activity," I murmured more to myself than anyone.

"I don't think so, Sweetheart." Luka's hand closed around the sword at his side.

"Someone give me a sword," my voice rang out over the chaos. The daggers sheathed under my gown were less than ideal for this fight. I thought a sword was a necessary wedding accessory but *no*—I had to leave Minerva in my chamber. Several people scrambled around me, offering me swords. I took the first one I saw and broke into the fray, Luka at my side. Glass crunched under our feet as we ran towards the window as two more beasts appeared through the hole. Black blood rained across my dress as my borrowed sword pierced the Dhampir's chest. Its screech pierced my ears as I withdrew my sword. The Dhampir swiped out with its arm, the sound of tearing fabric reached my ears as its claws tore at my dress.

"I liked this dress," I grit out as I thrust my blade into the Dhampir again. It let out one last gasp before crumpling to a pile on the floor.

I turned, spying Luka as he removed his sword from a Dhampir's chest, blood sprayed from the wound, but still, the creature stood. Several other guests had jumped into the fray, the sounds of fighting echoed in the room as we all worked to fight off the beasts.

Screams echoed off the walls, I turned finding a Dhampir ripping into a guest, its irregularly long fangs piercing into the guest's shoulder as it gripped them tightly in its claws. I ran toward the Dhampir; it was oblivious to my arrival as it spat flesh on the marble floor before going back in for a second bite.

The guest's form was limp in the Dhampir's grasp as I sent out a wave of magic, freezing the ground beneath the Dhampir. Its feet slipped out from under its mutated form, the now dead body of its victim falling to the ground beside it. Before the Dhampir could attempt to stand I rammed my sword through its chest.

The room around me fell silent as the last beast fell, but screams still echoed in my ears.

I panted as I turned and surveyed the room. Massive forms, soaked with black blood, lay in a pile at our feet. People were huddled under the tables, some peeking out over the top to see what was going on. Broken glass was scattered across the floor, littered across the limp bodies of several guests. Black and red blood was splattered on the marble floors and across the tables, staining the white tablecloths with death.

This was not at all how I imagined our wedding would go.

Panic seized my chest as memories of last fall flashed to the forefront of my mind.

My city in ruins after the attack.

Bodies crushed under the rubble.

*Again.* It was happening again.

"It's not your fault." I jumped as Luka's hand brushed against my hip. The words *I know* got stuck in my throat.

"We need to get everyone somewhere safe." I turned to Declan. "I don't think these are the last of them." I tried to make my voice appear calm as I surveyed the room.

"I agree," he said as he surveyed the room.

"What can we do to help?" Several people had approached us: Zienna, Caterina, Endora, Caspian, Arlo, the Kings from the Aquatic Court, and several others whose names I didn't know.

"This is an attack on all of us," Ceto declared. "Whoever sent those creatures knew we'd all be in attendance here."

"We're at your service," Caspian stepped to his side.

"Thank you." I looked around at the people gathered around me. "All of you. But first and foremost I need to make sure we get everyone out safely."

"I can do that," Kara interjected.

"We can't forget someone tried to poison you and Luka," Declan interjected.

Fuck. He was right.

"We can help with that." Caterina made her way through the destruction, Endora at her side.

"Endora has a special kind of magic that is helpful in getting information out of people in a timely manner." Her and Endora shared a look. I had never heard of such magic, but I'd be curious to learn more about it at a much more convenient time.

"Thank you, that will be extremely helpful. Those that are innocent can be given safe lodging if they desire until we have made sure the city is clear. Any found guilty of crimes can be sent to the dungeon." Cateriana dipped her chin.

I looked at Kara. "You know where to bring them for safe keeping?" She nodded, and I took her hand in mine. "Be safe." She squeezed my hand before turning towards the room.

"Anyone who doesn't want to stay and fight, please follow me," she announced to the crowd.

Murmurs broke out before people hesitantly moved out from underneath the tables and chairs and followed Kara out into the grand entry, Caterina and Endora following behind.

"Your Majesty, shouldn't you go to safety as well? Let us protect your home and you," Ceto argued.

"I'm honored by the sentiment, but I would not ask anyone else to fight a battle I would not fight myself."

Luka stepped up beside me. "Lennox is being too kind, my wife isn't one to miss out on an opportunity for revenge." My chest warmed at his words. *His wife.* And I did love an opportunity for revenge.

The Aquatic Kings nodded. "Noted Your Majesty. We will fight alongside you."

"Thank you." I gave them a warm smile. "Declan?" I turned towards him, confident he could direct us in a proper plan of attack.

"We don't know if any more Dhampirs might arrive, or if anyone will arrive with them. The monsters are vicious, but can easily be disabled by one or two people." Declan proceeded to fill in the rest of them with everything we knew about the monsters, their weaknesses, and things to look out for.

"Anything else you want to add?" He asked, looking at Luce. She shook her head. "I think you about covered it."

We all turned our attention back towards the winged male. "Does everyone have weapons?" Everyone nodded. "Good. Aim for the heart, and don't let those fuckers get you."

"Spoken like a true general," Zienna commented.

"The best," Luka added.

"Are we waiting here for more to arrive?" Arlo asked.

"Some of us should stay here and the rest should go into the city."

"Split us up, Captain," Zienna said.

Declan split us up into two groups, Luka, Declan, Nico, Luciana, Caspian, Zienna, and I along with the Aquatic Kings and a handful of others would take off toward the city. Arlo, along with the rest who had volunteered would remain at the palace, defending against anything else that might breach the walls.

"We will protect your palace, Your Majesty," Arlo said as Declan finished dividing the group.

"Thank you," I told him, and I meant it. "Thank all of you for being willing to help protect my people." Luka took my hand and squeezed it. "I love Lethenia, but as I'm sure you all understand, the people of Alethens, this is my home. These people mean so much to me. Thank you for helping protect them."

"For Alethens." Ceto stepped forward, raising his trident.

"For Alethens," Alon repeated, echoing Ceto's movement.

All throughout the room people raised their weapons and chanted.

"Lennox, are you ready?" Declan asked as I continued to

scan the room, marveling at the support of the people around me.

"Yeah." I took one last look at the people volunteering to protect my city. "Let's go."

# 62

# LENNOX

We saddled our horses and took off towards the city. Declan led the charge on his black steed, the rest of us trailing behind him as we whipped through the woods.

My head snapped to the left as a roar broke through the stomping of hooves. Before I could shout out a warning, the Dhampir came crashing through the woods. I called Odin to a stop, clamping my thighs tight around him as his front legs reared off the ground to avoid the Dhampir.

The Dhampir in front of us pivoted, leaping over Caspian's horse, swiping at the duke with his claws and slamming him to the ground. Caspian's horse reared back before taking off into the dark woods. Red blood seeped through the duke's clothes where the Dhampir's claws had met their mark. He lay motionless on the ground gasping for breath.

Yells rang out from the group ahead of me, I couldn't see too far in the darkness, but the growls reverberating through the air told me enough.

"Odin stay!" I leapt from my horse, sword in hand as I ran toward Caspian. The beast's teeth ripped through his leg with its back to me.

I wasted no time burying my sword in the Dhampir's back.

Its shriek echoed in my ears as its claws clamored for the sword, attempting to pull the steel from its chest. Had I missed its heart? I removed my sword as the Dhampir continued to shriek, its red eyes burning. Before I could strike, the Dhampir ran toward me. I stumbled back, my foot catching on a rock.

I landed on the forest floor with a grunt, a curse slipping from my lips as the Dhampir leapt for me. I gripped my sword in my hand as I rolled out of its path, moving to stand before the Dhampir could track where I had gone.

It turned toward me, a growl slipping from its unnatural jaw as it swiped out with its claws. Blood was seeping from the wound I had inflicted on its chest, but it didn't appear to be slowing. The other Dhampirs we had encountered died easily, this one was a different story.

A chill found its way down its spine.

Was whoever was creating these abominations making them stronger somehow?

I blocked the Dhampir's claws, the sound of their scratch against the steel of my blade causing me to wince. I swiveled, the Dhampir following me as I danced around it, paying no attention to the person approaching from behind.

Luka's sword was cutting across its neck before the Dhampir could even turn.

The Dhampir's severed head fell to the ground with a sickening thud.

"The only way to kill them is to behead them," Luka panted.

"Fuck!" I scanned the woods around us, bringing a ball of fire to my palms as I scanned for the rest of our group. Decapitating these beasts was a lot harder task than a sword to the chest. Dozens of Dhampirs swarmed the woods.

Nico was in his wolf form, as was Zienna, her coat the same dark chestnut as her hair. The two worked back to back, ripping the heads from the Dhampirs as they came for them in a constant stream.

Declan stood alone, piles of dead Dhampirs surrounding him as he pressed his boot into a still-living Dhampir's chest before thrusting his sword through the beast's neck.

Where was everyone else? My gaze landed on the Aquatic Kings fighting side by side, Ceto's hand was pressed to his side, as he struggled to fight one-handed, Alon kept one eye on him as he continued to keep a Dhampir at bay.

Behind them, laid two mutilated fae bodies.

*Three we had lost three already.*

And where was Luce?

I could feel my panic rising as more Dhampirs broke through the trees. Too many, there were too many, we couldn't take them.

The pressure in my chest increased. These people had followed me out here and they were dying. I had to stop this. I closed my eyes, a plan forming in my mind. My magic pushed and pulled against my skin to the point of pain.

I opened my eyes, twitching my fingers before closing my hand into fists. My nails bit into the skin of my palm as the ground beneath me shook. A fissure in the ground formed at the tip of my boot, spreading out further until it reached the first Dhampir. I threw out my magic, opening my palms in a burst of magic as the ground opened up, swallowing the Dhampir whole.

Slow, this was too slow.

Fuck. I couldn't do this quickly without risking the lives of everyone else.

"SHIELD YOURSELVES!" I screamed into the forest. Declan whipped his head in my direction, his brows pulling together. "NOW!"

I felt out with my magic, sensing for other magic in the darkness around me. I could feel it, six or seven different imprints of magic. Not everyone, but enough. I felt Luka's magic wrapping around me as he shielded the both of us.

Now. I had to do this now.

"I'm here." He stood behind me. "You can do this."

I dipped my chin. I didn't have a choice. I searched for my magic, pulling it together inside my chest as I inhaled. It rushed for my fingertips as I exhaled, but I didn't let it out, not yet.

I let the world around me disappear as I closed my eyes.

The sound of fighting, screaming, and roars dissipated.

The trees fell away one by one. Everything faded to white until there was nothing.

The Dhampirs. I only wanted the Dhampirs.

As I inhaled, each of them appeared, one by one frozen in time. My magic snaked out toward each of the beasts, I could see it, thin luminescent golden threads slithered out from the ground I was standing on, breaking off as I felt for each of the Dhampirs, wrapping itself around each beast.

Once each thread was connected, I slowly let the world back in, I could still only see the Dhampir, but they moved, no longer frozen in time.

My magic pushed against my fingers.

*Now.* It demanded.

A scream tore from my throat as I opened my palms, throwing out my magic in a burst.

My palms burned at the heat of my magic as the world around me shook.

The ground cracked and fissured, swallowing some of the Dhampirs whole as others erupted into balls of flames.

I pushed out another wave of magic, gritting my teeth at the force. I stumbled back, falling into Luka's firm hold.

His hands braced on my hips and I continued to push out my magic. The Dhampirs surrounding the Aquatic Kings erupted into shards of ice, the pieces ricocheted off the barriers surrounding them as the shrieks of the Dhampirs echoed through the forest.

More, there were still more, I could feel them. With Luka grounding me from behind I let out one last burst of magic, pulling from everything I had, using every drop of magic I could muster.

My throat ripped raw from the scream that tore through it as I let out the magic.

The forest blurred as my magic crested over it like a wave.

I released more and more magic until there was nothing left.

My chest heaved, it was the only sound in my ears as the roar of my magic ceased.

Slowly I opened my eyes.

The Dhampirs were gone.

All evidence of them and the havoc my magic had caused was gone. Not a trace of the Dhampirs remained. Everyone stared at me, seemingly frozen in place.

"Holy fuck." I turned at the sound of Luce's voice from behind me.

"Luce." Some of the pressure in my chest released at the sight of her. "You're okay."

She smiled tightly. "I can't say the same for Vivienne though," she added softly as she glanced over her shoulder.

Four. Four deaths.

"It could have been more," Declan argued.

But it was still four too many.

# 63

# LUKA

I had no idea how much time had passed since we left the palace. It was still dark so it couldn't have been too long, even if the exhaustion pulling at my limbs tried to tell me otherwise.

I slung my arm around Lennox as we exited the stables and headed towards the palace, after the death we had experienced tonight I needed to feel her, feel her breaths, to know she was still here, that she was still alive when so many others were not. After our run-in with the Dhampirs in the forest, we headed into the city, splitting off into pairs and scouring the city for any other signs of the abominations, coming up empty. Hopefully, the ones we killed in the woods had been the last of them.

For now.

Caterina had sent word the palace had been ridden of Dhampirs and the interrogations were complete, but they had found some guests trying to sneak out before their turn; they were now being held, waiting for us to question them.

"We should get a couple hours of sleep before we question the intruders."

"We can't sleep," Lennox argued.

"Lennox, you can't help if you're exhausted."

"I know but—"

"There's no but." I pulled her tighter to my side. "We can go check in with everyone, but then we go get a couple of hours of sleep. The people in the dungeons will still be there in the morning."

"Fine." She yawned. "But only a couple of hours. If only someone hadn't kept me up all last night." She poked my side.

"Hey—that's on both of us." I smiled. "And if I remember correctly you were the one who invited me back to your room."

"Our room," she corrected.

Warmth spread through my chest. "Right, our room."

"If I knew you two were going to be so sickening when you were happy together I never would have helped you get together," Nico said from behind.

Lennox ignored him, resting her head on my shoulder instead. I kissed her forehead, finding a spot that wasn't splattered with blood as we continued towards the palace.

"A bath might be nice too," Lennox added.

"Are you saying I smell or something?"

"Of course not. But I do prefer you without being covered in rotting blood."

"Are you sure? Because I think I quite like this version of you. The bloody bride suits you."

She shook her head. "Sure."

I didn't say anything more, but I truly did think she was beautiful. Her dress was torn. The white fabric at the bottom was now stained with red and black blood and covered in dirt. The same blood was splattered over her face and chest.

Half her hair remained in the intricate updo, the other half had fallen loose around her face and down her back. Somehow through it all her crown remained on her head. Somewhere she had acquired a sheath for her sword and it was belted over her gown.

My beautiful, fierce wife.

"This was some wedding, huh?"

"Sure was memorable, that's for sure." She poked me gently

in the side. "Good thing we took matters into our own hands last night."

"Good thing."

"Where is everyone?" Nico asked as we entered the palace, Zienna and Declan following closely behind. The grand hall was empty and the entire place was quiet.

"Hello?" Lennox called. "Hello? Where is everyone?"

"Most everyone went to bed." Arlo appeared from the dining room. "I said I would stay up until you arrived."

"Everyone is okay?" The concern in Lennox's voice was evident.

"A few injuries from the couple of Dhampirs that snuck in after you left, but no more casualties. We were prepared."

Lennox stiffened beside me. I knew what she was thinking. We were not so lucky in our pursuit.

"There were a few that tried to sneak out before interrogation, they were captured swiftly and detained."

"Caterina sent word about them. They're in the dungeon I assume?" Declan asked.

"Yes. They are under high guard until you are ready to see them."

"Did Caterina find anyone else guilty in her questioning?"

Arlo shook his head. "Not that I know of, but I'm sure she will have a full report for you in the morning."

"Perfect, thank you," Lennox responded.

"If you don't need anything else from me, I'll be off to bed now."

"Please, go get some rest. We will see you in the morning," she told my grandfather.

"You get some rest too, your Majesty." He gave Lennox a firm nod.

"I will."

My grandfather looked at me. "I trust you will make sure she sticks to her word?"

I gave him a slight smile. "Yes, I already told her as much."

"Look at you, making a fine husband already." His face softened. "I'm sorry your wedding ended up being such a disaster." It was hard to reconcile this male in front of me, the caring grandfather, and the male that might have had a hand in murdering Lennox's family. We needed to figure out his role in this sooner rather than later.

I pulled Lennox to my side and gave her a small smile. "We can't change the past."

"No, you can't." My grandfather sighed deeply. "Goodnight." With that, he dipped his head and left.

"Bed. Now." I steered her in the direction of her room.

"But—"

"No buts. Everything is in order. Sleep and then you can go into High Queen mode."

"Fine."

Before she could protest further I picked her up and used my last bit of strength and sped us to our room, leaving the rest of our group behind.

She let out a sigh when I closed the door behind me.

"Bath and then bed," she murmured.

The bath was already filled with water as we entered the bathing chamber. I set Lennox on the edge of the tub. Sitting on my knees, I removed the sheath at her waist first. The sword clanged to the floor as I released it. I drifted my fingers over the bare skin of her back before they skated over the top of her bodice.

"May I?"

Wordlessly she shifted, twisting so I could access the back of her gown. I undid the buttons one by one, letting my fingers drift over her skin as the buttons moved lower and lower. Once the last button was unclasped I motioned for her to stand. She obliged, allowing me to slip the dress the rest of the way down her body until it rested in a pool at her feet. Even speckled in blood and exhaustion weighing at her limbs, she was stunning.

I couldn't believe she was mine.

She placed her hands on my shoulders as she stepped out of her dress. I placed a kiss on her stomach, causing a shiver to wrack her body.

"My turn," she said.

I stood, her hands moved to the hem of my shirt, and slowly she lifted it over my body. Her hands moved to the top of my pants, once they were loose she slipped them down my legs.

I held Lennox's hand as she stepped into the steaming tub and followed in behind her. I groaned at the feeling of the scalding water on my aching limbs.

I leaned back in the tub, Lennox falling between my legs.

She passed me a washcloth and we washed ourselves, scrubbing at our blood-speckled skin until it was raw and the water was an unsettling color. When we were both clean she leaned back against my chest.

I wrapped my arms around her, placing a kiss on her now clean shoulder.

"We should get out before we fall asleep."

She sighed, leaning her head back against my shoulder and closing her eyes.

"Can't we sleep here?" she murmured.

"Sleeping in water isn't recommended."

"Fine." She huffed. I placed several kisses on her neck, unable to resist the perfect skin exposed to me.

She leaned forward and I exited the tub, wrapping a towel around my waist before offering one to Lennox. I helped her out of the tub and dried her off; she shivered as I ran the towel up and down her body.

"Don't get too excited," I chided. "You need sleep."

"Are you sure we don't have time for something else first?"

"Sleep first." The blood rushing to my cock thought otherwise.

"Sometimes I hate it when you're so protective."

"Someone needs to look out for you." I picked her up and

carried her to the bed, placing her gently on top. I returned to the bathing chamber—grabbing us each a robe.

"Thank you for looking out for me." She wrapped her arms around my torso as she kneeled on the bed.

I wrapped my arms around her in return. "I've always got my eyes on you, Sweetheart."

Her lips drifted over my jaw before finally meeting my own. I gripped her hips, drawing her closer as her hand drifted to my hair.

"Sleep, Lennox. Don't think you can distract me from the fact that you need to sleep."

Her hand drifted lower. "Are you sure I can't distract you?"

"Lennox. You need sleep." She was going to be the death of me.

"Fine." She sighed.

She kissed me one more time before falling back onto the bed. She put a little extra sway in her hips as she crawled towards her side.

I scrubbed my hands over my face and adjusted my aching cock. It was technically our wedding night—*no.* Sleep was more important tonight.

I shuffled in next to her. Pulling her against my chest and the covers over us. I placed a kiss on her temple. "I love you."

Her arms around my waist tightened.

"Until the stars turn to dust."

"Until the stars turn to dust."

☪

The sun was shining in my eyes sooner than I hoped. My limbs still ached with exhaustion as my eyes squinted against the sun. Based on where the sun sat in the sky I guessed we had gotten a few hours of sleep. Enough to get us through the day, but not enough to quell the bone-deep exhaustion after the events of the previous days.

"Not yet," Lennox grumbled from beside me.

"You can go back to sleep if you want. You don't have to get up yet if you don't want to."

She didn't open her eyes as she spoke. "I have to go and be High Queen. There was an attack of Dhampirs at our wedding reception. Someone tried to poison us. There are intruders in our dungeon."

"Fuck." I scrubbed my hand over my face, attempting to rub the sleep from my eyes. "We have to get up, don't we?"

"Probably would be best."

She rolled so her arms laid haphazardly over my body, her head on my chest. "Making me sleep was a good call. I'm still exhausted, but I needed it."

"So you're saying you're not mad I made you sleep for a few hours instead of fucking you for hours?"

She scoffed. "Well, I wouldn't put it that way." She danced her fingers up and down my chest.

"Lennox Adair, you insatiable creature."

Her hand moved lower until it gripped my cock. I groaned as she stroked up my length.

"What can I say?" She removed her hand from my cock and swung her leg over my waist so she was straddling me. The robe she had slept in was loose, the tie coming apart from her movements while she slept. Slowly, she moved her hips, rubbing herself against me. She tilted her head back as she continued to move. I slipped my hands under her robe gathered at her thighs, resting my hands on her hips to guide her movements.

As she moved her robe parted further, revealing one of her perfectly rounded breasts. I sat up and took her nipple in my mouth, flicking my tongue over the tight bud.

"Fuck, Luka. I need you. Now."

My mouth moved up her chest, kissing and sucking my way up to her neck. "Take what you need from me, Lennox."

The little moan that slipped out of her mouth sent blood directly to my cock. She lifted her hips, taking my cock in both of her hands and directed it to her soaked center. I hissed as she slid the tip of my cock inside her.

She bit her bottom lip between her teeth as she pushed down another inch. Without warning she slid the rest of the way on my cock, throwing her head back in pleasure as I continued to suck on her neck.

"Astria's tits, you feel so good squeezing the life out of my cock."

She panted, tipping her head to meet my gaze. "The only tits you should be talking about while you're inside me are mine."

"Noted, Sweetheart." With that, I moved my mouth to her breast, kneading her other one with my hand as she started to move again.

"More, I need more." She panted. I lifted her hips, she whined as I slipped out of her.

"Patience," I scolded. With one movement I flipped us so she was lying on the bed. She reached for me, but I was faster. I took her hands and held them above her head. "This is about you. Let me please my *wife*." Her eyes burned with desire as she squirmed underneath me. "Do you trust me?" I asked.

She nodded. "I need you to say the words, Lennox."

"I trust you," she said without hesitation, causing a burning sensation to spread in my chest. I wasted no time removing the sash from her robe, her breathing hitched when she realized what I was going to do.

"Give me your hands."

She held out her hands and I tied them together with the sash, tight enough so she couldn't get out, but loose enough it wouldn't be painful. Once they were tied I fastened the end to the bed frame, rendering her at my mercy.

Her eyes were heavy with desire, her chest and breasts heaving as I admired my work. "I don't think you've ever looked so beautiful. Tied up and naked at my mercy. My beautiful vicious creature."

I cupped her cheek before kissing her. Slowly at first before deepening the kiss as she writhed beneath me.

"Please, Luka. I need you inside me."

"Not yet. I'm starved."

She whimpered as I kissed my way down her stomach before finally closing in on her dripping center. She bucked beneath me as I gave one long lick up her center before closing my mouth over her clit and sucking.

"Fuck!" she screamed. I continued my feast, taking my time licking long teasing strokes up and down her dripping core. Delighting in her sweet taste.

She whimpered as she pulled against the binds, her hips bucking up to meet my mouth. If there was one thing Lennox Adair lacked it was patience. As much as I'd like to tease her until she was begging, we did have important things to attend to.

Another day I'd take my time. We had the rest of our lives in front of us.

I flicked my tongue over her clit as I plunged three fingers inside her. Her back arched off the mattress as I thrust my fingers in and out of her, her hands pulling at the restraints. Her legs locked around my head, her heels digging into my back, forcing my face farther into her heat.

Her body trembled under my ministrations.

"Are you going to come on my tongue, Sweetheart?" She whimpered. "Tell me, Lennox." I removed my fingers from her. "Use your words." Lust clouded her green eyes, but there it was —that Lennox determination I loved so much creeping through.

I shook my head, smirking slightly.

In every other aspect of our lives, I'd give in to her. Give her what she wanted. Let her be the bullheaded female I loved.

But not here. Not now. When it came to sex with Lennox there was a balance. I wanted the power now.

I placed a sharp slap on the inside of her thigh. She yelped, her hips bucking off the bed as her cheeks darkened.

"Use your words, Lennox."

She set me with that determined gaze again.

"I could leave you tied up here all day. Tied up, empty, and wanting."

Her chest heaved.

Fuck I loved her.

She bit her bottom lip. "Fuck me Luka."

"Good girl."

## 64

## LENNOX

A scream tore from my throat as Luka's tongue speared me.

Goddess above he was a fucking tease. My body was coiled tight, my release having been kept at bay for too long. My hips jolted off the bed, my heels digging into Luka's back as his tongue moved. He sucked at my clit at the same time he thrust his fingers back inside me.

I tugged against the restraints binding my hands above. I wanted to touch him. My fingers itched to run my hands through his hair and tug.

I'd experimented a lot in all my sexual adventures, but never had I trusted someone enough to let them have control and tie me up.

Until Luka.

As much as I loved being in control, it turns out I equally enjoy giving it up to Luka.

In certain circumstances.

Being tied up while he had his mouth between my legs was one of those circumstances.

His fingers pumped in and out of me with force as his tongue licked and sucked at my clit.

My release barreled through me. My throat rubbing raw from the scream that escaped me.

I licked my lips as I watched him bring his fingers to his mouth, licking myself from his long fingers.

"Luka, please. I need you inside me."

His eyes were wild with desire. He had shown me control, but I knew that thread was thin. He needed his release as much as I did.

He gripped himself, running his hand up and down his cock several times causing my heart to pick up speed and my thighs to clench.

"I can't wait another second to be inside you."

"So don't."

In one breath he was inside me. I gasped as he filled me to the brim, his cock hitting so deep inside me it stole the air from my lungs.

"Stars above Lennox." I thrust my hips in time with his movements. He leaned forward, his fangs scraping against my neck as he sucked and nipped at my skin. One hand thumbed at my breast while the other worked at my binds. The moment the tie was loosened my hands were on him, pulling him closer before bringing his lips to mine.

His hips picked up speed, the sound of skin slapping on skin and our moans filling the room as my release continued to trickle up my spine.

I protested as he pulled all the way out, my mind trying to keep up with what he had in mind next.

"Up." His hands gripped my thighs, pulling me down the bed an inch. "On all fours."

I rolled over, leaning on my elbows, my bare ass in the air ready and waiting for him. I looked over my shoulder at him, finding him raking his eyes over my body. I wiggled my ass slightly at him.

"What are you waiting for?"

His eyes darkened, as he ran his hand up my spine, sending a shiver dancing through my body.

He dragged his cock through my wet center, teasing me once again before he finally pushed his way in.

I ground my ass up against him as he gripped my hips and filled me to the hilt. His thrusts were slow at first before they picked up speed. Each thrust and slap to my ass sending my release building higher and higher.

His thrust became sloppier as he chased his release.

His hand roamed between my legs, strumming my clit as he pumped inside me.

With one more brutal thrust and strum at the bundle of nerves, I came, Luka coming with me, his release filling me.

I let myself fall against the pillows, my hair sticking to my sweat-soaked face. His release dripped down my thighs as he pulled out of me. I rolled onto my back as Luka fell in a heap beside me, pulling me into an embrace.

"Well, I guess we're going to need another bath."

I laughed. Rubbing my sticky thighs together. "You think?"

He rolled on his side, propping himself on one arm so his face was framed by the golden rays of morning light behind him.

"Or maybe you skip the bath. I like the idea of you walking around all day with my cum dried on your thighs." He leaned forward, nipping at my ear. "Then everyone would know you're mine."

I shivered. If we didn't have so much to attend to, I might give into his idea. But walking around all day painted with his cum while I talked to the neighboring royals sounded like a bad idea.

*Terrible idea.*

It would take all my self-control in the first place to keep my hands off of him. I didn't need that reminder too.

I ran a finger down his chest. "Another time."

"I'll hold you to that."

"Until then we'll have to find another way to mark you as mine."

"You don't need to, Sweetheart. Everyone already knows."

☪

A while later, both of us cleaned up and dressed, Luka and I made our way from our room in search of everyone else. I was surprised no one had come looking for us during our morning wake-up—hopefully, that meant everyone was catching up on their sleep.

Luka pulled me towards the kitchen, but I stopped him. "Can we stop in the dining room first?" He hesitated, the concern evident in his eyes.

"Are you sure?"

"I need to see it."

"Okay." We made our way silently to the dining room, my stomach twisting in knots with every step closer we took. The doors were shut when we arrived. I took a deep breath before pushing open the double golden doors.

The room looked the same as when we left it last night. That felt like days ago. Someone had used magic, it looked like a combination of earth and ice magic—to roughly seal the broken windows. Vines and trees wound through the broken panes with ice frozen in between the cracks, creating a makeshift wall. Light filtered in fractures through the panels of ice. I would have thought it was beautiful if I didn't know the circumstances behind the structure.

If Dhampirs hadn't created the hole in the first place, leaving a trail of ruined bodies in its wake.

Beads of shattered glass still littered the floor, dried blood flaking on the floor in dried splatters and rivets. One of the tables lay in shards as if someone was slammed down in the middle.

There were several large pools of dried blood on the floor.

At least someone had removed the bodies that had once laid in them.

"I need to find someone to clean this up."

"There are more important things than getting this room cleaned up right now."

Luka was right, but my eyes fixed on the dried pools of blood where a body once lay, the thinner spot of blood burning itself into my mind. I needed it gone. I wouldn't be able to focus knowing the blood of my people who had died in my palace walls stained this floor. I needed this room cleaned up and sealed off. I didn't want to step foot in here for a long time. Or ever again.

And the people—where had they been put? Did we know who they were? Had their families been contacted? I'd go tell them myself if they hadn't been told already. Where were their families? Had they been here too? Or were they waiting at home, wondering where their loved one had gone?

Luka tugged at my hand. "Let's go find someone, maybe there will be someone in the kitchen. We can eat and get everything sorted out, but you need food."

My body was numb as I let him lead me from the room. I hadn't eaten since yesterday afternoon before the ceremony and my stomach gnawed with hunger.

He put his arm around my shoulders, pulling me into his side. "You did everything right last night, remember that. There's nothing you could have done to prevent what happened."

I let out a deep sigh, some of the tension leaving my shoulders. "I know," I forced myself to say. Every instinct in my body screamed to blame myself—to let myself bear the burden of the lives taken last night. But Luka was right. There was nothing I could have done to prevent the events from last night.

Still, the losses weighed heavy on my soul.

☾

I sat on a stool in the kitchen, having finished eating the breakfast Luka had insisted upon. He dismissed the staff we found in the kitchen, asking them where to find a few things before asking them to leave and find someone to clean up the dining room.

Eventually, Gulia found us.

"Your Majesties! There you are!"

"Good morning, Gulia." Luka greeted the female.

"Sir Declan has been looking for you. I told him if I found you I would send you to the study to find him."

Luka and I shared a look. "Let's go."

We quickly made our way to my study, finding Declan and Luce sitting in the armchairs.

"The newlyweds finally made it out of bed I see," Luce sing-songed.

I rolled my eyes. "We've been up for hours."

"Exactly," Declan added dryly. I gaped at the harpy, his dark hair was pulled back today, accentuating his chiseled face.

"I expect those kinds of comments from Luce and Nico, but from you Declan?" I clicked my tongue but he said nothing.

"He's tired of us already," Luka whispered as we sat on the couch.

I smiled before turning my attention back to the group. "What have you found out this morning?" I looked at Delcan.

"Not much more than we heard last night, Luce was filling me in on the events that happened here."

"My mother found me last night before I made it to my room and gave me an update. Everyone she and Endora questioned were innocent, nothing she was able to get out of them connected them to the poisoning or the Dhampir attack. With the exception of the ones they found trying to sneak away. She assumed they caught on to what she was doing and tried to escape before they were questioned. They claimed they didn't have anything to do with the Dhampirs, but the poison was another story."

"And those are the ones being kept in the dungeon?" Luka asked.

Luce took a sip of her drink. "They are ready and waiting for your direction."

"And the innocent people? What is the status on them?"

"Some decided to go back to their homes last night after being questioned, others stayed here through the night. My mother and Endora were checking in with them again this morning to figure out their next steps."

"Good." Knowing my people were safe lessened some of the tension wracking my body. "We will have to make sure and check up on them later, make sure they are still all doing well and that no one has any lingering injuries."

"I'm sure my mother and Endora would be willing to check up on them."

"I need to." I needed my people to know I cared about them.

"I know it's important to you, but you have a lot of other things to concern yourself with, let them help," Luce insisted.

"Luciana is right." Luka placed his hand gently on my thigh. "What if Caterina goes and checks on everyone today and she can let them know you will stop by later this week, once everything is settled around here."

"Fine," I conceded. I didn't like having to wait, but I had so much to attend to.

"We have some traitors to interrogate anyways, don't we?"

# 65

# LENNOX

Twenty minutes later the four of us were in the dungeon, the heavy cement door slamming shut behind us, the lock clicking back into place as we strode down the hallway.

"Good morning, Caio," I greeted the guard.

"Good morning, Your Majesties. Are you here to see the prisoners?"

I nodded. "Is there anything more you can tell us about them?" Luka asked.

"The three of them were ready to talk their way out of here this morning, they claim they were sent here by some group, but meant no harm, they were only sent to spy."

I shared a look with Luka. If they were sent by the Vanir, we'd easily be able to confirm such by searching them for the mark. But I had a hard time believing they were sent here only to spy.

"After we detained the female we found this on her." Caio handed me the empty vile. It was miniscule. I was almost surprised they didn't miss it, it was only slightly bigger than my fingernail.

"You think she's the one who tried to poison us?" I surveyed the bottle.

Caio shrugged. "I don't know. That's above my pay grade."

"Let me see it." Gently, Luce uncorked the top, brought the vial to her nose and sniffed. Her face scrunched at the smell. "That's it, that's the poison that was in your drinks."

"Now we need to figure out who she's working for." She had to be with the Vanir, we needed to get her to admit it.

"Declan and Luce, why don't you two go see what you can get out of the other prisoners." I dipped my head toward the cell behind me. "Luka and I will deal with this one."

Without another word, we separated. The door to the cell creaked open as Luka and I made our way in. I blocked out the musty smell that invaded my nostrils, instead focusing on the female in front of me. She lay on the straw cot. Her hands were bound together by the magic-enhanced cuffs, which were chained to the wall. She must have put up a good fight last night if they thought it necessary to keep her chained to the wall.

She was a tiny thing, barely taking up any space in the small cell. Her hair was dark, shaved on one side and fell in a long straight curtain on the other side. She was dressed elegantly, her dress was a deep blue with a high neckline and long sleeves with silver embroidering. The fabric pooled around her waist slipping around her thighs as she sat with her knees bent. Had she been a wedding guest? I didn't recognize her but that didn't mean she hadn't been a guest. Or she had poised as a guest to make her way into the palace—the perfect cover. Slip in, poison us, and slip out. She would have done it if it weren't for the Dhampir attack.

It looked like she had gotten into it with whoever detained her—whoever found her trying to slip from the palace. Her lip had been split, it was already healing, as well as the black eye she was sporting.

"I was told I might get to see the queen," she rasped, "but I didn't expect I'd get a personal visit from Her Royal Majesty herself. And her consort." She looked at Luka. "What an honor."

"You did try to sneak away from the wedding celebrations without saying hello."

She laughed, the sound gravely in her throat. "Is that what you called that blood bath? A wedding celebration? Maybe you are as bloodthirsty as they say you are. We know your husband is." The way she sneered at the word husband made me want to slash my sword across her throat.

Luka's fingers brushed over the small of my back. *Not now.* They seemed to say.

"Who sent you?" I asked.

Her dark eyes fixed on me. "I think you know."

Luka cursed.

"Prove it," I demanded.

She brushed her long hair behind her ear and turned her head towards the light. "See for yourself."

I took a step forward, my hand on my sword as I bent to examine her closer. Sure enough, inked behind her rounded ear was the symbol of the Vanir in white ink.

"Our people will not rest until the crown rests on one of our heads." Her words lacked conviction.

"Your people?" Luka questioned. "You are nothing but a disgruntled band of outlaws working towards an impossible goal."

"I would have been successful if it weren't for the witch bitch!" She spat, struggling against her chains as she attempted to stand. "No one should have been able to detect the poison before it was too late."

I silently thanked Luce for her constant thirst for knowledge.

"Why do you want me dead?"

The female contemplated for a minute before speaking again. "If I tell you what you want to hear, will you promise to make my death quick?"

I reared back at her words. "What?"

She crossed one ankle over the other. "If I did manage to escape and get back to my people, I'm dead anyhow for coming back a failure. I'll tell you everything you want if you make my death swift. How you choose to go about it is up to you, but I want a quick end."

"Deal," I said before Luka could protest.

"You're making a deal with an assassin. Someone who tried to commit treason against us," Luka argued. "Are you sure that's a good idea?"

"We've been searching for information on the Vanir for months with no avail. If she's willing to give me information I can give her a quick death if that's what she wants."

"Okay." I expected him to argue more, to question my intentions, but he didn't. Instead, he took a step back, allowing me space to do what I needed to do.

I sliced my palm with a dagger at my side. "Give me your hand—"

"Oriza."

"Oriza." She held out her palm, her shackles clanging as I dragged the blade over her skin before taking her hand in mine.

I muttered the spell, feeling the magic working its way through my arm.

"I, Lennox Adair, promise to give you a quick death if you, Oriza, promise to give me the information I need."

Her dark eyes met mine. "I need you to repeat the promise," I told her. "It will seal the deal so neither of us can break our promise."

She repeated my words. "I, Oriza, promise to tell you all the information I can give on the Vanir in exchange for a quick death."

Magic zapped through our joined hands, causing Oriza to jolt back, hugging her sliced palm to her chest. "What are you?" Her voice was quiet in the cell.

I stood, wiping my bloody palm on my leathers. "Since your breaths are short-lived I figure it won't hurt to let you in on Lethenia's best guarded secret." I turned and smiled at the female. "I'm half witch."

"Holy stars," she murmured. "That's why you have a witch in your circle."

"My cousin," I confirmed. "But enough about me. Tell me about the Vanir."

"What do you want to know?"

"Why are they after Lennox?" Luka asked from his spot leaning against the wall.

"I made a deal with the Queen, not you," she spat at Luka.

"Careful how you speak to your High King or I won't hesitate to bury my dagger in your thigh."

"You can't." She smirked. "You made a deal."

"I made a deal not to drag out your death. A dagger in your thigh won't kill you. It will only hurt like fuck. But if you talk to my husband like that again there won't be time to take back your words."

I pulled an old wooden chair from the corner—wanting to be on Oriza's level, but not willing to sit on the floor of the cell.

I sat in the chair and leaned back, crossing one leg over the other. "Talk."

Oriza crossed her wrists over her bent knees. "What do you want to know?"

"The poison—why try to poison me and Luka?"

"It was mainly supposed to be for you and your sister. The Vanir want to eliminate the Adair line. They tried to kill the two of you before you got married." *Obviously.* "But since that didn't work, they believed Luka could be persuaded to work in favor of the Vanir. But if he would have drank the poison they wouldn't have been upset about that. If the crown was open, they'd make their bid for the crown." She swallowed. "They figured getting to your sister would be easy if you were gone."

The knot in my stomach tightened. They greatly underestimated Kara. "So you poisoned all three of our glasses?" I asked tentatively.

She shook her head. "I only got the poison into yours and

Luka's. I was going to try to find your sister's glass later in the night, but all hell broke loose."

Luka and I muttered in agreement.

"What else do you want to know?"

"Why do the Vanir want me dead so badly?"

"At its core, the Vanir are against the concept of having a High King and Queen. If there is going to be one, they want it to be a Vanir with the crown."

"Don't you think the Vanir are putting too much stake in the hatred between the vampires and the rest of the courts?" Luka asked.

Oriza shrugged. "That's not my judgment to make."

"It doesn't make sense—this level of hatred."

"They've lost sight of the vision they started with," Oriza said quietly.

"What was that?" Luka pressed.

She sighed. "When the Vanir originated—centuries ago—all they wanted was equality. They wanted their people—the vampires—to be treated as everyone else was. That vision was quickly lost when members became bloodthirsty. They saw the power that came with killing and they got a different type of blood lust. They thrived off of fear—no longer did they worry about true equality. They wanted the crown. With the crown, they could demand justice by force." She looked at Luka. "I'm sure you're all familiar with how the original rebellion ended."

We nodded solemnly. "Everyone thought the Vanir had snuffed out centuries ago when they were hiding in the shadows instead. The Vanir never ended. But they decided recently to make themselves seen again."

"That's how they've been able to keep themselves so hidden while coming back so strong." I looked at Luka. "They've been hiding for centuries."

"Why are you telling us all this?" Luka asked Oriza.

"I didn't have a choice in being a part of the Vanir."

"What do you mean?"

"I was born into the Vanir. My parents were members. Once you're in it, there is no way out but in death. I was forced to live in the shadows." She took a deep shuddering breath. "Living in the shadows is no way to live." Oriza looked at the ground before speaking again. "What else do you want to know about the Vanir?"

"Where can we find them?" I asked without hesitation.

"They're everywhere. They live in groups all throughout Lethenia—not only in the Blood Court. It's nearly impossible to find them unless you know their locations and know about their tattoos."

"Can you tell us the locations you know?"

"I moved to the Star Court about ten years ago, I was too young when we came here to remember where we were located before, even if I could, I doubt they're still there. But I can tell you about my base here."

Luka and I nodded, encouraging her to continue. "I've been living with a group of Vanir located on the northernmost tip of the continent. You have to travel through the Abode Mountains and on the coast there are several small villages scattered along the border." She looked at me. "People rarely travel through the mountains."

She was right, there was nothing of use on the other side of the mountains, so no one ever traveled there. Making it the perfect hideout for a secret organization.

"Who is your leader?" I asked.

"And where can we find them?" Luka added.

"I'm afraid that's a question I can't answer. They keep their identity safely guarded. Only the people in their trusted inner circle know their identity. As well as at their home base. From what I understand they move around a lot though."

"That makes sense," Luka murmured.

"Is there anything else you can offer us?" I asked.

She thought for several minutes.

"I don't think so. I'm sorry. This was one of my first jobs. They don't share much information with me yet."

The more I looked at her, the younger she looked. She couldn't be older than twenty and yet the Vanir sent her out here to poison the High Queen.

They had to have known it was a suicide mission.

"You going to kill me now?"

I arched a brow at her. "Not yet, I have a couple more questions. Why did you send the Dhampirs after us?"

Her brows furrowed. "Is that what those creatures are? You think we sent them?"

"Didn't you?" Luka and I asked in unison.

She shook her head. "The Vanir have nothing to do with those abominations. We've been avoiding them for months. They've killed many Vanir since they started appearing."

"If the Vanir aren't responsible for the abominations, who are?" We all shared a questioning look.

"What about Astria's journal?" Luka pressed.

"Astria's journal?" Oriza asked, her brows furrowing.

"Fuck," Luka swore. "The Vanir aren't the ones looking for Astria's journal are they?"

Oriza shook her head. "I might not know much, but I've never heard anyone mention a journal or book of any type."

My stomach hollowed.

Luka swore. "What does this mean?"

"It means we've been keeping our eyes on the Vainr this whole time, while there's another force at work." I looked at Luka. "It means we no longer have one enemy, but two."

Oriza whistled. "I'm not envious of you guys, that's for sure." I leveled her with a gaze.

"Any more questions?" She turned away from my stare.

I looked at Luka, who shook his head.

Well then.

I stood and reached for my sword. Luka stopped me with a

hand to my arm. "Do you think killing her is the best idea? What if we could get more information?"

I looked at Oriza. "I made a deal. I will stick to that deal."

"You didn't say you had to kill her immediately," he countered.

"I know." I looked at Oriza again. When we first came in she looked like a tough assassin. Now—now she looked like a sad young female.

"Keeping her alive any longer would be as bad as torturing her."

Luka removed his hand. He hadn't been trying to stop me, he only wanted to make sure I was certain this was the right choice. I appreciated it when he did that. I did tend to make brash choices, but this wasn't one.

Minerva whined as I removed her from her sheath—causing Oriza's gaze to flick up to meet mine. She stood, the chains shaking slightly as she wrung her hands. I met her dark gaze. "Thank you for all the information you gave. Rest well knowing it will be used to create a better Lethenia. To help try to end this strife between our people."

A muscle feathered in her jaw as a tear slipped down her cheek. I tightened my hand around the pommel of my sword until the metal bit into my palm. I focused on the sting. On the pain.

*She had tried to commit treason*, I reminded myself. She would be tortured if I let her go. I couldn't trust her to stay in the palace —even if she had given us valuable information.

I closed my eyes and thrust my arm forward. I winced at the sound of the gasp choking from Oriza's throat. I removed my sword from her heart letting it clang to the floor as I laid her lifeless body on the straw. Her blood coated my hands as I stared into her lifeless eyes.

It was what had to be done. I closed her eyes with shaking fingers before squeezing my own eyes shut. *This is what she wanted*, I repeated to myself.

A hand brushed over my shoulder, taking me from my thoughts. "Lennox, it's time to go," Luka whispered gently.

I wiped my bloody hands on my leathers, quickly turning and leaving the room. I made it several paces down the hallway before stopping and turning to Caio, snapping my mask of queen back on. "The body should be burned and set to rest in a dignified manner."

He nodded and at his confirmation, I turned and headed back out of the dungeon.

I could feel the panic clawing up my chest. Tears clouded my vision as I made my way to my room. I needed to get to my room.

"Lennox." Someone called but I ignored it. I needed my room. I needed to be alone. No one could see me break down.

The door of my office came into view and I bounded towards it. When I closed the door behind me I was met with resistance. I pushed again, but the door pushed back until Luka emerged.

He looked at me with such a soft expression, causing the last tether of my restraint to snap.

"She was just a girl," I rasped, tears clouded the edge of my vision.

"I know." He wrapped me in his arms. "But you did the right thing—that was what she wanted."

"I know, but it doesn't make it any easier. Oriza, and the people who died at the wedding yesterday—I feel those losses on my soul." I let their faces filter through my mind. I knew their deaths weren't my fault—but I had a hard time believing it. I was their High Queen, I should have protected them. I should have done better.

"We'll get through this." Luka held me until my breaths evened out again—my heart beating in time with his as I tried to reconcile my thoughts.

"I love you."

"I—"

"I know."

"Until the stars turn to dust." I should say it. Tell him I loved him—but I couldn't get my lips to form the words. I wasn't ready yet. *Soon.* Soon I could tell him how I felt. Even if he already knew—I wanted him to hear those words.

But not right now.

Not after I had taken the life of a young female.

Not when my hands were stained with Oriza's blood.

Not when people were dying on my watch left and right.

Later.

I would tell him I loved him later.

☾

Luka held me until I was ready to face everyone again.

He wiped away my tears and helped me clean Orizia's blood from my body.

I took one more deep breath before I let Luka lead me from the room.

We found everyone in the sitting room, chatting idly with plates filled with meats, cheeses, and bread littered on the table between them. Luka and I settled on the couch, I popped a piece of cheese in my mouth before leaning back, my eyes scanning the room.

"Where's Kara?"

They all shrugged.

"I haven't seen her yet today," Luce remarked.

"Neither have I," Nico pinched a piece of meat between his fingers.

A seed of panic took root in my chest. I took a deep breath to quell it. "Has anyone seen her today?"

Everyone shook their heads.

The seed of panic grew.

Declan stood from where he leaned against the wall near the window. "No one has seen her today?"

We shared a look. I could see the worry in his eyes. "When was the last time anyone saw her?"

"I saw her briefly last night, she was heading to her room after helping get everyone home with Caterina," Luce said.

"But no one has seen her since?' Declan pressed.

The room was silent.

I stood, the panic no longer a tiny seed but a sprouting worry. "She could be sleeping, it was a long day yesterday." I tried my best to keep my voice calm as I spoke, but fear seeped in.

I took off towards Kara's room. She was probably still sleeping. I felt Luka's presence behind me—but he said nothing. Not bothering trying to calm me. Knowing it was pointless until I confirmed where Kara was.

I knocked on her door with three rapid knocks. "Kara!" Nothing.

I knocked again. "Kara." My chest constricted.

I tried the door handle. It opened, I pushed open the door, Luka following behind me. "Kara?"

My stomach dropped at the sight of the empty room. "Kara?"

The bed was unmade. The sheets rustled slightly from the breeze filtering in from the open balcony doors.

She had been here. But where was she now? "Kara?"

I walked out towards the balcony. Maybe she had fallen asleep on the balcony.

Nothing. I walked back into the bedroom. Luka's face was pale as he looked up at me. "What is it?"

My eyes flicked to the paper he held in his hand. "Lennox." The hairs on the back of my neck rose at the tone of his voice.

I approached him. My boots crunching on something. I looked down to find broken glass littering the floor. The bedside lantern had been shattered. There were flecks of something staining the ground. The flecks were a deep red color. Blood—was that blood?

"Kara's not here."

"What do you mean?" Luka passed me the note.

"She's not here. Someone took her."

There was a roaring in my ears. I held the paper—the note in my shaking hands.

*If you want the Princess back, bring me the journal.*

The paper fell from my hands. Gently falling to the floor, landing on the broken glass. My eyes fixed on the white paper as the edge's darkened. The spot spread, blood slowly staining the parchment.

That's how it felt in my chest. My feelings slowly seeping in, staining me, tainting me.

My sister was gone. Taken by someone.

Who?

Where?

*Kara was gone.*

I fell to the ground. Glass bit into my knees as my skin shredded on the tiny shards of glass. The pain was nothing compared to what I was feeling inside. All these years—everything I had done was to protect Kara.

And I had failed.

This. Letting someone take her—this was my greatest failure.

Someone was screaming.

Tears tracked down my cheeks. Or was it sweat? I couldn't tell. I couldn't feel anything. My entire body was numb.

My sister was gone.

I slammed my fists against the wooden floor and the room shook around me.

This feeling—this bone-crushing feeling. The excruciating pain that ripped through my chest. It was familiar. That thought alone could have sent me to my knees if I wasn't already there. The last time I had felt like this—the last time I felt like this was the night of the vampire attack. When I realized they were dead.

Magic exploded from my palms as the pain rushed through me. Pain. That's all I felt. Soul-crushing excruciating pain.

"Lennox!"

My chest heaved violently. I was unaware of what was happening around me.

"Lennox," came a calm voice.

Arms wrapped in flames enveloped me. Legs coming on either side of me as I was pulled against a strong body.

Hands searched for mine, forcing me to relax my hands from fists to intertwine with theirs. Flames lick up our hands, our arms.

Our entire bodies were encapsulated in flames.

"I'm here." Luka held me to him. "I'm here, Lennox. I've got you." Sweat dripped down his brow onto my shoulder. "I need you to breathe." I couldn't.

"Yes, you can. Breathe in."

My body shook as I tried to get air into my lungs. "Good. Try again. Breathe in." He brought our intertwined hands to my chest. Placing one set on my heart and the other on my stomach.

"Feel as you breathe. Try again." I took another breath, getting more air in my lungs this time.

I don't know how long we sat like that. Each time I breathed my flames grew smaller until my heart leveled out and the last of my flames flickered out.

The floor beneath us was scorched, as were parts of the sheets falling from the bed.

"Can you get up?" Luka stood and offered a hand to me. When I was standing in front of him he wrapped his arms around me.

"She's gone," I choked out. "They took her." There was no stopping the tears now that they flowed. The sobs wracked my body violently. My legs wobbled beneath me. If Luka wasn't holding me up, I was certain I would have fallen back to the ground in a heap of tears.

"I know." He ran a hand down my hair. "We'll get her back. I promise."

"You can't promise that," I choked out.

"I might not be able to promise it, but I will try my damnedest, Lennox. You know that." He took a step back, holding my face in my hands as he looked at me. "I've got you." The look on his face—the sincerity and determination written in his expression—Luka. I still had Luka. No matter what happened, I still had him. I was not alone. I closed my eyes and pressed my head against his chest.

"We'll find her." He placed a kiss on my forehead. "We'll find her."

That was the last thing I remembered before I slipped into the darkness.

# 66

# LUKA

I stood, carrying a sleeping Lennox in my arms.

I wasn't sure if she was sleeping or if she had passed out from the stress of the last day, but either way, I was glad she was resting. I knew the moment she woke we'd be on our way to get the journal from the Galtains.

She'd be upset with me for even letting her sleep, but she needed it. I knew she wouldn't rest until Kara was back safely in her arms.

I tried my best to calm my own racing heart. Everything had gone so wrong. The Dhampirs, everything we learned from Oriza, and now Kara disappearing—her being taken—that was something else entirely. Everyone knew how protective Lennox was of Kara. If we didn't get her back in one piece—I shuttered. I didn't want to think about the consequences.

When I opened the door, Luciana, Declan, and Nico were waiting in the hallway.

Declan's wings were spread wide as he leaned against the wall, arms crossed over his chest. Luce and Nico sat on the floor, rushing to stand as I opened the door.

"What happened?" Delcan's voice was as steely as death as they all looked to Lennox's sleeping form.

"She's sleeping. She passed out. I think it was from the stress of it all."

Luciana's eyes slid to the room behind me. "I take it Kara wasn't in there?"

I shook my head. "Let me go lay her down and I'll explain everything."

They followed silently behind me as I made my way to Lennox's room. I set her gently on the bed, slipping the covers over her, before returning to everyone in the hall.

They all looked at me expectantly.

"Kara was taken." I told them, not wasting any time.

Luciana paled. "By who?"

"It's whoever wants the journal. They left a note saying we needed to retrieve the journal if we wanted to get Kara back." I pulled the note out from my pocket, having grabbed it from the floor of Kara's room. Declan took the note from my hands and read it before passing it to Luciana.

"What are we waiting for?" Delcan asked.

"I want to let Lennox rest, it's not a coincidence she passed out." I looked between the three of them. "We all need a good night's sleep and we can take off to the Blood Court in the morning." I looked at Luciana. "Can you get us there?" She nodded.

"I'm going to examine the note, see if I can find any traces of who might have written it," she added.

"That's a good idea." I scrubbed my hand over my face.

"You need sleep too," Nico argued.

"I'll sleep when my cousin is back home safe," Luciana snapped.

Nico was unfazed. "But you won't be able to help us get her back if you're too exhausted to expel a single spell. You need sleep too."

Delcan clenched his fist at his side. "Enough arguing. First thing in the morning we leave. I don't care what the fuck you do until then."

Luciana straightened her shoulders at his demand. "Okay, I'll get going." She didn't look back as she departed down the hallway toward her room, Nico following after.

"I'll make sure she sleeps!" he called over his shoulder.

# 67

# LUCIANA

Kara was gone.

I gripped the blood-stained note in my hand. It was up to me to see if I could figure out who had taken her from a piece of paper.

Lennox was sleeping now, but when she woke she'd be inconsolable. I wanted to give her something. Some hint of where Kara was when she woke.

I was the only person who could.

But no pressure.

I gripped the back of the couch, my nails digging into the fabric as tension radiated from my body. I could do this. For Kara, I could do this.

"Are you okay?" I jumped at the sound of Nico's voice. I knew he had followed me, but I didn't realize he had followed me all the way into my room.

"I'm fine," I lied.

"Liar." I looked over my shoulder and glared at him.

"Your cousin was just kidnapped, no sane person would be fine."

"Whoever said I was sane?" I countered.

"I mean…"

"I need you to leave," I gritted, my grip on the couch increasing. I needed him gone. I wouldn't be able to concentrate with him here. I wouldn't be able to push my magic as far as I needed with him hovering over me

"I'm not leaving." He planted himself in one of the chairs in the sitting room. "I'm here to make sure you don't push yourself too far and get some sleep."

"I don't need sleep."

He raised a silver brow. "I beg to differ."

"Your presence will interfere with the spell," I argued.

"Doubtful." He crossed one leg over his knee. "That's never stood in the way before. Just think of me as moral support."

"Fuck off." I flipped him a vulgar gesture over my shoulder as I made my way to the chest at the end of the bed.

He was silent in the chair as I gathered my materials. I stacked the relics in my arms before making my way to the table by the window.

I set out my materials, referencing my spellbook, making sure I had everything before I mixed the relics in my bowl, trying to ignore the presence of the wolf in the corner.

When I couldn't resist anymore, I peeked at him over my shoulder. I silently cursed myself when I realized his gaze was set on me, watching me work. He gave me a lopsided smile. I shook my head and turned my attention back to my spell.

I took a deep breath, once everything was mixed, scanning the spellbook one more time to make sure I had committed the spell to memory.

Once I was confident, I brought the note left in Kara's room to the lantern on the table, carefully placing the corner into the flames. I watched the flame take over the parchment, the blood staining it dissolved into ashes, falling into the bowl under my hands. When all but the corner I was holding had turned to ash I let the paper fall into the bowl with the rest of the ashes. I brought my magic to my fingertips, splashing five drops of water into the bowl before pricking my finger and letting five drops of my blood fall in as well.

Using my finger, I mixed the relics in the bowl, the mixture having formed a soft paste of sorts. I scooped the material into my palm, coating the inside of my hands with the substance. Once they were properly coated I locked my hands together in a prayer position, closing my eyes and mumbling the spell.

After several minutes of chanting I could feel the substance coating my palms heat, the texture of the substance shifted, and it felt more grainy now as it absorbed into my skin.

My palms burned slightly as the magic worked its way into my hands, but I kept my palms pressed together as instructed, continuing with my chanting.

I could feel it now, the letter was a part of me. I could feel the paper, the ink, as it worked its way into my bloodstream. The texture of the paper grated against my skin somehow, my veins.

*Now where did you come from? Whose hands did you touch?*

Lennox, I could sense Lennox.

And Luka.

Both of them had held the letter.

More. I needed more.

I increased the speed of my chanting, pressing my palms together harder.

Who else had this letter come in contact with?

I tasted blood at the back of my throat.

*Kara.* My magic whispered.

The blood belonged to Kara.

My legs trembled. She would be fine.

My whole body burned as I continued to pull at my magic, searching for more traces of the letter.

*Who else? Who else?*

My jaw locked. *Who else?* I screamed into the abyss.

A figure formed in my mind. *There.* I followed the thread of magic toward them as they continued to manifest.

The figure was dark—but I couldn't glean anything else yet. They were sitting, there was something in their hand.

Was that who wrote the letter? Is that what they were doing?

I dove farther into my magic, it bucked against my call, but I continued to pull at it. I was so close.

Something dripped down my face, but I ignored it as I drew closer to the figure.

The tips of my fingers were edged in pain, I ignored it.

I was almost there.

*"Luciana."*

I ignored his voice. I tried to move my hands, but they refused.

Just a little farther. My feet remained planted in place.

*What the fuck*, I grumbled. I pulled at my magic again, but it refused.

*"Lucy."*

The illusion around me faded. My room came back into view around me as I fell to the floor.

"Luce," Nico gasped, catching me before I hit the ground.

I gritted my teeth. "Bastard, I was so close!" I screamed. "I told you, you'd break my focus!"

"I need to try again." I tried to stand, but couldn't, my legs refused to move.

"The fuck you will, Luce. You are not doing that again." I shoved him off of me, as much as I could without being able to move my legs.

"You can't tell me what to do."

"Luce, that spell, the magic was consuming your body. It was eating at you from the inside out." I furrowed my brows. "Your hands and feet were frozen, your lips were turning blue, your nose was bleeding profusely."

I brought my hand to my face, and when I removed it blood stained my fingertips.

"Do you even have any magic left?"

I searched inside, feeling for the well of magic that resided in my chest, finding only a small ember of it remained.

I had used it all. Every last drop.

I looked at my stinging hands.

"That's what I thought."

"I didn't mean to, I was—I was so close." But yet again I had failed. I slammed my fists against the floor. "Fuck!"

I stood, the sensation in my legs finally allowing me to do so. "Fuck, fuck, fuck!" I took the bowl that had held the relics, throwing it to the floor. It landed with a satisfying crash, the pieces flying across the wooden floor.

With a heaving chest, I turned back to the table and grabbed a jar in each hand. I threw both of them, they crashed to the floor, shattering glass and relics across the floor. What good was this magic if it could only lead me so close to answers, so close I could almost taste them, only to cut me off time and time again before I could get what I needed? Failure. I was such a failure. Could I do anything right? One by one I smashed the jars until there were none left on the table.

The floor was littered in glass and a mixture of the relics. My mother would kill me if she knew I was wasting relics this way.

But I didn't give a fuck.

I wanted them gone.

I summoned my magic, intending on using wisps of air to clean the mess, but came up empty.

Even now my magic failed me with this simple task.

I stared at the mess on the floor. I always made such a mess of things, didn't I? Streams of water made their way through the shards of glass, soon there was a small river in the middle of my bedroom, carrying away the glass and relics until they disappeared off the balcony, leaving the floor spotless, like nothing had happened.

"Thank you." I didn't bother to look at Nico. "I don't have any magic left. I can't even clean up my mess so I can't try the spell again." Even if I tried again later it wouldn't work. Not without another item linking me to whoever took Kara.

I crawled into bed. Not even bothering to pull the covers up over me as I curled into a ball and hugged my knees to my chest.

The bed dipped beside me. "You're not a failure." Nico's voice was clear but soft. "You did everything you could."

"Exactly," I muttered. "I did everything I could and it still wasn't good enough."

I jumped at the feeling of his calloused palm on the bare skin of my arm as he rubbed up and down several times, before wrapping his arm around me. His front was warm against my back, warming my chilled skin. I didn't have it in me to ask him to leave, so I said nothing and let him hold me.

"You are good enough, Lucy," he said finally.

Those were the last words I heard before I let sleep consume me.

# 68

# LUKA

Lennox slept through the night. I guessed it was the most sleep she'd gotten in a long time. I was expecting her to have a nightmare or two, but she never stirred. She was exhausted—too exhausted to dream even.

Me on the other hand—I felt like I hardly slept. I was too worried about Lennox.

Worried I would wake up to her gone, having gone for Kara on her own.

Every time I felt myself falling asleep, I jerked myself awake, looking to find her still asleep beside me.

A little before sunrise she stirred awake. I sat as she blinked back the sleep from her eyes, holding my breath, waiting for her to remember what happened.

"Luka?" She mumbled as she stretched her arms over her head. "What happened?" Her brow furrowed as she tried to recall the events that led her here.

"Kara!" She gasped, sitting up abruptly and ripping back the sheets.

I laid a hand on her arm. "Lennox calm down."

"Calm down?" Her nostrils flared. "My sister has been taken and you're telling me to calm down? I—" I could see the panic starting to take over her features. "You let me sleep! I was sleeping while my sister is Goddess knows where…" Her breaths became short and uneven as she clawed at her chest.

"I—I—"

I crossed the bed and grabbed her, pulling her against me as her panic consumed her body.

"I'm here. We will find her. Lennox, I promise you we will find her."

I could feel her tears soaking into my shirt as sobs wracked her body.

"You let me sleep." She pushed me away. "You let me sleep." Her panic was turning into anger now, I could hear it in the roughness of her voice. "You let me fucking sleep!" She hit my chest, trying to push me away. "For fucks sake Luka! Why did you let me sleep." She turned from me, her hands balling in and out of fists.

She was angry at me, I knew she would be, but I needed to get her to calm down.

"Lennox. I need you to breathe."

"I can't. I can't. Kara's gone and I—"

I took her hands in mine, unballing them from fists and linking our fingers together.

"Breathe." I stared at her as she refused to meet my gaze. "Lennox, I need you to breathe. I need to see your eyes, Sweetheart."

She finally met my gaze, her emerald eyes were glassy as tears stained her cheeks. The sight caused a fissure through my heart.

"You passed out in Kara's room. I knew you wouldn't allow yourself to rest until we found her so I let you sleep."

She looked away from me, shame written on her features.

"Lennox, I need you to look at me." She took several deep breaths before looking at me again, fresh tears staining her cheeks. I wanted to wipe them away, but I needed to help her control her magic so I kept our hands intertwined and brought them to her face, wiping away her tears with the back of my hand.

"You passing out was your body's reaction to needing rest after everything over the past few days. I knew you needed sleep so I let you sleep. Blame me all you want, but I'd do the same thing again." She said nothing but continued to meet my gaze.

"I updated everyone on what happened. We all agreed we'd head out to the Galtains first thing this morning. Once you are calm enough we can get ready and go."

I held her hands until finally, her breath evened out.

"Thank you," she rasped. I finally let go of her hands, wiping another tear from her cheek before pulling her to me. "We'll find her. I know we will."

I hoped we would. Because if we couldn't find Kara—I didn't want to think about what that would do to Lennox.

I left Lennox to bathe alone; when she emerged from the bathing chamber the color was back in her face. Although I knew she was a wreck on the inside, I could tell she had pushed past the shock and sadness and had moved on to anger. Pure determination to get her sister back.

Vengeance was written on her features.

Everyone was already waiting for us when we arrived— almost a parallel to yesterday afternoon. Before we discovered Kara was missing. But the tone was much more somber today.

Had it only been days ago we had gathered here to celebrate Lennox's and my wedding?

Lennox wasted no time before asking, "What's the plan?"

"I was thinking you and I should head to the Blood Court and visit the Galtain family." Lennox looked at me, surprise written on her features. "The three of you can wait here and get everything ready while we're gone. We don't know what we're dealing with and we need to be prepared." I looked at Declan and he nodded. "And Luciana, I'm assuming you can do a spell to locate Kara?" She nodded.

"I used a lot of magic last night, it's still replenishing, but I can try to scry. I should be able to find her location easily."

"Lennox?" I looked at her.

She swallowed. "It all sounds good. Thank you." She took my hand and squeezed. "I do have one request." We all looked at her expectantly. "I get to kill the fucker who dared to take my sister from me."

☾

Luciana transported us to the forest, depositing us in the clearing outside the Galtain family's cabin, claiming she'd be back in an hour to get us.

"I need her to teach me how to do that," Lennox mused as we trudged through the woods. I almost opened my mouth to disagree—to remind her of the potential effects of using Ichor Magic. But I had to admit, her being able to transport without Luciana would be convenient. And if Lennox set her mind to it, there would be no changing it.

"Maybe she could teach me too."

Lennox threw me a look over her shoulder. "Worth a try don't you think?"

"No harm in trying," she admitted.

The cabin came into view as we continued through the snow. Our boots leaving tracks behind us. Smoke billowed from the chimney—hopefully, someone was home.

Although maybe it would have been easier if there was no one here. We could steal the journal without them knowing.

We each took in a deep breath before Lennox knocked on the door.

Silas' surprise at us appearing at his door was evident, but he wasted no time in ushering us out of the cold.

Malina and Auden stood from where they sat by the fire-place to greet us. "Lennox, Luka, what do we owe the honor?" Malina asked.

"Shouldn't you be celebrating your wedding?" Silas added.

"We're not here on good terms I'm afraid," I admitted

The family shared a look of worry. "Well, why don't you take off your coats and sit here by the fire and warm up while you tell us why you're here."

We didn't argue, quickly shucking off our coats before sitting by the fire.

"I'm going to get right to the point." I braced my hands on my knees. "Lennox's sister, Kara, was taken." Lennox sucked in a breath from where she sat next to me.

Malina gasped. "I am so sorry my dear." Her gaze softened as she assessed Lennox, surely now noticing the differences in her demeanor since the last time we were here.

"But why are you here?" Silas asked. "What does this have to do with us?"

Lennox's voice was rough as she spoke, "Whoever took her left a note. They said if we wanted her back we needed to bring them the journal."

The air in the room thickened to the point it was almost painful.

"I know how important the journal is to your family. But you have to understand, this is my sister at stake here." Lennox's hands trembled in her lap, I took one of them in my own as she continued, "Once we get her back I'll find a way to get the journal back to you I promise." I squeezed her hand, we hadn't discussed this. "I need to get my sister back. I need to make sure she's safe and then I will get the journal back to you. You have my word."

Silas and Malina shared a look. "We will give you the journal. Of course, we will."

Lennox's shoulders dropped, tension visibly leaving her body. Malina stood until she was in front of Lennox, kneeling in front of her chair and taking her hands in her own. "We can still share the contents of the journal by sharing the stories. The people in our stories have long since passed. Your sister is still alive. We will gladly give you the journal so you can find her."

"Thank you," Lennox rasped, a tear falling down her cheek. She quickly wiped it away with her hand.

"Why would you do this for us?" I asked.

Malina turned her attention to me. "She is my High Queen. She could have come in here and demanded we hand over the journals, but she didn't." She looked back at Lennox. "Lennox, you came in here with an open heart, asking for help. I admire that deeply."

Silas returned with the journal, handing it to Lennox. I watched as she ran her fingers over the leather bindings.

"Give me a second," she told the family as she stood and pulled me away.

"I have an idea," she whispered. "I need you to tell me if it's too crazy or not."

"Let's hear it."

"What if I used a spell to replicate the journal? That way I can leave the original journal with the Galtains and I can manipulate the duplicate and remove random pages so whoever's hands this journal ends up in they are unable to recreate the spell to end vampires."

I ran my hand through my hair. "Do you think that would work? Would anyone be able to tell it was a duplicate?"

"Maybe an experienced witch, but they'd need to suspect it was a duplicate. If it's Astria's journal it will already feel and smell strongly of magic. It's worth a shot. Besides, by the time they find out it's a fake we will hopefully be far away with Kara in safety."

"Do it." She let out a sigh of relief. "How are you going to conduct a spell without the Galtain's finding out?"

"I'm not going to. I'm tired of hiding my heritage. Let all of Lethenia find out I'm half-witch. I don't fucking care anymore."

"Okay, let's do this."

We returned to the living room, where the Galtain family waited expectantly.

"I have a plan," Lennox declared. "A way we can both have the journal. I'm going to conduct a duplication spell—that way I can leave you with the original journal and I can take the duplicate and still get my sister back."

"You're going to conduct a spell?" Silas looked between the two of us, brow furrowed.

"You're a witch," Malina breathed.

"Half witch," Lennox confirmed.

"Holy stars," Silas remarked. "How?" Lennox quickly explained her history, before listing off the ingredients she needed to complete the spell.

Malina and Silas scurried around the kitchen, finding each of the items Lennox needed and placing them on the small round table in the center of the kitchen.

Once everything was assembled, Lennox set the book in the center of the table while she mixed the ingredients together before igniting them with her flames.

"Don't be alarmed." She looked at the couple. "The book will appear like it is burning, but I assure you it's not. It's part of the spell." Lennox returned to her work, sprinkling the smoldering ingredients over the book.

The edges of the leather curled as the ashes spread over the book. Lennox placed her hand over the smoking book as she closed her eyes, mumbling the spell under her breath. Flames erupted around her hand, the book dissolving to ashes under her hold, but the flames remained contained, appearing to not even touch her skin.

Malina gasped as the book disappeared, grasping Silas' arm as she continued watching Lennox work.

Smoke clogged the air, Lennox's burning hand disappearing behind its veil. The smoke dissipated when Lennox stopped speaking and brought her hand back to her side.

When all the smoke was gone it revealed two identical journals sitting side by side.

"How do you know which is which?" Silas asked.

"This is the original." Lennox picked up the book on the left and handed it to Silas. "I can tell because I conducted the spell. Otherwise, it's near impossible."

Silas turned the book over in his hands, examining it and the duplicate. "Marvelous," he murmured. "Thank you."

Lennox smiled tightly. "I wish we could stay longer, but we should go," she said. "I hate to rush out of here so quickly but—"

"No," Malina interrupted. "You need to go. Go get your sister back."

"Thank you," we both told them as we donned our coats. "We owe you."

"You owe us nothing," Silas said. "Keep leading us strongly, our queen."

"And come back and visit with that sister of yours when this is all over," Malina added.

Lennox stilled in the doorway before looking over her shoulder at the couple.

"I will," she promised.

The cold wind stung my cheeks as we exited the house.

Surely an hour had passed and Luciana would be here soon. This weather chilled me to my bones, despite trying to use my flames to warm me. Lennox hugged the duplicate journal to her chest as we made our way to the clearing.

"You did a good thing in there," I told her.

"I tried," she mused. "I still feel like shit though." She sighed and she pulled her coat tighter around her neck. "I hate asking them for anything."

"I know but—" She held out a hand to silence me.

"Do you feel that?" I strained my ears against the howling of the wind.

A figure crashed through the trees to our right. I pulled Lennox to my side as we both reached for our weapons.

"How do these fuckers always manage to find us?" I growled as I assessed the Dhampir prowling towards us. There was only one, but that didn't mean there weren't more on the hunt.

This one looked different though, with more human features. Its face looked mostly human, with the red eyes typical of Dhampir and its elongated fangs.

"Beats me," Lennox gritted as she took off towards the Dhampir. It snarled at Lennox before bounding towards her. They met in a vicious clang of steel and teeth. The Dhampir let out one of its high pierced shrieks as Lennox's sword found a home in its shoulder.

I ran up beside her, slicing my sword through its chest the moment Lennox removed her sword.

Black rancid blood splattered across my face. The liquid was hot against my face in the winter chill, but the Dhampir still stood.

I grunted as I pulled back my sword as the Dhampir swiped out a massive claw. Lennox stumbled back into the snow, a scream of pain tearing from her as she gripped her leg.

I ground my jaw and ran towards the Dhampir as it prowled towards Lennox where she lay in the snow. Her red blood streaked the snow as she stumbled away from the beast.

If that fucker thought he stood a chance against Lennox Adair...

Her daggers flew through the air—embedding in the Dhampir's thick chest. The Dhampir paused before ignoring the daggers, removing them from his chest one by one and discarding them on the ground without even flinching.

The Dhampir set its sight back on Lennox, continuing its pursuit. Lennox might be injured, but there was still plenty of fight left in her. I could see it in her eyes.

She glanced at me, giving me a wink before turning her attention back to the Dhampir. I crept up behind the creature, waiting for the right moment to take the final blow.

The monster was getting closer to Lennox. Each step was precise as it approached her. Only when they were both breathing the same air did she swipe up with her sword, hidden in the snow beside her, thrusting up into the Dhampir's chest. It roared—the sound shaking the forest around us as I rushed forward—embedding my own sword in the Dhampir's back. It twisted towards me, trying to reach the sword, oblivious to the fire sparking to life behind it. Lennox's flames engulfed the Dhampir and it shrieked louder. I reinforced Lennox's flames with my own, our combined fire melting the snow underneath the Dhampir, but we continued until all that was left was its ashes in the patch of dead grass. I brought my flames back inside of me, staring at Lennox across from me as her chest heaved.

Magic prickled in the air around us, and we both turned to find Luciana materializing beside us.

"Once again, you're late to the fight," I told her.

She looked around the forest. "What was it?" She asked.

"Another Dhampir."

"Fuck," she swore.

"Let's get out of here before another one finds us." I looked around the forest for any signs of more abominations.

"Did you get the journal at least?" Luciana asked. Lennox nodded as we both headed towards our swords that now lay in the ashes of the beasts—the metal untouched despite our fire burning the monster to ashes.

"Now let's go get my sister."

# 69

# LENNOX

"Did you figure out where Kara is?" I asked Luce before our forms were fully even corporal again.

"Yes."

I gave her an expectant look. "Her location shows up in the woods about a two-hour ride north of the city. They must have some kind of camp set up there at the base of the Abode Mountains."

"What the fuck happened out there?" Declan stood from the couch as he took in mine and Luka's blood-splattered appearance.

"What do you think happened?" I threw him a glare. "One of the Dhampir found us again."

"Did you get the journal at least?" Nico chimed in.

"Of course, I got the journal." I reached into the pocket of my leathers, pulling out the duplicated journal.

Nico took a step back and held up his hands in surrender. "Sorry, I didn't know if the fight deterred you."

I took a deep breath, trying to calm my swelling emotions. Kara was gone, but I didn't need to take it out on my friends.

"We got the journal and one better." I set the journal on the table. "I duplicated the journal and left the original with the Galtain's."

"Brilliant," Luce whispered.

I flipped through the book, picking random pages throughout and ripping them out, making it look like several pages had been ripped out and throwing them into the smoldering hearth.

"And that's why you are the queen," Nico mused. I huffed a laugh and shook my head. I threw the remaining pages in the fire before slipping the journal back into my pocket. "Are we going by horse or is Luce transporting us?"

"Do you two want to bathe before we go?" Luce waved a finger towards Luka and me, her nose scrunched as she assessed us.

I looked at Luka. "I don't see the point when we're likely going to be covered in blood again."

"She has a point," Luka agreed. "If we're all ready we should go."

Everyone nodded in agreement. "Luciana should transport us," Declan said. "That way they won't be able to see us coming."

"Can you handle that?" Nico looked at Luce with concern in his eyes.

"Yes, I can do it," she snapped.

We all looked at her questioningly. She huffed a breath. "I ran my magic out last night; he's being a mother hen." She crossed her arms and looked at Nico. "I'm fine now."

"If you're sure..." I asked carefully. I wanted to get to Kara as quickly as possible, but not at the expense of Luce.

"Yes, I'm fine. Let's go."

The world shifted around us before I could question her anymore.

☾

I pulled my cloak tighter around me as the winter chill formed around us as we appeared at the base of the Abode Mountains at the Northernmost tip of Lethenia.

The mountain's snowy peaks loomed above us. I had never been this close to the mountains. Or any mountains, despite living only a few hours ride from them. I could see them looming in the distance, but up close—they were breathtaking, even despite the circumstances. I saw no sign of any dwellings or camp of any sort yet, not even smoldering flames from a fire. Scrying wasn't accurate to a precise location, but instead of giving a general location, I hoped we weren't too far off.

"I'm guessing they're located in one of the mountain passes," Declan mused. "We won't be able to see them until we get closer."

We all trudged through the snow, a bubble of silence surrounding us to continue to keep our arrival a secret. I used spurts of my magic to keep my body warm as we continued along the mountains. Goddess, I hated winter. I was used to the mild winters of Alethens, this type of cold should have been illegal.

Finally, we made it into a mountain pass. A large dwelling came into view on the path. The building was long, stretching between the two mountains with trees surrounding it on both sides. Its flat roof was covered in a thick layer of snow. The walls had been patched several times over the years. Pallets had been fixed to the sagging parts of the structure.

This had Vanir written all over it, but from what we had learned from Oriza, this was not the Vanir's doing. *Unless the Vanir were working with this other force and Oriza was unaware.*

"How do we get in?" I surveyed the building from where we crouched behind the shrubs at the mouth of the pass.

Two guards stood outside the door, a multitude of weapons strapped across their bodies.

"Do you think we could get in through one of the makeshift

patches? Maybe we could get one off the building easily," I mused.

"It's a good idea, but it might bring attention to us and take too long. And we have no way of knowing what lies inside. We could be walking into a trap," Declan said.

I let out a sigh. "This whole thing might be a fucking trap. Maybe we go in the front door. The note said I needed to bring the journal to get Kara back. They must be expecting us. So maybe we just go in."

Declan was quiet as he thought over my idea. "That might be our best bet if we go in willingly and give them the journal— we might walk out unharmed with Kara."

"Or we might not walk out at all," Luce added.

"But it's worth a try." Luka shifted, his boots crunching on the snow.

"Lennox is right. We try to go in. But it should only be some of us, the rest stay out here in case things go wrong."

"Goddess above. This is insane. You can't expect them to let you walk out unharmed after they kidnapped Kara!" Luce's voice rose with every word.

"Shh." I hit her on the arm. "I know it's not ideal, but we have to try."

"Well, I'm not walking into a trap. I'll stay out here, ready to help once everything goes to shit."

"I think I should go in. Alone."

"No," Luka growled. "There is no way I'm letting you walk in there alone."

"It should be the three of us," Delcan said. "It makes the most sense and shouldn't set off any alarms. "The Queen, her husband, and their guard."

"Okay." I looked at Nico and Luce. "You two stay out here and watch for anything unusual. If we're not out by sunset, come in after us."

They murmured their agreements.

I turned to Declan and Luka. "Let's get my sister back."

☾

Luka, Declan, and I backtracked slightly, making it appear as if we had come directly to the mouth of the pass. The guards were instantly at attention as we appeared, each of them releasing their swords from their sheaths with a whine that echoed in the silent passage.

We approached with empty hands held in the air.

"I'm High Queen Lennox Adair, I'm here for my sister. I believe she is being kept here." The males lowered their weapons but didn't sheath them. They dipped their heads slightly. "We've been expecting you, Your Majesty."

We followed behind them as they led us into the building. The hallway was narrow, it was a tight fit to walk through side by side. My shoulder continuously brushed with Luka's as we walked, Declan at our back, his wings tucked in tight so he could fit. The path was silent at first, but as we walked farther sounds filtered in. Were those nails scratching against a wall?

I shuttered as what sounded like a scream or a moan of pain, rang in my ears.

Doors appeared on either side of the hallway now. Small windows were carved into each door with thick bars over the openings, reminding me of the cells in a dungeon.

A body slammed against one of the doors. Letting out a hiss as we passed.

Luka jumped. "What was that?"

"Not that it's any of your business, but it's one of the mistress' experiments."

"Experiments?" I mouthed to Luka. The word sent a shiver snaking down my spine.

As we continued to walk more and more sounds came from the cells. Some crashed against the doors as we passed, others remained quiet in their cells, slumped against the doors.

What kind of experiments were they? They all looked normal. As normal as any prisoner might look. In the hall beyond, one of the prisoners was hanging its arms through the bars, hissing and growling as it scratched at the walls.

I sucked in a breath as we passed it. Claws, it had claws that were scratching against the walls, leaving deep gouges in the cement.

And its eyes were fully red. Its eyes reminded me of the eyes of the Dhampir... and the claws—*Stars above*. Was this mistress creating the Dhampirs? Was that her experiment?

I looked at Luka, his face was pale, making me assume he had come to the same conclusion I had.

Eventually, we came to the end of the hallway where it split in two directions. To the left, there was a chorus of growls and screams. Goosebumps peppered over my skin as I turned my back to the sounds and followed the guards down the path to the right.

Those growls—I knew those growls. I had heard them this morning, had heard them as they burst through the palace windows after our wedding.

Dhampirs were down that hall. Fully manifested Dhampirs had been either captured or were being made here.

I tried to block out the growls, *the screams*. I was here for Kara. I needed to get Kara out of here and then we could figure out what was going on in this building.

The guards opened the door at the end of the hallway, revealing a large open area. The room was empty, save for the makeshift throne sitting in the center at the far end. Boxes and other discarded metal items had been fixed to create a large square platform, with steps built in and encased in ice. Each of the four layers leading up to the throne resting at the top.

The throne was a simple structure made of ice. Not nearly as magnificent as the female residing in it.

Her sleek black hair swished around her chin as she looked up as the door opened.

The female's deep red lips curved into a vicious smile as she took us in. "I see you got my note," she crooned. Her voice was as smooth as velvet, but she didn't move from the throne as the guards continued to usher us toward her.

"I'm so glad you made it." We halted as we approached the base of the throne, forced to look up at the female atop it.

Luka's hand bunched into a fist next to mine.

"We didn't have much choice did we?" I said through gritted teeth.

The female clicked her tongue. "You did, I had heard rumors you cared deeply for your sister, but you never know if a rumor is true or not. Turns out this one was."

"Where is she?" I hissed, my voice low.

Her hands gripped the ice throne, her blood-red nails digging into the ice. "Seems the rumors about your less than pleasant temperament were true as well."

"Sorry if I'm not in the best mood, life has been a little hectic the past few days."

Her blood-red lips curved into a smile. "So I hear. A wedding, several murders, a kidnapping. Such fun."

"Where is my sister?" I ground out. I could feel my magic rising, pushing against my fingertips.

"She is here. She's fine. Once we're done talking, I'll have one of my guards fetch her."

"Get her now." I met the guards' gazes. "I am your High Queen, or did you forget that?" I seethed. The males had the nerve to look nervous, but instead of getting my sister, they looked behind me, at their mistress on the throne behind. I swallowed a growl.

"Do you have the journal?"

I reached inside my leathers, pulling out the leather-bound book. "So, you can listen." She clapped her hands together enthusiastically.

I tossed her the journal and she caught it swiftly. "I still want to talk—we have much to discuss, *Your Majesty.*"

"If you bring my sister out now, I promise to stay and talk."

"Fine." She gestured for one of the guards. "Go fetch the girl." He nodded before leaving for the door behind the throne.

The female flipped through the book, my heart beating fast as she did.

"Aren't you curious as to what my name is?" She set the journal on the arm of the throne.

"Asking the name of our enemy isn't something we're fond of," Luka remarked.

"Enemy?" The gold ring in her nose crinkled as she spoke. "Whoever said I was your enemy?"

"You kidnapped the princess," Declan stated.

"You're being dramatic." She waved a hand dismissively. "I only borrowed her to get your attention. I want to work together."

I scoffed. "I find that hard to believe given the circumstances."

Her golden eyes glimmered. "Did you catch a glimpse of my pets on your way here?"

"You claim those abominations?" The disdain was clear in Luka's voice.

"No, I don't claim them. But I do take responsibility for them." Her dark eyes glimmered. "I created them."

"Why?" My magic pushed against my fingertips. "Why create such vicious beasts and release them into the world?

"It was never my intention to create monsters. Or to release them into the world. The ones roaming about are the ones that escaped. From the smell of you"—She crinkled her nose, causing the ring to shimmer—"you've come in contact with them before. They are not easy to tame."

"No, they're not," Luka bit out.

"What was your intention, if not to create monsters?"

"I am trying to destroy the true monsters." Her gaze slid to Luka.

"My name is Adreona, by the way. I'm the head of the Panateia. Our organization aims to rid Lethenia of vampires."

# 70

# LUKA

Ice slid along my veins as Adreona's words processed. *We aim to rid Lethenia of vampires.*

Not cure vampirism. Rid the world of them.

"How? Why?" Lennox stammered.

"The why is for another time"—She waved a pale hand dismissively—"but in simple terms, vampires are nothing but bloodthirsty monsters. They are a danger to themselves and others. They are a curse upon our continent. I believe it is my destiny from the Goddess to rid our world of them."

Lennox scoffed from beside me. "I can assure you, Astria has done no such thing."

"You dare to question my destiny?" There was a steely edge to her voice.

Lennox was silent. Not the time to fight this battle. Lennox would have words with Astria later that was for sure.

Our attention turned to the door opening behind the throne.

"Kara." Lennox ran to her sister, throwing her arms around her as Kara stood motionless.

"What is this?" Lennox gestured to the chains encircling Kara's hands.

"A precaution. They will be removed once you leave the building. I still need to ensure you cooperate."

Lennox snarled at the female. "Release her now." The guard behind Kara pulled her close, keeping her near as Lennox stared down Adreona.

Flames flickered at Lennox's fingertips as she removed her sword from her side. The whine of metal echoed through the empty room.

Adreona laughed, the sound cold and cruel. "Be careful young Queen. I hold all the cards here."

"Are you sure about that?" Before Adreona could open her mouth Lennox was rolling across the floor, her legs kicking out beneath the guard holding Kara. He fell to the floor and she climbed on top of him. Her knees pinning his arms to his sides as she pressed her sword to his throat.

Her hair fell in front of her face as she looked up at Adreona. "If you've heard rumors about me, you know I won't hesitate to kill him."

"Oh, I know." She smiled. "Do it, he's useless anyway for letting you disarm him that quickly."

Lennox hesitated for a moment before she slid her sword across the male's throat. She stood, as the guard gurgled, choking on his blood as Lennox returned to my side, sword still in hand.

"I'll burn this whole fucking building to the ground if you don't let her go," she snarled.

"Would you? You'd kill all the innocent people in here? Your friends?"

"We would make it out," she countered, I knew she was calculating a plan in her head as I was. Trying to find all possible exits, how we'd escape once we grabbed Kara. Our best bet might be out the way we came. If we could let loose some of the Dhampirs on our way out they'd be a good distraction.

"But would they?" Adreona gestured behind her, as the door

opened, revealing Nico and Luce, escorted by two guards, their hands tied in front of them.

I could feel Lennox's magic festering. She clenched her hands into fists, breathing hard through her nose.

"I'll kill her," she murmured under her breath. "I'll slit that bitch's throat for this."

Panic flared in Luciana's eyes as she took in Lennox.

"Lennox no!" The witch warned, but she was too late. Lennox flung out her arm towards Adreona, a spear of ice flying through the air.

Before the ice could touch the female, it melted to a puddle on the floor. Lennox's brow wrinkled, but she tried again, only for the same thing to happen.

"If only you would have listened to me, you insolent child," Adreona growled. "Your magic is useless against me."

Despite Adreona's warning, Lennox tried again, throwing out her hand, but nothing came from her fingers.

"This place puts a damper on your magic, rendering it all but useless."

We all turned at the sound of the door opening behind us again. Guards filtered into the room, each of them guiding a restrained Dhampir into the chamber.

There had to be close to twenty Dhampirs being led into the room. Dread settled low in my gut.

"I'll make you a deal, High Queen." Her voice slid down my spine like a snake. "Make it out of here alive and I'll let you all go."

"Fuck," Nico swore.

We knew how to take down Dhampir, but this many, without any magic…

For the first time, I thought we might not make it out alive.

"The deal was I bring you the journal and I get my sister back."

Adreona raised a dark brow, "I have the journal and you

have your sister back. I never said anything about you making it out of here alive."

I looked at Lennox, but her gaze was fixed on Adreona, determination written across her features. I squeezed her hand three times before she looked back at me.

"We can do this," I said, trying to reassure her as well as myself. "I love you."

She smiled softly. Squeezing my hand back. She opened her mouth, but Adreona's voice rose over the room before she could speak.

"Release the Dhampirs."

Chaos erupted as the guards released the Dhampirs. The guards ran, filing back into the doors they came from as the Dhampirs roared and took off toward us.

"Help!" I turned my head toward Luciana and Nico as they screamed and ran toward us. "Our restraints!" They bellowed as they ran toward us with wide eyes. The guards had abandoned them, left them for dead with their hands still restrained. I rushed toward them, and Lennox toward the Dhampirs.

"Do you still have weapons?"

"They only took the ones they could see on us," Nico said as I slashed my sword through his bindings.

The moment he was free he shifted into his wolf form, whatever magic was diluting our elemental powers didn't tamper with his shifting abilities. He wasted no time ripping into a Dhampir that rushed him.

I turned my attention back to Luciana, I had never seen her look so panicked. "It will be okay," I told her as I cut off her ties.

"I'm not so sure." She let out a deep sigh before setting her shoulders, her eyes scanning the room. "I need a sword." Her gaze landed on the guard lying dead on the floor. "Cover me?"

I nodded. Luce palmed the daggers strapped to her thighs before breaking into a run, me at her heels.

"On your left," I warned Luciana. The Dhampir pounced, its claws clamoring for Luce. This one looked like the first one I encountered after the market, its face less human than the recent ones we had encountered. It was worth a try to see if a blade to the heart would be enough to kill it. Luce kept running, I embedded my blade in the beast's chest from behind. I didn't look back to watch it fall as I continued after Luciana.

We made it to the guard, Luciana grabbed the sword, turning back toward me, her eyes going wide. "Look out!" She warned.

I ducked in time as a Dhampir lept for me. It met Luciana's sword as it leaped, falling to the floor dead. "Thank you," I breathed.

"Anytime."

We made our way back to the fray, taking down any Dhampir that crossed our path.

As another Dhampir fell at my feet, I kicked it aside, scanning the room for Lennox. Nico was still in his wolf form, his silver coat splattered with black blood, Luciana had joined Delcan and they fought back to back against a horde of beasts. They kept coming. No matter how many I killed, more kept coming.

But still, I couldn't find Lennox.

Or Kara.

Where was Kara? Wherever Kara was Lennox was.

I scanned the room. Adreona still sat on her throne, a satisfied smile on her face as she surveyed the room. A guard stood by her side, still holding Kara hostage. I searched the throne for Lennox. Where was she? I turned my attention back to the area surrounding me, searching for any sign of blonde hair among the bodies of the Dhampirs.

Nothing.

Another Dhampir descended on me. I kicked it in the chest, giving me a moment to prepare before it struck again, shoving my sword clear through its throat.

The Dhampir gurgled as I removed my sword.

I made my way through the room, searching for Lennox.

A Dhampir swiped out with its arms, its claws coming dangerously close to my arm as I pushed my sword through its heart this time.

The dead Dhampir sagged to the ground as I removed my sword. I turned my attention to the throne, once again searching for my wife.

*There.*

There she was, climbing up the back of the throne.

Adreona's gaze met mine. Fuck.

I looked away quickly, but not quick enough. Adreona's gaze searched the floor, searching for Lennox. Her eyes widened with panic, but she was too late.

Lennox stood behind the ice throne, holding her sword to Adreona's throat.

*That's my girl.*

The sounds of fighting faded; I looked over my shoulder as my friends slayed the last of the Dhampirs.

"I'll enjoy watching the blood drain from your body," Lennox drawled as she pressed her sword into Adreona's throat. Crimson dripped down the female's pale neck.

"If you kill me your sister dies," Adreona rasped.

I turned my attention to Kara at the same moment Lennox did, my throat going dry at the sight of the guard holding a dagger to Kara's throat, a mirror to Adreona and Lennox.

Lennox was deathly still behind Adreona as she watched the male move with her sister. Her eyes fixed on that dagger.

Without hesitating, Lennox removed her sword from the female's throat.

"Smart girl," Adreona crooned.

"Why are you doing this?" Lennox pleaded as the male continued to hold the blade to Kara's throat. She moved away from Adreona, making her way down the stairs of the throne to my side. "I gave you the journal. What more do you want from me?"

"Do you think me stupid?" Adreona spat. She stood from

the throne, wiping the blood dripping from her neck with the back of her hand, but the wound continued to bleed. She flung the journal at Lennox's feet. "There are several pages ripped out. Where are they?"

Lennox's gaze stayed fixed on Kara. "I don't know. I received the journal like you asked and came straight here."

"Liar," she hissed. She gave the guard a nod. Kara whimpered as the blade pressed into her skin, a thin line of blood dripping down her neck.

"Please," Lennox pleaded. "Don't hurt her. She did nothing. Let her go. Take me."

The female's eyes flashed.

"Lennox," I warned.

"Take me in her place."

"And why would you think I'd want you instead?"

"I'm the queen. You could use me as a bargaining chip. I'm a skilled warrior. Use me to kill your enemies. I don't care. I'll do anything if you let my sister go." Panic constricted my chest as she continued to plead. She couldn't do this.

The gleam in Adreona's eyes made my stomach churn. "I did find something interesting while your sister was here. She possesses witch magic. Do you possess this same magic?"

Lennox swallowed. "I do. Mine is stronger."

"Perhaps you could be of use to me. I require a willing witch to help with my experiments, my current one is of little use these days."

"Lennox, no," I pleaded. "Don't do this, we will find a way."

She took a deep breath. "Release my sister and we can talk."

"Lennox, don't do this."

Adreona nodded to the guard. Kara sagged as he removed the dagger and Lennox let out a shuddering breath.

I took Lennox's hand in mine. "Lennox," I warned. "Please." She looked over at me. Her eyes were lined with tears as her face contorted with pain. She squeezed my hand.

"Trust me, Luka, please trust me."

# 71

# LENNOX

My heart felt like it was ripping in two as I looked between my sister and Luka.

But I knew what I needed to do.

*Trust me.* I told Luka.

I didn't look at him as I slipped my hand from his and took a step toward the throne. I didn't dare look back at him or I might give in. Choose him. Choose myself.

"Bring her to me," Adreonas' voice echoed through the room.

"Release my friends first and I will come to you willingly." I approached the base of the throne.

Adreona narrowed her eyes. "Fine."

"Bring the sister to the other witch. Release them, but keep an eye on the vampire."

I kept my back to my friends as I approached the throne. Kara's eyes searched mine as we passed on the stairs, but I kept my gaze forward. I couldn't look at her or I might not be able to do this.

"You sacrificing yourself for your sister, for your friends, is not something I anticipated." Adreona ran an icy finger down my cheek, I forced myself not to wince. "I look forward to working with you, Lennox."

Her calling me Lennox was a slap to the face. While I was here, I was no longer the High Queen. I was nothing but a pawn in her game.

"Get the shackles." A cruel smile curved up her lips. "I don't want to, but you must understand Lennox, I cannot trust you yet." The sounds of the chains clamoring as the guards climbed the stairs sent a shiver down my spine.

"Lennox!" Luka's voice broke through the roaring in my head. I closed my eyes as the guard fastened the shackles around my wrists.

"LENNOX!" Luka bellowed. A tear slipped down my cheek at the sound of his voice.

I opened my eyes and found him, one last time. I could look at him one last time.

"Let me go!" he snarled. Declan and Nico held him back as he thrashed against their hold. "She's *my wife*. Let me go."

*My wife*. My knees threatened to give out at those words.

His eyes met mine. "Don't do this," he begged, falling to his knees as they continued to hold him. "Lennox. Don't leave me."

My chest heaved, the pressure was too much. This was all too much. I couldn't leave him, but I had to. For Kara, I had to.

"I'm sorry," I choked out. "I'm so sorry." The words felt like sandpaper in my throat. Maybe someday I'd make my way back to him and we'd finally get our happy ending.

Someday.

Maybe.

"Luce." I turned to my cousin, her gaze was firm, but her eyes were glassy. "Please. Get him out of here. Make sure everyone is safe." She nodded solemnly. My chest cracked in two at what she was about to do for me.

I let myself look at Luka again. "I'm so sorry. Luka, I—"

"No," he growled. "You don't get to say that now. Not like this. I'm not letting you leave with her."

I looked at my feet, holding back the words I wanted to say. Maybe it was better this way. "Please forgive me," I told him. He continued to thrash against Declan and Nico. Oblivious to the witch approaching him.

He had no time to react as Luce pressed her fingers to his temples.

In a heartbeat, he was slumped against Nico and Declan.

"Brilliant idea." Adreona clapped behind me. "You will be such a treasure, too bad your friend can't stay too."

Panic coursed through me. Would she try to keep them?

"If you want me to work with you willingly, let them go unharmed. Right now." I wiped away my tears with my arm, my chains jingling.

"Fine, you're no fun." She waved a hand at my friends, *my family.* "Leave. Now." Declan and Nico held Luka's limp body between them. They all gave me one last look before they turned towards the door.

"Wait," I called out.

They paused, and I ignored the glimmer of hope in their eyes. "Tell Luka I love him." A tear slipped down my cheek as magic zinged through my body. I felt it pulsing through me, moving like a living thing as it made its way to my heart, caressing it softly. Whatever spell was on this place must have ended.

"Tell him I have loved him for a long time now, I was too afraid to say it before and now it's too late." I choked out. Even if he didn't want to hear it like this, I still wanted him to know. He deserved to know how I feel about him. A sob wracked my body as my heart compressed in my chest. A whip of magic clenched it tight. My marriage mark tingled, a zip of magic tickling my palms as they were held together by the restraints.

I used to think my heart was in shards, incapable of loving and being loved. But I was wrong. My heart was still in me. It had been made whole again by him, and right now it threatened to crack straight open. Goddess, I loved him. I loved him so much. I loved him so much the feeling rattled my bones.

I straightened my shoulders, wiping my tears with the back of my arm. "Tell him I will try my best to find my way back to him."

Kara shuddered, but it was Declan who spoke, "You can tell him all that." He looked to Adreona behind me before looking back at me. "You'll be back with him soon. I promise you, Lennox."

A seed of hope threatened to take root in my chest, but I quickly diminished it.

I had no hope I'd be leaving here anytime soon.

# 72

# LUKA

My body ached. The pain in my chest was almost unbearable. It was that pain—that ache, that tug, that pulled me from sleep.

Goddess, how long had I been asleep?

I reached my arm out in the bed beside me, surprised to find the space where Lennox should have been empty. I strained my ears to try and hear her—but the only sound in the bedchamber was the breath of someone else sleeping. Their breaths were too heavy, too deep to be Lennox.

I sat up, finding my friends in the sitting area...

Why were they—it all came back to me. "Lennox." The pain in my chest intensified.

Lennox had given herself to Adreona to save Kara—to save us all. And I had passed out? What had rendered me unconscious?

"You're up," Declan mused from where he relaxed in the chair. His hair was down and loose, there were deep circles under his eyes.

"I need to go to her." I pushed back the sheet and made my way to the bathing chamber. I had to get to her as quickly as possible.

"It's not that easy," Declan countered as he followed me into the bathing chamber. The large white wolf sleeping on the floor rustled, magic flashed and Nico was standing in the bathing chamber. I ignored him as I looked around for my weapons.

"We go back to the abandoned building and we get her back. Simple."

Declan laid a hand gently on my arm, causing me to stop my search and look at him. The expression on his face sent worry scurrying about my system.

"You don't understand, Luka. She's not there anymore."

Nico's expression was a mirror of Declan's. "We went back after we brought you back here. They cleared out the space. They knew we'd go back for her."

I took a shuddering breath, rubbing my hand over my chest —over the spot where pain radiated.

"Luciana will scry, she will find where she is."

The two shared a look. "What?" They were both silent. "Spit it the fuck out." I ground out. Pushing Declan away from me.

"She tried. It didn't work," Nico admitted.

"Then she'll try again." I pushed past them back into the bedchamber.

"She's been trying for two days straight." Nico followed behind me. I stopped, closing my eyes against his words. *Two days.* I had been out for two days. Lennox had been in captivity for two days.

"She tried until her body gave out on her. She passed out a few hours ago. She thinks whatever block on magic they had on that building they now have on Lennox."

It would have been too easy, wouldn't it? Too easy to conduct a spell and find her and bring her back to me. Adreona didn't want us to find her.

I bunched my hands into fists.

But I would find her.

I would rip the realm to shreds until I found her again.

# 73

# LENNOX

I leaned my head against the cool cement of the wall of my cell.

The guard who had brought me here had called it a room, but you didn't get locked in rooms. There was at least a bathroom. That was a luxury for the cell. And I had a table to eat the meals they brought me. Not that the meals were anything worthwhile. But at least it was food.

Adreona hadn't called upon me since we had arrived here. Wherever here was. She knocked me out after everyone left. I woke up here. In their new headquarters.

At least my shackles had been removed.

But there was still something snuffing out my magic.

I traced my fingers over the new markings on my hand. The delicate snaking vines that wrapped themselves around my marriage marking. The red and gold vines swirled until they became one.

I had no idea when they appeared.

I traced the lines to distract myself from the pain that never ceased from pounding in my chest.

I looked up at the sound of the door opening. Surprised to find Adreona strolling in, holding my dinner plate.

She looked me up and down, a clear look of disgust as she took in my appearance and my choice to sit on the floor.

"When we begin our work you will be required to be presentable," she sneered before setting the plate on the table and taking a seat in the chair crossing one leg over the other.

"Cheer up, girl. We will have such fun together."

I didn't meet her stare, instead tracing the mark on my palm.

She sighed. "We still need a few more days to finish setting up our new headquarters. We will begin work in a few days. That should give you plenty of time to mope about being separated from your mate. I expect you to be in a better mood then."

I snapped my head up to meet her gaze. "What did you say?"

She narrowed her eyes. "Did you not realize the vampire was your mate?"

*My mate.* Luka was my mate. How? When?

"What did you assume the mark on your hand was?"

"It's new. It appeared once I arrived here," I rasped. My throat was dry as I spoke for the first time in days.

Her perfectly arched brows rose. "How interesting. I imagine the mating bond must have snapped into place sometime the other night. Those kinds of things are triggered by something."

My mate. The pressure in my chest intensified. Luka was my mate.

And I had been separated from him.

"Anyways. Rest up, Clean yourself. I will call for you in a few days."

I didn't register her leaving the cell. Those two words on repeat in my mind.

My mate. Luka was my mate.

All this time. That pull to him. Our bond.

Tears slipped down my cheeks.

How had we gotten here?

I hadn't let myself have hope before, but now—Luka was my mate.

I would make it back to him.

I would claw and fight my way back to him only stopping once I made it to him or I turned to stardust. Whichever happened first.

He had fought for me.

Now it was my turn to fight for him.

### THE END BOOK 2

# ACKNOWLEDGMENTS

I honestly can't believe I'm here doing this again, writing the acknowledgments for my second book. I'm sorry, but what?

First and foremost, thank you to my family and friends. I would list you all out, but there are so many of you. You know exactly who you are. I would not be here, doing this, if it were not for your support. Please keep asking me about my work, how things are going, and just anything about my writing. You asking those questions and making those little comments mean the absolute world to me, even if I don't make it seem like it. I'm still learning how to take a compliment and acknowledge that I'm an author. I'm trying my best.

But I beg you, please stop bringing up the fact that I write spicy scenes and trying to read them in front of me.

To Abby and Emily, your constant, unwavering support of this dream of mine means more to me than words could ever express. You are truly my biggest fans every single day, even when I'm not a fan of myself. My besties for the resties, I love you SO MUCH.

To my editors, Caitlin and Kayla, I cannot thank you enough for the work you put in to help me get this book where it is now. I could not do this without you and I am so incredibly thankful to have you in my corner. Thank you for sticking with me even when I was stressing you out and breaking your heart throughout this book.

To my amazing team of beta readers, Bekah, Niamh, and Tiffany, you read this story when I still referred to it as a steaming pile of garbage. You helped me realize it wasn't all garbage, hyped me up, and helped me make it better. You helped me realize this story had more potential than I even imagined. I cannot thank you enough.

To my street team and ARC readers, thank you for being here supporting me, and hyping me up. Your love for Lennox and Luka and their story means the absolute world to me. You are the reason I can keep doing this.

To Maribeth, my original book bestie, and the rockstar behind Legends Literary management. Thank you for all of your help with the release of Queen of the Crimson Throne. You made my job so much easier, and I'm so thankful for that (and you).

To everyone from BookTok, Bookstagram, and Threads, everyone I've had the joy of connecting with, thank you. Thank you for sharing my book and helping it reach more eyes. And just your general love and support of me. I LOVE YOU. To my fellow authors I've gotten to connect with, you help me feel not so alone in the scary world of authoring, thank you for that.

I would not be me without thanking Taylor Swift. Her songs are the soundtrack of Lennox and Luka's story. And I could not tell you how many times I watched the Eras tour movie while editing this book. It (and wine) truly got me through edits.

To my dog Leia, (yes, she gets another acknowledgment) thank you for always staying cuddled by my side (like you are right now) even when I was screaming in frustration over this manuscript and for licking away the tears from all the crying I did while writing this book (crying in a good way).

Finally, thank you, reader, for picking up another one of my books. I would not be here if it were not for you. I am eternally thankful for you helping me make my dream come true.

# AUTHORS NOTE

I promise I'll keep this one brief (she said before she rambled aimlessly).

When I started drafting Quen of the Crimson Throne, I was worried from the start as to how I was going to get the romantic storyline and the overarching fantasy plotlines I had in mind to intertwine and their arcs to intersect. I struggled writing the first drafts of this book, more than I struggled writing book one and it terrified me.

But when it came down to it, I did it. And I think I did it really fucking well. I had so many expectations for this book. In my mind, book one was laying the groundwork for everything that was set to happen in book two. And I was excited to finally get to write it.

There were so many scenes in Queen of the Crimson Throne that I had been dreaming about for over a year, finally getting to write them—I can't even explain that feeling.

I am proud of myself for writing Queen of Blood and Stardust—for achieving my dream and publishing a book.

With Queen of the Crimson Throne, I'm not just proud of myself, I'm so incredibly proud of this story that I created.

I've never been more proud of something I've created in my entire life than I am of Queen of the Crimson Throne.

When people tell me they've read Queen of Blood and Stardust and they liked it I smile, nod, and say, "Thank You," but in the back of my head I'm thinking, *they're lying.*

Maybe that's my imposter syndrome or maybe that's my anxiety but either way, I'm working on it.

But when it comes to Queen of the Crimson Throne, when people tell me they like it, I actually believe them. I believe in this story with my whole fucking heart.

And if we're being honest I'm bawling my eyes out right now writing this because I'm so proud of how far I've come. I've grown so much as a writer in working on this book and I can say with full confidence how proud I am of myself and this story.

I'm just so thankful every day to have the opportunity to write these characters and their stories. To explore their complexities while also learning and growing myself through them.

I love this book so much. Queen of Blood and Stardust will always be my first baby, but Queen of the Crimson Throne is my favorite, and I hope it will be yours too.

# ALSO BY KAITLYN SWANSON

☾

## *Queen of Blood and Stardust Series*

Queen of Blood and Stardust

Queen of the Crimson Throne

Queen of Blood and Stardust Book 3, Coming 2025

# ABOUT THE AUTHOR

Kaitlyn has always loved writing. Writing a book has been a dream of hers forever, she just never imagined that dream would come true in her twenties in the form of a fantasy romance novel.

When Kaitlyn isn't writing she enjoys relaxing by one of Minnesota's lakes with her golden retriever Leia by her side and Taylor Swift playing in the background.

Follow along with what she's doing next
kaitlynswansonbooks.com